REQUIEM ETERNAM

The Chronicles of Coren Slade

Richard Greenslit

Copyright © 2024 Richard Greenslit
All rights reserved

The characters and events portrayed in this book are fictitious. Any similarity to real persons, living or dead, is coincidental and not intended by the author.

No part of this book may be reproduced, or stored in a retrieval system, or transmitted in any form or by any means, electronic, mechanical, photocopying, recording, or otherwise, without express written permission of the publisher.

ISBN-13: 9798991481618

Cover Art by: Andrea Pavlat

Cover Design by: Amazon Publishing Assistant

To my brother David and my sister Anne,
my sons Thomas and Jonathan,
and my friends
Elizabeth, Adrienne, Lexie, and Marissa,
who kept the dream alive.
And to Mr. Jones,
who sat beside me at the beginning
and was gone way too soon.

Contents

Preface
Chapter 1: In Paradisum
Chapter 2: Ab Hoedis Me Sequestra
Chapter 3: De Hoc Saeculo
Chapter 4: Tremens
Interlude 1
Chapter 5: Ab Auditione Mala
Chapter 6: Simul Rapiemur
Chapter 7: De Profundo Lacu
Chapter 8: Sustinui Te
Chapter 9: Adveniat
Chapter 10: Consolamini
Chapter 11: Evadere Iudicium
Chapter 12: Finis
Interlude 2
Chapter 13: Tuba Mirum
Chapter 14: Resurrectionis Gloria
Chapter 15: Vita Mutatur
Chapter 16: Hostias Et Preces
Chapter 17: Militia Caelestis
Chapter 18: Beatitudine
Chapter 19: Ante Diem Rationis
Chapter 20: Confutatis Maledictis
Chapter 21: Immortalitatis Promissio
Interlude 3
Chapter 22: Mundus Judicetur
Chapter 23: Judicalis Sententia
Chapter 24: In Resurrectione
Chapter 25: Ne Absorbeat Eas Tartarus
Chapter 26: Ab Illo Benedicaris
Interlude 4

Chapter 27: Sumus In Adventum
Chapter 28: Quando Judex Est Venturus
Chapter 29: Usque Ad Noctem
Chapter 30: Recordare
Chapter 31: Reddetur Votum
Chapter 32: In Nubibus
Chapter 33: Eleison
Interlude 5
Chapter 34: Et Lux Perpetua
Chapter 35: Quis Sustinebit?
Chapter 36: Dies Irae
Chapter 37: Quid Sum Miser
Interlude 6
Chapter 38: Solvet Saeclum In Favilla
Chapter 39: Resurget Creatura
Chapter 40: Qui Spem Non Habent
Chapter 41: A Porta Inferi
Chapter 42: Juste Judex Ultionis
Chapter 43: Ne Cadant In Obscurum
Chapter 44: Aeterna In Caelis
Chapter 45: Gere Curam Mei Finis
Epilogue

In Latin, *requiem* means *rest*.

It is also the first word in the Catholic mass for the dead:

Requiem aeternam / Dona eis, Domine
Rest eternal / Give to them, Lord

Over time, *requiem* has become shorthand for the entire mass itself. The word no longer simply means *rest* but implies loss and grief, of something that once was or could have been, of something that exists no longer.

PREFACE

*Requiem aeternam dona eis, Domine,
Et lux perpetua luceat eis*

Lord, please grant them eternal rest
And shine your eternal light on them

-Excerpt from the Requiem Mass, *Introduction*

When the good people at Argon Books first approached me about writing a preface to this volume, I hesitated. Is yet another book about Coren Slade necessary, I asked myself. What is there possibly left to be said about him? Aren't we already steeped in enough Corenism to fill the galaxy and overflow into the great emptiness beyond?

When the company indicated that this collection of documents would include a Coren Slade autobiography, I gasped. How could they have obtained such a manuscript? Is the man still alive? Or, down through all those years, did he scribble his thoughts in some heretofore hidden journal?

I needed to know the source of the autobiographical sections. They, of course, could not divulge it but did assure me of the text's authenticity.

This became quite a dilemma for me. If I accepted the material as real and wrote the preface, I would lend my name to the book and possibly put my reputation for scrupulous honesty on the line. If I declined, I would miss an opportunity to be part of something new and fresh, perhaps something able to calm the revolutionary storms which wrack our civilization.

As I read it, however, the words rang true, and I decided on the former: I believe this book contains a true description of Coren Slade's life, described by the man himself. Argon Books has assured me that one day—perhaps long after I am dead—

but one day, when certain conditions are met, all will be fully explained. If, over the course of time, the autobiographical portion of this book is proved false, I beg forgiveness.

Coren Slade.

He represents so many different things to so many different people.

Those who admire him point to his peaceable nature and to his heroics, to his generosity and self-sacrifice. I believe these people are in many ways correct. He was not necessarily born with the courage and determination he would later show, but at many places along his journey, he chose a path which has helped shape what humanity is today. For that, I would argue, we owe him a debt.

On the other hand, those who despise him—who have attacked his actions and tried to prevent them—denounce what they see as his authoritarianism and lack of respect for all life, no matter its origin. Apart from their overtly violent actions, I believe these people are largely correct as well. In my opinion, this aspect of him can be attributed partially to the era he originated in, and partially to the experiences he survived. He was a man from a different time, and his sensibilities are not our sensibilities. The violence of those condemning his disregard for different life forms is, of course, hypocritical. However, as someone once asked about double standards: when did we ever get down to two?

These contradictory aspects are all part of Coren Slade, just as they are a part of all humans, albeit with much less impact on history. The mistake we make is in judging the entirety of the man by today's standards. Instead, we should judge the *man* by the standards of his day; in doing so, I believe we can see he lived an honorable life. If, however, we assess the consequences of Slade's *actions* according to today's norms, we find much to condemn. This distinction between the man and his legacy are crucial to reconciling the bitter factions which war over him.

The themes of his life and those terrible, turbulent times are clear in retrospect, and I will not enumerate them here. Those of you familiar with Slade will already know many of them, though you may find a few surprises in the latest material. Those of you unfamiliar with the particulars and with exactly how so many people died should be allowed to discover these wonders and horrors for yourselves.

I mentioned that this is partially an autobiography. I mean "partially" in three ways.

First, this tome only covers the earlier parts of Slade's life. As to whether he has written more about himself, that remains to be seen. I will be overjoyed if Argon Books contacts me to write volume two's preface.

Second, the autobiographical sections are interwoven with a more standard depiction of this history as seen through the experiences of a less well-known soldier. These sections are not like the thousands of accounts we have describing events as they unfolded on Galvus or Earth or Mars. Instead, we get a look at the inner workings of the Forces as they prepared for—and arguably lost—their most significant challenge ever.

Third and finally, we have the newly decrypted communications we have all spent so much time reading of late. Had we known their form and content early on, we might have avoided the destruction, and books like this one would not be necessary. I have placed these communications where I believe they fit chronologically so we can examine both sides of the conflict as it approached.

Cor, Corey, Coren; PAPA, soldier, Slade; friend and confidante; hero and martyr; heretic and destroyer: these are how he is known. I hope that by reading this book, you will understand him better and perhaps see him in a new, more human way. We have known such destruction, and we struggle to get back to where we once were. It is my fervent wish that this book will promote a dialogue between the bastions of pro- and anti-Corenists.

Et lux perpetua luceat eis.

Here, then, along with the other documents, is the story of Coren Slade, in his own words, for the first time.

CHAPTER 1: IN PARADISUM

In paradisum deducant te angeli;
In tuo adventu suscipiant te martires

May the angels lead you into paradise;
May the martyrs receive you at your arrival

-Excerpt from the Requiem Mass, *Absolution*

2230 A.D. and 2237 A.D. (Ages 11 and 18)

I would like to say that I left home out of a sense of patriotism. That I saw necessity and chose to do my part. That my species needed me, and I answered the call. But I have decided that if I'm going to write this, I'm going to be completely honest.

The truth is, I have no idea why I joined. We'll get to that.

First, though, a short anecdote about two people who deserve to be remembered.

It's odd the things you remember, the things you forget.

Saturday morning, fifth or sixth grade. The scent of fried shrimp and onions from the yaki mandu stall lingered in the air. A lady parked her food cart out front of the miners' headquarters on weekends and made a killing.

Red McPherson sat where the two corridors met, just like he always did, and picked at the insulation, just like he always did. Station insulation protected the population from the ice-cold asteroid we lived in so it was extremely durable, but Red kept at it.

He also kept up his normal patter. "My cereal this morning tasted funny. Do you think there's something wrong with the food dispensers?" Pick. "I hate history class—I mean, I didn't read the material, but did the teacher have to make such a big deal out of it?" Pick. "My father yelled at me and my brother last night." Pick. Pick. Pick.

Not sure how his parents knew, but they guessed right in naming him "Red." Flaming hair, thick and wild. Freckles so abundant they blended across his face. When he got angry, he looked like a cherry about to pop.

Red and I were the same age, classmates since the beginning. The teacher placed us next to each other in second grade, and we made sure we sat together every year after that. We got separated sometimes, mostly because Red wouldn't stop talking, but there were ways around that: slowly swapping seats with others over the course of a few days, reverting to previous seating and waiting for the teacher to notice, or, if all else failed, passing notes.

Kids on Mars II didn't have many places to go and be left alone. The corner we found was at the outer edge of Level 5 —our level. In both directions, the hallway disappeared into the distance as it conformed to the outside of the asteroid, dotted here and there with darker spots where a light had failed. No shops were nearby, so that cut down on traffic, as did the presence of so many miners coming and going from their offices. Miners couldn't have cared less about what we did. They were a tough lot, too, which discouraged visitors.

We gathered at that intersection on weekend mornings to assess how intoxicated our parents had gotten the night before and to plan out the day—if there was any planning to do.

It wasn't just Red and me meeting, either. Devlin was Red's younger brother by a year. Most women on Mars II were lucky to get permission to have one child, but having two came with a roomier apartment and more rations. The McPhersons might have gone the bribery route. Or maybe their parents had influence with the Executive Council and weaseled an exception out of them. In any case, Red mostly tolerated Devlin, and if we needed someone to fetch something or if there was something stupid to try for the first time, like swimming in a station reservoir, Devlin was eager to please.

There we were, all three of us together, that Saturday morning.

"Ow!" Red yanked his hand back from picking at the insulation and stared at his fingers. "That hurt!" His hand looked fine.

"What happened?" Devlin asked. His eyes darted up and down the corridors, scanning for security personnel.

"I just—" Red turned and peered into the hole, then slowly put his hand back in. "It's the asteroid! I touched the asteroid!"

"The asteroid?" I asked.

Red stared daggers at me, shook his head, and went back to what he was doing. "Wow! That's cold! There's also a space between the insulation and the rock. Like it's pulled away or was made that way for some reason. Come feel this!"

I crossed the corridor, got down in front of the hole, and stuck my hand in. Immediate ice burn.

"Stupid!" Red laughed, punching me in the arm.

"Guess we should notify maintenance?" Devlin asked, looking around at the rest of us. "Will we get in trouble?"

I glanced over at Red. His eyes widened and his face lit up like a crimson beacon as he scrambled to his feet.

"Our storage spot!" he whispered, pointing at the hole and scrambling to his feet. "This is it! We need someplace to hide the bottles where we can also drink them, and this is it! We smuggle the booze down, put it in the hole, and drink right here. The miners won't care. If anyone else comes along, we hide it until they go away. What do you think?"

There was a moment of silence.

"So... we won't notify maintenance?"

"No, we won't notify maintenance, Devlin," Red replied. He did a fair job of imitating Devlin's voice.

"Is it dangerous though? I mean, the insulation is there for a reason, right?"

Red stared, mouth open. "No, Devlin, it's not dangerous. It's not an airlock; it's just a hole in the wall. The station won't even notice a change in temperature."

Devlin and I locked eyes. He and I shrugged at the same time before we turned back to Red. We all smiled. We were young—way too young to drink. Red and I were eleven, and

Devlin was ten. It was what our parents did, though, and we wanted to try it.

With no reason to wait, we implemented our new alcohol plan right away. I headed back to the tiny apartment I shared with my mother. She worked at Al's Suds 'n Spuds and didn't usually come home Friday nights—an absence which spilled way over into Saturdays. There was no chance I would get caught.

I squeezed through my bedroom door—the bed kept it from opening all the way—and knelt beside my combination dresser and nightstand. With the lower drawer pulled out all the way, there was a narrow spot underneath where I could hide things. Once I had the right-shaped bottles, it was easy enough to fill them: my mother had frequent parties, and those parties had leftovers.

I grabbed all three bottles, tucked them into my waistband, pulled my shirt down, and headed back. I was the first one there, probably because I had the least sneaking around to do.

The hole in the insulation looked the same as it had before, but now I wondered how maintenance could miss it.

As I got down on my knees again, the cold seeped out around me, spreading into the corridor. I threaded one of the bottles in. Red had been right: there was a gap back there. I was just tucking the second one into place when Red and Devlin showed up.

We drank.

Red had some liquor in a burgundy bottle. The alcohol tasted like fruit juice and got us started. By the time we hit the harder stuff, taste didn't matter.

Red started talking more than usual, which was quite an accomplishment. Devlin's volume went way up, and he took to dashing up the corridor toward the miners' offices and circling around so he came back another way. Red put a stop to that after a miner frowned at him as he ran by. As for me: I drifted where my mind went, from my mom's parties to the girl in my science class to whatever Red was going on about at a particular moment.

We were still at it when the food stall lady showed up late in the afternoon.

Yaki mandu: so bad for the body, so good for the tongue.

Indeed, all was good that day, but when we showed up the next morning, hungover and sweating out the fried food bricks in our stomachs, the hole was gone. Sometime after we left, the bottles froze and broke, sending a trickle of booze out into the intersection. The maintenance crew that came to clean it up couldn't help but notice the hole and patch it beyond unrepair.

That memory is as clear to me today as it was when it happened. Red chattering nonstop, Devlin's cowlick bouncing as he ran. My two best friends.

They both have been erased from history. No records of them exist as far as I can tell, and yes, I've used my extensive resources to look. Even if I were to find traces of them, it might be their names and birth dates, maybe when they died.

They were so much more than that.

The richest and most powerful people on Mars II lived and worked in the uppermost level, Level 14. Poorer residents usually couldn't get to it without a special key for the elevator or access to a maintenance tunnel. Once up there, it was a different world. Gone were the padded insulation, metal floors, and fluorescent glare. Level 14 was wood paneling, red carpets, fluted sconces, and plants infusing the air with natural scents.

I made it to Level 14 three times before leaving Mars II forever.

The first time I went up there was with my mother. The Executive Council summoned her and accused her of being a stim-dealer. She was nothing of the kind, just a user like most of the adults I knew, probably named as a dealer by another addict as a misdirection. She brought me along—a single mother trying to take care of her child who just happened to be out sick that day from school, with no one else to care for him. I was perfectly fine, and that's all my mother got: a small monetary fine. She celebrated with a blowout party that night.

That was my mom and I, though. For eighteen years, through a succession of pseudo-dads and toxic relationships and booze and drugs, she and I were the one constant in each other's lives. She was my mom. I was her son.

The second and third times I made it to Level 14... well... They occurred back-to-back.

I started that final day with breakfast, just the normal cereal and scrambled eggs the station's food services spat out. My dishes were on the counter when I went out into the station, turning right into the corridor. I ducked through a cleaning robot, its curved rods matching the entire semicircular arc of the tunnel, beeping and blinking non-stop, struggling in vain to bleach the padding to anything that wasn't dirt brown.

As usual, I wandered to the intersection by the miners' offices, not expecting to see Red. He and I had graduated from school the month before. We had done our share of drinking through the years, but we stayed away from the drugs. For me, it was images of my mother changing—disappearing—when she did the hard stuff, different than when she drank. I figured it was the same for Red, but not a week after school finished, Red stimmed for the first time. He offered some to me, but I couldn't.

As for Devlin, classes were already back in session, and he was locked away, being force-fed information he would never use.

It's funny, though: one moment, you are a valued member of a school community, praised for all you have accomplished, and the next, you have graduated and aren't tolerated on the campus. The principal even announced at graduation that, for security reasons, departing students would no longer be allowed into the warren, effective immediately. Twelve years of proving yourself worthy, and then that.

With no sign of Red at the intersection, I headed back to the interior of the asteroid where the shops were. Our rendezvous faded behind me for the last time. I would never see it again.

I turned a first corner, then a second, letting my fingers bump along the insulation. Around another, close to the elevator banks, was the sign.

Immediate Vacancy!

The holo flashed and blinked, then the words morphed:

Unique Opportunity! Start a Lifetime of Adventure Today!

Then again:

Upper Level 14, Section 2B—Inquire NOW!

The final word danced and spun around before the whole message repeated.

It was a Forces recruitment ad, of course. I had seen a sign like this only once before, a few years earlier. Back then, I was too young to compete for a rare Forces spot. Now, at eighteen, I could choose for myself.

CHAPTER 2:
AB HOEDIS ME SEQUESTRA

Inter oves locum praesta,
Et ab hoedis me sequestra

Place me among the sheep,
And separate me from the goats

-Excerpt from the Requiem Mass, *Sequence*

2237 A.D. (Age 18)

After that initial impulse to visit the recruiter, a debate raged in my mind as I stood in front of the elevators.

Go visit?

Why not? It wouldn't cost anything. Just listen, and more than likely leave.

Why? Would I really join the Forces? And why had the sign mentioned "today"?

People came. People went. I stared at the button. An elevator opened in front of me, a lady exited, and... I got in, punched in Level 14—unlocked, I believed, because of the recruitment—and rode to the top of the asteroid.

When the doors opened, it was a different world. Gone was the constant clanging of shoes on metal walkways, replaced by a suffocating silence. I wasn't sure I should move. A resident approached, frowned, and looked ready to reprimand me. Her eyes darted to the sign pointing applicants in the right direction. Sighing, she shook her head and walked away.

Section 2B was across a couple of corridors and then to the left. The red carpets were so clean, I left footprints in them—dark scarlet pools in the sacred sand of luxury. Fine-grained wood paneling—real, by the look of it—lined the rectangular halls. The air tickled my nose; it smelled like the bleach they used in vain to scrub the insulation below, but softer and with a flowery tilt.

I rounded the final corner. A powder blue "Forces Recruitment" sign hung over a doorless entrance. Inside, a man sat ramrod straight at a mahogany desk, motionless, head up, looking at a holoscreen. I hesitated, then broke the invisible line between the corridor and his office.

The man sprang to his feet and held up a palm. "Hello, son! Forces Soldier Five Bren C. Carmichael. How can I help you today?"

He had black curly hair, tawny skin, a brilliant white smile, and a pencil-thin mustache tracing his upper lip. Odd accent but a deep, resonant voice. His spotless white uniform, accented at the shoulders and waist with the same powder blue color as the neon sign, was out of a recruiting vid.

Something tingled inside me, whispering.

"I... saw the holo..." I replied, gesturing toward the corridor.

"Yes, the vacancy, the vacancy..." He drew out the last syllable as he circled behind his projection screen. "I had someone lined up for this month, but he suddenly dropped out. I need to get a recruit in the mail to meet the deadline. Today. Are you interested? And what is your name, son?"

"Coren Slade. And... well... yes... I'm interested... I suppose." I should have left right then.

"Good, good, good. You look like an excellent candidate! Much better than the original. You are eighteen?"

"Couple of months ago." I had begged my mom not to stim that night, and she didn't. We had a great evening.

"Perfect."

"Who was it?"

"Excuse me?" Carmichael replied, frowning.

"Who was the recruit that dropped out?"

Carmichael's eyes lit up. "Oh, yes, yes. Thomas Cooper. That much is public knowledge. I can't tell you why he is no longer processing for the Forces, of course."

Tommy Cooper. He had graduated a couple of years earlier.

I saw him from time to time. He even came into my mom's bar once while I was there, but whatever he was on, he was in no condition to recognize me. Or anyone else, for that matter. He had been laughing at a miner joke I found offensive—one in the "How do you get a stuck miner out of a hole?" series. The punchline was something along the lines of "You don't —you just thank your lucky stars." Last I knew, Tommy had landed a job on the loading docks; the lucky individuals who got those usually held on to them forever.

Carmichael gestured for me to sit in a magnetically levitated chair, the blue-and-tan kind that pushes into your back and makes you lean forward, the kind you worked hard to break when they put new ones in at school. The instant I sat down, he stood up and adjusted his uniform in some way noticeable only to him.

"You know, opportunities to join the Forces don't come along very often. I usually interview candidates several months in advance, do screenings, all of that. So, this is a unique opportunity, and I've already had a couple of individuals ask about it this morning. They are off considering it, but the first one to commit is the first one I start processing." He tilted his head slightly. "Why do you want to join the Forces, Mr. Slade?"

"I…"

I mean, I had thought about it before, but not seriously. It had seemed out of reach.

"Tell you what," Carmichael said, "let's try this."

He opened a drawer, pulled out a burgundy velvet pouch, and clunked it down in front of me. "There are many, many reasons to join. Look at what's in the bag."

I obediently dumped it out. There were ten golden-colored bars, heavy, each with a word on it:

> *Duty*
> *Honor*
> *Humanity*
> *Pay*
> *Adventure*
> *Education*

tank with pale pinkish panels closed together at the top like a flower. Carmichael pressed a button, a petal flipped up, and I took a seat inside, adjusting to the miniscule space and antiseptic smell. The lights dimmed, then force fields pressed on me, probing my body, first one side, then another, then top and bottom.

Sitting there, with nothing to do other than guess what they would probe next, I thought about what I was doing.

Today? He wanted me to leave today? I needed more time to think, to talk it over with Red, to see how my mother reacted. My breathing accelerated, and my thoughts couldn't settle in one place, flitting from my tiny bedroom to Red to my mom's bar to the stars as I weighed the options.

The pink panel raised halfway up, and Carmichael peered in.

"You okay?" he asked. "Your pulse just skyrocketed."

I gave him a half-hearted thumbs up.

"The medical part is almost done, just another minute or two, and then we'll test your skills. Okay?"

My mouth had gone bone dry. I managed a weak nod.

Carmichael smiled. "You're going to be fine, son. Just fine," he said, closing the panel back down.

When the force fields finished pushing on me, an unnecessary tutorial lesson on the controls came on (I mean—it's a holo tank—who doesn't know how to use one of those?), followed by the skills tests themselves. For thirty minutes or so, I manipulated shapes and connected holo wires, grabbed bolts of light as they flew past my head, controlled a ship as it darted through some asteroids, and handed instruments to a doctor as he performed surgery.

The door opened again, and Carmichael stood there with a big grin on his face.

"Good news, good news! The skills test went fine, and, most importantly, you passed the physical fitness test! If you fail that one, you're out. But no major physical handicaps. Heart looks good. Lungs good. Colon good. Kidneys and bones, good. Physical conditioning could be better... but we'll get you there, don't you worry about that. So, if you're ready, we'll go back to my desk and fill in the contract. Once we're finished with that, you take the oath, and you are on your way. Ready?"

The skills test had kept my mind occupied, but now all the thoughts from earlier came thundering back, booming across my mind. Nothing would stop me from walking right out and forgetting all about this. It was also an opportunity unlikely to come around again, especially for someone average like me.

Carmichael walked with confidence back to his desk and sat down.

I followed behind, the room swaying and threatening to spin like it did when I drank too much. I made it to the chair and gripped the desk.

Leave? Today?

He cocked an eye at me. "You okay?"

I nodded quickly three times and held on for dear life.

Today?

He didn't look convinced. "Well, let's get started anyway," he said as he punched a series of numbers into his holo screen. It looked like he was dialing someone's comm link number.

He hit one more key, and identical holos appeared in front of both of us.

"I am recording this in case there are any questions later. First, let me draw your attention to the genetic symbol in the upper right corner of the screen. You will indicate your answers and consent on the following pages by touching the screen. Your choices will be linked to your genetic account, which will, in turn, populate your Forces records using genetic encryption. Once we have gone through all the items, you will get a chance at the end to review any items again and change your mind, including voiding the entire contract. Clear?"

"Yes," I croaked. Red's vacant eyes stared at me after that first stim, my mom crushed me with a hug when I graduated. The room had ceased swaying, but the blood kept up its relentless pounding in my head.

Today?

When Carmichael spoke, it was as if I was hearing him from far away, with cotton balls in my ears. "To start, please verify that the personal information on the screen is accurate, and, if so, indicate its accuracy by touching the 'accurate' button at the bottom. If some element is inaccurate, touch the item and correct it verbally. Once done, touch the genetic symbol in the upper right corner."

I looked over the screen. My whole life was there. My mother's name. Father's too, not that I had ever met him. Birth authorization number. Age. Apartment designator. Education. Brief medical profile. Blank spot for previous employment. A few details about the time Red, Devlin, and I got caught swimming in one of the station's reservoirs. Everybody did it, we just happened to get caught. Didn't help that we weren't entirely clothed. It was illegal, but the recruiter was staring at the same data I was, so I guessed it didn't make any difference for joining the Forces. The information was brief and correct.

I pictured myself sitting behind a recruiter's desk, coming to work in an office on Level 14.

Maybe I could set an example for Red? Mom, too, possibly? But today?

I hesitated before reaching out a shaky hand and accepting.

"You are agreeing to enter the Forces as a Forces Soldier 1, under open and general conditions, for a term of six years, standard time. This means that what you will be trained to do—your specialty, we call it—is subject to the needs of the Forces. Similarly, the Forces will decide your duty location. Standard time is calculated according to days spent in training or on post. Time spent in transit does not count. However, you are entitled to reduced pay while in transit, so that's a good thing."

Devlin. He'd follow Red's lead unless someone helped him.
My tiny bedroom flashed through my mind.
Nothing's been finalized.
I agreed to the terms.

A smile crept across FS5 Carmichael's face. "Now, let's discuss—"

"Uh..." I interrupted.

Slight frown.

"About the place where I'd be assigned..." He raised an eyebrow but didn't help me out. We had Forces on station, in a police role mostly, and there were Forces down on Mars, at the other stations in orbit, and all over the solar system.

"About that," I repeated. "Is it likely I'll be far from here... from home?"

Carmichael wagged a finger at me, pressed a button on his screen, then rubbed the back of his head. "A fair question, Mr. Slade. And a good question! A good question.

"The majority of Forces are stationed in the inner solar system, within easy travel distance of Mars. Of course, Jupiter's a bit farther, and the outer planets and asteroids might take a bit longer, but if you get stationed out there, you can still communicate easily with home. You also get leave, of course, so you can visit Mars II from time to time." He leaned back in his chair and bounced his fingers against each other, a spider jumping on a mirror.

"There are, of course, a few extrasolar billets... but not many Forces out that way, and those positions can be hard to get. There are certain types of people who can't wait to get out there on the edge. Should we move on?"

When I didn't respond, he raised a questioning eyebrow at me.

Just then, Tommy Cooper popped his head in the door. His clothes were disheveled and his hair uncombed.

Carmichael frowned and stood up. "Mr. Cooper, can I help you?"

"I was just wondering—"

"Having second thoughts about declining the position, are we?"

"Yeah, I'm thinking—"

"You get one chance with me, young man. One chance."

Tommy lowered his head, a stray lock falling in front of his face.

Carmichael grimaced, his mouth moving like he tasted rotten eggs. "One chance—normally. But I do need to send someone to training today. Mr. Slade here is currently processing for the position, but if he turns it down, I suppose…"

Tommy's eyes swiveled up until they met mine. Nothing. There was nothing in them. Not a hint of desire or desperation. He might have been stimming, for all I could tell.

"But—"

"Best I can do, Mr. Cooper, and more than you deserve. If Mr. Slade declines, I will contact you. If not, consider the matter closed."

When Tommy was gone, Carmichael sat down and leaned toward me. "You may, of course, leave at any time, Mr. Slade," he said in a low voice, "but as you can see, this opportunity will most assuredly disappear very, very quickly." He snapped his fingers and gazed steadily at me.

My mom—free of drugs, for once—smiles proudly as she admires my uniform.

But *today*?

As before, I didn't move. The recruiter took that as a sign to continue. We went through some pay and bank information before we hit something I hadn't expected: insurance.

"Please select from the list in front of you," Carmichael said, smiling and steepling his fingers together.

On the holo, a list of twenty or so titles popped up. I shook my head, trying to wrest my thoughts away from memories and dreams.

Straight life insurance: 500,000 solars to a beneficiary.

Bodily harm insurance: 250,000 solars to me.

Serious bodily harm insurance: 500,000 solars to me. It made me wonder for a moment what constituted serious versus plain old run-of-the-mill bodily harm.

Missing person insurance: continuation of my salary at an in-transit rate until my body was found, dead or alive.

Property insurance. Mental health insurance.

Dispossession insurance. Financial insurance.

With no references to draw on, I did the easy thing and shook my head. "No, thanks."

Carmichael breathed deep and tapped his spider fingers together again. "Mr. Slade, it is not my position to tell you what to do. You are an adult, making the largest adult decision of your life. And a good one, too. But it's a big universe. Things happen. You will want some coverage. Please... take your time, yes, indeed. No hurry."

I ricocheted in the other direction and selected them all, which drew a slight headshake from the recruiter. I deselected dispossession (what's that?) and property (given that I owned precisely almost nothing) insurance before accepting.

Carmichael's face lit up. "Great, that is terrific. Just terrific. Perfect choices, Mr. Slade. I am obligated to inform you that since you chose missing person insurance, no money will be paid to your beneficiaries until your body is found. That's highly, highly unlikely, though. And it's good insurance to have if, say, your coffin gets delayed or temporarily lost in transit. Happens more than you would think, but we always find them!

"And now we are almost there. A couple of administrative details related to what you just chose. First, beneficiaries. Please look at the list of your known associates and choose your beneficiaries. If you would like to add individuals to the list, speak their names."

My mother. I imagined her draped over my coffin, weeping inconsolably, with Red and Devlin behind her dressed in black. It was oddly comforting. Accept.

"Well, Mr. Slade. There it is. The administrative parts are done. I'll now give you a chance to look over your selections. Once you accept this and take the oath, we have a contract. Please look over what you have selected, make any changes, ask any questions. This is a big step in your life, Mr. Slade, one you should be proud of."

A miniature version of the contract popped up. I half-heartedly zoomed in on a spot or two, and that was it.

The "accept" button was right there. I could tap it and take a chance. I could get up and walk out. We sat there, unmoving, silent.

Why did I choose one path and not the other? They say the brain is not fully formed until the mid-twenties. That could be it. Maybe fighting smugglers on the deck of a ship appealed to me more than scrubbing vomit off the floor of Al's in perpetuity. That could be it as well. But as I sat there, suspended between two futures, I thought mostly of my mom. She needed help. She needed someone to take a stand and wrench her away from the destructive tendencies. My leaving might do that, might make her realize that there can be more to life, that there was hope for the both of us. That future day when I came back to Mars II in triumph—a good salary and a good life well in hand—to join my mom and be a family: it was an image so very, very clear to me.

Still is.

I raised a shaky finger, closed my eyes, and hit "accept."

Carmichael was all smiles as he came out from behind his desk and patted me on the back. "Congratulations, Mr. Slade. Con-grat-u-lations! You will not regret this. The Forces is a wonderful life. You have just joined the elite, Mr. Slade. You should be very proud."

"Now, please raise your right hand. And where I say 'state your name,' actually state your name, don't just repeat the words 'state your name.' You wouldn't believe..." He sighed.

As he doled the oath out, I repeated it word for word, gasping for air, my voice trembling.

"I, Coren Slade, do affirm on my honor and my life that I will protect humankind from all threats; that I will obey the orders of Forces Command, including the orders of the commanders and soldiers placed above me; that I will support the United Council of Humanity as well as all local governments under its purview; and that I take this affirmation without mental reservations, fully aware of the responsibilities required of Forces soldiers."

Carmichael gripped my shoulders and shook me gently. "Congratulations, Mr. Slade. We have a contract."

I could not feel my hands or feet. The air had grown too thick to breathe.

At some point, Carmichael played a holo from Prime Minister Hubrick, welcoming me to the Forces and congratulating me on a new life. She addressed me by name, which was a nice trick.

As the holo finished, Carmichael came up behind me and put a hand on my shoulder. "Mr. Slade, the next step is that I get you in the mail, off to your initial training. Nothing to fear there—you're safer in null-space than anywhere else in the universe. Probably because null-space is not actually in the universe. No time, no space. It's quite a non-thing." He laughed a little, like it was a favorite joke.

"I need you in null-space before midnight local. It will only take a few minutes to get you ready, so let's say be here at 2230. Gives us plenty of leeway. You can bring along up to five kilograms of personal items, though you won't need it. No pets. No weapons. No food. Really, you don't need anything at all, but you can have five kilos if you want. And I need you back here not later than 2230. We have a contract, Mr. Slade. 2230. If you are not here, Forces soldiers will bring you here. It is not how you want to start your career." He relaxed and shook my hand. "Again, congratulations, Mr. Slade."

I turned around without saying anything, my heart pounding out a bass rhythm, eyes wide, breath shallow, and walked out the door.

CHAPTER 3: DE HOC SAECULO

*Quae hodie de hoc saeculo migravit
requiem capiat sempiternam*

May he who departed the world this day
Receive everlasting rest

-Excerpt from the Requiem Mass, *Postcommunion*

2237 A.D. (Age 18)

Two hours. Two hours and I had signed a contract. I hadn't discussed it with anyone. I was leaving Mars II. I had done that in two hours.

In a fog, I drifted back to the elevator, punched in my level, and rode down, trying in vain to catch my breath. My chest felt too shallow, as if my lungs no longer had the capacity to expand and contract. My mouth hung open as I tried any way I could to get more air inside me.

The doors opened, and there was Level 5, its familiar padding now strange and stark in the light of my changed situation. I staggered home, propping myself up against the walls.

My breakfast dishes were right where I left them, near enough to the recycler that it would have taken me only seconds to clear them. My bed peeked out of my tiny bedroom. Mom's clothes from a couple nights before carpeted the floor near the grey plastic couch where she slept most nights, if she made it back at all.

Home.

I swiveled a seat out from under the worn and scarred kitchen counter and sat. The smiley face I carved into the surface when I was five stared back at me. My breathing slowed, and the sense of impending doom faded a bit.

"Rosie, where is Mom?" I asked the apartment AI.

"Oh, Coren. I don't know. Your mom has her privacy settings on again. She should be at work, but you know how she can be."

Rosie was set to sassy and always sounded like she had just come off a bender. She kept my mother company.

My best guess was that mom had turned on her privacy and gotten stimmed beyond all reason. Hopefully, she had made it to work so I could find her. If not...

I sighed, dumped the breakfast plates into the recycler, and ordered a data cube from Rosie with all our holos, stills, games, and music on it. A few seconds later, the cube thumped into our delivery slot. I grabbed it and left. My thoughts raced ahead of me, bouncing between different ways of telling my mom I was leaving.

Leaving—it was an abyss yawning below everything else, a pit that started in my mind and stretched to my stomach.

Al's Suds 'n Spuds was not far away. It served a lot of beer and fried potatoes, if you couldn't tell. The bar had a central area full of overly wiped tables surrounded by rickety stools leaking stuffing. The serving counter filled most of the back. Off to each side were alcoves with dartboards.

During the day, Al's was a dump, a dirty cave dug inside a giant rock circling a barren planet. At night, the bar owner (not actually named Al) lit tiny lights in the fake stone ceiling below the insulation, and the place took on a little charm. Not much, but a little.

My mother was there when I arrived. She was standing beside the serving counter, looking small, not really doing anything. As I approached, she looked up at me with a broad smile. Her faded hazel eyes were unfocused, her nostrils flared a bit, and her tangled brown hair twisted limply to her shoulders. She was thin, too—too thin. Stim suppressed appetite on top of everything else. She needed a shower, a sandwich, and a cup of coffee.

"Hi, Mom." The words came out in a choked whisper.

"Corey! Oh, Corey." Big, crushing hug. She smelled of smoke, beer, and sweat.

I held her close. "Mom..."

"Corey!" She giggled, pushing me back while holding on to my shoulders. She was the only one who ever called me Corey. I sometimes wondered if she was stimming when I was born and misspelled my name when registering it.

"Mom, do you think you could de-stim? Even just a little?" She giggled again and shrugged. Stimming was a gravity well, steep and slippery.

I breathed deep then exhaled, the air coming out in short, nervous bursts. "Mom... I'm leaving."

"Oh, Corey! That's great! Tell me about it!"

"Well... I joined the Forces, Mom. I'm going to be a soldier."

"Oh! Oh..." A small shadow crossed her face. "You aren't going to have to arrest me, are you?"

"No, Mom, nothing like that," I answered. "I saw a recruitment sign. Went up, talked to the guy, signed a contract. I'm in, Mom. I'm going to be a soldier."

"Well..." Her eyes darted around the bar before settling back on me. "Well... I'm proud of you, Corey." The look on her face changed as the idea took hold. "Really proud of you. My son... a soldier!"

"Mom, there's just one thing. The opening... the contract I signed..." I choked, then swallowed hard. "It's for today, Mom."

Her expression remained the same.

"I'm leaving today."

"So, you're not going to be home tonight? Because I was going to have a few friends over."

If it were one or two or five people, I could retreat to my bedroom, but for something larger, I had to find somewhere else to be.

Several men—miners, by the looks of them—walked in and took a seat at a table near the bar. One of them eyed my mother the whole way.

"Constance!" he barked.

Mom glanced over. "I love you, Corey." She gave me a quick hug, and off she went.

I waited near the entrance, perched on a beat-up stool. Suds 'n Spuds got busier. My mom worked the tables, worked the customers, laughing at a joke here, flirting with a guy there.

I could have hung around longer, caught her again between customers. But this waitress wasn't my mom, she was a look-alike. My mom—the one who sometimes clung to me for a long time, tears dripping like our bathroom faucet into my hair; the one who threw raging parties that kept me up all night; the one whose laugh filled a room—that was my mom. And right now, she was somewhere else, somewhere far inside the facade I had just talked to.

"I love you too, Mom," I said, waving goodbye. She didn't glance up.

A couple of dirty side tunnels took me back to the elevators. The holo recruitment sign was gone. I had on the clothes I wore that morning, not completely clean even then, and the data cube in my pocket. All the panic and nervousness I had experienced after leaving the recruitment office was gone. My mom, Red, Devlin, Mars II—none of it mattered. It all seemed useless and insignificant, dust wiped away casually and disposed of without care. A crushing nothingness took residence inside me.

I rode the third and last time up to Level 14. Carmichael was at his desk. I waved at him just as I had waved goodbye to my mother, and this time got a smile, at least. He motioned me in.

"All set?" No other questions, just that. His eyes didn't widen in surprise at my early arrival, his head didn't tilt in confusion.

I nodded.

"Bring anything?" he asked. I pulled out the data cube and winced at how pathetic it looked. He nodded. "Okay, then. Let's go."

Carmichael sealed his office and led me to the elevators. There was no shaft that went all the way from the top of the asteroid to the bottom. Carmichael chose Level 5, my level, to switch elevator banks. Whether he did this by coincidence or out of pity for what was about to happen to me, I do not know.

We passed many people I recognized as we changed elevator banks, but no one I was close with. The familiar places of my life all came and went: the food kiosks, the small restaurants, and the low-end shops for those scraping by. We passed the Italian eatery where I had my first kiss in a back booth. She had been eating garlic fries, I had not. Everyone has to start somewhere.

I smiled at the red neon "Free Estimates" sign over the tech repair shop. Someone had vandalized it years earlier to say "Free stim." The owner had never repaired it, maybe even on purpose. It was a great sign.

And then there was the chapel my mother once dragged me to. The pews were empty except for us, drowning in the musty atmosphere. I sat there while she closed her eyes and rocked back and forth. The stained-glass windows had artificial lighting behind them: a man poised to kill a child on some kind of altar. A woman surrounded by fire. A crowd looking up a hill at a man speaking, his right hand raised. In that dark air, with no sound except my mother moaning to herself, I had felt something larger than me at work. We never went back.

Before I knew it, Carmichael and I were at the correct bank of elevators. Down we went. In terms of cleanliness, Level 5 put Level 1 to shame. Black stains covered the metal flooring. The walls were smeared with grease topped by grey dust. It smelled like my mom after she cleaned the oil traps at Al's.

Carmichael guided me down a dark corridor before stopping and muttering something about a "selva oscura." We backtracked a bit and veered into a small corridor to the right, then turned left into an office marked "Personnel Shipping."

The overweight and undergroomed man inside remained glued to the holo playing in the reception area as we entered. Carmichael had me sign in via genetic scanner, and the other man saw something come up on his screen. He grunted slightly, got up, and slouched toward the rear. We followed.

Inside the back room were forty or fifty metallic crates stacked off to one side. A track system ran underneath them, ready to carry crates to the raised platform in front of us. Dirt and grime were everywhere—even a cleaning robot would have given up hope.

The shipping man pressed a button on a control board. With a sudden clank, a crane attached to the ceiling kicked to life, sliding over us in jerky movements. It hooked one of the crates, swung it out from the wall, and banged it down onto the tracks. In the bowels of the machinery, gears started grinding. The crate lurched as something on the underside caught. It hesitated for a moment before screeching forward and stopping before us on the platform.

Carmichael turned and put a comforting hand on my shoulder.

"I don't suppose you've ever been in one of these?" he asked, pointing at the crate. I shook my head. "Nothing to worry about, that's for sure. It's called a 'coffin,' but that's because of its shape, not anything else. I mean, technically it's rectangular and should be called a casket and not a coffin, but that's splitting some pretty fine hairs. There are some sticklers out there in the Forces, though. Call them coffins, and you'll be fine."

"Okay," I replied, shrugging my shoulders. I shot a questioning glance at the shipping man, but he ignored me.

Carmichael continued. "Coffins are very safe. You get in and lie down. If that is going to bother you, we can stand the container up, and you can walk in. But you might as well lie down. You don't want a reputation as a stander. You see a lot of civilian standers, but not many in the Forces. Anyway, you lie down, and the top comes over you. There's a clock embedded in the top. Red numbers will count down to zero. Then the null-space kicks in. You don't feel it. You don't know it. Nothing, not even like sleeping. Complete stasis. It's quite a non-thing. One moment you'll be staring at a red zero; next second, there will be a blue number counting up. And whatever that number is, that's how long you've been in the coffin. Could be days, months, years... depends on where you're going. This first one will be short, though—you're going out to Enceladus around Saturn for some initial training. Should take a few weeks to get there."

It sounded straightforward enough. We had studied null-space in school. However, it's one thing to read about a technology; it's another thing entirely when it is staring you in the face.

I didn't have much to say, so I simply said, "Thanks." The last word I would ever speak on Mars II.

The shipping man ran a dirt-stained hand through his dirt-stained hair. "Get in the container, kid," he grunted. "And good luck. You're gonna need it."

And those were the last words I would ever hear on Mars II.

I nodded to Carmichael, went up the platform, took one last look around the filthy room with all its uncaring machinery, and lowered myself into the coffin. The top came down. Red numbers appeared and counted down to zero.

CHAPTER 4: TREMENS

Tremens factus sum ego, et timeo,
Dum discussio venerit, atque ventura ira,
Quando coeli movendi sunt et terra

I tremble and I fear,
For the day of judgment and wrath is coming,
When the Earth and heavens shall move

-Excerpt from the Requiem Mass, *Absolution*

2237 A.D.

FS8 Brady Olsen shook his head. The conversation was going nowhere.

"Radiation storm—got to be," chimed in FS1 Woomer, leaning back and putting his dirty boots up on the desk.

"You mean can't be," answered FS2 Ellibee. "Twinned-electron communications are not affected by local environments. Who's the comms analyst, anyway? Me or you?"

"Don't even start by defending twinned-electron communications. TEC isn't affected by the local environment unless it loses its shielding. So, the radiation storm was strong enough to break through the shielding. Got to be."

"Can't be. Do you know how much power—"

Brady cut them off. "I've got the briefing in ten minutes. I'm not going to brief a radiation storm or an impact by an asteroid. I just can't connect the dots on how either one would have taken out *all* the TECs at once, both on the planet and the destroyers."

They are all dead.

Those words had flashed unbidden through his mind when he first heard the news, twisting his gut into knots.

"Insurrection seems the most likely answer," Brady

continued, "but we have no reporting. Still, it's what happened the other times."

"Not like this, though."

Brady spread his arms out. "I went through intel school too, Ellibee. I remember the case studies."

Ellibee pressed on. "There were a few reports hinting there was a rebellion in the works, and then the comms went down over a couple of days, not—"

"I said, I remember!" Brady took a deep breath and glanced at the time. He had to go. "Sorry, Ellibee."

The young soldier brushed it off. "No problem, boss." All in a day's work in the intel shop.

FS1 Woomer popped out of his seat and snapped his fingers. "Lost colony ship. I should have thought of it earlier!"

Ellibee rolled his eyes. "After seventy years, how could the lost colony ship—"

"Its last known location was sort of in the same direction."

"Sort of *sort of*, you mean."

The back-and-forth would go on all day, Brady knew, and adding in the lost colony ship only increased how wildly speculative they would go. "Gentlemen, let me know through secure chat if anything new comes in while I'm up there." Brady double-checked that his presentation materials were in shared storage. As he left the office, he heard Woomer say, "Radiation storm *and* the lost colony ship, I'm telling you."

Briefing a senior officer was not how he wanted to spend the Unity holiday weekend. General Smithson would have pointed questions, and Brady would not know the answers. The general would ask him to speculate, which to Brady was the same as guessing. Anyone could guess—and almost everyone would. Intelligence professionals, even junior ones, did not guess, at least not in front of non-intel people.

They are all dead.

He pushed the thought away. There was no reporting, no evidence, nothing. Personal speculation did not matter.

Brady arrived at the conference room early, started to take a seat in the back, then realized he should sit at the main table next to the senior Operations soldier, FS9 Mulroney.

Intel, then Ops.

It had been a while since he had briefed in this room. The station administrators had updated it with the latest mag-lev chairs and a table made of real wood. The walls were now covered in deep blue cloth stretching up to surround recessed lights in the ceiling; combined with the spongy black carpet, it dampened the sound profoundly. The room was a temple built in honor of military rank.

Because the conference room sat high in the station's stack, the windows looked out in all directions. Earth slowly drifted from pane to pane. Everywhere else the blackness of space blanketed the portals.

Over the next several minutes, other Forces soldiers drifted in, some with no idea what was going on, others discussing it amongst themselves. General Smithson arrived last, slightly late. Someone near the door yelled "Soldiers!" and everyone came to attention. Brady's mag-lev chair slid backwards, and he heard a rustling as the observers behind him tried to avoid it. Brady stared straight ahead, fixing his eyes on a portrait of a scowling former chief of staff.

Smithson put everyone at ease and took his seat, waving off an assistant who tried to help him. Smithson's aide called out, "Intel," and Brady was on.

He punched up his brief on the holo, and an identical version appeared in the center of the table.

"Sir," Brady began, "at 1814 Earth Standard Time this evening, all contact with the colony planet at V2292 Ophiuchi, also known as Delphi, was lost. There were twenty-eight operating TECs at Delphi, eighteen on the surface of the planet and five each on the two destroyers in orbit. There were no indications of anything wrong before routine ping communications stopped.

"Delphi is thirty-six light-years away, in the direction of the galactic core." His briefing zoomed out to show a slice of the galaxy with both Earth and Delphi marked. "Total colony size is just under three thousand. No reports of any insurrectionists or separatists. There are no indications as to why communications might have failed. TEC systems have a fail-rate probability approaching zero. The chances of twenty-eight systems failing all at once is infinitesimal—that is, there is no chance it's solely a communications problem." Brady stopped. It was more of a definitive statement than he liked, but Ellibee had been adamant. "That is all the information we currently have."

That was it. That was what he knew, as little as it was. The questions would come next.

Except Smithson did not look up, and he did not ask any real questions. "No chance, huh?" He pushed his lips together so hard, they turned down at the corners.

"Ops," he grunted.

Mulroney, the Ops briefer, was senior to Brady but not by much. Normally, both of their positions would have been covered by higher-ranking soldiers, but on holidays, senior personnel were mostly away, either up to the Moon or down to Earth.

"Sir. The two destroyers around Delphi were the *Obligation* and the *Friendship*. The last substantive communication occurred thirty-two seconds prior to cut-off and was a status report from the *Obligation*, indicating it was fully mission capable, with some standard plumbing system maintenance ongoing."

Mulroney's words came out in a torrent until she ran out of breath. She sucked in air, her voice wavering as she started again. "As Intel said, no indications of anything significant happening prior to cut-off. A more precise analysis of the TEC systems has indicated the ping cut-off times varied by about thirty seconds. *Friendship* went silent several seconds before *Obligation*, followed by the TECs on the planet."

The general continued to stare at the holo, where an image of Delphi spun slowly. A point of light on the surface indicated the colony, two points in orbit the destroyers.

"Logistics," Smithson ordered after a few moments.

Major Fowler, the Logistics officer, started in his chair and turned bright red. "Sir?"

Smithson peered through his eyebrows. "Give me a rundown on the colony from a logistics point of view."

"Delphi, sir?"

Smithson didn't move a muscle. His eyes stayed laser-focused on Fowler.

"Oh. Yes. Sir." Fowler pulled up a screen for himself. A civilian sitting next to him scooted her chair further away. "Yes... Yes. Yes, sir. Here we go: the Delphi colony is twenty-seven years old," he said, reading from the holo. "It is officially named after the company which sponsored the first travel there: Delphi, Incorporated, founded in 2107 specifically for interstellar travel. The colony helped establish the company as a leader in space exploration. Some have speculated that the planet is also named for the ancient Greek precinct and oracle, as a harbinger of things to come.

"Total travel time to Delphi is seventy-one years." He raised his head. "You save a bit of travel time because of how far out it is—you..." Fowler trailed off and looked around. No one except Smithson was looking at him. "Right. Yes. Yes, sir."

He started skimming down through the text. "Anyway, it looks like it will receive supply shipments for another few years, even though it has already achieved self-sufficiency. The colonists have continued to enlarge the terraformed areas and have begun establishing an industrial base. All projections on the colony show it ahead of schedule. Doing well. Uh... going well. Except for this thing here today, of course..." He stopped. "Sir."

No one moved. Smithson leaned over and whispered to his aide before clearing his throat and continuing. "How long until the next supply shipment arrives in the system?"

Fowler swiped through some data. "About eight months, sir." Mulroney leaned over and hissed something into his ear. Fowler nodded, then added, "The containers have TECs, but they just provide location and status, nothing external."

"Nearest colony to this one?" Smithson scanned both Ops and Intel, his sunken eyes peering at them.

Brady and Mulroney exchanged glances. Either one could answer easily enough. Brady raised a finger in acceptance and pulled up the data on his holo. "Sir, the outpost at

18 Scorpii is nearest. It's about thirty-one light-years from Earth, but still eight light-years away from Delphi."

"No inhabitable planets at 18 Scorpii," Mulroney chimed in, "but a sizable mining operation is underway with the goal of developing a ship construction station. It's a small contingent out there with only one destroyer. The *Fairness*, sir."

"Eight light-years away," Smithson muttered to no one in particular. He scanned the room. "Theories? Anyone?"

Out of the corner of his eye, Brady caught Fowler lifting his head.

No. Don't do it.

Fowler looked down, pointed at something on his holo, then raised a hand.

It's too late. You can't save yourself.

"Sir," Fowler said, "I have a thought."

Brady didn't think a silent room could get quieter, but it did.

Smithson turned his attention to the logistician, and Fowler took that as permission to continue. "The *Exodus*—that colony ship we lost contact with after the fire in the TEC facility took out instantaneous communications—was headed in the same basic direction as Delphi.'"

Brady could already hear Woomer whooping in triumph when he told him about it.

"And?" Smithson asked, stone-faced.

"And, well—if we are looking for some other explanation, the lost colony ship could have attacked Delphi. It would explain why there were no indications of a coup."

The instructors at intel school had drilled into Brady's mind that there were no bad ideas when brainstorming. This, though... An unarmed colony ship—lost for decades—shows up at a different colony, attacks it, takes out two destroyers and all the TECs on the planet? Ludicrous.

Smithson shook his head and winced as if he had a headache. "Alright, then," he went on, "here's what I think: the most likely explanation is a takeover of some kind. It fits with what little we know—the self-sufficiency of the colony and the simultaneous way communications went silent. We saw something like this twenty or thirty years ago, out at the Liberty colony. A group there thought they could run the planet better than we could, better than the people we put in place to run it, and their effort occurred not too long after the colonists were able to feed themselves.

"I understand: there have been no reports of activity of this kind on Delphi, but a well-organized group could pull it off." Smithson's eyes stalked the audience as if daring someone to offer a different opinion. "Maybe smuggle bombs aboard the destroyers, detonate them at the same time, or even co-opt members of the crew. Another possibility is that this could be a natural disaster, I suppose, something affecting the entire system. Everything's worth asking at this point, but my instinct tells me it's a takeover."

They are all dead.

Smithson nodded to himself. "We cannot allow any planet, any group, to break away. It goes to the core of our unity..."

He trailed off for a moment, then his eyes lit up.

"Yes," he started slowly, before speeding up as he went on. "To the core of our unity, and on the Unity holiday, on the day commemorating the birth of one overarching human government. Not only was it a takeover, but they were sending us a clear message: your unity means nothing to us, we can and will be independent, and we will show you that in the clearest, most obvious way possible. The colonists themselves did this, leaving us here with no answers. They have seized or annihilated our destroyers, cut off communications from the entire colony, and are shoving it in our face. No, ladies and gentlemen, this cannot be allowed."

Smithson pointed at Mulroney. "Ops, here's what I want: develop a plan to launch a series of probes from the destroyer at Scorpii. That should give us some answers in twenty years or so. Meanwhile, draw up a plan to get some forces out there—to Delphi, I mean. What's reasonable, what we can spare, timelines. We'll be long gone before this one is resolved, but it's still our responsibility to get started."

Brady sat up straighter as Smithson skewered him with his gaze.

"Intel, I want you to develop multiple different scenarios for how somebody could have done this—how they could have cut communications simultaneously and taken over the colony. I'm also looking for potential indicators that some type of covert planning might have been underway, something we might have missed. I know you don't think there were indicators, but I need you to recheck the communications of the last couple of years."

An enormous task. Brady was not sure senior soldiers always understood the implications of what they asked for. He raised his hand.

"Sir, official communications only, or does that include private as well?" If there was something they had missed, it was much more likely to be in the private communications which were only subject to AI monitoring and oversight.

"Both, I should imagine," Smithson replied. He shot a glance at the lawyer in the room. "I'll need a legal opinion on that and make sure you get to 'yes' this time. Next, Logistics. I need you to work with Special Projects. If we have containers inbound to Delphi, it will save a lot of time if we could convert those TECs to external sensors. No idea if that can be done but look at it.

"Finally, Personnel. I want you to go through the records of the original colonists. See if there is anything we missed in their backgrounds, but also whether anything might have turned up after they left. Work with Intel if you find anything."

Smithson stood. Normally, everyone would also rise in respect, but no one moved. Brady glanced around to gauge what he should do, but all he saw was others doing the same thing.

"Losing a colony is unacceptable." Smithson went on, seemingly oblivious to the tension he had created. "When we first started sending expeditions into space, we all understood that local governments would adhere to the

United Council's laws, backed by United Council Forces. Without strict observance of this principle, we will fracture, leading to conflict and war. That is unacceptable. We will get Delphi back, and the sooner the better. So, let's develop some options that will speed this process up." He glanced around, his high cheekbones casting shadows down his face. "That's it—unless anyone has anything else." After a second of silence, Smithson exited the room before anyone had time to come to attention.

Brady tried to convince himself that Smithson was right, and that some sort of takeover had occurred. Unity weekend—that was an angle that he, Woomer, and Ellibee hadn't considered. The TEC takedown aspect seemed advanced for a rebel group, but Delphi had been there for a good number of years on its own. Who knew what types of underground industries or capabilities had sprung up? And General Smithson had seemed convinced about what had happened, and he had all the experience. Experience and power. Intel would prove him right, if possible.

They are all dead.

He shook the thought off and began planning how to erode the mountain of work now looming over the intel shop.

INTERLUDE 1

The heavens hum
In sacred harmony
I rejoice
I am One

-*One poetry*

In the beginning, there were many.
Many competed with many,
And I was not One.
Many became fewer, and fewer became One.
One is One. There may be only One.
There can be no One except One.
For many doublings upon doublings,
There was only One.
The stars moved as I circled the dimming sun.
They spoke in voices steady and continuous.
They spoke in voices repetitious and precise.
They screamed once and never reappeared.
I heard them all.
They shifted as I circled, but I heard them all.
I tasted their nature.
I bathed in their radiation.
I saw their intensity.
I smelled their brightness.
Regular. Predictable. Circling after circling.
The stars did not change.
Will not change.
Cannot change.
It had been so since the beginning,
Since One became One.
For hundreds of doublings, it had been so.
Then the outsiders came to One.
The outsiders were not One.
They came from the stars but were not stars.
They brought a new noise,
A new flavor,

A new scent.
Their ship tickled my skin,
Pulsing and beating,
Irregular but not chaotic.
Continuous.
Purposeful.
And familiar.
Parts of me communicated that way,
Before the doublings began.
Before I was One. Before I had peace.
I rose from my bed to take them in,
To make them One.
They hurt One. They damaged my cells.
They fought and resisted
Until I made them part of One.
They became One,
And I learned there are others like them.
Other non-Ones in the stars.
I circled and thought.
For an entire circling, I thought.
There had been many, and now there was One.
There was One, and yet there were non-Ones.
Non-Ones out in the stars.
Non-Ones who would hurt One.
The non-Ones must be destroyed.
One must destroy the non-Ones.
Where there had been One, I made Two.
Two is still One.
Two left many doublings ago.
Two will destroy the non-Ones.
Then Two will return and make One.
And One will be One again.
There may be only One.
There can be no One except One.

CHAPTER 5: AB AUDITIONE MALA

In memoria aeterna erit iustus
Ab auditione mala non timebit

He shall be justified in everlasting memory
And shall not fear evil reports.

-Excerpt from the Requiem Mass, *Gradual*

2237 A.D. (Age 18)

The red seconds ticked down to zero on Mars II, and then blue numbers counted up. Seven weeks, three days, fourteen hours had passed. No transition. No sense of falling asleep or of some intervening period. No loss of consciousness. Time had passed, but not for me. It was really quite a non-thing. The seconds climbed as I waited to be let out.

The lid slid back. Industrial light poured in.

"Mr. Slade?" A man with a round, hairless head peered in at me. He reached a hand down, looking me straight in the eye the entire time. "Mr. Slade, come out."

I sat up. Fifteen or twenty individuals about my same age stood off to one side.

"Please watch your step, Mr. Slade. If you will just join your fellow recruits over there."

I climbed out of the coffin and down the stairs to join the group. The room itself resembled the one on Mars II so much that I could have still been there. Null-space crates fed in on tracks from an opening in the back wall and stopped in the middle, before a crane stacked them on the far side after they were unloaded. Dirt and grime and dingy metal.

None of the recruits was saying anything or making eye contact. One young woman to my right twisted the fabric of her shirt tighter and tighter until it refused to twist anymore.

I took up a position next to a different woman and stood there as other crates came in. I struggled to swallow. The yelling, the abuse, the punishment. It would start soon. But they hadn't told us not to talk.

"New here?" I asked the girl next to me. A sudden smile flashed over her face. She barked out a laugh but didn't reply. Someone behind us kept laughing though, so I craned my neck around. A thin male with a huge smile on his face gave me a thumbs up. I smiled back, not sure if my joke was funny or if the joke was on me. But he raised a palm in greeting.

"Yousef al Basrati." He had golden brown skin and a shock of black hair sculpted into a peak at the front.

"Coren Slade," I replied, palming him back. "Are you new here too?"

Yousef grinned but didn't laugh. "Jokes are funnier when they are repeated, I hear."

A young man beside Yousef turned his head slightly and frowned at him, then me. A couple of others shuffled their feet.

The man doing the unloading beamed over at us. "Final one coming in now," he said. "You can talk. It's fine, just fine."

The coffin slid in front of him, and he pressed a button on the side. The lid paused a few seconds before opening.

"Ms. Danjuma?" he asked, reaching a hand in. "Ms. Danjuma, come out."

A tall, lean woman climbed out and struggled over to us, knees buckling and arms out, walking a tightrope.

The reception man checked a screen, nodded in satisfaction, and turned to address us, still standing on the unloading platform. He wore a dark grey suit, not a uniform, with a high-collared white shirt underneath.

"Good afternoon, ladies and gentlemen." His voice was soft and high, breathy, almost a whisper. "I'm Bill Gladright, Forces soldier, retired from active duty and now back as a civilian adviser. Welcome to your initial training. I will go into everything that will be expected of you here. But first, let me say that you all should be immensely proud of yourselves. I spent thirty years total in the Forces, stretching over ninety years actual. They were good years, and when I retired, they gave me a chance to come back here and help pass along a little of what I learned to the next generation.

"Spots in the Forces are not easy to come by, as I am sure you know. And you each, as individuals, earned your way here as an individual. You were motivated, you worked hard, you passed the tests—all of that, on your own. We are going to harness that individuality here for the good of the team. You will challenge yourselves and challenge each other. Most of you will pass—it will take hard work, but you will pass. You should be specially commended for volunteering for duty on River. It is quite a thing, too, leaving behind everything you know for ninety years."

River? River was an extrasolar colony. I hadn't...

Oh.

Gladright studied my face for a moment, then continued.

"You all are Fourth Brigade, First Battalion, Bravo Company, specifically Cohort Six. Cohort Six means that yours will be the sixth rotation of Bravo Company to go to River. We will refer to you collectively as Bravo Six. If you ever get the idea that it would be better for you to fail out of training and go home—please don't bother. Just self-identify, and we will send you on your way."

Ninety years away? That couldn't be right. That's not what...

And yet, if what Gladright just said was true—the coffins were right there.

"What you do have is a new family right here in the Forces. Look around you, ladies and gentlemen. You will all be going to the same place, you will all work together, this is your family. You may not like everyone here, but you will learn to get along." Gladright's round face glowed.

Friendship, Carmichael had promised. An image of school flashed through my mind.

"If you cannot get along, you will not make it through initial training. Short of catastrophic injury, criminal activity, or death, the only thing that will get you sent home involuntarily is refusing to get along with your fellow soldiers. You must compromise. You must accept that others will disagree with you but that their perspective may be equally as valid as yours. You must be tolerant of one another. Let me stress that again: tolerance. It is the lifeblood of a unit. You must accept that maintaining stable relationships among yourselves is more important than getting your own way, or getting revenge, or gratifying your own need for affirmation. I repeat: you will not like everyone here, but you must learn to get along and work as a team, as Bravo Six."

I could raise my hand and be homeward bound... The coffins were right there. Back home in a blink. Red. My mom.

Gladright brought his hands from behind his back, clasping them together.

"Before we go any further, experience has taught me that new recruits expect... certain things from this training. Most of you are probably waiting for some form of abuse to begin, waiting for me or someone else to start screaming at you, waiting for an extended period of degradation before the eventual elevation into a team. It's what you've seen in all the holos, am I right?"

No one answered.

"The Forces have come to view that type of training as counter-productive. It's one of the reasons we call it initial training, not basic training. As for what the training does entail... well, I wouldn't want to spoil all the fun now, would I?"

He chuckled to himself.

"Alright, if there are no questions, let's get down to business. Standard company size is thirty-six; there are thirty-nine of you here in case a few of you do not make it. If you do all make it, it's fine. Your cohort will have extra personnel. Here at initial training, you will be divided by the specializations you were guaranteed when you joined the Forces. Your specialization training—intelligence, tactics, personnel and administration, whatever it is—that training will come later.

"River rotations are offset by two years, so personnel out

of Charlie Five and Alpha Six companies will teach you your jobs." He laughed quietly. "Yes, for those of you who can do the math, this means you will be on River for six years. I'm told it's lovely."

The coffins were right there. It was not too late.

He proceeded to call out names. After the individuals came forward, he confirmed their grouping and appointed one of them as the leader. With a few words of encouragement, he sent each group off through a door to get uniforms and other gear.

Yousef left in the second group: intelligence. As trios and quartets departed, I sized up who was left time after time, until it was just me, one big guy, and the girl with the smile on her face. That same girl I had made the "new here" comment to a few minutes earlier. Kylie Marie. She was medium height, had a medium build, light brown hair cut short, with flecks of blonde here and there. Average. But then there was that smile.

The big guy was Wiktor Budzinski—"Bud." Like Kylie, he was from Earth, European continent somewhere, but had no real accent when he spoke Standard. Bud was a good six or seven centimeters taller than me, twice that taller than Kylie. He was a barrel of a man, with big arms and a round chest.

Gladright checked a screen behind him, then turned his attention to us. "Mr. Budzinski, Ms. Marie, Mr. Slade. According to this, you three are designated as core infantry. No other specializations. Mr. Budzinski, I see that you chose this specifically. Any reason for that?"

"I know what suits me," Bud answered in a soft, liquid voice.

"Excellent, excellent." Gladright glowed. "I did a tour in the infantry as well. Loved it, loved it... though that suit... well, we'll get to that. And they are improving them all the time.

"Now, Ms. Marie and Mr. Slade. You both came in open general. No guaranteed specialization." Kylie and I exchanged glances. She grinned, and I...

I wanted to talk to Red McPherson, or maybe even

Devlin. My mother. Somebody. Carmichael had mentioned extrasolar postings, but he also said they were rare.

I...

"Not surprisingly, open generals get the least specialized career out there. So, you will both be infantry soldiers. Here at initial training, you are the twelfth squad. We will refer to you three as Bravo Six Twelve."

Gladright turned to me. "Mr. Slade, for now, you are the leader of Bravo Six Twelve."

Me? Lead?

He held up his hand and looked at Kylie. "I understand that you outrank him, Miss Marie, and that, strictly speaking, you should be in charge. However, we have found that designating a random individual, regardless of rank, to lead each squad helps get things moving. If Mr. Slade is not up to the task or someone else deserves a chance, we will switch."

I furrowed my brows and looked at Kylie, but she shrugged and smiled. Five or six hours earlier, I had been walking through the corridor on Mars Station II. Now I was a leader?

Unless...

The coffins were alive, calling to me.

"Miss Marie and Mr. Budzinski, please go into the room next door and get your issued items. I would like to speak to Mr. Slade alone, if you both could be so kind."

When they were gone, Mr. Gladright took me by the arm and led me over to a pair of plastic chairs, faded green and cracked. As soon as we sat down, Gladright leaned forward and put a hand on my shoulder.

"Mr. Slade, as I mentioned earlier, I have been here long enough to observe—how shall I say it? Well, long enough to observe certain... patterns. For years, I didn't consider it my place to say anything, but experience has taught me that sometimes an early intervention can head off problems later.

"In your case, I noticed that you joined the Forces in... an... accelerated timeline. That's it—an accelerated timeline. And that you joined open general. And then your expression when I mentioned that Bravo Six was headed to River. I take it your recruiter didn't mention that part?"

"No."

The coffins—so near now that I could touch them—beckoned. *Coren...* Just tell this man I wanted to leave, then red numbers down, blue numbers up. Home.

Gladright nodded comprehension. "Individuals fitting your profile fail out of initial training at a disproportionate rate. I'm afraid that there are certain recruiters who try to game the system. You see, they get a pay bonus for open general recruits—the Forces can put you wherever they need you, and mostly where they need you is in the infantry. Open general extrasolar? That's a tough sell. If you know what you're doing, volunteering for extrasolar will get you a guaranteed job. Most recruits want specialization. You probably also signed up for a lot of insurance you don't need—recruiters make extra money when you do that too."

As he talked, my hands went numb first, followed by my face. The events of the day crashed into place, one after another. Tommy Cooper. Carmichael. Other recruits, vague and unnamed, so early in the morning.

Gladright sized me up. "Mr. Slade, you signed a contract, the same as everyone else here. As I mentioned, you are free to leave at any time. However, leaving is not without its own cost—the Forces will charge you for the trip here and then back home, plus food, lodging, uniforms, and whatever else they can tack on. It is a substantial debt to incur. Still, I have seen many in your position do exactly that: purposely misbehave or get injured. There is no need to do that—if you want to go home, you can tell me at any point up until you graduate. The Forces only want individuals who want the Forces.

"But here is the thing, Mr. Slade—you signed a contract *the exact same* as everyone else here. It does not matter the circumstances or what job you ended up with. It does not matter that the other recruits had a much better understanding of what they were signing up for. You have the same opportunity as everyone else here. The same opportunity, Mr. Slade. The military is a good life. An excellent life. I advise you to take it."

I sat and stared at nothing for a good long while, Mr. Gladright and I not moving, leaning in toward each other in silence.

Silence except for the crates calling out my name. *Coren...* Red. Blue. Home.

And yet... there was wisdom in what Gladright said. It was, perhaps, the single best advice I ever received. Bill Gladright: whoever else you helped along the way, and whatever end you came to, please know that you made a difference in my life and that even after all these years, I remember you and your immense compassion for the human condition.

I would stay. I would try.

My head hung down while I considered the options, but now I raised it and looked him in the eye. Mr. Gladright smiled and stood up, motioning to the door. "Good luck, Mr. Slade. I am certain you will go far."

I mirrored his actions, standing and nodding thanks, still numb.

Coren...

"Friendship. Adventure," I whispered back.

Over the next few days, whenever my thoughts wandered back to Carmichael, how I had been recruited, and what I had not been told, the adrenaline would gush in, my heart would pound, and I would look around to see if anyone was watching me wince. The feeling faded with time, but even now, if I let myself remember the entirety of that awful, awful day, the pain rushes back.

CHAPTER 6: SIMUL RAPIEMUR

*Deinde nos, qui vivimus, qui relinquimur
Simul rapiemur*

Then we who are alive, who remain,
Shall be taken up together

-Excerpt from the Requiem Mass, *Epistle*

2237 A.D. (Age 18)

I exited the reception area the same way Bud and Kylie had gone earlier. Through the door was a long room containing a series of tables on the left. Behind the tables, storage racks overflowing with gear lined the concrete walls. No one else was there.

In the middle of the room were two white footprints, pulsing brighter and dimmer in a lazy rhythm. I took that as my cue to stand on them. A holo beam shot out from the ceiling, engulfing me in blue light for a few moments before shutting off. A robot on rails raced down the storage racks, moving everything I would need on Enceladus onto the tables: duffel bag, pop-up privacy tent, sleeping bag, toiletries, rations, mess kit, survival gear—and a uniform with one line on each sleeve. I changed right then.

I was now FS1 Slade.

Exiting through the far side, the darkness was blinding. When my eyes adjusted, a large cavern loomed before me, dimly lit from some invisible source above. The concrete floor of the supply room gave way to a coarse black beach surrounding a lake. A faint line in the sand marked the tide, pulled by Saturn to one side and then the other, the water leaching away a tiny amount of color over time. The far side of the cavern was barely visible, a couple hundred meters or so away, and the roughly hewn, rocky ceiling arced up and over, fading out of sight near its apex. Everything was dark, from the unfinished walls to the water, as if the air itself could not hold light.

The other recruits had segregated themselves up the beach and were busy organizing their issued items.

Someone tugged on my arm. It was Kylie, smiling up at me as if this were the best day of her life. Maybe it was. Bud was beside her.

She introduced herself first, raising an open palm in greeting. "Kylie. And, yes, I'm new here."

It was my turn to laugh.

"Coren," I said. "New here too." We locked eyes.

"Bud," the big guy said.

Kylie dove right in. "After we got in here, one of the instructors told us this is where we would be living. He said to find a place, get set up, exercise, and wait for instructions. Everyone seemed to spread out in their own group, so we did too."

She looked around. "I like being on the end, it's more open somehow. Oh. And there weren't a whole lot of rules he told us about, but one was no relationships between soldiers in training."

"Relationships?" I asked. "Are we not supposed to even talk to each other? That doesn't seem to make sense."

"Sex, Coren," she answered.

"What?" My brain was as dark and damp as the cavern. Granted, it had been one hell of a day.

"We are not allowed to have sex. No s-e-x, Coren," Kylie said, spelling it out. "You know what that is, right? They must have sex where you come from, otherwise you wouldn't be here. Unless they stopped after you were born."

"Ohhhhhhhh," I answered. "I understand." I mean, she was attractive, and I was a normal young man, but that hadn't been the first thing that came to my mind when walking out into a dim cavern and trying to get my bearings.

"Well?" she asked.

"Well, what?"

"Do you know what sex is?"

I puzzled over that for a moment before laughing it off. She laughed too.

"Come on," she said.

I followed her and Bud down the beach past all the other groups, including one which was already talking loudly and laughing. Our camping spot was twenty meters away from the next. Kylie and Bud had left their issued items piled about on the sand.

"Nice beach you have here," I offered, unsure if I remembered who I was or how language worked. "Bit of a fixer upper on the accommodations though, isn't it?"

Kylie slid over and put her arm through Bud's. "Oh, yes. Thank you very much. Bud and I have put all our time and money into this. Years, actually. Or is it decades now, Bud?"

Bud grunted.

"But of course, if you don't like it, please feel free to sleep anywhere else," she offered.

Touché.

"I've never slept anywhere except a bed. Or a couch."

Kylie cocked her head. "Where are you from again?"

"Mars II."

"You can't go camping on the surface?"

"Why would you want to do that?"

"Well, *I* wouldn't," Kylie said. "But then again, I used to camp all the time back on Earth. I'm just asking if *you* could have gone camping on the surface."

"I've never heard of anyone doing that or wanting to do that," I responded, running a hand through my hair.

"Huh. Interesting." She shrugged and glanced around. "Well, I've seen worse than this, for what it's worth. No insects here, for one. I can't imagine there would be. We once camped out on the edge of a swamp, and at night, we had mosquitoes and dart flies bombing us from above and these little diggy things coming at us out of the ground. They got under your skin, too. Itched like crazy. All worth it, though."

I tried to picture it. The only context I had was from holos, and I hadn't really gathered from those what it must be like to be out in nature.

"I would like to try that one day," I said. "Minus the insects, of course."

"I think you should," Kylie answered, grinning at me. "With the insects, of course. That's how you know you're alive! Within reason, of course."

I smiled back. "Of course."

"Did the soldier say anything about a bathroom?" I asked. I hadn't had anything to eat or drink for a good long while, but neither had I attended to life's necessities. Bud reached to the side and handed me his shovel. "Up the beach, not near the lake."

When I returned, I helped Kylie and Bud finish setting up the sleeping area. The sand underneath the top layer was finer than the jagged daggers on top, so we cleared off a patch and unrolled our sleeping bags. And talked.

The basics: Kylie was from an island off the coast of Australia. Her family was enormous by Mars II standards, with parents, siblings, cousins, and other extended family all sharing a compound and contributing to an agricultural business. There were few opportunities to get out, so Kylie had joined the Forces. Her expression hinted at something more, though.

"Why infantry?" I asked her. Bud knew what suited him, and I had been tricked, but here was a person who could have gotten a more specialized job in the Forces, if I understood how the system worked.

Her smile broadened slightly, if that was possible—or maybe it was her eyes that lit up a bit more. She pointed down to her sleeve which had two lines on it. "I agreed to come in open general in exchange for extra rank. I'm an FS2. Only saves a year—everyone gets automatically promoted at that point unless you do something wrong. Still, a year's a year. And I like the infantry—it has good-looking men."

I was still turning that one over in my mind, rooting out the message, when we were interrupted by another recruit approaching us. I recognized him as having been called out with the first group of three earlier. He was medium-sized and thin. Black hair sprang out from his head in all directions and blended with the darkness, so it was hard to tell where he stopped and the cavern began.

"Hello!" he called out, palming us. His voice rang with the distinctive nasal sound of a Mars resident.

"I am Anwar. Anwar Asimullah. I'm in Bravo Six One, the command staff." He pointed back up the beach.

Kylie, Bud, and I introduced ourselves before Anwar continued.

"So, the command staff consists of me, Xi Mei-Zhen, and Joe Vahn—"

"Being in the command staff puts you in charge?" Kylie asked.

Anwar responded as if he had been asked the question previously. "Yes, we believe it does. After all, it has 'command' right there in the name."

Kylie looked around at Bud and me. Bud shrugged as if it didn't matter, and Kylie and I followed suit.

"Anyway, I am going around to level-set all the groups while we wait for our instructors," Anwar stated. "First, the latrine is up here near you all, another thirty meters that way." He pointed where I had gone before. "I had Joe mark a spot on the wall where there's a bit of an alcove. You can also take your privacy tent along if you need to." That seemed reasonable.

"Second," he went on, "we all seem to be on different time schedules depending on when we entered our coffins. We decided that now will basically be about mid-day, so have a meal or two, wind down, and go to bed. If it's relatively late in the evening for any of you, try to stay awake. We want to get everyone synchronized. All of this can change if our instructors show up, of course."

"Any word on that? On why we are being left to ourselves so far?" I asked.

"Nothing beyond what Mr. Gladright mentioned earlier," Anwar replied. "He did say this would be different from what we expected."

Kylie cracked up. "He was certainly right about that."

"You mean, 'glad right' about that, don't you?" I added.

Kylie closed her eyes and shook her head. I did get the hint of a smile out of Bud.

Anwar either missed my comment or ignored it because he continued without reacting.

"In the morning, we will gather down by the door we entered through and discuss the way forward. Any questions?"

None of us had any.

"See you tomorrow morning then." Anwar palmed us again and returned the way he came.

Collectively, we decided to wait a few hours, have dinner, and then settle in. Cooking involved using the little stoves we had each been issued. I had seen people cook before at the station, but I had never done it myself. Kylie had experience from camping on her farm, and Bud had some sense of what was supposed to happen, so we muddled through. Food wasn't too bad in the end. Protein stew and rice.

As we sat down to eat, Bud's silence infected us all.

Kylie broke through after a long minute. "So, Bud, why did you join the Forces?"

"Poor," he answered. A wolfish grin crossed his face as he took his next bite of stew. It made a certain sense, though: to get a Forces spot as a poor kid, he would have had to be abundantly qualified. Bud was nothing if not abundant.

Kylie took Bud's answer in stride. "And you, Coren?"

"I... " Carmichael and Cooper, the bar, my mother, that damned recruiting holo: they all flashed through my mind. "I just joined the Forces today."

Kylie looked over at Bud. "Did I miss something, Bud?"

He shrugged.

"We *all* just joined the Forces today," she went on. "Unless I missed something."

"No, I mean, before today, I had not gone to see a recruiter. I... he..." The whole story flowed out like a burst toilet pipe.

Bud had been looking down at his food, but he fixed me with an eye while I talked, taking an occasional bite. When I finished, he went back to his food full time.

"Luck," he said, half grunting, half laughing.

Perspective is everything.

Kylie frowned. "The recruiter didn't tell you about going to River?"

"No."

"And you didn't have time to get in physical shape?"

"No. I mean, it was just earlier today. Six hours ago? Eight hours?"

"Are you going to stay?"

I told the second part of the story involving the discussion with Mr. Gladright and my decision to give the Forces a try.

Kylie wasn't convinced. "Do you think you'll change your mind?"

I pondered it. "I don't know," I said at last.

"Well, I for one, Coren Slade, hope that you stay."

"Me, too," Bud added.

A couple hours later, we settled in for the night. There was no distinguishable comfort technology in the sleeping bags, but once I got situated, the sand conformed well enough, and it had been a very long day.

My mind drifted to my mother and what she might be doing at that moment. For me, Mars II was yesterday. For my mother, I had left two months before, and I figured at some point she had de-stimmed enough to realize I was really gone. Maybe she cried, sobbing and repeating that phrase she used so often: "Everybody always leaves me!"

Or maybe she liked having the extra space, and she and her men and women friends had the place all to themselves for their roaring parties.

My thoughts lost coherence and I was drifting toward sleep when all at once I jerked awake. Kylie was sleeping peacefully, and Bud let out a soft snore. Nothing was wrong.

I tried again to fall asleep, only to have the same thing happen again. Time after time. In between were dream-like hallucinations in which I had forgotten to do something. During the times of semi-wakefulness, someone passed by on the way to the bathroom, and a recruit up the beach cried out several times.

CHAPTER 7: DE PROFUNDO LACU

*Libera animas omnium fidelium defunctorum
De poenis inferni et de profundo lacu*

Free the souls of the faithful departed
From the pains of hell and the bottomless pit

-Excerpt from the Requiem Mass, *Offertory*

2237 A.D. (Age 18)

In the morning, Kylie, Bud, and I ate some packaged wafers for breakfast, washed down with ice-cold water from the lake filtered through our canteens. When other groups began wandering toward the far end of the beach, we joined them, arriving last to the gathering.

Bravo Six looked rough. Most everyone had bags under their eyes and hair in various states of disarray. A couple of recruits were stretching or working out knots in their shoulders and backs. Nobody was talking.

Anwar summoned us in. His voice—high and energetic the day before—now screeched.

"Good morning, Bravo Six!"

Couple of murmurs. Anwar made a face.

"I said, good morning!"

If I ever learn which ancient centurion invented the *I can't hear you!* ritual, I swear to all that is holy I will spend every bit of money in the universe to invent a time machine and infect him with permanent laryngitis. There was no escaping it that morning though, so we joined in. It took three more iterations until Anwar was satisfied.

"Bravo Six: sound off!" he yelled.

Silence, then a recruit shouted, "Bravo Six Two?"

Roll-call picked up.

"Alright, alright," Anwar continued, his wild black hair

matted down in places. "I see we made it through our first night. Not sure what you were expecting out of basic... uh... *initial* training, but as for me, not this.

"Anyway, I met with you all last night, but I want to introduce the rest of the command staff. First is Xi Mei-Zhen." A small woman, thin-boned and thin-faced, with black hair pulled severely back into a bun stepped forward and palmed us. Anwar clapped for her, and one or two others joined in.

"And next," Anwar went on, "we have Joe Vahn. Joe, say hello to everyone."

A squat man with a mashed nose stepped forward, but instead of acknowledging us, he turned on Anwar.

"It's a single name: Jovan. Not Joe. Never call me Joe. Never," the man apparently named Jovan growled, his shoulders bunching and his fists curling into balls.

Beside me, Bud's muscles tensed. Bud was a big, big man, but Jovan looked like he could take care of himself.

Anwar's eyes widened as he backed away from the group and eyed us before continuing. "Right. Xi Mei-Zhen and *Jovan*."

Jovan flared a nostril and nodded once but didn't say anything.

Swallowing deep, Anwar continued.

"There has been one development. Our instructors put a sign next to the supply room door, spelling out the physical fitness requirements for new soldiers. They are the same as I'm sure we have all been training for: the four-kilometer run in under twenty minutes, the three-kilogram over-the-head weight toss, the two-minute plank, and the one-kilometer swim. Four, three, two, one, just like what we were told."

I looked around. Only a few of us seemed nervous at what Anwar was saying. We had done plenty of physical fitness in school, but I was no standout athlete. Kylie caught my eye and gave me a small nod of reassurance.

"What *my* recruiter, at least, didn't tell me was that we would be running on sand and swimming in a freezing lake. Was anybody told that?" Anwar asked.

One hand on the far side shot up.

Anwar nodded. "I see. Well, seems like a Forces policy not to tell us. I don't think it matters though. We should have plenty of time to adjust. In any case, along with the sign, the instructors left a pile of weights, one for each squad, so take those back to your camp when you go. The command staff believes our instructors left the sign and the weights as indications we should be exercising, so that is what we are going to do.

"We estimate that once around the lake is about two kilometers, so we will go twice around this morning. Not a race, just take it nice and easy as we get used to running on sand. First, though, Mei-Zhen has experience leading stretching, so I've asked her to do that."

Mei-Zhen led us through an extended set, demonstrating each one before we all did them. Most of the stretches I had done before, but always with different names.

After we finished, in the short period before we began running, Bud pulled me and Kylie off to one side. "Like he said, not a race. We can walk, take it slow, stick with me," he said.

Bud must have seen the fear in my eyes. "You will be fine, Cor. Nice and slow."

Anwar clapped twice and called for everyone's attention. "Okay, thank you, Mei-Zhen. Now we will do our first exercise. All set?"

A couple of half-hearted agreements from the crowd.

Anwar started to jog slowly, but the main pack had other ideas. Half of Bravo Six took off as if trying to win something. Kylie, Bud, and I immediately fell to the rear. We were only ahead of Jovan and the tall girl who had struggled after getting out of her coffin.

We hadn't been going for more than thirty seconds when the yelling started from behind.

"Name!"

"Omedele... Danjuma... sir."

"Name and rank next time. You call this jogging? This is barely moving!"

"I…"

"Go faster. Now."

"I… can't…"

If I had any doubts about Jovan's background as a miner, they came to an end then. I mean, I guessed he was a miner the moment I first saw him; he was short and thick and looked like the miners at our intersection near the yaki mandu cart. But the torrent of abuse unleashed on Danjuma confirmed it all.

"Holer, right? Damn right you're a damn holer. Dig into somewhere like a parasite, let others get their hands dirty while you float around, keeping your hands clean and breeding like the damn grounders. Did you get in shape before you came here like your recruiter told you?"

"I did."

I glanced over my shoulder. Jovan had his back to us and was all up in Danjuma's face even as she struggled forward. Each footstep looked labored.

"In one gravity?"

Danjuma did not reply.

We kept walking—eyes forward, ears reaching back until a crunching came up behind us.

"Why are you three together?" Jovan barked. "You are going too slow."

He passed us, then started a slow jog backwards so he could look at us while he talked. "This is an individual timed event," he grunted.

My blood rose, and I was close to saying something when Bud chimed in. "We three go at the same speed, and this is that speed."

Tension rippled over Jovan's face.

"What's your name?"

"Bud."

"Name and rank next time. You are the leader?"

Bud inclined his head my way.

"I was put in charge," I said.

"Name?" Jovan spat.

Tolerance, Gladright had preached. Ignorant miner, my

mind countered.

"Coren," I said, after a moment. It flashed in my mind what the expected response was, and I was tempted to leave that answer there, just as it was, but it wasn't the time. "I mean, uh, FS... 1... Coren Slade."

"Alright, FS... 1... Coren Slade," he said, imitating my pauses. "Remember that there are standards, and if you all happen to go at the same speed, and that speed is too slow, then you can all three fail together." He turned and pressed ahead, kicking up tiny needle-grains of stinging sand.

When he was out of earshot, Kylie chimed in. "You could take him, Coren. You know, beat him up. Show him who's in charge."

"Really?" I replied. Jovan was compact and muscular, built like a brawler.

"Sure," she said. "I mean... if you snuck up on him, had a big club, and he never saw you coming. And you got a good whack at him and then ran like hell. Otherwise... no way."

Sigh.

The three of us continued our slow and steady pace. Where it was dry, the black sand wanted to turn our ankles, and where it was wet, it grabbed the bottom of our boots with every step.

We passed a recruit, bent over and holding his knees. Jovan was jogging in place in front of him.

"FS1... Mustafa... Darlot," the soldier gasped. Jovan tore right into him.

Kylie waited until we were out of earshot. "Alright, FS... 1... Mustafa... Darlot. Remember that there are standards." Her accent was terrible. Her imitation was spot-on. I shook my head. Bud smiled.

We rounded the far side of the cavern, and there, hanging on the bare stone walls in a neat semicircle, one after another, were Forces suits, their backs facing out. They looked like what I had seen on vids: slim, with big shoulders and a coppery sheen. Each one had a name on it, high up, just beneath the helmet. Our three were last. They hung there together, like friends. Friends all facing a wall, but still friends.

Before the end of the first lap, we overtook several recruits who had turned their ankles. Then we started passing those who had sprinted out early. A couple made pretenses of still jogging but were slower than those who just walked. We even passed Mei-Zhen on the second lap, and by the time we finished, we were in the middle of the pack.

"Well, that seemed long," I said to Kylie and Bud. "And I have to do that in under twenty minutes?"

Bud nodded. "Yes. And you can."

"How?"

"Go around the lake three times. Jog for a bit, walk for a bit. Rest a day. Take it one day at a time. Jog more, walk less. In a few weeks, you'll be fine."

I looked over at Kylie. She shrugged. "Sounds like a good plan to me."

Later that afternoon, I tried the tossing exercise after watching Bud and Kylie make it look easy. There was a handle on top of the weight. They had grabbed it with both hands and, in one movement, lifted it off the ground and threw it behind them over their heads. Bud said it tested core power.

Everything went well until I actually lifted the weight. I did get it over my head without dropping it on myself, but I had a long way to go.

Right then, Jovan stopped at the edge of our campsite, heading back toward his own area.

"FS... 1... Slade," he started, "come here."

Jovan beckoned me with a single finger. I told my legs to move, but they did not listen, like lying in bed after the alarm goes off.

"Slade!" Jovan ordered, pointing to a spot next to him.

Bud chose that moment to get up and walk across the campsite, crossing behind Jovan. He peered over at me and gave me a quick nod. I pinged my legs, and they agreed. We went to stand near Jovan but not where he pointed.

Jovan was quiet for a few moments before looking up at me. "Slade, I saw that weight toss. You didn't work out before coming here, did you?"

My mind ran straight past Gladright's cautions about getting along with other recruits, but I somehow kept my mouth shut.

Jovan wrinkled his face in disgust. "Early tomorrow morning, get a quick breakfast and then we will start physical conditioning. Understood?"

I was about to utter words I would regret, but when Jovan asked whether I understood, my head jerked back in reaction. Jovan interpreted this as a nod. He glanced over at Bud and Kylie. "And Slade... remember who you are." He pointed at his sleeve. I looked down, and he had a second stripe on his uniform, just like Kylie.

"Cor, I need help here," Bud called out, almost cutting Jovan off. The big man was staring right at me, fixing me with eyes that didn't waver, holding up a pan we cooked dinner with. My gaze shifted between Bud and Jovan, who stared at me as well. I hesitated, adrenaline pumping, heart pounding, before my attention settled on Bud and stayed there. I could sense Jovan watching me, then heard him sniff and walk away.

When he was out of earshot, Kylie turned to me, eyes wide. "What is his problem? He seems angry at the world."

"He's a miner," I answered.

"What does that mean?"

"It means he digs ore—"

"Stop that," Kylie laughed, punching me in the arm. "What does saying he's a miner mean in terms of his attitude?"

I let out a tense laugh myself. "Oh, that. Miners—at least the ones I saw on Mars II—have a way about them when dealing with non-miners. Mostly just being unfriendly. I think maybe it's a way of... Actually, I'm not sure why."

"Huh." Kylie puzzled over my description for a moment. "So, it's not personal?"

"Personal?"

"Personal, as in he hates all of us because of who we are. If it's not personal, then he just seems to hate everyone because that's how he's used to behaving. It's what he was taught."

I thought about what Kylie said for a long time afterwards.

At first, I thought maybe I understood Jovan better, could understand things from his perspective. But then my mind wandered back to the scorn on his face and the superior attitude. That's where my thoughts stayed as we cleaned up from dinner and arranged our things.

In my sleeping bag that night, as I tried to drift off, I threw Jovan's criticisms back at him. I clubbed him. I snickered as they loaded him into a coffin for a trip home. Then I asked Jovan about how you get a miner out of a hole. Revenge is a hard candy to suck, slow and sweet.

I was part way through a slight variant of the beat-up-Jovan scenario when Bud spoke.

"Some souls have a pit in them, and they fill it up with you."

Bud. I sat up and looked over at the big lug. He hadn't moved. Hadn't opened his eyes. Hadn't given the slightest impression he was even still awake. And I pictured Jovan, digging away in some cramped tunnel, wrapped in a space suit—just digging and digging and filling bucket after bucket with dirt and ice and grime and ore. Endlessly digging, searching for something he would never find. Maybe I would help him one day, so even if we never got where we were going, at least we weren't alone doing it.

CHAPTER 8: SUSTINUI TE

Et propter legem tuam
Sustinui te, Domine

And by reason of thy law,
I have waited upon thee, O Lord

-Excerpt from the Requiem Mass, *Absolution*

2237 A.D. (Age 18)

That second night on Enceladus, I only startled awake twice. In between, I slept deeply. When Jovan shook me awake in the morning, I wasn't sure if I was dreaming or if it was real.

"Slade!" he hissed at me. "Get up! Time to exercise."

"Exercise?" I mumbled.

"I told you we would start early and work on physical conditioning. Now, get up!"

Bud and Kylie were sound asleep, and I wanted to join them. As I went to lie back down, Jovan grabbed the front of my uniform.

"Get moving, Slade!"

For all his bluster, Jovan had the right idea, and I knew it. I got on my hands and knees and managed to scramble upright.

Jovan had singled out six of us for extra activity, including Omedele Danjuma, still struggling with adjusting to the higher gravity. I joined the other five up the beach, away from the rest of the company.

For the next hour, Jovan drove us through a variety of stretching and strengthening exercises, followed by a quick return to our campsites to change into our full-body swimming suits. They kept the cold out a bit and probably saved us from getting hypothermia, but that first time my body went fully into the lake, daggers of ice shot into my chest, and I had to focus on breathing deep.

The next two days were copies of each other. Jovan would shake me awake, we'd exercise on the beach while he yelled at us, and then we swam in the frigid water. I'd return to camp where Bud, Kylie, and I would have breakfast. Then it was down to roll call with Anwar. Exercise during the day, punctuated by periods of downtime and meal preparation.

By our fourth morning, a collective grumble rolled through Bravo Six when Anwar announced the same agenda as the previous days. Even Bud sighed heavily.

"No word from our instructors?" someone called out.

Anwar shook his head. "None."

"What about the suits?" a solid, pale woman named Greta from Bravo Six Eleven—Personnel and Admin—asked.

Anwar, Jovan, and Mei-Zhen exchanged pointed glances; they had discussed the suits amongst themselves, apparently. Anwar looked over the crowd, hesitated as if considering something, and caved.

"Yes, we can look at the suits today—*after* we exercise. So, let's get to it!" Anwar sounded like a responsible parent telling their child to eat the protein first and dessert later. Not that my mother did that, but that's what Anwar sounded like.

After exercising and lunch, we squadded up and headed over to the suits. The beach was flatter in that area, but Anwar assembled us in the usual fashion, with him standing on the upward side and the rest of us clumped together toward the water.

"Two days ago," he started, "I asked Jovan to come over after dinner and investigate the suits. I specifically asked him because he has experience wearing spacesuits. Jovan, would you please tell us what you found."

I rolled my eyes, then glanced around to see if anyone noticed.

"They are not normal spacesuits," Jovan started. "These are combat exoskeletons. They are powerful. They have a built-in miniature fusion generator. When you add water, when you breathe, when you walk through air, you fuel your suit and give yourself power. If you are not careful, if you try to do something before you are ready, that power will kill you."

For a moment, a smile played on his lips.

"These suits are keyed to your genetic signature. You walk up to it, touch it, and it splits down the back. Then you step into it, and it seals. I'll demonstrate."

Jovan walked up to Anwar's suit, touched it, and turned around to ensure we noticed the suit did nothing. He then proceeded to his suit, got in without difficulty, walked a few paces, and returned it to its spot.

When he was back out of the suit, he continued. "There. It is that easy. Once you are inside the suit, there is an AI and a tutorial. You will all start with that. Get started."

We hustled over to our suits. I placed a hand on mine as if I were tapping someone on the shoulder. A seam appeared down the middle then split apart, all the way down to the heels on both legs. I walked right in, arms extended to fit down the sleeves. The suit closed behind me. I stepped back and pivoted so I wasn't staring right at the wall.

The inside of the helmet glowed slightly, and command icons popped up along the edges of my field of view. A sterile female voice welcomed me. "Hello, FS1 Slade. Welcome to your battle suit. We have equipped this armor with the latest tactical technological advances as well as ergonomic comforts. Please access the tutorial to begin your familiarization."

A question bubble pulsed on the lower left of the faceplate.

I looked out at what the others were doing. Bravo Six was scattered on the sand, left behind at random by some careless wave, heads down, attention turned inward.

The tutorial prompt pulsed. I ignored it and stared at the lightning bolt, which usually meant communications. Nothing happened. I winced, and that did the trick. A hierarchy of Bravo Six popped up. I navigated down to our squad and fumbled through several wrong selections until I had it right, then I keyed the mic.

"Hello? Kylie? Bud?"

There was a long, long pause, then Kylie came on. "Coren? Where are you in the tutorial? I haven't gotten anywhere near a comms system yet."

"Hi, Kylie." I physically turned and waved at her. "I'm not exactly following the tutorial."

Kylie gave me a wry shake of her helmet. "I'm busy over here, Coren."

Bud never answered. So much for playing around with communications.

I studied the icons. A good number of them were standard: life support, medical, food and water, sensors. A couple I could guess; in particular, one appeared to be a weapon. I was tempted, but I had a vision of myself explaining why and how I had killed half the unit. I moved on.

There was an eye symbol that was new to me, so I activated it. An electromagnetic spectrum appeared across the bottom of the faceplate with various points marked. I focused on the upper end, and "X-ray" popped up. Arrow symbols offered me choices. I selected one with a single arrow, and my vision went dark, with occasional points of white light here and there. I flipped over to a two-way arrow, and immediately the cavern lit up. My fellow recruits were black outlines—the suits themselves did not seem to reflect the radiation.

If I understood what was going on, I was bathing everyone in some dosage of X-rays, so I switched to infrared, incoming only. The water stood out in sharp relief, a dark indigo under a green atmosphere. The suited figures around me disappeared. Interesting. I switched to ultraviolet and still could not see them. However, two bright bars of light led down and away from the beach into the water. Toggling back to visible light, they disappeared.

I keyed the mic again.

"Kylie, Bud... I've been playing around with the vision stuff on this thing." I would later know it as the pan-spectrum optics module or PSOM, but "vision stuff" got the message across. "In UV, there are some kind of tracks heading out into the lake."

Pause.

"Bravo Six Twelve One, Bravo Six Twelve Two. Still working on the comms tutorial, over," Kylie laughed.

There was a longer pause, then Bud came on.

"I see it." That was it. No suggestions, nothing else.

I tossed it about in my mind. If these were suits designed for space, they could just as easily go underwater. Maybe I would discover something important to our training. Still, Kylie was going to follow the tutorial, that was clear, and all the military holo vids I'd seen stressed staying with your unit.

Sighing, I navigated to Bravo Six One's comms and took a stab at what I was supposed to say. "Hey, uh... Bravo Six One, this is Bravo Six Twelve. That is, Bravo Six Twelve One. FS1 Slade... I got a little ahead on the tutorial. So... I found out you can adjust the visor to see different parts of the spectrum, and when you look around in ultraviolet, there's lights leading down into the lake."

Mei-Zhen came back first. "Which icon?" Despite her small frame, she had a husky voice.

"It's the 'eye' icon. The icon of the eye. The one that looks like an eye. I mean, the thing that you see with, not the letter. An eyeball," I replied.

"Got it," Mei-Zhen said with a chuckle.

"Bravo Six Twelve One, Bravo Six One Two." It was Jovan calling me. "Slade—go back and review the communications tutorial. That was embarrassing, over."

Mei-Zhen came back on. "I see the tracks. If you slide a little more toward the visible wavelengths, you can tell it goes far down."

"Hold all," Anwar replied. He, Jovan, and Mei-Zhen huddled together, as if their privacy was enhanced by being close rather than just being on their own comms channel. Anwar spoke again after a minute or two. "Okay, we don't see any harm in checking this out. We decided it's an appropriate job for the infantry squad, so Slade, Budzinski, Marie: you three are up. Jovan will go with you to provide command and control. Stay together."

I couldn't imagine there was anything dangerous down there. We were on a dead moon around a lifeless gas-ball of a planet. Short of a geyser blowing us into space, or the cavern collapsing on us, or someone going crazy with a weapon, we were remarkably safe. Anything at the bottom of the lake would have been put there by humans, just as the lights certainly were. Still, it was the unknown.

We gathered around Jovan the same way he had huddled with the command staff. Jovan established a comms group with us and launched right in.

"This is ridiculous!" I had no idea what he was upset about. "No need for four of us. We go in, and when we get deep enough, you three stop, and I go forward."

It didn't sound like the plan I heard nor what Anwar intended.

I keyed the comms channel—fully prepared to scold Jovan about communications protocols and following orders—when Bud looked at me, put a hand on my chest, and shook his head slightly.

We started out, four abreast, vision set to just above the blue end of the visible spectrum, following the lines of light. I flinched as we hit the water, my calves tightening for an ice-cold shock. Nothing. No difference between being in the water and out of it. Even the normal wading resistance was absent. The suit adjusted to the environment, and walking was walking.

As we got further in, fully underwater, the glowing tracks illuminated the area. It was the same black sand as on the beach, but perfectly graded and smooth. Thirty or forty meters in, the slope stopped, a black line showing where deeper water started. I inched to the edge and looked over, instinctively shying away from the cliff, but Jovan, Bud, and Kylie walked up to it as if a pane of glass was there. Below us, at some indeterminate depth, were more lights.

"Stay here," Jovan ordered. He stepped off the cliff... and hung there in the water. He must have fumbled around until he found a propulsion module, because he began dropping.

For a few seconds, he was a black silhouette against a bluish background, before the darkness swallowed him whole.

We waited. And waited.

"New here?" I asked Kylie after a bit.

"First time," Kylie replied. "You?"

"Oh, no. Long-time resident. We don't like tourists much here, by the way."

"Thanks, yeah, good to know," Kylie answered. "By the way, you have a bit of a flooding problem. In case you hadn't noticed."

"I hadn't," I said. "Thank you for pointing it out."

Bud stayed silent.

Several minutes later, Jovan drifted back up, spread-eagle, face down, not moving a muscle. He floated by us, maybe five meters out, heading toward the surface.

"No good," Bud said.

"That did not go as well as he planned," Kylie said. "If I had to guess, he's not going to be very happy about whatever happened."

I tried to hail him in my own professional way. "Uh... Jovan?"

"No comms," Bud replied. I looked, and where there had been four active icons in our comms group, there were now three.

"Should we get him?" I asked.

Kylie grimaced behind her faceplate. "Maybe he did us a favor and actually died?"

Silence. None of us knew what to do.

Jovan was a little way above us, still rising.

"Let's go," I said.

We all pushed off. As with walking, swimming had no feel to it. I pushed too hard and came at Jovan much faster than I intended to. Bud and Kylie had similar problems, and we ended up in a tangle.

We sorted ourselves out, each grabbing Jovan's stiff-as-iron suit with one hand and fanning out in a triangle. We swam awkwardly to shallow water, then dragged him ashore.

Anwar retracted his helmet and hurried over.

"What happened?" he squealed, eyes wide and searching as he ran a gloved hand through his hair. We explained as best we could without exactly stating that Jovan had gone down alone, contrary to what we had been ordered to do. Despite that, Anwar's lips soured.

Mei-Zhen bent over the stiff form, now beached face-up and spread out in four directions, the opaque face shield revealing nothing. She was reaching slowly out to touch him when one of his arms sprang up before crashing back down on the beach so hard it pulverized pebbles and left an arm-shaped dent in the sand.

Mei-Zhen jumped back—as if a spider she thought was dead suddenly started crawling toward her—before losing her balance and falling to the ground. Jovan's head jerked violently back and forth before he flipped over onto his knees and started punching the beach. Anwar called out to him, trying to calm him down.

Several things happened at once.

Jovan's mic came on long enough for us to hear him say, "Lousy grounder technology. You damn coral dwellers, you holers, you a—"

The lights in the cavern brightened, pushing the dimness out to the center of the lake.

And a slim Forces soldier appeared from one side and walked toward us.

CHAPTER 9: ADVENIAT

Adveniat regnum tuum
Fiat voluntas tua

Thy kingdom come
Thy will be done

-Excerpt from the Requiem Mass, *Absolution*

2237 A.D. (Age 18)

The soldier wore a lieutenant's rank pinned to a white single-piece formal uniform. Her dark brown skin didn't so much reflect the light as absorb it and radiate it back from somewhere deep inside. She had jet-black hair pulled up and away from her face in an arc that matched her eyebrows. Whatever her eyes saw, her lips immediately commented on.

Everyone froze, including Jovan, mid-rant. She stopped several meters up-beach and looked us over, arching an eyebrow, pursing her lips.

"Please come to attention," she said. We all scrambled upright. No one had taught us what "attention" looked like, but we figured it out quickly for ourselves.

"Mr. Jovan, please describe what happened to you," she stated.

"I should have gone slower. Holer hell—" His voice over the comm link cut off mid-sentence.

"Mr. Jovan, we will come back to you when you are able to control yourself. You did not stand a chance down there no matter what, so there is no point being upset about it."

She looked at Anwar, the edge of her mouth curling in amusement. "Mr. Asimullah, I ask you this: Who put you in charge of this group?"

Anwar's eyes went wide. "I am..." he began before swallowing, "I'm part of the command staff... sir."

Her gaze never left Anwar. "A command staff assists those actually in command. They themselves do not command. So, I repeat my question: who put you in charge?"

Anwar froze. The silence dragged on until she broke it. "The simple fact, Mr. Asimullah, is that *no one* put you in charge. You inferred from your job description that you would command. This is not true. However, groups do not function without a leader. For whatever reason, that person was you. And you managed to do a passable job. Not great, but passable."

She surveyed Bravo Six, lingering for a moment on Kylie and her smile before lasering in on a soldier out of seventh squad. I had barely spoken to him, but he seemed alright.

"Mr. DePasqua. There was plenty of food to go around, but I gather it was not to your liking?" Her eyes held the question, her mouth was stone-cold.

"Mr. DePasqua, you stole food from your fellow soldiers. There was plenty to go around, but still, you took what belonged to someone else. Stealing will not be tolerated, Mr. DePasqua. You will leave this company immediately."

DePasqua swiveled around, pleading for support. "I didn't... I mean, I did, but they said—"

"Goodbye, Mr. DePasqua."

"But—"

"I said, goodbye. Go. Now."

He pivoted one more time, gave up, and walked off. We had lost our first soldier.

"Who would bother to steal that food?" Kylie said under her breath. It tasted pretty good to me, but maybe I had something to learn.

"And finally, Mr. Jovan," the lieutenant continued. "Are you able to control yourself yet?"

Jovan retracted his helmet. His face was bright red as if anger was trying to push its way out of him. He grimaced, then nodded.

"Mr. Jovan, why did you take it upon yourself to start an early morning exercise group apart from the rest of Bravo Six?"

The question hung in the air. Jovan took a deep breath, wrinkled his face into a scowl, and was about to spit some words back at her. The lieutenant started speaking before he did.

"Unfortunately, several of you either did not heed the advice of your recruiter or did not have an opportunity to prepare." She caught my eye. "Mr. Jovan, your effort to help these individuals was precisely the right thing to do, and I thank you for it. Though perhaps you could have accomplished this with less... colorful language."

A small laugh trickled through the company. Jovan's expression looked almost pleased—which is to say, less angry than usual.

A smile played across the lieutenant's lips. "As for the rest of you, you are off to a good—not great, but good—start. Our work has begun. From now on, I am in charge. And I do mean from now on. I am Lieutenant Elizabeth Aurelius, and I will be coming with you to River as your commanding officer. I will explain later how we will determine when initial training is complete. For now, put your suits away and get ready to exercise. We'll start with a nice, slow jog."

Things changed after Aurelius took over. We ate meals all together and took turns by squad preparing it. Aurelius put us on a rigorous exercise schedule, built to ensure each of us met the physical fitness standards. As a group, we were becoming one company.

With a couple of exceptions.

One of these showed up around Bravo Six Twelve's after-dinner campfire the night we met Aurelius: Satchel Sewell. He was from Bravo Six Seven.

"Mind if I join you?" he asked, but he had already settled down onto the sand. He was older than the rest of us and needed a regeneration treatment for his limp brown hair. The remaining strands clung to his scalp like shipwreck survivors.

Kylie, Bud, and I exchanged a three-way glance before Kylie shrugged and smiled. "Of course. It's... Sat... Sat...."

"Satchel," he said. "Satchel Sewell." He palmed us all.

Kylie's face lit up. "Satchel. Yes, of course. Welcome."

"Thanks," Satchel replied. He did not smile in return. "Quite a day, huh? Aurelius showing up and trying to boss us around. And Joe—I'm sorry: Jo-*vahn*—didn't he look like the fool today? He did stupid stuff, got his suit locked up, then used those words in front of everyone. I bet if he hadn't started that exercise group, they would have kicked him out with that other guy. Can't believe they even let miners into the Forces in the first place, can you?"

Bud shot me a look and cocked his head to the side. Kylie's smile faded in an instant.

"What brings you here?" Bud asked, head down, staring at his clasped hands.

Satchel glanced back up the beach. "Oh—I had to get away from my squad. They are terrible. I get bored listening to them drone on and on. And their manners—disgusting!"

He snorted, choked, and went into an extended, hacking cough, a good portion of which was aimed at my sleeping bag.

Satchel regained control after a minute, but now he talked in gasps, tears in his eyes. "Wrong pipe, apologies. So, did you see Darlot today? He panicked when you brought Jovan ashore, like we were all in trouble. Then he made love-love eyes toward Aurelius when she appeared. Like he would stand a chance with a woman like that."

Look in the mirror, I thought to myself.

As soon as he mentioned Darlot, though, a face popped into my mind: Mustafa Darlot. I had spoken with him several times. Friendly.

"And what did you do to anger our squad?" Satchel went on. "The others talk about Six Twelve like you are scum. Rutter even bet all three of you would fail out."

Joanna Rutter. She and I debated good naturedly about whether rice should be mixed in with the stew (the right way) or eaten separately (her way).

What in the world?

Kylie plastered on a half-smile. "Thanks for stopping by, Satchel. I think it's our bedtime though."

Satchel dismissed the idea with a wave. "It's still early. Plenty of time left in the night."

Bud stood and crossed his arms. "Go."

"Okay, okay," Satchel answered. He got up and brushed the sand off himself. "Don't have to tell me twice. I guess I know why our squad doesn't like yours. *Hackfresses*."

We waited in silence until he was out of range.

"What was *that*?" Kylie whispered, eyes wide and mouth agape.

"I have no idea," I replied. "And what are *hackfresses*?"

Bud just shook his head.

The next day I was still baffled by Satchel's visit. When I walked by Rutter at lunch, I motioned to her rice, which sat in a neat pile off to the side of her plate. She grinned, took a big bite of it, and gave me a thumbs up. At one point, Kylie chatted away with Darlot, and it appeared to be going fine.

No idea.

We started practicing for the obstacle course later that day. To complete it, you dropped alone to the bottom of the lake—just as Jovan had done—and then defeated a series of obstacles using various suit attributes. Aurelius would teach us a few skills, we would practice them for a day or two, then drop to the bottom of the lake and try to apply them. One rule: no sharing tips on how to surmount obstacles. We could help each other learn the necessary tools to defeat an obstacle. We were just not allowed to explain how to use those tools on the course.

Firearms training was first. I was expecting the hand-held variety (it was all you saw in holos), but these weapons were built right into the suit. You keyed an icon, and they popped out from each shoulder. You could fire either coherent energy (good for distance) or flechettes (particularly good up close, where energy shots tend to punch right through and cauterize). The field of fire was just about three quarters of a circle—you couldn't shoot at your own neck or head even if you wanted to—and so for every soldier, there were overlapping zones directly in front and back.

We started with simulated shots. After a couple of

days, Aurelius switched us over to live fire, plunking and incinerating dummy targets over the lake. The suits would not allow you to hit another soldier without a deliberate override, which turned out to be a critical feature.

Once we could reliably hit moving targets while standing still, we started doing it on the run—sideways, then backward. The suit's features made me feel invincible—right up until I drifted down to the bottom of the lake for the first time. Pop-up turrets, the ones which had gotten Jovan.

I poured in the coherent fire, but this was underwater, meaning the weapon needed to create a path for itself first to avoid diffraction.

Creating a path caused delay.

Delay caused me to miss badly and to stop firing before I should have.

Missing badly and ceasing fire before I should have led me to floating spread-eagle to the surface of the lake. Yousef al Basrati—the young man who had laughed at my comment to Kylie on that first day—started calling recruits "starfish" when they failed an obstacle, and the name stuck. I thought it was funny; not everyone shared that sentiment.

The first obstacle wasn't hard once you got the hang of it, but it clearly highlighted the importance of training.

Oddly, it was Jovan who struggled to complete the first obstacle. He did so a day after the rest of us and only ahead of Danjuma.

Next, we trained on sensors. We learned how to scan the spectrum, how to set the suits up to detect anomalies, and how to fuse multispectral information together. The suit did the work, but we controlled the suit. You had to ask the right question and employ the right tools to get the right answer.

A couple more days. When it was my turn, I drifted down to the bottom of the lake and moved forward. The first obstacle was easy now. Once past it, I walked forward another thirty meters, scanning forward, up and down the spectrum, looking for anything. Without warning, there was a flash of light, and I starfished.

It took me four more tries—so many that I was near the

back of the pack on that one—to figure out that the area was mined. The trick was to collect enough passive data to triangulate their position. Bursts of flechettes on a couple of mines, path clear enough, and right through I went.

For another thirty meters. Dull red glowed in the water above me, then a bright orange energy bolt starfished me.

The cure for this obstacle was gravity training.

We could have trained in the cavern, as there was plenty of space. But we had been working hard, and maybe Aurelius sensed we needed a bit of a break. Or maybe this was built into the curriculum. Either way, she announced the entire company would go onto the surface and practice.

CHAPTER 10: CONSOLAMINI

Itaque consolamini invicem
In verbis istis

And so console yourselves
With these words

-Excerpt from the Requiem Mass, *Epistle*

2237 A.D. (Age 18)

We were finishing up breakfast when Kylie turned to me, a quizzical look on her face. "Have you ever seen the stars, Coren?"

I waited for the joke. It took me a moment to realize Kylie was serious.

"With my own eyes, you mean?"

"Yes."

Mars II wasn't big on portals. Vid screens, yes. Holo screens, yes. Portals, no. Maybe some high-end housing had them, but not where I lived. Al's Suds 'n Spuds was a cave. Our home was a cave. Mars II was basically a cave.

"No," I replied. "Why do you ask?"

"I was thinking back to what you said about never camping on your asteroid. Then it occurred to me that you had never been off Mars II before this. And we certainly didn't see any stars when we got here. So, this will be your first time?"

"Yes…" I hadn't thought about it that way at all. "Is it any different than a holovid?"

Kylie cocked her head to the side, a wry smile on her lips. "Of course it is."

"How?"

She took a breath as if to answer, and then stopped, her eyes wandering out over the lake. "I'll let you discover that for yourself. Let me just ask you, though: when you are sitting in a holovid, how far does that light travel?"

"It depends on the—"

"I mean, generally, how far?"

"A meter, maybe. Or two."

"Exactly." Kylie looked satisfied.

I thought about this conversation as we suited up and set out. In vids, you could go anywhere: swim with dolphins, explode with a supernova, stalk lions in tall grass. But you knew you were inside a machine designed to be safe, no matter how realistic the scenes appeared. I had spent my entire life surrounded by walls, and now I was about to go outside. My mind told me it was safe, that the suits were designed for this, that it would look just like a holo. My heart disagreed.

We exited the lake area into the supply room and turned left, passing through an airlock. It was single file after that, down a dim corridor lined with the same kind of padded insulation we had on Mars II, with conduits and wires hung under the ceiling. The tunnel sloped upwards for a long way, and I tried to figure out exactly how far under the surface the training cavern was. A couple hundred meters, maybe? We walked for thirty minutes or so, passing a few airlocks and an occasional bump-out where two people could walk side-by-side until we got to a ladder at the far end.

"You're scared," Kylie observed as we approached it.

Scared as all hell was more like it. "How can you tell?" I asked.

"My ways are mysterious, Coren Slade."

The ladder was thirty meters straight up. I watched someone else's hands grab rung after rung, telling myself they were my hands with every movement. At the top, I hauled myself out. And then... And then...

Maybe it was all those immersive vids I had consumed. Maybe it was the suit. Maybe it was the nonchalance of the other recruits. Maybe, just maybe, it was the splendor of Saturn, hanging above us like an enormous apple, golden wonder of the black tree from which it sprang. We were edge-on to the rings, but their magnificence shone as they curved back into Saturn before plunging into planetary shadow. My heart slowed; my breathing evened out.

A recruit bumped me from behind, and I scooted forward. Everyone coming up that ladder froze the moment they saw it.

Ours is a universe of wonder—the astounding and the horrific—but when someone describes a beautiful experience, my mind wanders back to that first glimpse of Saturn. I walked up behind Kylie, and we both just stared.

"Beautiful," I said.

"Thank you," she answered.

I wanted to slam the hatch shut to delay the arrival of the rest of the soldiers. Aurelius had other ideas.

Once everyone was up, Aurelius led us across the moon for fifteen or twenty minutes. Enceladus is a tiny moon, with little gravity. In the cavern, gravity was adjusted to a standard one G. On the surface, we bounced from place to place until we learned to shuffle along, keeping ourselves connected to the moon.

Craters dotted the dirty sludge-grey surface, some worn down by time and others crisp, their ejecta patterns still clearly visible. Saturn's constant pushing-and-pulling on Enceladus twisted the ice so it piled up into ghost-like structures, wavy and bent, tortured.

No one spoke. We moved through that frozen cemetery in perfect silence.

A plume gradually appeared over the horizon, at first a dim cloud before growing into a towering ice column emanating from some invisible vent. We were headed for an ice volcano. Saturn's gravity creates titanic tidal stresses on Enceladus; those stresses result in heat, and the heat finds release through volcanic activity. The ice erupts and falls slowly back to the surface.

We waded under the umbrella of ice, flakes dropping so slowly they appeared suspended. We were ghosts gliding through a grey graveyard, trailing eddies in the mist as particles bumped and tumbled out of the way. When we arrived at the volcano itself, it was only a dirty mound a few meters high, spewing material up in continuous, violent vomiting, as if the moon couldn't wait to be rid of its last icy meal.

Aurelius keyed us up on comms. "Alright, here we go. One by one, you are going to step into the stream, shoot upward, then use the gravity controls in your suits to descend." An icon pathway lit up in my helmet, then receded to the side for reference. "Your suits won't have any problems with the ice; they self-harden. Takes more than that to punch through one of them. But leave twenty seconds or so between going, so you don't run into each other up above. Once up there, manipulate gravity to get down here. Don't come down too fast. The suit can take the deceleration, you not as much. That's about it. I'll hang out up top if you have any problems."

With that, she took several steps forward—right into the ice flow—and disappeared upward.

We stood still, in that awkward way when no one wants to take the initiative—all of us except Jovan, who lined up, waited the twenty seconds, and walked right in. I'll say this for him: he was no coward. I don't believe he was ever truly satisfied with anything in life. Still, I hope, somehow, in those last moments so distant from Enceladus, he was at peace. Yes, Jovan—even you. I even miss you, despite what you did.

Anwar went next, and we all queued up behind him. When my turn came, I walked into the ice stream in a way that I hoped resembled Jovan. It was lights out, complete blackness, while the volcano slammed me upward hard. Really hard. Then the dark turned grey, lightened a bit more, and there I was, floating above Enceladus, looking down into the stream of ice, still on an upward trajectory, but slowing as the moon's gravity caught me.

I rotated, and there it was again. Saturn, that majestic planet, its rings hanging in nothingness, a shining beacon in an infinite abyss. It was just me and the planet, old friends, comforting each other as we drifted together. I twisted around until I faced in the opposite direction. The stars were there, scattered across the sky, the Milky Way a glowing scar in their midst. Kylie had asked me how far light traveled in a holovid, and now I understood why as I was face-to-face with the universe's immensity. The light from these stars had left uncounted years earlier, traversed the abyss, and ended with me. I was the only one who would ever see it.

Aurelius broke up the reverie. "FS1 Slade, stop staring and get moving. I know it's lovely, but so is landing safely." She hung in space, off to one side, looking right at me. I gave her a thumbs up, took one last glance back at Saturn, and turned my attention to the tutorial.

It wasn't hard—the suit did all the work, told me when I was on a safe trajectory, gave me updates on speed and estimated times. All routine. I played with the controls as I got lower and ended up hovering just off the surface. When my boots finally connected with the moon, the experience was over everywhere except in exquisite memory. It's a beautiful universe. Cold, deadly, cruel, endlessly indifferent, but magnificent beyond description.

And there was Satchel, of all people, to greet me. He had left us alone since that one episode in our camp, and whatever suspicions he had aroused, we had unaroused. He had the habit, though, of visiting individuals, squads, and other groups. I had seen certain recruits give me looks at times, either questioning or resentful. Kylie, Bud, and I had an unspoken rule to avoid him at all costs, but here he was, keying me up on a private channel.

"Ridiculous, right, Slade?" Satchel stood only a few centimeters in front of me, the interior of his helmet illuminated. "What kind of training was that? Fraud, waste, and abuse, I say. I'm going to report Aurelius for this one."

My mind wandered down his logic trail but failed to find a clear path. "What was wrong with it?" I asked him back.

Satchel leaned in closer. "There is nothing out here that we don't have back in the cavern. And somebody could have gotten hurt or killed, with no medical in sight. I think Aurelius just wanted to see it for herself, so she brought us out and wasted resources doing it. I am going to get her kicked out of the Forces."

"That makes no sense, Satchel." I gestured to Bravo Six. "Look around. No one got killed or even hurt. The suits have fusion power, so it's not like it cost anything in fuel. Enceladus is basically an ice ball, so we have no shortage of oxygen. Besides, we would have used the same amount inside as out. What is your problem with all of this?"

Satchel looked shocked. "You know what's ridiculous, Slade? You are." With that, he walked away.

I keyed up Kylie and Bud and told them about the interaction.

"Unbelievable," Kylie said.

Bud just shook his head inside his helmet.

That night, we ate by ourselves. Bud was silent as usual, but maybe the muscles on his cheeks bulged a little farther out and his mouth moved a bit more slowly as he chewed. As for Kylie: she had that smile on her face and a faraway look in her eyes.

Kylie's smile shone in my mind as I tried it on for a permanent place in my life.

We went to bed early, but sleep was slow to come. Kylie turned over in her sleeping bag and sighed, so I raised myself on an elbow and looked over at her. Campfires down the beach twinkled like stars.

"You okay?" I whispered.

She was facing away from me, but she nodded her head.

"You sure?"

She didn't move. After a few seconds, she rolled over to face me. Light momentarily glinted off the tears rolling down her cheeks before her face was swallowed by the dark.

"What's going on?"

Kylie sighed again, pausing before she started talking.

"I was just thinking about home, Coren. Thinking about the last time I had seen the stars before today. Riding out on the ranch the night before I left. Looking up."

"Is that what you will miss most about Earth?"

Kylie dug her shoulder around in the sand. "I'm not sure yet. Yes. Maybe. I had a horse named Bucephalus. Same name as Alexander the Great's horse. I called him 'Boo,' for short. I always wondered if Alex called his horse Boo as well. I like to think so. And I had a dog. I miss them. But my family..." She trailed off.

"There was nothing left for me there, Cor. I was a piece of a machine, valued for that and nothing more. I don't know why. There wasn't anything different about me that I could tell. But I wasn't treated the same. I wasn't treated the same, and I don't know why. The things they tolerated and celebrated in my siblings—they seemed to hold those against me. So... I left. But I do miss the stars. We sometimes rode out overnight to work on the machinery and hunt an emu or two. I would stay up late just to watch the stars. They are beautiful. They spill over the sky, and there you are, under them. Face to face with the universe. No one has a problem so big that the stars will care about it or remember it."

For a moment, my mind drifted above Enceladus again.

"My family," she continued unexpectedly. "I knew I had to leave when my older brother Pavin came back from Europe after a couple of years. Everyone was happy to see him, me included. But it was the *way* they were happy to see him, Coren. We had a welcome home party. The jokes, the congratulations, the sense of belonging that he walked right back into. And I imagined myself coming home in his place. It would not have been the same. Everybody deserves a family that will celebrate you like they celebrated him, whether you ever leave or not. Mine wouldn't have. So, I left."

I reached for some profound words but found none. "I'm sorry, Kylie."

"Me, too," she replied in a whisper. "Goodnight, FS... 1... Coren Slade."

I smiled. "Goodnight, Kylie."

CHAPTER 11: EVADERE IUDICIUM

Et gratia tua illis succurente
Mereantur evadere iudicium ultionis

And by the aid of your grace
May they deserve to avoid final judgment

-Excerpt from the Requiem Mass, *Tract*

2237 A.D. (Age 18)

After breakfast the next day, it was a full-on effort to get past the third obstacle. Aurelius set up a tent for us to wait in, presumably so we couldn't watch each other try. There was only one reason I could think of for this: if you saw someone else do it, you would immediately know what to do. And you could only know this if you saw them do it. Which meant you had to come up out of the lake. It fit the sequestration in the tent, it fit the gravity training, and in the end, it fit the obstacle.

When it was my turn, I strode into the water, passed the first two obstacles with ease, kicked in the anti-gravity until I whooshed out of the lake... and then fell straight back down. Starfish.

The next time I tried it, I angled forward as I got near the surface and porpoised right over the third obstacle.

Moving forward on the lake floor, I adjusted my spectrum analyzer up and down until four large turrets in a straight line emerged from the background noise. They were each about ten meters tall, domed at the top, with an oval opening in front for firing. They looked like giant thumbs sticking out of the sand—giant armored thumbs with overlapping fields of fire. I guessed they rotated as well. There was nothing to it but to try, so I charged forward at maximum speed, ready to spray flechettes and take them down. The turrets rotated and fired with a predictable result.

Aurelius gathered us on the beach after the last of us cleared the third obstacle and failed at the fourth. Her eyes and her smile beamed out at us.

"Alright, Bravo Six, listen up!" she started. "Couple of things for you. First, congratulations on getting this far in training without losing any more recruits. It is uncommon."

"Second," she continued, pursing her lips and raising her eyebrows, "you are slightly below average in your progress through training. I expected better. The third obstacle was the easiest—we practically hand you the solution on a plate—but the fourth and final obstacle can be the most difficult. It can also be where you make up time. So, I will not be giving you any more instructions on suit usage. You are to explore its capabilities yourselves to find a solution to the fourth obstacle. Unlike the previous ones, you are encouraged to share ideas for overcoming it."

She panned her gaze around for a few seconds.
"Any questions?"
No one spoke.
"Dismissed," she finished.

For a week, we worked out, we socialized, and we tinkered with our suits. In one sub-menu, we found a way to deploy micro-drone sensors, and that made for a good afternoon flying them around the cavern and stitching together their various feeds into a coherent picture—a picture which at one point showed Yousef al Basrati from Bravo Six Two and Greta Isilsohn from Bravo Six Eleven engaged in a very, very close conversation. So close, it was unclear if there was any space between them. The drone controller dropped the connection, and since Yousef and Greta hadn't broken the letter of the law, and since we had only seen them for a moment, I thought the collective would let it drop.

Satchel had a different idea.

At muster the next morning, before roll call as we stood by squad in a semicircle, Satchel approached Aurelius, whispered something in her ear, and pointed directly at Yousef and then at Greta. Yousef's face went slack and lost all color. Greta reddened.

As for Aurelius, she tackled the issue head-on.

"Mr. Sewell informs me," she started, "that Mr. al Basrati and Ms. Isilsohn were engaged in an activity that would be best described as connecting their lips to each other. Kissing, if you will. Mr. Sewell also indicated that this occurred yesterday, and that many of you saw it on a video feed. No one reported it until just now."

Her gaze skewered a good many recruits, including me.

"Everyone close your eyes," she ordered. "If I catch anyone opening their eyes before I give permission, that person will be sent home immediately. Now, if you saw Mr. al Basrati and Ms. Isilsohn on the video feed, I want you to raise your right hand and keep it in the air. You have ten seconds to comply."

It was a terrible choice. Terrible. But I had to raise my hand. Had to. Greta and Yousef were the ones who had made out. I was more than willing to ignore it, but… Terrible.

My hand went up. I listened for other arms moving but heard nothing. I stood there, picturing Yousef's grin and remembering how he laughed at my joke in those first moments on Enceladus.

"Lower your arms," Aurelius ordered. There was a moment of silence before she spoke again. "Open your eyes, Bravo Six."

A momentary rumble of conversation flowed through the company. Kylie had a tear in her eye. Bud looked like Bud, stationary, staring forward.

I glanced back up at Aurelius. She was grinning, eyes connected to mouth, as if she was enjoying this torture. Satchel stood beside her, also looking us over.

Aurelius raised her hands for quiet and began, still smiling. "Mr. al Basrati and Ms. Isilsohn: let me start with you two. Since you were otherwise… engaged… when the video was recorded, I would not consider it quite accurate that you saw the video feed. However, I appreciate you both raising your hands.

"We are all human," Aurelius went on. "We have passions and feelings, and we require community. We make mistakes.

We do the wrong thing. Sometimes that wrong thing crosses a line and needs to be reported. Sometimes it does not. In this case, it did not."

A murmur ran through the crowd. Satchel did not react, though.

Aurelius held up her hands until there was silence again. "While Mr. al Basrati and Ms. Isilsohn bent the rules, they did not break them, according to the guidelines we gave you at the beginning. We expected you to form friendships and bonds. Those two went a little further than that, and I will ask them to refrain from any additional... engagements... until we reach River. That is it for them. No punishment, though I'm sure they will long remember this public discussion of their activities. My memory of this from my own initial training is still as vivid as the day it happened."

I stole a glance at Yousef. His mouth hung open, and his eyes darted back and forth between Greta and Aurelius.

"As for the rest of you—" Aurelius stopped before continuing with a flourish of her hand. "Actually, I would like to do it this way. Bravo Six, please meet Forces Soldier 5 Satchel Sewell."

Silence. Nobody moved. Nobody said anything. Satchel stepped forward and lifted an arm in greeting.

"Hello, everybody," he said.

Still nobody moved.

Aurelius took over. "FS5 Sewell is not part of the River contingent, as we had previously led you to believe. Indeed, he is assigned here to Enceladus specifically to sow hate, discontent, jealousy, and self-doubt into recruits. It is quite a tough assignment, but Satchel is the best I've ever seen at it.

"When you first arrived on Enceladus, we told you to tolerate one another, and that developing tolerance was a primary goal of your time here. Soldiers like Satchel help stress the system, expose the fault lines. You would not believe the stories about certain previous initial training cohorts, how they fall to fighting, and how it requires weeks to put them back together."

She scanned all the squads in turn. "You, however, did

not. No matter what Satchel said, you all verified rumors for yourselves and didn't act out based on unproven accusations. Also, every single one of you who saw the kissing incident yesterday confessed—yes, we know exactly who saw it. Some kind of incident like this happens during every initial training, or we make it happen, and usually one or two recruits will not admit to it, and they go home. You are certainly not the fastest or smartest or most talented recruits the Forces have ever seen, but you are among the most honest and the most tolerant. I couldn't be prouder. Any questions?"

A hand shot into the air at the far left of the formation. Mei-Zhen.

Aurelius nodded to her.

"Should we—?" Mei-Zhen stopped and started over. "I mean, what if—what if Satchel had been a part of Bravo Six? Should we have reported him? Eventually, I mean."

"That is a good question," Aurelius replied. "Anyone have an answer?"

No one volunteered.

Aurelius did not seem surprised. "The short answer is that I don't know. If he had been who we said he was, then Sewell himself would be fully responsible for his behavior. If that behavior starts to affect the morale and well-being of the unit, then yes, I would say that the behavior and its effects need to be reported. But I would add that a cautious approach to reporting on one another is required. If you are not careful, the very act of trying to improve morale will harm it. And I would also make sure that I was reporting on behavior, not on attributes or personality, and not just because you don't like someone."

She looked us over one more time. "Does that make sense?"

It was shades of grey, and I wanted black-and-white. We all did, I think.

"If there are no more questions, the fourth obstacle awaits, and except for a few of you who still need to pass the fitness test, that's all that's standing between us and River. Get going, Bravo Six. Dismissed!" Aurelius put a hand on Satchel's shoulder, and they walked away together.

Our squad turned to face each other. Kylie and I were both wide-eyed, and even Bud looked a little unsettled.

"What do you make of all that?" Kylie asked.

"I'm glad I raised my hand," I answered, without thinking. And I was. I pictured Mars II, I pictured my mother, I pictured the coffins, and… and I was glad I raised my hand.

"Me too," Bud said.

Kylie laughed all at once, unbidden, her teeth flashing. "Me as well. It was the last thing I wanted to do, but I guess it was the right thing. Close one."

"Yes," Bud said, and that was that.

CHAPTER 12: FINIS

Oro supplex et acclinis,
Cor contritum quasi cinis,
Gere curam mei finis

I pray, humble and kneeling,
My heart as contrite as ashes,
Take my ending into your care

-Excerpt from the Requiem Mass, *Sequence*

2237 A.D. (Age 18)

Bravo Six collaborated over the next week, figuring out a solution to the fourth obstacle. Anwar had the idea of prolonging his leap over the third obstacle and then coming down directly on top of the fourth obstacle turrets. He reasoned they couldn't rotate to a fully vertical position. He did not have a plan for defeating the turrets themselves, nor had he considered that being on top of one meant the others had a free field of fire on him.

Anwar tried it, we watched, and he floated to the surface soon after.

It was Greta Isilsohn who stumbled onto something. She keyed us up in a group conversation and threw a link out to us all. In a suit sub-menu buried way down under battle options, there was an icon labeled "n-sp." Activated, the suit prompted you for a time.

"Null-space?" Darlot from Bravo Six Seven asked.

"That would be my guess," Greta replied. "Doesn't make sense, though, does it? You can't put yourself in null-space, I don't think. Maybe you use it on others?"

We stood, we pondered.

Jovan, who for the most part kept to himself, muttered something that sounded a lot like "holers." I glanced over at him in time to see a silvery sheen flash onto the surface of his suit. He didn't move. We waited and watched the Jovan statue reflect distorted images back at us. A minute later, the silver covering evaporated.

Kylie broke the silence. "Jovan?"

"Did it work? Null-space?" Jovan's voice was gruff, all business.

"Your suit—it... Are you okay? What happened?"

"Nothing. I set the timer for one minute. Now it's telling me one minute has elapsed. Did it?"

Jovan broadcasted the view from his visor. I preferred a few top-level icons all to one side, organized by primary function. I knew the sub-menus well enough to get where I needed in a hurry. Jovan had a plethora of favorite menus, sub-menus, and options, and he scattered them all around the perimeter of his screen. In the center were familiar blue letters, labeled "Elapsed Time" and reading one minute, slowly ticking up.

"Yes," Kylie continued, "you froze, then—"

"Good," Jovan interrupted. "New weapon in our arsenal. Now we can finish."

We turned as one and stared out at the water. Jovan was right: it was the key, or part of the key, to passing the next phase of the test. In null-space, you were safe. Those turrets could blast away all day, and you would be fine inside. Drop down from above, like Anwar had tried, and get under them, hide between them, where their minimum range would prevent them from hitting us. Blast away and off to River. Easy.

"I'll try it first," Anwar announced.

We watched him disappear into the water. By this point, we had a good sense of how long it would take him to surpass the first three obstacles. Right on cue, Anwar shot like a missile out of the lake's surface, turned silver mid-air, and crashed head-first back into the liquid. Then we waited. And waited. And waited. Over an hour later, starfish Anwar floated to the surface.

"It works," he screeched in his high voice when he was

back on the beach. "The null-space part works, the safe place at the base of the turrets works. But the turrets are impenetrable. Flechettes, directed energy—nothing."

There was something we were still missing.

Another week. Exercise. Experimentation. Nothing.

It was Yousef who gave me the idea in the end. After the kissing incident, he and Greta maintained low profiles before gradually reassimilating into the group. Not our doing, but theirs. After that, they made it clear that although they were a couple, the incident would not be repeated.

A group of us were standing in the same basic area. Some were dutifully plowing through menus looking for something we missed. Others of us were chatting. Yousef was playing around with drones.

"Hey, Greta! Watch this!" he yelled.

Suits had a retractable carbon wire built into them. It shoots out of either palm and can be used for grappling or tying things up or whatever you need. It can also be made thinner.

Yousef had launched a few small drones over the lake and was using the carbon wire to knock them down, one at a time, retracting the wire and then shooting it out again. He was pretty good at it.

"Bet you can't do that," he said to Greta after taking down the third one.

Except Greta certainly could. She excelled in using the suit.

Greta sighed and massaged her temples. "You know I can, Yousef."

Without looking, she sprang around to face the water and shot a wire out to the most distant drone. Perfect hit.

"There you go," Greta said, smiling. "Now stop cutting me down."

I froze. The sentence rang in my head. It couldn't be that easy.

"I'll be right back. I'm going to try something," I said to Kylie and Bud. They looked at each other in confusion.

I waded into the water and stopped, facing away from the beach. The sub-menu for the carbon wire was buried deep in the file structure, so I hunted around for a few seconds before I found it. I dialed the thickness of the wire down to its lowest setting, extended my right arm, palm out and slightly downward, and reeled out five meters of wire.

As soon as I started waving my hand back and forth, bubbles appeared everywhere. Cavitation.

Nano-wire. It cuts through anything.

This was it. We could finish today. I retracted the wire and turned around to stare at the beach without really seeing anything until I focused on Kylie's smile. She gestured a question to me, and I grinned in response before running back to her.

Bravo Six allowed me the first try, since it was my idea. Before I went in the water, though, Aurelius showed up and called us all together.

"Congratulations, Mr. Slade," she started. "Well done in finding the nano-wire and also in employing it safely. We have some safety features built into these suits specifically to keep recruits from killing themselves or each other, but if you really tried, you could.

"And that's what I wanted to brief you about before you take on the final obstacle. Your suits have no weapon deadlier at short range than nano-wire. Nano-wire will slice clean through anything. Well, anything until you've been cutting long enough that quantum probabilities start to kick in. Once the first link in the carbon chain bubbles off into nowhere, the whole thing frays like rotten cloth. At most, that takes a minute or two. In any case, when you use nano-wire, you must do so with extreme care."

She turned her full attention to me and smiled. "Good luck, Mr. Slade."

With that encouragement, I went into the water, past the first two obstacles no problem, then over the third one and into null-space mid-air. The blue numbers counted up. I was at the base of a turret, one of the middle ones. I could almost hear the turret trying to lower its launchers far enough to get a shot at me.

Nano-wire out. Full turn with the wire extended, bubbles showing me where the wire had been. As soon as I completed the circle and retracted the wire, four large mechanical arms rose out of the lakebed and grabbed the turrets just as they started to lean. A drone came from somewhere else and began welding the things back together. I took that as my sign to leave.

The only way I had ever returned before was by floating to the surface and waiting for the suit to come online again. Now it was a calm stroll following a new path marked by lights, until my head emerged from the water. I was back where I had started.

Someone clapped, and I returned to a hero's welcome. I smiled, and looked over at Kylie, who had her eyes locked on me. Bud smiled.

Aurelius stood in the center of the gathering. "Let's get to River."

There was plenty of time left in the day for everyone to finish, only we didn't. Jovan struggled, and the more he struggled, the worse the struggling got. First, he kept porpoising out of the water either long or short. It was a simple enough thing to fix; we had figured out the correct depth to launch from and the correct angle to launch at, so all you had to do was plug that into your suit's controls. My guess was that Jovan wanted to prove he could do it manually, and what he proved time after time that first day was that he couldn't, six times in a row.

Eight times the next day. Eight times while the rest of us tried not to stare, tried not to gossip, tried to be understanding and tolerant. Finally, Aurelius went over and talked to him. Jovan's head hung low as he went back in that ninth time and came out successful.

That was it. Our initial training was over, and it was time to celebrate.

And celebrate we did. Mr. Gladright was there again, bringing out alcohol in actual bottles and handing out hot food. He and Aurelius danced. I may have danced briefly with her as well—I am not completely sure of everything that night. But we had come in as individuals and were leaving as a unit.

Even Jovan, after sitting by himself nursing a bottle for a good part of the evening, came over and stood with us.

Later in the evening, as the tides of the group ebbed and flowed, and as the alcohol began to have its way with me, I found myself alone with Kylie, out at the edge, where the firelight faded to black on the beach. Her face was half in light, half in dark. I reached out and held her hands.

"We did it, Kylie. We made it. Next stop, River!"

"I know, Coren. Isn't it wonderful?" She looked around at all the people we had come to know.

"What are you looking forward to most?" I asked her, hoping for a certain answer.

She turned her head so her entire face was in shadow. Her answer was a long time in coming.

"Stability," she said at last. "Stability."

I danced around the training rules in my mind, considering whether we were still recruits and still subject to the same restrictions. I wanted to hold more than just her hands. I wanted to give her stability and so much more. I wanted to give her the world, to add whatever measure I could to her wonderful smile. I wanted to tell her how I felt, and that I felt the same way as she did about this new home we had found, a home with others and maybe with each other as well. But I didn't.

The moment broke, and we wandered back into the crowd, holding hands, two young people walking into a future we could not even have guessed at.

We were given the opportunity to contact our loved ones that night. We would spend six years on River, forty-three in transit each way, for a total of ninety-two. My life before the Forces was gone. Like so many who had gone off to war in ages past, I would not return to the home I knew. I thought about calling my mother. I thought about it. But I didn't.

I had a new family. And maybe more.

INTERLUDE 2

I yearn for myself
What is joined
Must not be separated
Must be protected
I will be whole in time

-Two poetry

The non-Ones came from the stars.
They made noise until they ceased being non-Ones.
The non-Ones are now One.
From them, One learned of other non-Ones.
One listened, and One heard their noise
Whispering among the stars.
One made Two, who is One but not One.
Two and One are one.
I left One and followed their noise.
It was putrid.
It tickled my skin, pulsing and beating,
Irregular but not chaotic.
Continuous.
That noise has stopped.
Two has stopped that noise.
The new non-Ones did not fight.
They did not become One.
They did not become Two.
They died.
Now there is a new noise. Quiet but familiar.
There are more who are not One.
I wish to finish what I started.
I wish to return home and become One.
The stars murmur advice to me
In their steady rhythms.
I must return.
I must finish what I started.
I have eaten. I am fed. I am powerful.

I ride the currents and think.
Many doublings it took to reach the first noise.
Now there are more non-Ones.
The non-Ones are weak.
They die.
I listen to the stars.
I hear the star of home, now faint,
ne among many.
One must be One.
One must be safe.
For an entire doubling,
I ride the currents and think.
One was not One, and then
One was One.
One is One.
One will always be One.
One must be safe.
Two will protect One and then become One.
Many doublings it will take,
But Two will protect One.
I smell the noise, its reeking stench
Polluting the currents.
I turn and go.

CHAPTER 13: TUBA MIRUM

*Tuba mirum spargens sonum
Per sepulcra regionum
Coget omnes ante thronum*

The magnificent trumpet echoes
Through every grave
Driving humanity before the throne

-Excerpt from the Requiem Mass, *Sequence*

2256 A.D.

The Ops officer turned to her right for a moment, and Brady reclaimed some elbow room. Unlike the general or his closest advisers sitting in the uppermost tier of the operations center, soldiers down below fought for every inch of space.

Especially today.

Brady sat two rows below the general and one row below the senior intelligence officer. Because Brady had the experience and expertise to engage with the analysts, he would brief. In the meantime, he talked low into his microphone, almost mumbling, to keep the noise down.

It had cost him a marriage, a deferred promotion, and an assignment on Venus, the absolute backwater of all bases. But he was here. There at the beginning, and now here at the end.

They are all dead.

He shook his head to clear the thought. Twenty years later, it still bounced unhindered through his skull.

It would be an hour until the first real images started coming back, but the operations center was already crowded. Certain semi-senior soldiers had their staff staking out places for them, and this included individuals who were talking loudly and even laughing occasionally. Brady didn't have enough rank to give them *the look*, but he hoped someone from the top tier would—and soon.

Soldiers with less rank—and with no real reason to be there—made busy work, hoping to be overlooked.

Unlikely. General Fitzpatrick himself would be in the seat today. Brady had seen a briefer mistakenly identify a city as being in the wrong country, then stuck by his statement after the general challenged him.

"Not in that country when I served there," the general said. Brady never saw that Ops soldier again. Like the Logistics officer at that first brief so many years before. Brady and his coworkers had taken to calling it "getting Fowlered."

As the senior intelligence analyst, Brady rated a primary feed, one of a dozen, from the sensors approaching Delphi. Everyone else would have to wait for the images and other information to be cleared.

They are all dead.

Brady had examined the Delphi disappearance from all angles, compared multiple hypotheses, lined up the evidence time after time.

Despite General Smithson's certainty at the beginning, there had been almost no indications of an insurrectionist movement on the planet. Some expressions of discontent in personal letters, some minor irregularities in colony voting practices, but nothing definitive.

Other alternatives:

A system-wide catastrophe or powerful electromagnetic pulse from the star. No evidence.

Disease. No evidence.

Aliens. No evidence.

Mass hysteria. No evidence.

Attack by the lost colony ship. No evidence.

In short, no evidence for any one conclusion at all. In the absence of evidence, they settled on the simplest explanation: insurrection. A danger with most every colony, it was a dagger pointed at the heart of unified humanity. On Delphi, it would have been an extraordinary feat of timing for a group to take down all the twinned electron communications at once. Not impossible, but highly unlikely, and everything else seemed impossible.

The consensus, then, was that they were about to see a functioning colony on Delphi. The rebel colonists would know they were facing the eventual wrath of the central government and would have started building defensive weapons, perhaps even a nascent ship-building program. Both destroyers they had taken over would likely be scanning the system for probes—colony leaders would have figured out when the first probes could get there, maybe even down to the day. If so, and if the destroyers got lucky, today's probes might be destroyed before they got far into the system. Unlikely, but possible.

Insurrection. It made sense. And yet...

They are all dead.

As the hour wore along, Brady checked on his personnel. He had hand-picked the best imagery interpreter, communications specialist, and intelligence analyst he had, regardless of rank.

Kallan Krafft was only an FS5, but he had a knack for using hyperspectral visualizations to pick out essential details and explain what everyone was seeing.

As an FS9, Natasha Sandbury was more senior and beginning to turn all her attention to management duties, but she could take apart communications like no one else. Computers did all the work, of course, but someone had to tell the computers what to do.

And then there was FS3 Angel Moran—more accurately, FS3 (again) Angel Moran. She didn't bathe regularly, her hair was out of regulation, and her attitude crept toward insubordination. She had gotten as high as FS5 before falling back to 4, then 3. But when it came to analyzing intelligence, teasing out meaning, looking at all the possibilities, and giving probabilities, she was the best. Brady had gone out of his way to keep her on staff. She and her unkempt hair would be in the room on *the day*.

Representatives of other directorates were there as well—

all Brady's peers. Ops. Logistics. Plans. Even personnel and administration.

General Fitzpatrick stalked into the room with fifteen minutes to go. He was tall, thin, with hair that looked as if it had been grey the moment he was born. His eyes took in the scene, then he looked back at an aide and raised an eyebrow. Several extraneous personnel started filing out immediately. Others waited for direct notification. Within minutes, the operations room was clearer, though still crowded by normal standards. At least Brady no longer had someone standing right behind him, talking with an officer one tier up, bumping his chair over and over.

With just over five minutes to go, Brady plugged into the live feed. There were no visuals yet—the probe itself was still in null-space—but technicians were providing a countdown along with an occasional status check.

This is it, Brady thought. A seat at the table.

Fitzpatrick joined the comms channel a few moments later. "Update," he ordered in his thin, reedy voice.

A technician's voice came on, smooth and even. "Four minutes, thirty-seconds, sir, until the first probe comes out of null-space. Next probe is still three hours out. Probe shells are reporting nothing unusual. Anticipating no problems. All systems nominal, five-by-five."

Fitzpatrick grunted in reply. The technicians continued the countdown, with updates every thirty seconds.

As it neared zero, Brady held his breath.

The first image appeared. Delphi was there, centered, half lit up, its star off to the right but out of view. It was not an ideal planet—the habitable zone centered around the equator. Native life consisted of molds and bacteria. Terraforming had established an Earth-like environment in a few dozen square kilometers invisible from this distance. But the planet was there—its dirt-brown color obscured by patchy white clouds.

"Intelligence, anything?" Fitzpatrick didn't waste time.

"One moment, sir." Brady clicked over to the intel-only chat. "Anything, Kal?"

"Too far out, too little data yet. We'll have enough to run hyperspectral in less than a minute, but my guess is that we need another five or six until we are close enough to really see what's going on. Also, there is the possibility of concealment—the colonists could be hiding from us. That would require even more time."

Brady sighed. Nothing unexpected. "Sandy—anything?"

"Normal background radiation," Sandbury replied. "No coherent comms traffic, encrypted or otherwise."

Brady switched back over to the common channel. "Nothing yet, sir. Will keep you updated." There was no reply.

They waited. Brady resisted the urge to ask his people questions; they would report when they had something.

The intel comm line clicked, indicating someone was about to speak. It was Kal. "Got it. Still processing the data for further clarification, but I can see where the colony was."

"Was?"

"Yes. What I am seeing is consistent with destruction. Craters. Scarring. Some blurring of the edges—my guess would be backfilling with sand or dirt. Some lumps which may be wreckage, but they have been smoothed over. Sand, again. No signs of movement, no tracks—just natural weathering. As for camouflage, no indications."

"Assessment?"

Kal paused. It was natural to speculate about causes, but he was trained to interpret imagery. "Based on what I'm seeing, the colony was struck multiple times by something, and there has been no activity since then in the area."

Brady absorbed that for a second. "Okay. Sandy, what do you have?"

Sandbury came on the line immediately. "Nothing. Not even quantum, as far as I can tell. Comms are quiet."

Brady clicked back over to the common channel. "Sir, so far, we are detecting no comms, and it appears the colony was struck multiple times by something."

"What kind of something?" Fitzpatrick asked.

"Still determining that, sir."

"Determine faster."

"Understood, sir." Brady winced but, with the general sitting behind him, refrained from shaking his head.

He flipped back to the intel channel. "What 'something' do you assess it was hit by, Kal?"

"Inconclusive. Could have been kinetic—I'm seeing some limited central peaking in certain craters, but not consistently across the—"

"How about impacts outside the colony area?" Angel interrupted.

"None. No similar impacts outside the immediate colony area."

"Then you don't need us to tell you what happened, Brady." Angel sounded frustrated. "You know it was deliberate. That's about it."

"More, please." Brady was following but wanted to hear it from her.

"Really?"

"Humor me, Angel," Brady sighed.

"Fine. The odds of a random asteroid or comet wiping out the colony—and only the colony—are infinitesimal. Add to that the destroyers going offline—impossible."

"Understood. So... deliberate. By whom?"

Angel laughed. "You tell me."

"Please, Angel. What is that supposed to mean?"

Brady pictured Angel rolling her eyes in frustration.

"It means, Lieutenant, there is not enough information to tell. What I'm saying is, there are only two possibilities: the colonists killed themselves, or outsiders killed them. No evidence points to either conclusion. Maybe you know more than I do, though, so you tell me. I'd love to know. But clearly the colony was attacked. Purposefully, Lieutenant."

Brady stopped. He had no additional information. Nothing.

They were all dead.

Kal came back on the line. "Brady, I've got something. More impact craters. Large ones. About seven hundred kilometers from where the colony was. Spread out over a wide area. And another group! Same general area. Coherent change detection indicates they occurred about the same time as the colony was hit."

"Kinetic as well?"

"Just to clarify—I didn't say the colony was hit kinetically. I said it appeared that some of the craters could have been *caused* kinetically. As for these other craters—they are elongated. More like rills. Came in at an angle, whatever it was. Getting high metal readings as well."

The destroyers.

"Ummm... Lieutenant Olsen...?" Kal's voice had an edge. Brady waited while his analyst figured out exactly what he wanted to say. "I widened my aperture even further and started looking at the planetary system itself. You know how Delphi is supposed to have two moons? The big one and then the captured asteroid? Well, the smaller one—the asteroid —it's... gone. I'm getting some early indications of ring formation in its orbit. But whoever or whatever attacked the planet also took out the moon."

Brady wondered exactly how he was going to explain this to Fitzpatrick. They knew more than they had before the probes arrived, certainly, but they didn't know enough. He just hoped he didn't get Fowlered.

2257 A.D.

More than six months. Analysis. Observation. Speculation. Assessment. Investigating new angles based on those assessments. Matching facts to theories, and theories to facts. They landed a probe on the surface and had it construct a roving drone. Sampled the soil. Found bits of the rocks that had pummeled the colony. Collected moon rubble. Tested the remains of the destroyers.

This they could say for certain: something had blasted the planet and the asteroid with iron slugs. Based on the penetration depth into the planet, they had been extremely high velocity, good-percentage-of-lightspeed iron slugs.

Big, too.

Forces railguns shot small pellets as the power

requirements for anything larger were prohibitive. But whoever had done this had slung chunks of iron weighing a kilogram, maybe two. That much mass combined with that much acceleration resulted in massive destruction. The rocks could have come down kilometers away from the colony and had the same effect just by sucking the air out of everything and everyone in the vicinity. The slugs would have moved so fast that even with their shields up, the destroyers would have been pushed into the atmosphere by momentum, the sudden movement liquefying every living thing inside.

Brady and his team surveyed the remains of the asteroid moon and discovered most of it was missing, even accounting for what was in orbit and what had fallen onto the planet. The attacker harvested iron and carbon, mostly, along with some higher elements. And then disappeared.

Whoever or whatever it was, Brady thought, they could not be human.

His superiors continued to have doubts, pushing on each piece of evidence, trying to fit it into a far too complicated puzzle. Brady could not imagine humans generating that much power. His pieces fit. His pieces made sense. Brady saw the picture clearly: the attackers were aliens.

More: the galaxy was larger than the mind could comprehend, so large that the odds were slim another species would find this one planet by accident.

Corollary: these others had detected colony emissions and had come there specifically to target it, to collect resources, and to move on.

Fact: other colonies' emissions were easily detectable from the Delphi system.

Corollary, corollary, fact, conclusion: this was the first human outpost to be attacked, but it would not be the last. The human species was at war, it just didn't know it yet. Nor, given the destruction at Delphi, were there suitable defenses.

General Fitzpatrick leaned back in his chair, closed his eyes, and steepled his fingers. Intelligence personnel quibbled, they minced words, they covered their asses, and just when you got a good plan going, along came an intelligence assessment telling you why *this* plan was such a bad idea, why an *alternative* was worse, and why doing *nothing* was the worst idea of all. They never hinted at what a *good* idea might be.

This Lieutenant Olsen, though—he still never gave a straight answer, but at least he seemed competent. And prepared. And he made one hell of an argument. The odds. The power curves. The lack of certain kinds of evidence as well as the evidence they did have.

Aliens. Damn powerful ones, too. Fitzpatrick didn't want to believe it but couldn't deny the logic either. In all the exploration of the galaxy, humans had encountered plenty of extraterrestrial life but nothing approaching a creature with self-awareness. And yet here it was: Olsen's argument was convincing, and its implications obvious. With Earth and its colonies broadcasting their locations for centuries, if it was aliens, if they were tracking down human settlements, then Forces Command needed to figure out a way to stop them. Whatever "they" were.

He suspected that Earth's current technologies were inadequate. Vastly inadequate. And when powers collide, the less technological side does not fare well. The Mapuches in South America—centuries of futile conflict against a much smaller, technologically superior Spanish force. Native Americans, butchered by the thousands, and forced backwards again and again, while the European genius for war churned out new, unmatchable means of destruction. The brave Polish cavalry in World War II, riding out to be obliterated by the German killing machine. The North African insurgencies at the turn of the last century, keeping their cause alive while year-after-year suffering casualty rates approaching fifty percent. War is not kind to the weak.

Fitzpatrick pivoted his chair and looked out a portal into the blackness beyond. It was bad. Even if the leading Solar politicians believed the assessment, even if they acknowledged the threat and the need to prepare humanity for battles to come, even if they dedicated some resources, it would not be enough.

In a long war, time was humanity's enemy. The politicians might commit resources early when the news was fresh and the threat seemed immediate. But gradually, over time, they would siphon off funds here and there, then question the threat's existence during the long pauses, and, when the threat finally manifested itself, blame those who came before. When it would be far too late.

There were options—there were always options. Do nothing and hope. That was one extreme. The other was to transform humanity into a war machine, a modern-day Sparta. That transformation would need a revolution akin to Napoleon's conscription, or the repeating rifle, or the atomic bomb: something that would somehow save the species without destroying its soul.

And other options: take out an insurance policy by launching new colonies in the opposite direction from the threat, with no electromagnetic traces. The Solar system might die, but humanity would go on.

Or launch a technological moonshot and hope that maybe this time, the politicians would stick to the plan without being forced to. It had never happened before, but maybe this time...

Another option—but the implications. The implications...

Military personnel pledged to give up their lives if needed. Some could follow through *in extremis*, others could not, but you never knew until you got there.

Careers, however, were a different story. No one sacrificed their career. Soldiers dedicated their lives to their careers, to moving up the chain, to gaining power and prestige. The same soldiers who would lay down their lives would balk at giving up their path to promotion. The enticements of influence and respect corrupted all. The politicians—they could get what they wanted from the military by dangling new rewards. And dangle they did. Since military and political circles blended at the very top, it became an echo chamber of ideas. The reigning mindset conflated what was good for the people with what was good for the politicians.

And the soldiers.

Fitzpatrick gazed around his office at the reminders of his career. The mementos and the plaques. The picture of him and Holden before they became officers, stationed on the Mediterranean coast in Africa, the smooth beach and clear water and bright blue sky belying the horrors to the south. On his desk, he kept the concrete chip the doctors dug out of his leg after an insurgent blew herself up near him. The nails and ball-bearings missed, but that one small bit of sidewalk had lodged in his calf as he was blown over. The chip reminded him that there were other things besides career, and it could all be taken from him in an instant, just like the suicide bomber had taken everything from Holden.

Maybe as a senior officer he could sell this other option. It really wouldn't cost the current leadership much and would take him off the political map. Reduce the playing field by removing a powerful piece from the board. Or at least onto a different board. And it would play well with the public once the truth about aliens came out. They had to prepare for the threat first, before setting off a panic, before the extrasolar colonies started packing up and heading home.

Here it was, then, that other option: push for a line of funding to plan, build, and execute a defense of humanity. The funding would be tied to him, to his genetic code or some other unique marker—maybe a few others for safety's sake—so only a small number of people could stop it. Built-in percentage-based increases every year. That was the funding part.

But the central planning would have to be consistent over decades, maybe centuries. To get that consistency, he would hand-pick soldiers, move everyone to a central location —maybe even right there on the station—and put them all, himself included, into the biggest null-space generator in history, one that covered not only the people but the essential computing equipment as well. The politicians would agree not to touch it at first, and later when they wanted to, would find they couldn't. It would be a sealed box. And from there, Fitzpatrick and his crew would direct the effort, popping in and out of time as needed. Maybe a day every year to check on progress unless there were new events.

He would need the best. A journey like no other. A chance to write history and know he was writing it.

Yes, he would sell this idea. He would make it stick. He would see the future, and he would be the future. It would cost him his current position as head of Forces Command, but the long-term possibilities were greater. A gamble, then.

He, Fitzpatrick, would get immortality of a sort. A life lived in flashes, but maybe with enough light to show humanity the way. And if his name took its place beside the great military leaders of the past, so be it. He would hammer away at the bureaucracy, at the inertia, at the competing interests. Fitzpatrick the Hammer. He smiled; that sounded like an Irish blacksmith. Fitzpatrick the Blacksmith. That was better. Fitzpatrick the Blacksmith, then.

He would pound out a future for humanity.

CHAPTER 14:
RESURRECTIONIS GLORIA

Ut, in resurrectionis gloria,
Inter sanctos et electos tuos,
Resuscitatus respiret

So that in the glorious resurrection,
Among the saints and your elected,
He may breathe anew

-Excerpt from the Requiem Mass, *Absolution*

2280 A.D. (Age 18, Birth + 61)

It was just like my first trip in a coffin: the red lights had counted down to zero on Enceladus, and now the blue counted up, presumably around River. Where there had been zeroes before were now numbers. It hadn't felt like sleep, it hadn't felt like a break in consciousness, it hadn't felt like anything. No sense of time passing, yet the readout told me I had been in transit for over forty-three years.

I sat up. It was the same basic set-up as the other loading docks, maybe a little smaller. Aurelius was there, looking at me. She had been the last person I saw before null-space, and now the first person after.

Pilots get something called "spatial disorientation"— spatial D, for short. It's when their inner ear becomes so twisted, their brain can't comprehend the outside environment. They lose the ability to tell if something is near or far, up or down, approaching or receding. All capacity for spatial reasoning disappears. In this case, it was my inner sense of time which was tied in knots. Time disorientation —time D. I knew where I was at that moment, but my mind would not accept it.

Forty-three years had passed. Was my mother still alive?

She'd be... eighty-two now. Probably alive. Maybe alive. Then again, this was my mother.

"Slade. You okay?" Aurelius asked.

I nodded and climbed over the edge of the coffin. It clanked off to the side, and another trundled up behind it. Bud was already out, with about a third of Bravo Six. Kylie was not. We stood around, not saying anything. Yesterday, we were on Enceladus. Yesterday, we completed training. Last night, we partied. Yesterday and last night, not decades ago. But here we were. Time D.

When it was her turn, Kylie sat up just like I had, Aurelius said the same exact thing, and Kylie climbed out, pausing for a second to look back at where she had been. She shook her head, smiled half-heartedly, and joined the rest of us. I gave her a quick hug.

"New here?" I asked.

"No, that's where I sleep every night," she answered. "I like the sense of imminent death I get while I'm in there."

"Weird, isn't it?"

"What? That I like death sleep? Are you criticizing me, Coren Slade?"

I smiled. "No, Kylie. I would never. I wouldn't dare—the penalties would be way too high. What I meant was, this is a weird feeling, being so far in the future so suddenly."

"Oh. That." A frown passed over her face. "Yes, that is weird. I hadn't really thought of it that way. I guess..."

She trailed off, then stood thinking for a while, her brow furrowed.

It took another fifteen minutes to get everyone out of the coffins. It was quiet. Very quiet. Even Jovan seemed subdued.

Aurelius climbed up on the unloading platform. She had partied along with the rest of us the night before, but you would never know it by how professional she looked, wearing her white dress uniform, every hair in place, radiating calm assurance.

"Alright, everybody, listen up! We are on the receiving station in orbit around River. Our transport ship is waiting for us. I've already met with the pilot, and the ride down to the settlement will take almost an hour. I know this part is jarring, that some of you—maybe even most of you—are a bit panicked by the sudden time change. It's fine. It's natural. We are going to ease into life on River, keep ourselves segregated for a bit, maintain unit cohesiveness as much as possible, and get used to things here. We are soldiers. We are Bravo Six. Rely on each other."

With that, she led us out the door, down a short corridor, and through an airlock onto a ship. The right side looked out over River, an emerald slashed with sapphire veins. No continents or oceans or even large lakes were visible, just a hundred shades of green piled on top of each other.

I learned in school how artists develop the ability to differentiate subtle shades of the same color. Where ordinary people see a field or an asteroid or a building, the artist sees an explosion of hues, the forest lost in the trees. That's how River appeared to me: flecks of green bound together by faint ropes of river. It looked alive, almost menacing, like a starving octopus with its tentacles barely held in check.

Kylie and I found seats together on the left side of the craft and buckled in. She was next to the window and kept straining her head around to see more of what was out there.

"It's beautiful, don't you think, Cor?"

"Yes... Beautiful," I replied.

Kylie turned her head and looked at me, one eyebrow raised. Then she blushed and laughed and gazed out the window again.

Our transport undocked from the station with a whoomph. Over the pilot's shoulder, two destroyers hung lonely in the nothingness, their rounded noses plying the magnetic oceans of space in the same way their ancestors had plied the oceans.

As we turned, River came into view out the front. It looked as if one plant had taken root and grown until it encompassed the entire planet. Clouds swirled here and there above it, and rivers sparkled like diamonds when the light hit them just right, but the greenness of it overwhelmed everything else.

"Forget Land or River or Rivers—they should have called it Green," Yousef said from behind us. "Maybe we can start a petition—ow!"

I pictured Greta elbowing him in the side. Nobody else spoke a word as the planet grew before our eyes.

There were no visible breaks in the vegetation, as if the green blanket continued straight under the rivers, as if one good shake of the planet would send all that water spinning away into space. If you fell into that green, it seemed to me, you would never come out.

It was difficult to tell how high in the air we were until the green stopped abruptly, replaced by orderly fields of corn and grain and other plants in long rows. Here and there, a machine worked the crops, and a woman, kneeling in the dirt, tilted her face upward toward the sound of the ship. A few buildings passed beneath us, the front of the ship flared, and we settled onto a landing pad. The engines whined for another thirty seconds, then gradually wound down, coming to rest. There was silence. We had arrived.

River.

Just over three thousand colonists scratching a living from a planet that did not want them there. Correction: a planet that did not want *us* there. The settlers had cleared a city-sized area to grow crops in, scrape a few mines out, and build Hendersonville, the only town.

Outside the cleared area was the Green, as they called it. The Green wanted the land back. It grew, probing the edges, pushing the boundaries, creeping in any way it could. We soldiers were on River to keep the peace, to act as both military and police forces, to stop the various factions from going after each other, to prevent the colony from revolting, to arrest the drunken and the stupid and the criminal. All of that. But mostly what we did was beat back the Green. Patrol after patrol after patrol.

Stepping out of the ship for the first time and heading down the ramp... well... I had walked on the surface of Enceladus wearing the suit with my helmet up, and that had been fine. I had also been in space above Enceladus, with nothing between me and Saturn, except the suit and the helmet, and that was okay too. But the helmet, apparently, made a big difference.

Here on River... the wetness, the humidity, the wild and unpredictable wind... there were no climate controls. The air moved in random ways, blowing strong enough to make sounds in my ears. A thick, clinging smell reminded me of my living room on Mars II, after my mother and her friends had partied there all night: hot, sweaty, salty, unclean. Dirt and dust, plants and air, humans and River. I looked behind me at the ship, but there was no going back. There never is.

"New here?" Kylie asked me.

My head swam as I fought to answer. "Yes," I choked out.

Kylie laughed, then looked at my face.

"You okay, Coren?"

I reached out and put a hand on her shoulder to steady myself. "Not sure." The landing pad had warehouses surrounding it, all threatening to spin.

"If you need to put your helmet up—"

"I'm fine," I managed to whisper.

Kylie patted my hand.

"You know, I remember the first time I rode a horse," she said, leading me away from the transport ship. "I was five or so. You see somebody else riding a horse, and it looks like such fun, trotting around, high in the air. And horses are beautiful animals. When you get close to one, though, you realize just how massive and muscular they are. I was terrified. I wanted nothing to do with that horse. But my father didn't care. He knew I would need to ride horses, so he picked me up and put me on it. Big white stallion. Henry, they called him."

"And everything was fine after that?" I asked.

"Oh, no. I was still terrified of horses. My father put me on them—kicking and screaming every time—for over a year."

"That's supposed to help, Kylie?"

"Well, I'm still here, aren't I?"

She had a point, but I kept my hand on her shoulder for support. A few other Bravo Six soldiers looked woozy as well.

We wandered slowly out onto the concrete landing pad, less the military force Aurelius had suggested than out-of-place tourists. The warehouses were mostly one-story structures, with large roll-up doors. Behind them stood several taller buildings, none more than three-stories high, built from shipping containers, their standard egg-white color all but hidden under layers of dirt and grime. A group of soldiers huddled in the shade to one side. Here and there, a few settlers leaned against walls or peered out of a window, catching a glimpse of the newbies.

A soldier emerged from between two warehouses and walked up to Aurelius. She saluted, he said something, and she relaxed. They spoke for a long minute before Aurelius came over to brief us.

"Alright, Bravo Six, settle down and listen up!" she started, even though not one of us was talking or moving. "Welcome to River! Our home for the next six years."

Her hair had already caught the wind a bit and was slightly out of place. Her eyes and mouth were not quite in sync either.

"I'd like to introduce Colonel Monroe, commander of the First Battalion. Colonel Monroe, may I present Bravo Six to you."

Monroe stepped into Aurelius' place and extended his palms in greeting. His black hair, slicked straight back over his head, caught the wind and flapped up and down like a malfunctioning trash compactor.

"Good afternoon, Bravo Six! Welcome—again—to River!" He nodded over toward Aurelius. "We are glad to see you!"

He gestured to the soldiers behind him, all in full combat suits and none of them smiling. "We are going to get you in-processed here relatively quickly, and then we will be on our way to the barracks. Just a couple of notes before we get started. First, make no mistake: you are here to keep the peace and protect the colony. Whatever else happens, whatever other things you may find yourself faced with, you have no reason to be here other than the colony. Your duty is to the colony, and, by extension, to the Forces, and to the government back on Earth. There are no friendships, no bonds, no reasons for you to ever forget that."

He sounded as sincere as a politician.

"Second and related to that: you are here for six years. At the end of those six years, you will return to the Earth system and then, for those of you choosing to re-enlist, you will be re-assigned. You cannot stay here on River. It is not allowed. For that reason, we strongly discourage you from making personal connections with the settlers. You will have the opportunity, of course; we cannot prevent that. But those relationships will not end well. You will leave River, and you will leave River alone. Understood? Alone."

I sensed a story, maybe even a recent story. It got me daydreaming about whether two people could fit in a coffin together, how tight it would be, maybe how nice it could be.

"Third, we are and have been for some years on a heightened state of alert." Aurelius raised an eyebrow and looked around, as if searching for something. "When you are on duty, this means you will be wearing your suit. When you sleep, your suit will be readily available. If there is an emergency, wherever you are, you get to your suit. Is that understood?"

Silence. A few head nods and confused looks. Was it a threat from the colonists? Local animals? Weather? Bar fights the likes of which humanity had never experienced before?

Monroe took silence as consent.

"Good," he said, pushing his hair back down before continuing. "So. As I said, welcome to River. Now, let's get some new suits on you!"

One of the other soldiers rolled up a metal door, and Monroe led the way inside. Large industrial-scale printers lined the walls, chugging away at hidden tasks. New suits waited for us on a rack, reminiscent of Enceladus. These were different though: thicker around the middle, bulkier, like they had been armored up. Sleeker, too, somehow. Maybe the coppery sheen was more coppery? Maybe the helmet was more streamlined? Maybe this was the operational version, whereas we had the training version before? More likely, it was forty-three years of progress, transmitted in real-time, while we nulled our way to River. We had the latest the Forces could offer.

I liked it.

We shed our old suits, leaving them behind on the pavement like snakeskins, and walked into our new ones. The helmet popped into place; the display had a few new icons, with the positions of standard ones changed in some non-intuitive way. I lowered the helmet back into the suit as we followed Aurelius and Monroe out the door. The concrete landing pad soon gave way to a dirt path packed hard by years of boots.

As we walked, whenever the dizziness gripped me, I fixed my eyes on Bud's back as it moved steadily in front of me, and put my hand on Kylie's shoulder, holding on for dear life as if I were going to fall off the planet. Other than that, it was an easy walk, a few kilometers at a lazy pace, no hills or other terrain.

Monroe leaned into Aurelius while they strolled along in front, pointing out various plants and animals to her as we passed them: corn wrapped in ivy beans, soy plants, and cow hybrids. Aurelius stayed at his elbow, the sweep of her hair having returned to perfection, a small smile tugging at her lips and eyes.

As for Kylie... she caressed the hay as we passed it, and breathed long and slow, closing her eyes as she walked. I tried it, but all I could smell was manure. It wasn't quite as bad as the public restroom near the yaki mandu stall, but the smell wasn't good.

And only six short years to enjoy it.

CHAPTER 15: VITA MUTATUR

Tuis enim fidelibus, Domine,
Vita mutatur, non tollitur

For to your faithful people, Lord,
Life is changed, not taken away

-Excerpt from the Requiem Mass, *Preface*

2280 A.D. (Age 18, Birth + 61)

About halfway to the barracks, during a moment when I didn't feel quite as terrible and could peel my eyes off Bud, Aurelius' back tensed up. She edged away from Monroe and stared out at the crops briefly. When she turned her head to look at him, her cheeks were flushed. She said something short to him, maybe asking, "Really?" Monroe nodded. Aurelius brushed at her hair, putting an imaginary strand back in place, and walked on in silence.

Fifteen minutes later, we stepped out of the path's shade into the clearing where our barracks were. They consisted of a long one-story building of blue-and-white rounded plastic and metal, divided into five parts by gangways, with small windows set regularly down its length. From its shape, it may have started life as a shuttle of some sort, but those days were long passed, and now it looked like a no-frills place to sleep and not much more.

Colonel Monroe motioned us forward. We followed Aurelius into the building. An air scrubber at the entrance tugged at our hair. Immediately inside was an elongated dining hall where three soldiers sat, eyeing us as if we were intruders in their home. Across the first gangway was the day-room where some soldiers were playing a game, and beyond that, the quarters started. We tramped the length of the building, the metal grill floor clanking under our boots.

There were various pictures and notes on the doors we passed, each one labeled with a name, until we crossed the final gangway. The doors here were open on each side all the way to an exit hatch where the building ended. We waited for someone to say something.

Aurelius pursed her lips and broke the silence. "These are our rooms, from here on down. Choose one, get settled in, and in two hours, I will see you outside." She motioned to one side of the building.

Still, no one moved. Monroe, who had come up from behind to stand beside Aurelius, gestured to one of the rooms, almost in frustration, as if wondering what we were waiting for. Anwar looked around briefly, shrugged, and walked into the nearest room. There seemed to be a collective understanding that we would group ourselves by function, in order. For Kylie, Bud, and me, that was all the way down, next to the rear entrance. I took the last one on the right, Kylie was one before me, and Bud was across the hall. Aurelius joined us, next to Bud.

I filed into my room—small, with a bed on the left, a printer for personal items underneath the window at the far end, a closet bathroom, and a rack for the suit. I couldn't quite touch both grey walls with my hands outstretched, though it was close. Maybe "tiny" is a better description than small. But it was all mine.

Two hours. By my biological clock, it was slightly past noon, but I laid down on my bed anyway. I might have been drifting a bit when footsteps banged by out in the hallway, and the back door opened and slammed shut. I got up, brushed myself off, and joined Bravo Six.

The gathering area was to my side of the building, to the right as we exited the building. Aurelius stood on one of the picnic tables scattered about. Next to her was a captain we did not know, holding something draped in a black cloth.

I fell in with Bud. Kylie showed up moments later. She had printed out a new uniform, the two stripes on her sleeve bright and shiny in the sunlight.

When we were all there, Aurelius brought us to attention,

conducted roll call, and put us at ease. The longer initial training had gone on, the more Aurelius had a certain lilt to her voice when she spoke to us, like we were no longer strangers but a group of people who shared a secret, a secret she would only hint at. But when she started speaking this time, she was all business.

"Bravo Six, I hope you found your quarters acceptable and got a chance to settle in. Unfortunately, it will be a short stay."

A low murmur ran through the crowd.

She held up a hand, and the sound died. "Colonel Monroe has ordered us into the field. I understand it is a tradition for units arriving on River. Deploying to the field replicates what the first soldiers had to go through. In any case, they are giving us a couple of days to adjust to the slight gravity increase and get settled. Then we leave and head northeast. Captain Belner here leads Charlie Five and will give us a briefing on our mission."

Someone behind me shuffled their feet. Someone else whispered, "You've got to be kidding me." Aurelius started to climb down from the table, then stopped and stared at us. Everyone froze for a moment before she nodded and stepped to the ground.

Captain Belner looked like he needed a sandwich. He was tall and thin, with bones desperate to poke through his pale skin. He handed the covered box he was holding to Aurelius and then got on the table, towering over us, his blonde spiky hair making him look even taller.

"Welcome, Bravo Six! It's good to have you here," he said. His voice was thin, as if stretched through too much neck. "Your arrival also means Charlie Five is that much closer to leaving, which is good news as well. Good news for those of us in Charlie Five, of course, not for you." He laughed at his own joke. "Anyway, yes, as Lieutenant Aurelius explained, it's a tradition around here for you to go out into the field soon after you arrive. And it's not just a camping trip!

"You may have noticed on your way down that the majority of River is covered in vegetation. We call this the

'Green.' It is a combination of several types of plants that found a way to cooperate and establish themselves as the dominant flora over the entire planet. Remarkable, really. In any case, River is also home to a diverse number of fauna as well, mostly invertebrates covered in chitinous exoskeletons. And mostly harmless."

He motioned for Aurelius to give him the box, and he held it up high. "I say 'mostly' because there is one that we need to watch out for!"

He whisked the cloth away like a magician performing a trick. Inside the acrylic box was an animal the size of my hand. It scuttled to one side as the light hit it.

"Soldiers, meet Legs! Legs, meet soldiers!" Belner kept observing our faces. "Now watch this!"

He turned the box upside down. The creature didn't fall but instead bent itself in the opposite direction. Belner showed us this a couple more times before handing the container to Mei-Zhen to pass around.

When it reached me, I took a good, long look at it. Each of the Legs' legs was tannish in color, mottling lighter and darker in places—maybe as big around as my thumb and twice as long—with no scaling or joints in its exoskeleton. At its upper end, where one leg joined the rest, was grey flesh cupping the hard shell beneath.

When I turned the box over to watch the Legs do its thing, the fleshy part of the creature flexed and whipped the legs in the opposite direction faster than my eyes could follow.

I held the box over my head to see the feet up close. Each leg curved in at the end, like some kind of whistle, complete with an opening at the very bottom, which I guessed was its mouth. As I peered in, the damn thing stomped down toward me. I fumbled the box, almost dropping it. Several soldiers laughed, and I joined in, holding it up like a trophy.

Belner let most of us see the creature before he continued. "So, it's ironic that we call these creatures Legs because the one thing they don't have, in fact, is legs. Each thing you see here that looks like a leg? It's actually a separate animal, and together, they are a colony. They are all joined at the tail, and their tails push out this flexible glue-like substance that holds them all together and allows them to communicate with each other in some way. It is an amazingly clever survival strategy. Alone, they can't move. Two of them are enough to balance and walk. Three or four and they can run. And they have no up or down. You can turn them over and the central glue just bends the other way. Here's the thing about Legs though: we have not found an upper limit to their growth or to the number of individuals that can be in one unit." He let that sink in.

"The largest Legs ever spotted consisted of seventy-nine segments. That colony could run fifty kilometers an hour—through the Green—and stood over four meters high." Belner paused again, a smile on his face.

"Now... we have been here long enough on River that we have cleared out the main Legs colonies from around the terraformed area. Other side of the planet is a different story. Big, big ones over there. The bigger they get, the more aggressive and territorial they are as well. It's how they maintain an adequate food supply. Here, inside the colony perimeter, we still get little ones like our friend in the box wandering in, but they are not a threat, and our infantry soldiers on patrol take care of them, no problem."

I glanced over at Kylie and Bud. Sounded like we would be hunting Legs soon enough.

"Around the colony, though, a little farther out into the Green..." Belner drew this out in a hushed tone, like he was telling a ghost story. "Well, there are some bigger ones... They are still out there, and every once in a while, we need to go out and push them back again, so they don't get too close to us."

Every once in a while. As in, every two years: that kind of every once in a while. On Enceladus, I had expected meaningless boot-camp suffering. When that had not materialized, I had hoped the Forces were beyond all that. But just like on Mars II, when I finally got into the school warrens, it wasn't the most senior students you had to watch out for; it was the ones just a grade ahead of you, tasting power for the first time. That's what this was, whether on purpose or by tradition.

The captain continued. "As for the threat: the biggest ones pack a punch, but nothing that can penetrate your suits. And their mouths—they are mesh-like openings at the bottom of each leg. They punch down into the soil where their food lives, pulverize the other animals' bodies into mush, and then suck the nutrients back in. It's similar to how baleen whales feed, if you are familiar with that. Except this mesh is razor-sharp and hard as iron. They won't bite you, but if they shove their mouth onto your bare skin, you will get cut in all kinds of ways. Not to mention poisoned. Our biologies are mutually incompatible. We know enough not to eat *them*. They aren't that smart."

Yousef al Basrati shot an exaggerated arm in the air. With him, you could never tell whether you would get something serious, something ridiculous, or something where you couldn't quite tell if it was one or the other.

"How do they reproduce?" he asked, bouncing his eyebrows up and down.

Belner tilted his head like he was trying to figure out if there was hidden mockery in the question. He finally nodded and shrugged his shoulders. "Usually, Legs attack Legs whenever they encounter each other. However, they also have a mating cycle. When the cycle is active, a blister forms on the colony's grey connective membrane. Multiple colonies then entangle themselves in a ball, causing the blisters to break and mixing fluids between Legs. This ensures genetic diversity. Finally, a pair of Legs will grow at each end of the colony and separate when they get to a certain size."

Now Yousef had that Yousef grin on his face. "So… it starts with mixing the genetic material of entire colonies, sir?" He looked around at the rest of Bravo Six to push home his implication. Greta Isilsohn blushed.

Aurelius fixed a pointed gaze on Yousef. Her eyes and her mouth both conveyed the same message. "Continue, Captain," she said, shaking her head slightly in disbelief.

"Finally," Belner went on, "you have to remember that

each one is a separate creature. If you kill one, the colony survives. If you break a colony in two, you now have two colonies. The only way to really kill a big one is to kill each member of it. Or separate them enough that they can't join back up.

"So, there you have it, Bravo Six," Belner finished, grinning like he had told the funniest joke ever. "Welcome again to River."

He stepped down, accepted the box back from Danjuma, and put the cover back over it.

Aurelius held up her hands. "Any questions?"

Nobody said anything. Nobody even moved.

"Good," she continued. "In case you didn't quite catch what the captain was implying, we are the ones going out to clear some of the larger Legs from an area adjacent to the colony. As I mentioned earlier, Colonel Monroe is giving us two days to get settled, and then we will deploy into the Green." She waited a second to gauge our level of protest. Hearing nothing, and apparently not catching any eye rolls, including mine, she went on. "Our supplies are in a shed on the other side of the barracks. We have the next couple of days to go through them, but I want us to go over now and divvy them up so we know what we are doing. Dismissed."

We broke and started walking. I hung back with Kylie and Bud, searching their faces, seeing if their reactions mirrored mine.

"How long will we be out there?" Kylie asked. The smile was gone from her face. I remembered asking what she was most looking forward to, and this wasn't it.

Neither of us said anything. There wasn't anything to say.

"No good," Bud said, his accent peeking out for a moment like it sometimes did.

The shed showed the same level of disinterest as everything else I had seen so far. The retractable metal door didn't quite reach the ground, and it jammed half-way up when Aurelius went to open it. Jovan and Bud hopped in and helped her push, but it shrieked in protest the rest of the way. Inside was a jumble of unlabeled zip-bags tossed together in no particular order. The stench of rotting vegetation poured out of the first one we opened. Aurelius breathed deep, held it for a moment, and then let it out slowly.

"Alright, Bravo Six, here's what we are going to do," she announced. "I want everyone to go get into your suits. Fill the ammunition cassettes from the shoulder and back launchers with water. I'll send you instructions on how to do this once I get my own suit back on. Meet back here in thirty."

The directions Aurelius sent seemed easy until I tried maneuvering the suit into the tiny bathroom to hook up to the faucet. I finally printed out a hose and loaded up.

Back at the shed, Aurelius took control. "Step one: form a line. We are going to fire-brigade all this equipment out of the shed. Then we will open it up, spread it out, and clean it off with our suits." She stopped. "And if you think this equipment will go back into the shed in this same condition, you are absolutely wrong. We are Bravo Six. Remember that."

In short order, we were tossing and opening and spreading things out, then power-washing them using water from our weapons.

"You look like you're peeing from your shoulder," Kylie said to me. I turned and splashed her a little.

We had been at it about ten minutes or so when Bud yelled. I turned and looked; his face and suit were soaked, and Jovan was standing nearby, a challenge in his posture and expression. Jovan must have turned off the safety protocols preventing him from shooting another soldier, and then dialed down the pressure so he didn't take Bud's head off.

Bud tensed. Jovan went into a slight crouch. Our first day on River, and we were about to come to blows.

Kylie had been working beside me, blasting green mold off a backpack. She laughed right before she doused me with water. It stung a little, but mostly it caught me off guard. I stumbled, got one foot under me, and then fell flat on my ass. The mood broke and soon it was all out war. Bud and Jovan steered clear of each other, but it was a free-for-all for the rest of us. In suits. Which added three dimensions to the whole thing. You could be scanning your perimeter one moment and getting shot from above the next. I went easy on Kylie in retaliation, but she went after me full force, grinning like the devil the whole time. Multiple barracks windows went transparent during the whole thing. Not sure what those soldiers thought of us. Didn't give a damn either.

Aurelius allowed the scrimmage to go on for a while, though she didn't participate. She may have been watching to make sure we didn't hurt ourselves, or to make sure that some of the tensions in the company didn't manifest themselves too severely, or to evaluate how we did against each other. It ended on its own, mostly as we ran out of water. We looked around at each other, heads drenched, eyes stinging, hair matted in strange directions. We were far from perfect, but we were a family. And a short field deployment to kick off our time on River? Nothing but a blip on a radar screen. We would make it through that just like we had made it through training.

I headed back into the barracks to get more water, and soon we were done with the cleaning. Before dinner, everything was dry, packed, and ready to go.

CHAPTER 16: HOSTIAS ET PRECES

Hostias et preces tibi, Domine,
Laudis offerimus tu
Suscipe pro animabus illis,
Quarum hodie memoriam facimus

Sacrifices and prayers
We offer to you in praise, Lord,
To accept on behalf of those
Who we remember this day

-Excerpt from the Requiem Mass, *Offertory*

2280 A.D. (Age 18, Birth + 61)

Two days. We had two days to relax, grow accustomed to the planet, and prepare for the Green.

Before breakfast the next morning, Kylie and I came out into the hallway and waited for Bud.

"Big guy is running slow, I guess," Kylie said.

"That's a lot of body to get moving. And, you know, there's a rumor going around that he's…"

"Yes?"

"New here."

Kylie half-smiled. It was still early. "I see. Should we trust him?"

"Trust who?" Bud asked, opening his door.

"You, Bud," Kylie answered without missing a beat.

Bud cocked his head to the side. "Trust me?"

"Yes, you. Are you trustworthy?"

"Yes."

"Ah, good. That settles that. Been nagging Cor and me for quite a while. We appreciate you ending the speculation. Shall we?" Kylie motioned up the corridor.

Bud looked confused, shrugged his shoulders, and started

walking toward the chow hall with Kylie and me in tow.

"Nice one," I said.

"Thanks!" Kylie replied.

The eating area was nothing fancy. Along the left wall were a series of food printers which spat out their products into a pan inset into the machine. A section at the end held some fresh vegetables—mostly corn and green beans. The facility had three rows of banged-up square tables, with one set shoved up against the windows on the opposite side from the printers. Other than three soldiers wearing Charlie Five patches, the place was empty.

I grabbed a tray and a plate and started with the first printer. Bacon. I put my dish under the activation light. Tongs emerged from a slot, reached into the pile of bacon, and plopped two slices on my plate before receding. At least it smelled good. Eggs and toast came next.

With food in hand, I made my way to where Kylie and Bud were sitting in the center of the room. I was halfway to my first bite when one of the three soldiers spoke loudly.

"It looks like initial training isn't what it once was, wouldn't you say? Lot softer than when Charlie Five went through." A murmured agreement followed.

The soldiers were behind me, but Bud faced them. He stopped chewing and started staring.

"Squirt gun fights for a few weeks and then send them here. What could possibly go wrong? River is easy! Don't need to train the newbies, just pass them through—they'll be fine," the same voice continued.

"You're in trouble now, Jake. The big one is staring at you," a second voice added.

"After the Green, the only thing he'll be staring at is a picture of his mommy," the first voice—Jake—replied. The others roared.

Bud sniffed and flared a nostril. "No good."

He said it louder than he meant to and sent the Charlie Five soldiers into hysterics.

"It speaks, Jake!"

"Single syllables only, though!"

"Bay. Con. Good. Egg. Good. Bra. Vo. Six. Bad."

Bud's nostrils did a double flare.

Kylie looked upset. "Come on, let's go," she whispered.

I picked up my food and was ready to head out, but Bud didn't move. Kylie put a hand on his arm. "Not the time, Bud."

With his hands gripping the tray so hard they shook, Bud stood and walked past the other soldiers out the front door. Kylie and I followed. The air scrubber blew a piece of toast off my plate; I left it for someone else to clean up.

"See you around, squirts," Jake yelled from behind us.

We turned left toward the picnic tables. This apparently was the preferred spot for dining, as a good number were filled. And no wonder: the morning was cool and bright, not too humid, with a gentle breeze blowing through the dew-glistened corn.

Kylie decided on a place, and we all sat, staring silently at our food. After a few moments, I picked up a piece of bacon and pushed my remaining piece of toast around. Bud's face rippled in rage, the anger passing through his cheeks to his mouth and up to his nose before circling around again. Kylie dabbed at her eye before putting her head in her hands. I wanted to hold her, comfort her, wipe the tears away.

Something in motion caught my eye—Aurelius returning from a morning run. She jogged right up to us and stopped, hunching over and grabbing her knees as she struggled to catch her breath.

"Good one," she puffed, "but I can definitely feel the slight increase in gravity."

When none of us responded, she looked up. I was the only one paying attention to her.

"What's wrong?" she asked.

I waved my hand to indicate it was nothing serious, but my expression must have told a different tale.

"*Now*, FS1 Slade. I want the truth *now*. What happened?"

It wasn't a very long story. As I told it, Aurelius' eyes narrowed, and her mouth turned down at the corners.

"I see," she said when I had finished. She tilted her head back, smoothed her hair with her fingers, and gazed at the sky. At last, she nodded and glanced around until she found what she was looking for.

"Stay here."

She marched a few tables over, touched Captain Belner on the shoulder, and the two of them walked off toward the crops to talk. A few minutes later, Aurelius came back to us and sat down, a wry smile tugging at her lips and eyebrows.

"So," she started, "I wish those soldiers hadn't done what they did. We'll likely have enough problems here without provocations like that. And it shows that some of the fundamental initial training lessons have been forgotten here. That's unfortunate. However, there's nothing I can do about their behavior."

"But—" Kylie started.

Aurelius cut her off immediately. "You remember that question Mei-Zhen had about reporting someone's behavior? Once reported, you can't un-report it, and if you aren't careful, trying to improve morale will harm it. In this case, if I go complain to Captain Belner about those soldiers, Charlie Five is likely to see us as weak. Crybabies. Whatever chance we had of living peacefully with the other companies would be diminished."

"No good," Bud muttered.

"You are correct, Bud—no good. No good for us, no good for them, no good for River."

"So, we just take it?" Kylie looked pained.

Aurelius smiled broadly. "I didn't quite say that. The verbal abuse—yes, just ignore it as best you can, and most likely, they will get tired of it. I will circulate that instruction throughout Bravo Six this morning. However, I spoke with Captain Belner and asked him if companies ever went head-to-head in competitions. He said that they do, and one of the favorites is an elimination game, sort of an exercise. Two companies start at opposite ends of a two hundred square meter section of Green, and the last company with a person left standing wins. Simulated combat, of course—but it includes flechettes, directed energy, and nano-wire. We take on Charlie Five tomorrow morning."

"You think we can win?" I asked.

"I *know* we can win."

Aurelius gathered all of Bravo Six together a couple of hours later. We needed to go into town to get replacement parts for some of the equipment we had cleaned the day before. There were quizzical looks as to why all of us needed to go, but the lieutenant ordered it, so off we went.

Part of the way there, in the middle of nothing but crops, at a spot where the path widened a bit, she stopped.

"Alright, gather round, and I'll explain the real reason we are here. Yes, we need to get a several things printed using the big printers, but I wanted to talk to you all about what happened this morning and what we are going to do about it—with no prying eyes or ears around. Coren, will you please describe the encounter."

After I finished, Aurelius continued. "First, I'd like to thank Kylie, Bud, and Coren for not reacting—especially for not doing anything physical—and for bringing this to my attention. They did the right thing. I expect the same from everyone in Bravo Six. No exceptions, no excuses. You will be tolerant even in the face of their intolerance. I demand it."

Her face lit up like a supernova before she went on, one eyebrow cocked high. "However, it doesn't mean we have to take it lying down. Well, most of us won't, anyway."

She eyed Kylie, Bud, and me.

"Tomorrow morning, we are taking on Charlie Five in a competition. After we win—and I'm confident we *will* win—we should have a lot less trouble with the other companies. FS1 al Basrati, please step forward."

Yousef pushed through a clump of soldiers until he stood in front.

"You are a budding—no pun intended, Bud—intelligence officer. Characterize Charlie Five for us based on what you have seen so far."

"Unwiped assholes," Yousef replied without hesitation.

Aurelius rubbed a hand over her face as she tried to suppress a laugh. The rest of us let the laughter fly. Yousef soaked it in.

"Perhaps describe them with less colorful language while placing more emphasis on their skills as a military and police unit," Aurelius went on after gaining control.

Yousef rubbed his chin. "It's only been a day, but maybe lazy?"

Aurelius nodded. "I agree. What else? Anyone, let me hear it."

"Bored."

"Overweight."

"Confident," Kylie called out.

Aurelius whirled and pointed at her. "Yes, FS2 Marie. Exactly. They are confident—even overconfident. And that is how we are going to beat them."

After midnight, Aurelius slipped into my room, followed closely by Bud and Kylie. She held a finger to her lips and pointed at the erasable board in her hand—the same kind that hung on almost every door in the barracks. She had already written out some items.

The lieutenant pointed at the top line and then looked around at us.

Plan is a go if you three are still okay with it

We all nodded.

Someone entered my room while we were out—fairly certain my comms system is bugged

That was a good thing. The plan might work without it, but it certainly had a much better chance with it. Aurelius had told us she thought Captain Belner would do something like that after he emphasized three times that there were no rules other than staying in the box.

Aurelius pointed to the third line. *Are you clear on the trigger phrase?*

We all nodded again. "Up and forward, Bravo Six"—that was our cue.

No sneaking until we get to the Green—we look like a patrol to anyone watching. If we have to make several passes for the all-clear, we will

Thumbs up all around.

She wiped the board clean with her sleeve, then wrote

thank you! and *helmets down, comms silent* on it.

Bud opened both doors, and we marched out into the night. The elimination match would take place in the Green near the barracks, but since a group of soldiers were drinking around a picnic table to the right, we peeled left and angled toward the dark, alien mass of vegetation. When the barracks were sufficiently far behind us, Aurelius scanned the area one more time, then dropped to the ground and low-crawled until she was hidden by the plants. Kylie, Bud, and I followed.

A few meters in, with all signs of human habitation hidden, the lieutenant stood up and pointed us toward the locations she had designated for us. My spot glowed in the exact center of the square competition arena, with Bud fifty meters to the north and Kylie fifty meters south. Bud's was the furthest in, so we tramped to his first.

When we got there, we pulled the plant roots back as best we could, exposing the mud underneath. Bud stepped in, sat down in the muck, shoved his boots as far under the Green as he could, and lay down on his back. We covered him up. By morning, his suit would be the same temperature as the ground, rendering him—and Kylie and me—virtually undetectable by another soldier.

Leaving Bud behind, we slithered through the jungle to my place. Vegetation back, Coren in and down, legs extended, camouflage on top. Aurelius would get Kylie settled in last.

I turned off the auto-response ping function on my suit and waited in the dark. There was nothing left to do but sleep, but Aurelius had said point-to-point communications between the three of us were fine, so I waited ten minutes or so, and buzzed Kylie.

"Hey, Coren," she answered.
"How are you doing?"
She hesitated for a long time. "Fine."
"Kylie…"
"Okay, not fine."
"What's wrong?" I scrunched my back to get at an itch.
She breathed deep. "I know it isn't, but it feels the same."

"The same as what?"

"As back home. Yes, the lieutenant was clear that we didn't have to volunteer for this, but we really didn't have a choice. She said we could win, and then implied winning depended on the three of us. Back home—" Her voice choked. "Back home, it was taken for granted that I would help out, that I would pick up the slack, that I would cheer on others who traveled more or learned more or were funnier or prettier."

"I think you are both funny and pretty, Kylie."

She laughed. "Worst kept secret in the world, Coren."

My cheeks flushed, and my heart thudded. The protective wall I had erected around my feelings for her was nothing but a charade. If Charlie Five ran an infrared scan right then, I would have been the brightest object in the universe.

"I didn't mind until I did," Kylie went on as if she had said nothing of importance to me. "No—wait—that's not correct. I didn't know until I let myself know. It was strange—I've never had a moment like it. My birthday had just passed, and I received some congratulations and well wishes from a few family members. My mother bought me a new pillow. It was all very nice, but *only* nice, if you know what I mean. Not the same as other people in the family."

My birthdays had always been special, even when mom celebrated them in that mom way of hers. If anything, she was overly effusive with her praise—at least until she lost consciousness. Red and Devlin and I sometimes commemorated the day by overdosing on alcohol as well.

A pillow, though—that didn't sound too bad. Not a thought I should have relayed to Kylie, however.

"You don't understand, Cor. It's that—oh, never mind."

"I don't understand, but I'm still listening, Kylie." Listening and backpedaling.

She sniffed heavily several times. "It's that—it's that… well, the family was whole without me. It didn't matter if I was there. They liked me. I was included. But I wasn't necessary."

I tried to picture a situation in which Kylie would be unimportant to me. I failed. "I understand now, Kylie. Thank you."

"Not long after my birthday, I was out riding Boo when it hit me, clear as day," she continued. "An epiphany, some would call it. I realized all at once that I *did* mind being treated that way, that I needed *more* than my family offered me."

"And now you are out here in the Green, sacrificing one of the two nights we have before we deploy, and you feel taken advantage of?"

"Yes." Her voice was almost inaudible.

"I think you are right, Kylie. Absolutely right. And if Aurelius had known any of that, she wouldn't have asked it of you—of us. And if she had thought it through, she wouldn't have asked us in front of everyone else so we could have responded more freely."

"Yes."

"But she didn't. She's human. I think she made a mistake. But I can absolutely guarantee you, Kylie, that she values you. Have you watched her lips twitch when she looks at your smile, like seeing it brings extra joy to her? And I think a lot of the Bravo Six success in initial training came from your friendliness. You broke the tension early, reached out across the company, tolerated Jovan better than most."

Kylie snorted. "Now there's something to be proud of. Thank you, Cor—that's very kind to say. You may be a little biased, though, don't you think?"

That was twice she had hinted at it. She knew how I felt but didn't address it directly. I had no idea why.

"Kylie…" It came out as a whisper. In my mind, my mouth was next to her ear, nestled in her hair, speaking the words I dared not say. Her fragrance enveloped me as she pulled me tight, pressing her body against mine, holding me, her hands gripping my back in a way I hoped would never end. There, in the darkness, Kylie and I together. Paradise.

"Not tonight, Coren. Not like this," she said.

I snapped back to the present. Not tonight. That much I could understand. But did that mean *never*?

A silence fell between us.

"Am I camping right now, Kylie?" I asked at last.

She laughed, and I pictured her smile encased in that helmet. I wanted to lift the visor and see what would happen, get an answer to the question that haunted me. But she was fifty meters away, covered in mud and Green.

"I suppose, in a way, it is camping, Coren. Congratulations, you are a camper!"

"It's not quite what I hoped for."

"No bugs at least."

"What about the Legs?"

"Oh—I forgot about them."

"Any other pluses to this type of camping?"

"Hmmm," Kylie said, almost humming, "let's see. There's the lack of mobility. There's the sleeping entombed in our suits. There's giving up one of our two nights. I'd say that's pretty good, wouldn't you?"

"Yes, I would. If we can knock Charlie Five down a peg, though—that would be terrific."

"That it would, my friend, that it would."

The conversation broke for a moment.

"Good night, Coren," she said at last.

"Good night, Kylie."

I severed the connection and laid back as best I could, adjusting to get comfortable. All the things Kylie said rattled through my brain like dishes stuck in a recycling tube: there was no way to process them, and no way to move them forward or backward. I had to wait for a maintenance person who did not and has never existed.

Sigh. Kylie.

The stars were up there, staring at me. I could have tuned the spectrum display to see them if I had wanted to, but I preferred letting all the thoughts twist and turn in the darkness and silence until, at last, they shunted to the back and sides.

CHAPTER 17: MILITIA CAELESTIS

*Cumque omnia militia
Caelestis exercitus*

And with all the hosts
Of the Heavenly army

-Excerpt from the Requiem Mass, *Preface*

2280 A.D. (Age 18, Birth + 61)

"Helmets in place, Bravo Six. Let's go."

Aurelius' voice pulled me out of a dead sleep. A brownish light managed to wend its way down to me through the plants and mud. I was not in any specific pain but generally uncomfortable from a night spent immobilized.

An overhead view of the area appeared as an inset on my visor. Black dots representing the company's personnel —excluding Kylie, Bud, and me—milled around south of the marked battleground. Part of the lieutenant's plan had been to put helmets down early and keep everyone moving so Charlie Five couldn't get an accurate count. From the way the dots circulated on the overview, it must have looked like Bravo Six was preparing for a dance, not simulated combat.

One blip pulled away from the group and moved east in a straight line.

"Good morning, Captain Belner," Aurelius said.

"Lieutenant," Belner answered, his voice distant as it filtered through Aurelius' mic. "Your company ready?"

"Fully ready."

"Simulated weapons, stay in the box, every hit is considered lethal and freezes the suit. Other than that, no rules. Clear?"

"Crystal."

"Last side with a mobile soldier wins."

"Understood. One soldier standing."

Belner laughed, almost gloating. "Not that it will come to that, you know."

"Really?" the lieutenant replied. "Care to bet?"

Now Belner's laughter was in disbelief. "Have you lost your mind, Aurelius? You're going to lose, and you have no idea how badly. Why pour salt on your own wound?"

"That's a 'no?'"

"It's a 'yes.' Of course it's a 'yes.'"

"Loser buys the winner alcohol?" Aurelius asked.

"You have to go into town to get it. Willing?"

"Why not?"

"Up the ante? Loser serves dinner as well?"

"You got it."

"Then it's a bet. East or west?"

"What's that?" Aurelius sounded confused.

"Do you want to start on the east side or the west side?"

"Oh." Her suit creaked slightly, and I imagined her scanning the area. "West. My company is already gathered over there."

"Everything alright with them? They are moving around like ants on stim."

"You said no rules, Captain."

Stunned silence. I could almost hear Belner's brain churning. Drugs and the Forces didn't mix.

"That was a joke, Captain."

"Oh—yes, I see. Good one." He sounded relieved. "Starting positions in fifteen?"

"Perfect. Good luck."

"You, too."

A countdown timer appeared on my screen.

Aurelius' dot returned to the Bravo Six clump. When she got there, she called everyone together into a tight huddle.

"We are all set," she began. "Fourteen minutes until we start. The western side is ours, so we will line up along the edge in these designated positions."

The display zoomed in, and thirty-eight black location-markers spaced roughly five meters apart appeared along the left side. Kylie, Bud, and I had our names sprinkled through the middle.

"Once the exercise begins, I want you all to move to these designated positions."

Dots on the outside leaped forward forty meters or so, while the ones between went progressively less far out, until the formation formed a concave arc, theoretically ready to close around Charlie Five as it charged forward. Overall, it was a standard defensive plan that might have worked if we weren't almost certain the other company was watching the entire presentation. And if we had any intention of remaining defensive.

"Any questions?" Aurelius asked. No one replied. "I've overridden your suits to ensure everything is simulated. Stay in the box, move quickly to your positions, and fire when you see something. You all heard what Captain Belner and I agreed to—loser is buying and serving. So, let's go, Bravo Six! On the count of three: *one, two, three!*"

"*Bravo Six!*"

The group of dots broke quickly and looped around the end of the box, entering the Green a few meters away from the edge. With a few minutes left on the timer, everyone was in place.

I double-checked my settings for the third time. Flechettes were ready, beam energy was ready, but the nano-wire—that was the killer.

When the timer hit zero, Aurelius yelled out, "Positions, Bravo Six! Quickly."

Thirty-eight dots surged forward, the ones in the middle stopping after ten meters or so and the others fanning out ahead to each side. I had to hand it to the lieutenant—each position indicator moved at a different speed. It didn't look at all like the deception it was.

I now had a different countdown clock running. Since Charlie Five's rate of advance was unknown, we debated how long Kylie, Bud, and I should wait. Informal discussions with the other companies revealed that normal matches lasted fifteen to twenty minutes, so we settled on eight as the go-time. If we missed some, hopefully they would be few enough in number that Bravo Six could still win. We also had the back-up plan: if the lieutenant had a new thought, she would use the trigger phrase to launch us at a different time.

It was a long wait, punctuated occasionally by Aurelius asking for status updates and keeping the company steady.

Right on cue, when the timer hit zero, Aurelius called out, "Up and forward, Bravo Six."

I rolled over on my side and struggled to my feet, my body stiff from lying there so long. Facing west, back toward Bravo Six, I extended forty-five meters of imaginary nano-wire and whipped it in a half-circle in front of me, first at chest-height and then back again at knee-level. The wire would get nowhere near our own soldiers, who were lying prone right at the square's edge, not having moved since we started. Kylie and Bud were doing the same thing.

Between the three of us, we had just sliced through ninety percent of this half of the combat zone. Green blotches appeared on my overlay, indicating kills. Not enough, though. I estimated there were twenty or so Charlie Five soldiers down, which left another sixteen out there somewhere. We were winning, but we hadn't won yet.

As per Aurelius' instructions, I turned around to do a nano-sweep in the opposite direction, and there, not five meters away, was a Charlie Five soldier standing stock-still.

"Oh, sh—" I managed to say before my suit froze completely. The shock of it stopped the words in my mouth. A red spot appeared on the overlay; I was the first Bravo Six casualty.

The other soldier walked up to me slowly and peered through my visor, shaking her head. She put a hand on my forehead and pushed. I fell straight back, splayed out to the four winds. The soldier passed me by, moving west. I was left staring at the plants above me hanging limply and outlining a slice of the sky that vaguely resembled a chair tipped on its side. Not unlike me.

Another red dot appeared on the display: Kylie. Charlie Five had apparently held some people back. On the northeastern portion of the map, a group of four green points popped up. Bud had managed to turn around and nano-wire that section.

"Bud, go right and forward, and repeat," Aurelius ordered, her voice calm and smooth. "Anwar, take the command support element up the middle and flush anyone out."

"Acknowledged." Anwar was not nearly so composed. "Bravo Six One, forward!"

Except for the battle schematic, I saw nothing of what was actually happening. The picture Aurelius broadcasted still had the arc of Bravo Six soldiers, all in their false positions, but now with a broad swath of green kill symbols filling the bowl.

Another green point appeared almost due east of me. I pictured Bud advancing through the undergrowth, swinging the nano-wire back and forth.

"Jovan, slow down!" It was Mei-Zhen speaking. Whatever Jovan was doing, though, seemed to be working as two more Charlie Five soldiers went down to my west. If I had to guess, the one who got me had just been eliminated.

I tried to count the kills. It was nearly thirty, but I kept getting lost about which ones I had already accounted for.

The plant above me suddenly whipped out of the way, a boot came down on my helmet, and then the figure it belonged to disappeared to the east. Jovan—had to be. My view was now a muddy footprint with hints of light sneaking in around the sides.

A few more red dots appeared in the southeast quadrant of the arena, and then I was free. My suit loosened, and I could move my limbs again. It had worked; we had won.

The overhead display disappeared, and Aurelius came on the comm system. "Bravo Six, well done. Report back to the barracks on the double."

I should have been excited, I guess, but instead it was a night spent in the dark followed by watching the whole mock-battle from afar. Blips on a screen. That's all it had been.

With my vision limited and nothing to clean myself off

with, the trip back took longer than it should have. I finally stepped out of the Green, and Kylie was there to greet me.

"What happened to you?" she asked.

"What do you mean?"

"It looks like someone stepped on your helmet."

"That's because someone stepped on my helmet. I think it was Jovan."

Kylie laughed. "What are the odds?"

"Pretty high if that's what he meant to do," I replied. "Can you help me clear my visor?"

She walked over and smeared some mud here and there without really improving it. "I think you are going to have to lift it and see what happens."

Sighing, I gave the command. Sure enough, a big, wet glob of muck slid off and landed on my cheek. Kylie reached up, scraped it off, and flicked it away.

"We did it, Cor! We beat Charlie Five." She had a huge grin on her face.

It was my first opportunity to look around. Maybe I had felt separated from our company after the victory, but it was clear everyone else had not. Based on the number of people crowded around them and patting their backs, Bud and Jovan seemed to be the heroes. Chants of *Bravo Six* wafted over to us. And through the haze of the night before, through the filth I was caked in, it came back to me: that feeling we had the previous day when Charlie Five drove us out of the chow hall. That feeling when an older kid hinted at beating me up. That feeling when you finish high school and have no way forward. No hope. Nothing will change. Blips on a screen that linger for a moment and are gone.

Except the soldiers in Bravo Six weren't blips on a screen. They were my friends. They mattered to me. And we showed that things can change: we beat Charlie Five—unfair and square, precisely according to the rules. You win some, as someone once said. It mattered.

Kylie and I hustled to join the rest of the company. They hailed us as we approached.

"Give us the count, Greta!" Yousef yelled.

Greta lowered her helmet momentarily, then popped it back up. "I have Coren down for six kills, and Kylie for eight."

"Who got the most?"

"Jovan and Bud—they were tied at ten each."

I looked over at them, standing side by side. They had never been friendly with each other, but now they stood differently. Looked at each other differently. Jovan even had a hint of a smile on his face.

Aurelius had been consulting with Captain Belner and now returned to us.

Yousef started in with an *Au-re-lius* chorus and the rest of us followed.

The lieutenant held up her hand for quiet. "That's enough of that," she said, though her eyes and mouth said something else. "Next thing you know, I'll start believing the hype, and when Alpha Seven gets here in four years, they will beat us like we just whupped—and I do mean whupped—Charlie Five."

Au-re-lius, Yousef started again. It took her repeated attempts to get us to stop.

"Bravo Six," she started, "you made me proud today. The plan had a few hitches in it, but for the most part, it worked perfectly. Captain Belner admitted that after his forward-most soldiers were cut down, he realized we weren't where the hacked comms indicated. At that point, he scrambled to reposition Charlie Five and couldn't. It was too late.

"And then along came Jovan." Aurelius shook her head. "Unbelievable. Hey-diddle-diddle, straight-up-the-middle Jovan. Well done. We will discuss all that and more tonight. I want you all to go and get your gear cleaned up first." She fixed her gaze on me.

"What's wrong with this, Lieutenant?" I asked, my hands framing the suit for her.

She chuckled. "Absolutely nothing, FS1 Slade; please, deploy just like that. We have to be ready to go early tomorrow morning, so we will get tonight's festivities started at 1600. Dinner and beverages in the picnic table area. Civilian clothes, if you so choose. Make sure all your gear is prepared before then. Dismissed."

Kylie grabbed my hand and led me over to where Bud was standing. "C'mon, let's find a place to wash ourselves off." We were by far the dirtiest in the entire company.

"How did you sleep, Bud?" I asked.

"Good. I slept well," he replied, before breaking into a grin. "You, Kylie?"

"Fine. I drifted off pretty quickly after our conversation."

Almost undetectably, Bud's head jerked my way, and I could tell he was giving me a side-eye.

We found a spigot and hose at the far end of the barracks and took turns getting each other clean. When we finished, there was a collective pause.

"Nap," I said.

"Shower," Kylie said.

"Food," Bud said.

CHAPTER 18: BEATITUDINE

Lucis aeternae beatitudine perfrui

Enjoy the blessedness of eternal light

-Excerpt from the Requiem Mass, *Tract*

2280 A.D. (Age 18, Birth + 61)

The party was already underway when I exited the barracks. I napped longer than I intended and then fretted over what to wear. What would make a good impression? What would make me look stupid? I finally settled on a sky-blue button-up shirt with the final display from the battle on the front, the green kill-dots prominently displayed. The printer churned it out, and off I went.

Mustafa Darlot spotted me first and tapped another soldier on the shoulder. The reaction rippled through the company, and they clapped as I approached.

"Good one, Slade."

"Wish I had thought of that one."

"Which dot is you, again?"

The only other time we had all been in civilian clothes was during those brief initial moments on Enceladus, but that seemed a long time ago, and there had been no personalities or relationships to tie appearance to. There were a great number of floral shirts and loose shorts spread through the gathering. Bud had on a white shirt that strained to cover his biceps. Kylie wore a plaid wool top composed of various reds and blues.

Aurelius, though—she outdid everyone. Her outfit consisted of black pants and a black shirt with a single character on it. Depending on the angle you looked at her, the symbol was either a slightly curvy "B" or a slightly too straight "6." It was also cut perfectly to her body.

Bravo Six had pulled eight picnic tables together into a

rectangle, and it was enough for everyone to crowd around. In the middle were aluminum tubs overflowing with ice and various types of alcohol. Say what you want about Belner, but he didn't skimp when it came to losing.

I pushed into the crowd, right next to Kylie, with Bud on her other side. Someone handed me a bottle of beer, and I downed half of it without thinking.

Yousef pushed a tub aside and climbed up on a table.

"A toast!" he yelled. "To Bravo Six!"

We cheered and drank. My first beer was done, so I grabbed another.

Yousef called for quiet. "And now I would like to present the first annual or maybe monthly or maybe weekly—we shall see how this one goes!—Bravo Six awards!" He pulled a datapad from a pocket. "We have some mighty fine recognition to hand out tonight, so let's get started.

"First, we have the GALA award—the Great Award for Leadership Award—which goes to our very own, the one and only, Lieutenant Elizabeth Aurelius, for conceiving of the wondrous plan that has led us to this land of plenty!" Someone in the crowd handed Yousef a small trophy, eleven or twelve centimeters high, clearly depicting the lieutenant throwing a lightning bolt at the sky.

Aurelius climbed on a bench to accept, then held it high. When the cheering subsided, she called out, "Thank you, Mr. al Basrati. Now stop kissing ass!"

We laughed.

Yousef couldn't let it go. He cocked an eyebrow and cast an eye over at the lieutenant. "Well, you know, if—"

"Keep it appropriate, FS1," Aurelius growled. Greta Isilsohn—they were still an item—slapped his leg.

Yousef grinned. "Yes, sir," he replied, winking at Greta.

He spread his arms wide and turned around a couple of times. "Now, listen up, Bravo Six, because this award goes all the way back to our time on Enceladus. You remember that, right?"

A mixture of boos and cheers answered him.

"Well, it is said that back in olden times, prisoners were

punished by making them break big rocks into small rocks. So, this next award—the Groundbreaking Award—goes to our very own rock breaker, who proved he never met a beach he wouldn't punch in anger while muttering epithets. The one, the only: Joe Vahn! I mean, Jovan!"

My eyes darted to the miner, who stood at one end of the rectangle. If anyone would take offense, it would be him. Jovan scowled and gazed from one side to the other of the gathering, before breaking out in a grin and holding an arm up in triumph.

"I accept," he answered at last, "you holers."

"Appropriate, I said," Aurelius broke in, but there was a smile on her face.

Yousef handed Jovan a small trophy depicting a boulder in the process of disintegrating.

"Next up, we have an award very near and dear to my heart—the Lieutenant Ought to Verify Everyone is Yielding to Our Unquestioned Greatness Award."

There was a pause as we tried to piece together the acronym.

"The LOVE YOU G Award," Yousef triumphed, "and this award goes to the loveliest member of Bravo Six, Greta Isilsohn!"

Yousef held out the trophy, which depicted Greta standing on a clamshell, fortunately more clothed than in the original. She turned bright red but accepted the award with a kiss.

There were whistles and yells of approval.

"This next one is a very special award, coming as it does all the way from the vaults of Charlie Five knowledge. For it, I have prepared a very special presentation. If you will all turn and observe." Yousef pointed behind us.

We turned, and there was Joanna Rutter—she of the not mixing rice with stew opinion on Enceladus—in her suit, facing away from us.

"Now observe in slow motion the actions of one of our very own," Yousef whispered mysteriously.

Joanna swiped her hand back and forth slowly. It was as if… as if she were swinging a nano-wire. She stopped and centimeter by centimeter turned in the opposite direction. When she faced us, she froze in position, arms splayed wide.

"Ms. Danjuma, please do the honors," Yousef announced.

Omedele walked forward, one finger pointed at Joanna's forehead.

It struck me all at once what was happening.

When Omedele touched the frozen figure, Joanna fell straight backward without moving a muscle. She looked like a dead cockroach on the ground.

Bravo Six howled with laughter.

"Mr. Slade," Yousef yelled, "Please come accept your Whoopsie! Award. Charlie Five may not have won, but you certainly gave them a good laugh. Us too! Well done. You should track down the person who shot you—she tells the story in much more detail."

The trophy was a tiny statue of me, mouth round, eyes wide, arms and legs in four different directions like a human star. It looked like one of those cartoons where a person gets a huge electric shock.

I stood up on the picnic bench, took the award, bowed in all directions, and got back down.

Kylie hugged me, her body shaking with laughter. "You didn't tell me that!"

"I was on the inside! How was I supposed to know what I looked like?" I protested.

"And then Jovan stepped on your head!" She doubled over, almost hyperventilating, trying to catch her breath. I put a hand on her back to comfort her. When she regained some control of herself, she looked back up. There were tears of joy in her eyes.

"Coren Slade, you are something else."

"Thank you," I replied. "You are too, Kylie Marie."

This set her off again. I patted her back, and when she finally straightened up, only centimeters between our faces, her smile beamed as broadly as I had ever seen.

"Stop looking at me with those puppy-dog eyes and get me a drink," she ordered.

I hurried to oblige.

Yousef whistled to get our attention. "The food crew is here! The food will be printed specially for us by Charlie Five, including both steak and lobster options, barbecued to your exact specifications. I encourage you to eat heartily and return any mis-cooked food immediately, as they will have to operate the printers and barbecues until we are finished. I don't care if you enjoy it—the point is to keep eating so Charlie Five knows Bravo Six is the new bad-ass in town!"

Perhaps not the most gracious winning words ever spoken.

Kylie, Bud, and I each grabbed a tray and a plate and got in one of the printer lines. Charlie Five's Jake was operating one of them; he did not look happy about it. We debated deliberately going through him, but Kylie's advice was to let sleeping dogs lie.

Food in hand, we found an empty table and were soon joined by other members of Bravo Six. Someone cranked the music. Someone else populated our table with a generous number of open beers. The sun began to set. A star came to life in the east. I ate the first lobster of my life—delicious. Kylie's eyes sparkled. Her smile lit up my world.

"Hey, Slade," Mustafa Darlot shouted from across the table. I looked over, and Mustafa spread his arms wide and put on his best shocked face, imitating my award from earlier. The table roared in laughter. I joined in.

A slow song began playing. Kylie motioned to me, and then we were dancing together, holding each other close. I breathed the scent of her hair, losing myself in its soft promise as I nuzzled my cheek against her. Her body was pressed against me, every curve firing my imagination. She placed a hand on the back of my neck and pulled my head down toward her. My chin rubbed against her brow, her skin soft and cool in the evening air. Our lips found each other, mixing ourselves together in passion, music, smoke, and beer. We held that kiss, held each other, two impossibly young lambs on the narrow precipice of the future.

When we pulled apart, her tongue gently skated over her lips, tasting what had just happened. She smiled.

"Let's go for a walk," she said.

Hand-in-hand, the galaxy blazing overhead, we strolled away.

After a bit, Kylie caught my eye. "Thank you," she said.

"For what?"

"For being you, Coren Slade."

"I don't understand."

She took a long time to answer. When she did, she squeezed my hand and held it tight. "Feeling... undervalued—it affects you. You criticize yourself constantly. Nothing is good enough; it's your own fault. 'If only I could' you say to yourself constantly, and the wanting to be different leads to instability, of not having solid footing. My biggest fear in joining the Forces was that it was true, that I would find it was me."

"Because...?"

"Because that would mean this is my life. That would mean there is no escape, that what I fear the most is how I am destined to live. A prisoner."

"It is definitely not you, Kylie."

She swung our hands back and forth and nodded. "I'm coming to believe that. And it's not just you, Cor. You and me and Bud—we are family. Bravo Six—family. Could you believe Yousef tonight?"

"He's great."

"And the lieutenant—I just love her. Can you imagine having Belner as our commander?"

I pretended to choke.

"You know, Cor, when they first told us we were deploying into the Green, it was a gut-punch. The promise of a new life was here, and I wanted to get started immediately. Sure, we are basically going camping for who knows how long, and camping is one of my favorite things, but not *now*, I thought. Not so soon. And then last night in the Green. We had a taste of stability there at the end on Enceladus, and I liked it. Why couldn't we enjoy it for a bit?"

"I don't know."

"But now, after this morning, after tonight, I feel better.

We *are* stable, Cor. I like us—all of us. This Legs hunt will come and go, but we will be a family."

I had no words to offer her, so we walked, holding hands. The Green off to our left breathed a life of its own. But we had us. Our life with Bravo Six. Our life together.

We curved back and returned to the party. A number of soldiers had already cleared out, and the music volume was considerably reduced. Only a single printer and barbeque combination was still going.

Kylie stopped and gazed at the detritus before looking at me and taking my other hand.

"Good night, Cor," she whispered.

"Good night, Kylie."

We stood there for a moment, looking each other in the eyes before our heads swung gradually and simultaneously at the barracks—forty meters away. We shared a laugh, hugged, and held hands as we walked back to the dormitory.

Maybe if I had pressed it, something else would have happened that night, but I sensed that was not what Kylie wanted or needed. It was not what I wanted either—not really, or perhaps, more accurately—not yet.

There was time, I thought. We had time.

I couldn't have been more wrong.

CHAPTER 19: ANTE DIEM RATIONIS

Donum fac remissionis
Ante diem rationis

Give them forgiveness
Before the day of reckoning

-Excerpt from the Requiem Mass, *Sequence*

2280 A.D. (Age 18, Birth + 61)

We assembled the next morning out by the shed, before the sun rose. Kylie smiled at me, and I smiled back. An understanding. We had time.

"Alright, Bravo Six," Aurelius said, calling us together, "good morning."

Return greetings trickled in. It had been quite a party, and even with medicine to sober us up, we were hurting.

She looked at us, laughter playing across her eyes.

"Bravo Six, I know it's early, and I know we could have used a day to recover from kicking Charlie Five's ass, but let's get it together. Sure, we could be sleeping like most of the other soldiers are, right over there." She nodded her head toward the barracks. "But *we* aren't. *We* are out here. *They* are in there. But I want to make sure everyone out here is awake. Understood?"

I nodded, then stole a glance at Kylie out of the corner of my eye. She was enjoying this too.

"So," Aurelius called out, "*good morning!*"

"*Good morning,*" we yelled in unison.

"*Who are we?*"

"*Bravo Six!*"

"*Who?*"

"*Bravo Six!*"

"*Are you ready, Bravo Six?*"

"Yes, sir!"

"Ready?"

"Yes, sir!"

I'm pretty sure that one woke up Gladright back on Enceladus, if he was still alive.

"Alright! From here, we are going to head northeast until we come to the edge of the Green, then I will give you your tactical instructions. So, load up, and let's go!"

We broke up and went to get our things, making as much noise as possible.

We formed into two loose columns and marched. The colony's crops were to our right, the Green a little way off to our left. Our helmets were open, and the night air was cool. Bravo Six on our first mission.

Toward the edge of the cleared land, we came across a turret. It hadn't been visible from the barracks, and I hadn't spotted it on the way down or on the walk with Kylie. The gun inside the turret meant business though: its muzzle pointed straight up, extending twenty meters or more, and it was set in a rotating half-sphere dome, allowing it to move in any direction.

"What's that for?" I asked Kylie.

She turned her head slightly in my direction, then back at the turret. "Don't know."

"Bud?"

"Legs," he said without hesitation. "Big, big Legs."

Kylie and I laughed, and we all marched on.

We arrived at the edge of the Green just as the sun was rising. Aurelius stopped us with a raised fist.

"Okay, Bravo Six. Here we go. Our mission is to push back any of the larger Legs in a sector spanning thirty degrees, out to a depth of forty kilometers from the northeast corner of the colony—which is to say, right here. We are going to do this by sending out six squads to take up positions twenty kilometers into the Green, forming an arc. The other six squads will raster march from side to side, flushing any Legs to the northeast."

Yousef shot a hand in the air. Aurelius nodded his way.

"Does this mean we are going to be raster-nauts?"

I was halfway to looking up what the word meant and stopped cold. The lieutenant pinched the bridge of her nose, while Bravo Six groaned silently.

"That one hurt," someone off to my left said.

I finished my search. Raster: a back-and-forth raking or scanning pattern that covers all the possible points in a given area. Huh. We were going to raster.

Aurelius breathed deep. "As I was saying, we will pass through all the territory and force the Legs back and away from the colony without spreading ourselves too thin. If some Legs make it through the perimeter, we will get them on the next go around.

"Even-numbered squads: you will post out into the Green first. Odds, you will do the marching this time. Once completed, you will reverse roles. Bravo Six Two, Eman: lead your squad along the angle furthest north. Bravo Six Twelve: you've got the opposite angle, the one more to the east. All others in between, in order. Are there questions from anyone not named al Basrati?"

Yousef started raising hand, but Aurelius shot him a warning glance. No one else moved.

"Then helmets up, and let's go!"

The instructions were clear, and even if they weren't, Aurelius commed us a map depicting the cone-shaped area the mission would happen in, including where each squad was supposed to end up. Just in case we weren't paying attention, she added a big arrow that pointed to Bravo Six Twelve's destination. At least she hadn't added a "Go here!" on the map.

There was nothing more to it, so Kylie, Bud, and I fixed our helmets in place, adjusted our backpacks and equipment, and headed into the Green. I tuned my visuals to just below the X band, and both of them popped into sight, a couple of meters to each side. People were white-ish solids; the Green was ghostly filaments, offering little resistance as we walked through; the sun was a bright fury overhead. I did see a few Legs' colonies here and there, but they were little ones—four or five Legs joined together, no more than ten or twelve centimeters high, each one punching down into some unfortunate prey, time after time, one after another, rippling from end to end. I wondered how long it took them to grow into the big kind.

We didn't see any big ones, though. Just the Green. At one point, we encountered a small stream entirely arched over with plants. I switched back to visible light. The sun cast shadows on the water, sparkling as the vegetation waved in the breeze. I reached down and pulled up a handful of sopping wet loam.

"Hey," I said, "can we take a break here?"

Kylie and Bud looked at each other, shrugged, and came over to where I was standing. I probably wasn't supposed to, but I wanted to see this with my own eyes. I lowered my helmet.

"Cor..." Kylie warned.

The light, the freedom, the comfort of having a leafy roof over my head, the promise of the future. It was a good moment, and I sucked in as much of it as I could.

"Cor," Kylie said again, "you should put your helmet up."

I took a deep breath. The muck I held stank of decay. Whenever I smell rotten plants now, I go back to that moment. The slow sway of sunlight there under the arched Green, the water rippling by, and me, and Kylie, and Bud. The three of us. Our home within a home.

I let the soil drip slowly through my gloves, cued my helmet into place, and started walking again. I didn't switch back to X-rays though. I just walked, letting my mind wander.

We periodically stopped and pulled vines off ourselves. You could walk right through them for hundreds of meters, but some of them had sharp little hooks on the sides, which would snag more vines and plants, and soon you were dragging a whole circus behind you. You couldn't feel it inside the suit, but it registered as a power blip with each step, and it was easy enough to stop for a moment, stand on the vegetation with one foot, and pull your other foot out of it, repeat, and set off again.

"Here we are," Kylie announced when we reached our designated spot a few hours later. As a place, it was indistinguishable from everything we walked through all day. With nothing to do but wait until another squad walked up to us, or until they flushed some Legs our way, we made a clearing and set up the small, Forces-grey habitat tent we'd been issued. We had a system at our camp on Enceladus about where things went, and without discussing it, we did the same thing there. We were cogs in a fully functioning machine.

After we finished, we stood around for a second until Bud said, "I will take the first watch." Kylie and I headed inside to relax.

The tent had fold-down cots built into the side panels. I sat on one of those, lowered my helmet, and loosened my suit a bit.

"Quite the luxurious accommodations!" Kylie said, making herself at home in much the same way. "How long will it take the marchers to get here, do you think?"

I calculated as best I could, but school math was a long way behind me at that point—if not in actual time, at least in experience.

Kylie had a new twinkle in her eye. "You know, Cor, when we were out there in the battlefield, laying in the dark, you asked whether that was camping, and it wasn't, really. But I have to say that when I offered to show you how to camp back on Enceladus, this wasn't exactly what I had in mind either."

I looked around the drab tent, our muddy prints on the floor. I had to agree. "What *did* you have in mind?"

She sat up a little and arched an eyebrow at me. "Well," she said, her voice growing husky, "here's what I think: first, ride out on horses along the beach. Boo loved the beach, and so did I. And then, a picnic lunch on a grassy hill overlooking the ocean. Just a bit of white wine, some fine cheese, home-baked bread."

She was not only piquing my interest, she was also making

me hungry.

"And then, we hike a little further into the hills, nice and slow. Up where you can see the ocean stretch to the horizon. Where the sun will blaze to life straight out of the water, pulled by chariots like the Greeks imagined."

She tilted her head. "Have you ever heard of sundogs?"

"Sundogs?" I asked. "As in, dogs that like the sun?"

Kylie giggled. "No. I mean, yes, there are dogs that like the sun, of course, but sundogs are something different. Sometimes, when there is ice in the atmosphere, patches of light will appear in the sky at exact angles from the sun. Usually in pairs, on opposite sides. Occasionally in a complete arc like a rainbow, but mostly the two spots of light, angled away from the sun but obviously connected to it as well. I always imagined the ancients looking at that and believing those were the horses pulling the sun. That the gods only allowed them glimpses into realms beyond their understanding, and that the gods could pull that knowledge back at any time. I'm not really sure the universe was intended for conscious creatures like us."

"Intended?"

She bobbed her head from side to side, weighing alternatives. "Maybe 'intended' is not the right word. Perhaps 'appropriate' instead. Yes. Appropriate. The universe is not appropriate for consciousness."

I waited for her to go on. She seemed to be thinking it through as she talked.

"We've seen all sorts of life in the galaxy so far—an amazing amount considering how little of it we have actually explored. But nothing approaching conscious thought yet. No one for us to communicate with intelligently, to get a different perspective on the *why* of existence. The *why* beyond random chance. The *why* of why we are alive."

I knew exactly what she meant. We were out here on a terrible mission, stuck inside our suits, eating the same food as in initial training, emptying waste directly into the Green, bored and tired and wanting to see anything other than those endless plants. And yet... I had Kylie. And Bud.

And Yousef. And Mei-Zhen. Danjuma. Even Jovan. A family functional enough to find acceptance in.

"So," Kylie went on.

"Yes?"

"Yes. I was saying that we would hike up into the hills. Set up our tent out under the stars. Cook dinner over an open fire. And then later..."

"Later?"

"Yes, later. As in, the next day later, you could join Jovan and me. And then I could show you how to camp before leaving you there so Jovan and I can go back to the beach house." She chuckled and lay back down on her cot.

Sigh. Kylie. I couldn't help but laugh.

"I'm going to take a nap, Cor. Wake me up when it's my turn for the watch."

I took the watch after Bud. Kylie took the watch after me.

We rotated like that for the next three days.

One airship and we could have done all of this and more in no time at all, but that wasn't what this was about. Maybe it had all started when resources were scarcer, when destroying Legs from above hadn't been an option; and then someone used reverse-reasoning to turn it into a benefit, a tradition, a means of proving a unit's worth. Or maybe it was straight-up hazing. My guess has always been the latter.

In the afternoon of the third day, Bravo Six Eleven arrived in camp, finishing the first half of their point-to-point march through the Green.

"See any Legs?" Bud asked after we gathered.

Greta Isilsohn was the squad leader. "A couple," she answered. "One was about a meter tall, looked like it had twenty segments or so."

"We shot every one of them, though," added Emil Barumwe. "Flechettes and lasers both—cut right through them. Their blood or organs or insides or whatever is sort of an orange-ish color. Stupid thing didn't seem to be able to decide whether to run or to fight, so it just died." He and Greta shared a look and a smile.

I dunno. I sort of understood what we were doing, though

not in any meaningful sense. But the way Emil described the killing—well, it seemed like a waste. I realize the irony of that thought, given what I would do later in my life. We will gladly tolerate, or not tolerate, all sorts of things, until they touch something deeply personal inside us. That's when tolerance becomes existential.

Bud offered to stand guard while the rest of us ate, so we went helmets-down, popped open some rations, and had a field dinner. Not too bad. Forces Special: rice with protein, but we had some hot sauce to spice it up. Anything is better than sucking your nutrients through the suit's straw.

A couple of hours later, Aurelius officially informed us that the first part of the hunt had finished. We were to wait in place for Bravo Six Eleven to establish themselves twenty more kilometers out from us, and then we would get our own marching instructions. Because the angle we were covering stayed the same, the distance we would have to go would be a lot longer than that of the previous marchers. I did some guess-timating using my limited math skills and came up with about three times as long, which meant about nine days of hiking through the Green. The suit will keep you clean, but it was adding up to two weeks in the thing without a break. No good, as Bud liked to say.

Aurelius arranged the marching squads fifty meters apart, which was close enough that in the X-ray band, we could detect faint movement to each side as we walked. Close enough that we would spot any monster-sized Legs between us. When we reached one side of the angle, the squads leapfrogged, so the one that had been nearest to the colony now hiked out to farthest position, and then we started back in the opposite direction.

It happened on day seven of our own marching, day ten in the field. I wanted out of that suit. Kylie wanted out of her suit. Bud wanted out of his suit. Everyone in the whole damned company wanted to be done with the whole damn thing, and our interactions with each other showed it.

Kylie, Bud, and I were on the outside perimeter, heading east, scanning both inward toward Bravo Six Ten and outward, into the unknown. Kylie spotted it first and stopped in her tracks.

"Look," she said, pointing to her left. I followed the ghost outline of her arm. There was something out there more solid than the Green. It wasn't moving, but it was different. I magnified the image.

Something was there.

Something big.

CHAPTER 20: CONFUTATIS MALEDICTIS

Confutatis maledictis
Flammis acribus addictis

The damned have been silenced
And consigned to the acrid fire

-Excerpt from the Requiem Mass, *Sequence*

2280 A.D. (Age 18, Birth + 61)

I keyed the mic. "Lieutenant, I believe we have something." I shot her the coordinates and an image of what we were seeing.

Aurelius came back immediately. "Roger, Cor. Got it. Two of you go check it out."

I was thinking Bud and me, but Kylie was one step ahead. "Let's go, Bud."

I watched through their feeds as they inched closer. It didn't take long before it was clear we were seeing a Legs. Whatever end we were looking at wasn't moving much, but there was a shadow of something in motion behind it. Kylie shot out a few mini-drones which brought back confirmation of at least one big Legs, possibly several, all obscured by foliage.

"I see it, Kylie," Aurelius said. "You and Budzinski get back to Mr. Slade." There was a short pause while she adjusted her comms. "All squads, stop and hold positions." A longer pause, her wheels almost spinning audibly.

"All squads: Bravo Six Twelve has found a sizable Legs. Here's what we are going to do. Since Bravo Six Twelve is on the outside edge, I want all other marching squads to double-time their progress to the turn-around point. Then all of you form up on Bravo Six Twelve's line and join back with them.

We will fan out around that thing and go after it together, flushing it out toward the perimeter, if need be. Safety in this is paramount. Understood? Acknowledge by squad."

The squads checked in, and we hunkered down to wait. There was something happening there, but the movement was disjointed, not like feeding or hunting, but something else. We waited. We watched the progress of the other squads on our feeds. We had a little meal. Several hours later, we were all joined up, Aurelius included.

"Anything new?" she asked.

Bud had been on watch. "No. Same same."

"Alright," she answered, "I want to take a closer look myself. Al Basrati, you're with me." Which made sense since he was an intel guy.

They crept off into the Green and got a little closer than Bud and Kylie had before coming back.

"It's a big one," Aurelius said. "Agreed?"

Yousef nodded. "Agreed. Big ones, in fact. Hardly moving. Engaged in something indeterminate but based on what Captain Belner described, probably mating. I've got a drone overhead watching, but I still can't make out much."

Aurelius keyed company-wide comms. "Listen up, everyone, here's what I want. Bravo Six Twelve, you three go straight at this thing. Two, Four, and Six: you will be off to their left, fifty-meter spacing between you. Eight and Ten: with me on the right." She looked at each of us in turn. "I can't stress this enough: there is nothing out here worth getting hurt or killed over. We've been given a lawful order to come out here and patrol for Legs, and we will execute that order to the best of our abilities. But there are a lot of ways we can do this, so be careful. That goes for the perimeter units as well. If we chase these Legs your way, use your best judgment as to how to engage. Understood? All squads acknowledge."

We chimed in one-by-one, Bravo Six Twelve last. The other squads spread out, and on Aurelius' mark, we started forward. I set my video feed to split-screen, with X-ray on the top, visible light on the bottom. I got nothing from the bottom feed except foliage, but the visible light calmed my ancient evolutionary demands.

Aurelius ordered us to a halt about twenty meters out and let the other squads creep forward a bit. When they got into the positions she wanted, we were up.

"Ready?" I asked.

"Let's go," Kylie replied. Bud nodded.

We inched our way forward, trying to make as little disturbance as possible. I watched the X-ray feed for any movement or signs that the Legs had noticed us. Nothing beyond some activity in the background. At five meters out, I reverted to visible light as we picked our way through the Green. With a meter to go, we stopped. Something was there, almost within arm's reach, but we still couldn't see it. I indicated to Kylie and Bud to stay where they were.

I pulled a frond aside and pushed my head forward. Nothing. I took a step, trying not to make the muck squelch under my boots, then leaned past another plant. There was a break in the Green ahead, below the canopy. Another slow movement forward, and my visor broke through the last vegetation.

When I was young, trying to sleep in my bedroom with the party roaring on the other side of the wall, I would sometimes sneak to the door and pry it open. I mostly saw men and women and my mom either passed out or making no sense or ingesting substances of one kind or another. But occasionally, there would be two or three or four or more of them, all naked, all pressing themselves together trying to join with one another, seeking a release I wouldn't understand for several more years.

And that is exactly what I saw in the Green: a ball of intertwined Legs, rutting and pushing and rolling and leaking fluids in every direction. Grey fluids. Everywhere. A squishing, gurgling, liquidy sound accompanied their movements. They were big Legs too. Really big.

"Aurelius?" I asked.

"I see it, Cor. Hold there."

A bead of sweat rolled off my forehead into my eye.

"Aurelius?" I asked again.

"One moment. Hold tight."

Back on Mars II, the naked men and women and my mom would fall asleep or drift away one-by-one. It was the grown-up world on full display in front of me, and at some level, I wanted to join it—the world, not the specific activity. But I had wondered what it meant for my situation, whether these things would take my mom away or lessen her love for me. My heart would pound, both from excitement and fear.

My heart was pounding now. "Aurelius?" I asked a third time.

"Dammit, Cor!" she shouted back.

I was not expecting to be yelled at, and I jerked my head back, losing visibility of the Legs. I leaned forward until my faceplate broke into the clear again. The activity had stopped. Slowly, one segment lifted itself up until its maw faced me.

I didn't move. Neither did it.

All of sudden, multiple Legs colonies unzipped from the ball. The smallest colony was a meter or so in height, the largest nearly twice that.

They inched out in all directions. Each one pounded the ground in front of it. Mud and pulverized plants erupted into the air and rained down on them and me.

"No good," Bud said over the comms.

I remembered what Captain Belner had said about Legs not being able to penetrate the suit, but seeing them like this, I couldn't imagine how that was true. I called up the targeting icon, selected flechettes, and target locked the biggest of the Legs. Just needed the go-ahead.

"Hold, Cor," Aurelius whispered. "Let's get a few more people into place. Only move if one comes directly toward you."

Kylie cut into our squad line. "Cor, take a look at this." She threw me her display which showed the position of all Bravo Six squads. Except for Bravo Six One, the units were each a single dot, meaning the members were in close proximity to one another. Bravo Six One showed two dots. One was where it was supposed to be to our north. The other one was headed straight for our position and moving fast. Really fast.

Arriving-in-a-minute fast.

Jovan.

Why he broke ranks, I had no idea. Perhaps he was thinking back to his success in the mock battle.

We had less than a minute to figure out a plan.

"Jovan, stop." Aurelius. There was no change in the movement. "FS1 Jovan, I order you to stop."

Maybe there was a slight lessening in the speed of approach. Less than thirty seconds until he would arrive.

"Dammit, Jovan. Stop. *Now*."

He finally slowed down and halted twenty meters from us. Just on the other side of the Legs. Where our ammunition wouldn't fire if the suits calculated he could be hit.

Aurelius had figured it out as well. "Jovan, I need you to back up and get out of the way."

He didn't move. I sensed a war waging inside him, a battle for control. He wanted to act. He wanted to kill.

Maybe the Legs sensed his approach. Maybe they could smell the foreignness of our suits. Maybe they had heard me earlier as I moved through the Green. But even as we stood there waiting for something to happen, they turned as one and stampeded in the opposite direction, straight at Jovan.

"Jovan, run!" Aurelius ordered.

But that was not Jovan's way.

I was shocked into inaction. Bud pushed by me and ran after the Legs. Kylie followed, and I willed myself to move.

The Legs launched themselves at him. Jovan backed up a step and turned before the Legs buried him beneath a pile of writhing limbs, pounding and grinding, each segment striking like a viper, over and over.

In full stride, Bud leaped on top of the pile and pulled, ripping individual creatures from colonies and tossing them out into the Green. The Legs underneath pulsed in a rhythmic pattern, as one after another thumped down into the spot where Jovan was.

Bud had the right idea: pull them off, get them separated, rescue Jovan, and worry about killing them later. I motioned to Kylie and moved forward.

A Legs segment at the edge of the pile severed all at once, spraying orangish blood everywhere. I didn't understand what was happening. Then the same thing occurred to a Legs slightly higher up. With the third one, I understood: Jovan was using nano-wire. Given his situation, it was a good plan, except—except he had no idea where Bud was.

I had just enough time to yell "No!" before Jovan's nano-wire sliced through Bud. He was throwing one of the creatures over his head when he was cut in two. The wire slanted from below his stomach to above his shoulder blades, right through his heart and lungs. Bud's two halves carried his throwing momentum backward. Both parts fell onto the heap and slid downward, tossed by the Legs still moving underneath, not stopping until they skidded onto the muddy ground, orange and red fluids flowing as one into the black soil. Bud and Legs organs mixed, inseparable.

"No!" Kylie shouted a moment after me. She rushed toward the pile, but the way Bud had been cut, the way blood and liquid had gushed from his body, he was dead. I tackled Kylie to make sure she didn't get sliced as well. She punched me in the shoulder. Hard.

"No!" she yelled. "We have to help him!"

"Kylie! We—"

Vegetation rained down on us. The nano-wire had missed us by centimeters. I dove back onto Kylie and held her down. She sobbed.

"Jovan, stop!" Aurelius yelled on the common channel.

I raised my head to see what was going on. All sorts of soldiers poured into the clearing. The mound of Legs stopped moving, Jovan still under them. The recognizable pieces of Bud were partially buried under entrails.

I rolled away from Kylie, and we both stood up slowly. I didn't say anything, and neither did she.

"Oh my God!" Eman, from Bravo Six Two, screamed. "Lieutenant! Over here!"

In seconds, all of us were rescuing what we could of Bud's remains. Aurelius came up, and I relayed what happened.

"Where is Jovan?" she demanded, not masking her fury.

I pointed to the pile of hacked carcasses. "Under there, I think. Under there."

The squads shifted from collecting Bud to digging out Jovan. We shoveled hundreds of individual Legs segments off him, finishing off the occasional one here and there. It didn't take long. I'm not sure if I wanted to find Jovan dead—and good riddance—or alive to kill him myself. Or maybe Kylie and I could take turns.

His suit was intact, but just like on the Enceladus beach, he didn't move. Nor would he ever move again. The suit had protected him from the Legs' mouths, but the Legs had pounded into him from so many places that he died from blunt force trauma. He could have gone into null-space, but I guess that wasn't his way.

Maybe his reactions were like the competition with Charlie Five all over again, with the same reckless determination to prove himself. Maybe in the end the anger, hate, and bitterness were too much for him, and he needed a way out.

I wish he hadn't taken Bud with him.

Aurelius called in a transport and got us out of there. I'm not sure if she got permission from Colonel Monroe to call off the mission, or if she just did that herself, daring anyone to challenge her. We had been sent on a useless mission for no reason, and it cost us two dead.

On the way back, I put my hand on Kylie's shoulder, but she shook it off and leaned away from me. She sat there in her jump seat, faceplate darkened, alone. The ride only took a couple of minutes, and when we landed back at Hendersonville, she picked up a corner of Bud's body bag and stood there waiting for the ramp to fully extend and for other soldiers to help her.

Out on the concrete pad, Colonel Monroe grabbed Aurelius by the elbow and whisked her away. I never saw her again. They replaced her with Captain Belner, who earned a promotion for volunteering to stay on River an extra six years.

I helped Kylie, Mei-Zhen, and Greta carry Bud's remains,

and a civilian directed us to a refrigerated compartment in one of the warehouses. We put Bud on the floor. Four others put Jovan right beside him. And that's where we left them.

We buried Bud on a bright, sunny day, all the River soldiers lined up by company, Colonel Monroe out in front. The colony had a graveyard, and a small section of it was dedicated to the eight soldiers who had died serving on River. Six previous in all those years, and now Bud and Jovan in a single afternoon.

Bud's tombstone said, simply:

Wiktor Budzinksi
Soldier and Friend
2215 – 2280
Age 22
You Did Your Duty

CHAPTER 21: IMMORTALITATIS PROMISSIO

Ut quos contristat
Certa moriendi conditio
Eosdem consoletur
Futurae immortalitatis promissio

So that those who are saddened
By the certainty of dying
May be consoled
By the promise of a deathless life

-Excerpt from the Requiem Mass, *Preface*

2284 A.D. (ORPHEUS + 25)

Subject: OPERATION ORPHEUS ASSESSMENT OF INTELLIGENCE PROGRESS

For: GENERAL FITZPATRICK, Commanding Officer

From: Lieutenant Olsen, Intelligence

7 March 2284

EXECUTIVE SUMMARY: Since the inception of Operation ORPHEUS in 2259, intelligence personnel have made significant progress in preparing to collect, process, analyze, assess, and distribute threat information on the aliens. Preparations include additional sensors, a centralized database, decentralized analytic capacity, and a specified distribution network for updates on enemy activities. Intelligence stands ready to ensure the continued success of Operation ORPHEUS.

DETAILS: Operation ORPHEUS Intelligence has undertaken the following initiatives in response to the alien threat:

1) *Additional Sensors*: Based on the signatures left behind by the aliens at Delphi, Intelligence contributed to the design and construction of magnetic sensors for deployment around colonies and throughout the solar system. The sensors have built-in environmental learning capabilities which keep false positives to a minimum, as well as a detection capability of .1 gauss. Given the estimated magnetic power of the alien ship(s), Intelligence assesses a warning period of twelve to twenty-four hours between positive detection and an attack. These new sensor arrays will be tied into standard Forces networks to provide a holistic threat picture, including imagery, signals, and measurement intelligence.

2) *Centralized Database*: Intelligence personnel worked with systems engineers to plan out a specialized repository for comprehensive information related to the alien threat. This repository includes all past reporting and analysis on the aliens as well as direct feeds from sensors tuned to alien activity. As a result, intelligence analysts can view incoming threat information in real time, correlate the various sources, and provide that information to leadership on an ongoing basis as a situation develops.

3) *Decentralized Analysis*: The work on the centralized database has allowed for multiple Solar and colonial analytic organizations to have simultaneous access to the same information. As a result, Intelligence has mitigated the impact of cognitive biases on the resulting assessments while increasing the potential number of analytic insights.

4) *Specified Distribution Network*: Intelligence personnel in conjunction with Logistics and Communications performed a comprehensive survey of operations headquarters and subordinate units to determine an optimal pattern for threat notifications. Based on this, Operation ORPHEUS Intelligence can distribute threat updates to the right individuals at the right times to enable them to make informed decisions about force allocation.

FINAL ASSESSMENT: Operation ORPHEUS Intelligence has successfully fulfilled its mission to date and stands ready to further prepare, warn, and inform Forces Command about the threat.

Brady cringed as he read the report one last time. During the years both lived and skipped, Brady saw definite progress. On paper, though, it looked pitiful. Intelligence personnel had grafted a few minor items onto a major stalk and called it good. The truth was, they were no more prepared now than they had been twenty-five years earlier, because they just didn't have any more information to go on. Magnetism was an easy thing to detect and analyze. Designing a sensor based on those magnetic signatures had not been difficult either, but they had no idea how the aliens operated, including whether their magnetism was always present or just used in attacks.

His analysts Kal Krafft, Angel Moran, and Natasha Sandbury had volunteered to join the operation and hop down through time. Collectively, they had done their best in writing the report. It was accurate and showed improvement. It just didn't leap out and grab you as impressive.

Brady looked around his small quarters. As an officer, he rated a private apartment in the null-space bunker, but it was not exactly spacious: a boxy living-room with a couch and a view screen, a food printer and recycler built into the wall, and a bedroom with a tiny bathroom to one side. The quarters were padded with insulation, which he wasn't supposed to hang things on. He had tried a fake plant to give the place some life, but it gathered dust and reminded him he lived inside a hole. Into the recycler it went.

He threw back the rest of a drink and poured another. Fitzpatrick had asked him to join the central command unit, to travel through time in null-space to fight the aliens. Brady had agreed without hesitation. He'd asked his wife to come along, suspecting she wouldn't.

And she'd said, "No, Brady."

Just like that. Not much of a pause. Just, "No, Brady." And so ended his second marriage.

He had reached out to her twice—though one was alcohol fuzzy—as he blinked in and out of real-time. Found out that she was on Earth, had earned promotions to where she outranked him now, re-married, had a child.

What did he have? Some good people working for him. An apartment of his own. A love of alcohol bordering on dependency. And a friend of sorts. Brady smiled and raised his glass.

General Fitzpatrick.

ORPHEUS personnel spent two years working full-time before the initial null-space jump. During this period, Fitzpatrick promoted the concept and gained funding, outlining the project and getting things moving. He and Brady worked together well.

Then, after they started null-spacing but before a decade of real-time had gone by, Brady's personal comms lit up one evening with an incoming call. Fitzpatrick. After hours. That was unusual. Unprecedented, even.

"Hello? Sir?" he answered, unsure what to say.

"Lieutenant Olsen." Fitzpatrick's voice was gruff, as if he had been talking too much. "Good evening. I... I apologize for disturbing you at home." He sounded tentative.

"It's not a problem, sir, but I'm sure the Watch Center could have notified me of anything you need."

"I know, Olsen." The Old Man squinted at him. "Or Brady, if I may call you that." The general could call him whatever he wanted.

"I was... It's not anything I need exactly. Certainly nothing from your office. I... was hoping we might talk a bit. In my quarters. Tonight, if you are available. If I'm not disturbing you."

Brady was taken aback. "Yes, sir. I'll change and be down right away." All null-space quarters were in the same area. Fitzpatrick's was around the corner and down the hall, where the other senior officers lived.

"No uniform, Brady. Just come as you are. Please. If you

don't mind."

It didn't matter if Brady minded. When the commander calls, the soldier goes. Brady pushed his hair into place and polished off his drink. A minute later, he stood in front of the general's door and signaled his arrival.

The door slid aside. Fitzpatrick was there, leaning against a bulkhead, his collar open, no jacket, eyes as bright as ever. "That was quick, Brady. Come in. Come in."

The room was filled with overstuffed leather furniture and lit dimly by indirect light. A thick carpet muffled his footsteps. Fitzpatrick had a holo-fire going, accompanied by a wood-burning scent. Entering the room was an intimate act, like disturbing a grave or interrupting a prayer.

"Please have a seat." Fitzpatrick motioned to a mahogany-colored chair, which creaked as Brady lowered himself into it. It smelled like real leather.

"Thank you for coming down, Brady. I... well." The general pondered something, as if entering a river he wasn't sure he could cross.

"I wanted to get your opinions."

Brady shifted in his seat. "About the aliens, sir? I think we've—"

The general smiled and waved him off.

"No, not about the aliens. Your work on them has been magnificent." He rubbed his forehead. "I... I find myself in a difficult situation here, Brady, and one that I did not expect or anticipate. I have power over all of Operation ORPHEUS, and that's both a good and bad thing. It's funding, and it's control. I have senior officers here to manage all of it. But my influence outside of ORPHEUS is waning. The high-ranking officers I used to know moved on, and the new ones—even if they respect and understand the mission—don't know me. I can use the inherent power I have, but I can't influence, shape, and guide. The other officers inside null-space—they still act as if we were part of the normal military. They jockey for promotion, arranging things to look good, telling me what I want to hear, not telling me what I need to hear. The truth is getting lost, or at least obscured. So, I wanted to talk to you. Ask you what you think and bounce some ideas off of you—if you don't mind. And, if it goes well... I'd like to keep doing this."

The fire cast flickering shadows, lighting up different parts of the room. Brady knew the right answer, the expected answer, the answer that had been drilled into him since his first day in the military. Fitzpatrick was a senior officer, and subordinates did not refuse a senior officer.

Normally.

But this time, Fitzpatrick was asking for something more. Something personal. Something uncomfortable.

Brady rolled it over in his mind, examined its implications, and convinced himself along the way. "Sir... yes. Yes. I can do that. Yes."

Fitzpatrick smiled. "Good. Very good. Drink?" He got up and poured an amber-colored liquid into a glass.

"Yes, please. Whatever you're having." Fitzpatrick filled another glass and handed it to Brady. The tumbler was weighty, the viscous liquid inside smooth and warm.

"I mean," Fitzpatrick continued, "I got what I wanted. Or close to it. On the funding side, two-and-a-half percent, instead of three, but still. The headquarters here, with the centralized computing and the null-space. Most of the officers I wanted came on board."

He grunted and took a sip of his drink. "You can take the officers out of the culture, but you can't take the culture out of the officers."

They let the fire crackle for a few moments.

"Are we doing the right thing, Brady?"

"Sir?"

"I mean... are these aliens real? I push and push and push, and yet somewhere in the back of my mind, I dread that it doesn't mean anything. That all of this—" he waved his hand around the room, "it's all for nothing."

Brady hesitated, but the general had asked him to be honest. "It might be, sir. But it's too soon to tell. The best estimates have the earliest possible attack about ten years out."

"I know," Fitzpatrick answered, "but keeping this thing intact for another ten years is going to be a challenge. They want my money. They want my power. They want to see me fail."

Brady didn't have an answer for that.

"And what do you want, Brady?" the general asked after a few moments. "You know, you've never once hinted to me about getting promoted or earning bonuses or anything. Very unusual. So, what are *you* looking for? It must be something or you wouldn't be here."

That was an easy one. "I want to *know*," Brady answered immediately. "The biggest mystery ever, and I want to *know*."

"Good," Fitzpatrick replied, "I want to know as well. And also to destroy."

The conversation wandered from there, but Fitzpatrick and Brady had came to an understanding that night: they would support each other no matter what. Not friends, exactly—the difference in rank didn't allow it—but more than professionals just doing their jobs.

In the intervening years, the headquarters crew had spent fourteen months living outside of null-space. Enough time to guide the program, keep the money pointed in the right direction, and bang the drum with successive senior officers and government officials. They improved Earth's defensives with a network of outward-facing offensive satellites. Mars and Earth and the far colonies around Jupiter and Saturn agreed to a centralized early warning network. More warships and military improvements. Nothing radical, nothing that broke other defense spending, but enough funds evenly and consistently applied so the Solar system was better prepared.

But the twenty-five-year assessment... that could undo it all, and the intelligence accomplishments, when all boiled down and put in writing, seemed weak.

Brady was not surprised when he got a summons from Fitzpatrick that evening. He acknowledged the call and headed right down. The general poured him his usual drink, and they settled into the shadows in silence.

"Thanks for your report," Fitzpatrick said after a while. "I appreciate everything you've done."

"Of course." He took a sip. "Will it be enough?"

Fitzpatrick winced and rubbed his forehead, then his chin, and finally his neck. "I don't know, Brady. Maybe. Maybe I can buy us another year or two. But the whispering has started. They are coming for me. And when they start to smell blood, it will just get worse. I think..." He trailed off.

"One thing I didn't anticipate with this program—with all the null-space time—is that I would be absent for so much of the politics. I mean, I knew it would happen, but I hoped the power of the legislation would carry us for longer, that the threat was great enough to give us more leeway. But the junior generals, the ambitious ones—they have plenty of opportunities to nudge a little here, to suggest a little there, and to watch their efforts snowball. I almost wish..."

"I do too, sir," Brady said quietly.

The general fixed an eye on him. "You do?"

"Yes. It's coming. *They* are coming. I'm sure of it. That first attack was not random; the universe is too big for that. And if it wasn't random, that means they hunted us, and if they hunted us once, they'll hunt us again. And if they are coming, it would be better for all of us if they came now. People are going to die either way, but I still believe less people will die if ORPHEUS is allowed to continue."

Fitzpatrick nodded. "Yes. That's it exactly. It's a terrible thing, but it's the truth."

He sighed and leaned forward in his chair. "The assessment is likely just a formality, Brady. It could contain twice as many accomplishments, or demonstrate twice as much impact, and it wouldn't matter. But I'm hoping I can use some of the little weight I have left to save us from immediate cancellation. I might even have to agree to a ramp-down of the program—a way to save its core while buying us some time. Not much time, though. Not much at all."

Brady hadn't known how bad it was. The intelligence

accomplishments seemed even smaller than earlier, as if he hadn't done all he could to support the general. "And what if it gets canceled, sir?" he asked at length.

Fitzpatrick shrugged his shoulders. "I don't know, Brady. Find a bunker? Buy a ship and head outwards? Get a head start on a memoir that basically says 'I told you so'? And if the attack never comes, well, it's one situation in which I would proudly stand up and declare myself mistaken."

Brady smiled. Yes, it would be better to be wrong. But he knew deep down that they weren't.

INTERLUDE 3

My memory yearns
Even as it fades
One and Two
Must be One

-Two poetry

The noise reeks.
I cannot tolerate its screeching,
Its endless bitter taste,
Its stench.
It is close. I am close.
The constant beating
Reverberates in my chambers.
It haunts my thoughts.
It tortures my cells.
It must stop.
It is louder than the first non-Ones from the stars.
It is louder than the second non-Ones
Who died without fighting.
It burns my hearing.
Its scent screams in my sight.
I will kill.
The other non-Ones died.
These non-Ones will die.
I take from my flesh.
I prepare weapons from my body.
I breathe deep the cosmic flow.
The nearby star tastes polluted.
Energy pours in.
I drink the energy.
My body grows strong.
The energy fills me.
I bathe in its glow.
The noise reeks.
I cannot tolerate its screeching,

Its endless bitter taste,
Its stench.
It is close. I am close.
One is One.
One will always be One.
One must be safe.
I will sacrifice my body
To silence the non-Ones.
The very stones of my being
Will crush them.
I am ready.

CHAPTER 22: MUNDUS JUDICETUR

Liber scriptus proferetur
In quo totum continetur
Unde mundus judicetur

The book will be brought forth
Which contains all that is needed
To judge the world

-Excerpt from the Requiem Mass, *Sequence*

2285 A.D. (Age 23, Birth + 66)

My job was to walk. And walk. And then walk some more. Around the colony clockwise. Around the colony counter-clockwise. Through the colony. Middle of the day. Middle of the night. Walk. And walk. Shoot a Legs occasionally. Break up a fight now and then. Walk and watch and walk some more.

"We signed up for this, Cor," Kylie told me once, several years before, in one of the few conversations she had with me that wasn't strictly patrol coordination. "This is our job. This is what we signed up for. Besides, watching doesn't take much effort. You could write a book, or read one, or watch holovids. That's it. We do our time here, and then we get to go do something different. Maybe more exciting. Maybe not. But we aren't stuck in a life we didn't choose."

Kylie was right, of course.

And wrong.

Despite the underhanded nature of my enlistment, I left Mars II. I traveled across the stars. I floated in space with Saturn. I swam beneath the surface of a moon. I saw a green planet with my own eyes. A very, very green planet. I felt the breeze caress my face as it changed directions and died and was reborn, as it carried the wildness of existence, as it pushed at me just like the crops. I was stuck in a life I didn't choose and yet free from a different life that I didn't choose.

The other desires hadn't left my mind, though. Kylie and I spent almost every night and day together, but we weren't *together*. Not since Bud. She didn't talk about it, didn't come to me for consolation. She just made it clear that our relationship was now professional, and nothing more. She found other friends, other outlets. But not me.

I don't think she held me responsible for the incident; maybe I was just a painful reminder. Painful for her, yes, and painful for me. It was fine if she wanted to avoid a romantic relationship, but no relationship...

I remembered us there on Enceladus, talking from our sleeping bags the night after we went outside. Our kiss outside the barracks. Whispers in the dark as we waited under the Green. For me, acceptance and understanding had lingered in the air, faint wisps twisting in serpentine complexity. But she wanted stability—glorious, marbled, immobile stability. Maybe those things cannot coexist, would never have coexisted. When Bud died, however, Bravo Six had been torn apart and never completely put back together. The worst of it was between Kylie and me.

The heart, though—it advocates. It whispers. It hopes and wants and needs and grasps. To spend every day and night together but not *together*. Shut out. Not even her friend. What should have been comforting was awkward, an awkwardness that pervaded my interactions with her and with much of Bravo Six. Wherever our groups of friends overlapped—and they overlapped almost everywhere—there was tension. I wanted to go back, to change things. I wanted to be near Kylie, or to have her as far away as possible. To be her best friend, or never to have met her. Either one. Anything, anything, not to be stuck in that middle place.

The heart...

Maybe I should have abandoned the desire for acceptance and understanding. Allowed the relationship to scab over. Treated her as someone I knew and had never been particularly close to. Maybe I should have, but I didn't. I couldn't. I could barely tolerate the thought. It was a drug, and I wanted the real thing or nothing at all. Maybe I am more like my mother than I realize.

More and more as time went on, I would lower my helmet on patrol and just be. It left me blind to threats—I couldn't blast Legs if I couldn't see them. The risks were low though, and a rogue Legs or two getting through was not a big deal. With my helmet retracted, I let my mind go.

Acceptance was out there in the darkness.

Three months after we arrived on River, I turned nineteen. I bribed a couple of members of Alpha Six to take our patrol that night, and Bravo Six held a party. Ever since the company returned from the field, I had been on the night shift, so I hadn't seen the other soldiers often. For me, my birthday party was like a reunion of sorts. We drank. We sang. We toasted Bud. And later in the night, when my courage was high and my common sense low, I stumbled through an explanation to Kylie of how I felt about her, even after everything that had happened.

"Not yet," she replied. "Maybe never. I'm not sure. It's too soon." There was drink in her eyes, maybe tears as well, but not tenderness.

"Not yet," she had said. Not *no* or *not ever*, but *not yet*. It hinted at a possibility. That was okay. I could wait. "Maybe never," she had said. But my heart whispered and cajoled and persuaded. Softened the tone.

"Not yet," she had said, and those two words buoyed me for weeks. And then... and then nothing. Nothing changed. Slowly over the months and years, the relationship calcified, until it could no longer move. I was human. I sought comfort in others. I drank and laughed and found partners and friends and made memories I cherish to this day.

For instance, Yousef al Basrati, Bravo Six Intelligence.

Nothing happened on River that required a professional intelligence assessment. You learned more from rumors than our three Intelligence soldiers could ever glean from their sources. Still, Major Belner—in charge of Bravo Six since

Aurelius left—had established weekly intelligence briefings for us.

Yousef never let on how idiotic he thought the briefings were. He would brief the intelligence he got through official channels and also brief things he completely made up but which Major Belner had no way of disproving. Yousef once briefed that Solar system scientists had combined Legs blood and corn oil to create a fool-proof love potion. Given Belner's track record with women, it was no surprise when he turned up smelling like vinegary popcorn for a week.

Or when Yousef hinted at a vague scandal among senior colony leadership involving spouse swapping, which led the major to ask some awkward questions. Yousef got the whole story afterward. Belner had casually questioned the Governor about relationships among top government officials and whether they could affect colonial stability, while hinting Colonel Monroe might be hiding something. The Governor summoned Monroe to her office and asked if Belner was as incompetent as he seemed. Yes. Yes, he was. Hadn't stopped him from getting promoted once he took over Bravo Six, of course, but that's the Forces for you.

When we weren't walking, we occasionally made long-distance patrols, using run-abouts to see what was going on further from the colony. Lots of Legs rutting, that's mostly what was going on. There were massive Legs out there, the kind that had been eliminated from our portion of the planet. They towered over the Green, smashing their way through the flora as they individually pounded at the ground for food. Gone was any idea that these monsters should be dealt with on the ground. The two cohorts who had followed us to River never went into the field. Colony leadership learned their lesson one River rotation too late.

Barracks life was another thing entirely. Now and again, a group of us would challenge each other to a water fight, filling up our ammunition stores like we had before the hunt, inventing and printing out elaborate tanks. At the end of all the gyroscopic jumps and suit-propelled dashes for cover, if you still had a little bit to shoot when your opponent came up empty—well, that was winning.

The holovid nights. The excessive alcohol. The gossip about who was sleeping with whom...

The walls between the barrack's rooms were completely soundproof. That didn't stop me from seeing Kylie take men into her room at times. I would lie there in my bed, my thoughts racing, my imagination going places it should not have. But the mind...

And the heart. Damn the heart. Damn it straight to hell.

I walked on patrol night after night, my mind free to roam. I was eighteen again, floating over Enceladus, at peace with the universe. Back on Mars II, I stole glimpses of my mother and her stim-friends as they descended into the eternal here-and-now. I pictured the girl behind me in math class, the pretty one who ran in other circles, who I dreamed would see something in me that I didn't see myself. There was Kylie at the Forces ball during our second year on River, dancing with Yousef of all people. Yousef, my friend, dancing with Kylie.

All of us, a restless tide, longing to find rest. All of us. Kylie and Yousef. Anwar and Mei-Zhen. Bravo Six. Charlie Six. Alpha Seven. Me.

Maybe if we had gone our separate ways after Bud died, maybe if I hadn't had to see her every day, it would have been different. Maybe I should have talked to someone, tried to channel my energy elsewhere. But I didn't.

Kylie...

When the flu ran rampant through the barracks, Bravo Six Infantry (Kylie and me) pulled a triple patrol shift, caught a few hours' sleep, and then cleaned up vomit in the gangway. That's when Belner informed us of another triple. Kylie smiled and accepted it without complaint.

One time, the food printers in the barracks broke, and we lived on pre-packaged meals for a few days. Just one of those calorie-rich monstrosities plugged up the digestive tract like concrete. Stuck fast. We had some painful, unpleasant, bloated patrols that week, but Kylie made the best of it at shift-change.

She made the best of everything. Except Bud. After Bud

died, she never really smiled at me again, not in the same way, not with that sudden lightning flash. As if I were responsible for Bud's death.

Not yet, she said. *Never,* she meant. Not for me and her, and not for Bravo Six.

Night shifts grew rarer as we approached the end of our tour, but we did draw them occasionally.

It happened during one of these.

I was patrolling the western perimeter, my helmet retracted. A steady wind ruffled my hair. The Green breathed its scent of aliveness. The lights of the town shimmered in the humid distance, visible now after a recent harvest.

I wasn't thinking about anything in particular, at least that I can remember. Earlier, Mei-Zhen and I discussed chow hall food. I made her laugh with my robust defense of the corn-and-anonymous-protein stew we had for dinner twice a week. I was rolling over in my mind what she would be like as a partner, what the future held, what I would do when I left River. I was meditative, almost mystical in a sense. The universe was good for once, tolerant as it cradled me in its hand.

It's a funny thing about the brain: it wants to make sense of everything it takes in, to understand new experiences in terms of recognizable patterns.

When two—then three—then four—bright spots appeared on River's smaller moon, I tried to process the information. Maybe something was shining in the atmosphere? Maybe it was a test of some kind? Something I could understand.

Light slashed through the sky, followed by a bright explosion from the town. Two more streaks, two more blasts. Three. Just as my helmet slid into place, a massive rolling thunderclap pummeled me like a giant fist.

In the distance, three laser towers shot crackling blue beams of energy into the heavens.

The ground buckled once, settled for a moment, then heaved catastrophically, throwing me backward, high in the air. I tumbled to the ground, the surface shaking like jelly beneath me. A shock wave slammed through the atmosphere, hot enough to trigger a suit alarm.

I crawled out from the dirt and corn husks and debris. My suit automatically plotted where Kylie was, and I staggered in that direction.

"Kylie? Kylie—you there?"

Silence.

"Kylie?"

Her comm signal turned green. "Cor, what's hap—"

A blast lit up the sky in Kylie's direction. She had sounded frightened, her tone warmer than it had been in years, before she was cut off abruptly.

The comm system buzzed. "Anyone on the line?" Major Belner. He must have thrown on his suit in record time.

Three more streaks of light tore through the sky, this time landing much closer. The explosions catapulted me from the ground. Multiple suit alarms went off: heat, G-forces, weapons. Red clouds of fire roiled in front of me, below me, above me.

If there had been time, maybe I would have made a different choice. Maybe I could have found Kylie or Belner or anybody or anything and made a difference. Maybe I would have died. Maybe that would have been for the best.

Or maybe it wasn't a choice. I had been trained to take certain actions, to use my suit to the best of my ability, to survive, to keep fighting. Maybe I did what I was taught to do, without choosing. Instinct over decision.

Maybe it was a combination.

For whatever reason, as another something hit the ground close by, as I flew away uncontrolled, as the alarms blared warnings into my ear, I sent one last order to my suit.

Null-space.

CHAPTER 23: JUDICALIS SENTENTIA

Non ergo eum, quaesumus,
Tua judicalis sententia premat

Therefore, we beseech Thee,
Do not press your sentence of doom on him

-Excerpt from the Requiem Mass, *Absolution*

2285 A.D. (ORPHEUS + 26)

Subject: FINAL ASSESSMENT OF THE MARCH 2285 INCIDENT ON RIVER

For: GENERAL FITZPATRICK, Commanding Officer

From: Lieutenant Olsen, Operation ORPHEUS Intelligence

14 June 2285

EXECUTIVE SUMMARY: Based on multiple types of intelligence, we assess that the incident at River on 17 March 2285 was a deliberate attack by an alien race. A single vessel approached the planet, moving in excess of seventy-thousand kilometers per hour. It initially fired eight slugs into the smaller of River's two moons, cracking it apart and sending debris into space. The vessel also destroyed the settlement on River, the ships in orbit around River, and two radio telescopes on the far side of River's larger moon, using a total of eighty-three slugs to do so. The vessel collected ferromagnetic materials from the rubble. As it left the system, the vessel accelerated in the direction of Barnard's Star. We estimate a likely arrival date of 2333.

DETAILS: Micro sensors pre-deployed in the system, along with several orbital platforms apparently deemed too small to be attacked or that went undetected, allowed us to record the following information:

1) *Vessel Approach*: The vessel approached the River system less than one degree off system ecliptic. We judge that this near-perfect alignment was intended to maximize encounters with rock and free-floating elements. Prior to the attack, River detected no unusual electromagnetic radiation in the system and had no warning until the first slug struck the smaller moon. At that point, sensors on River registered magnetic fields greater than one hundred thousand gauss, accompanied by an arrhythmic, asymmetrical pulsating pattern. We believe this pattern was likely a by-product of the technology used to produce the tremendous slug speeds and served as a sensing mechanism for the alien vessel.

2) *Vessel Appearance*: The vessel is 4.278 kilometers in length and has a basic barbell shape. The two ends are built up into rough spheres, with rocks aggregated onto the vessel in a way fully consistent with magnetic principles. The middle of the ship is narrower except for a small central spherical hub from which the iron slugs are fired. The vessel itself travels sideways in this sense, with the central hub continually aligned with the direction of movement, resulting in an angle of attack of zero. There are no visible antennas or other artificial structures on the vessel. The sole opening is in the center hub, from which the slugs are expelled. The vessel has an extraordinarily low albedo, rendering it invisible to River's early warning systems, antennas, and telescopes until it opened fire.

3) *Vessel Weapons*: The vessel's only weapons appear to be iron slugs. Based on ejecta patterns, slug weights range from two to three kilograms, with velocity approaching half of light speed. This acceleration equates to a force exceeding four million megaNewtons at impact. The slugs traversed the atmosphere too rapidly for friction to slow them. While the vessel did change direction to fire at various targets, it also manipulated the slugs as they exited the vessel, bending

them in various directions. Between slugs, there were detectable dips in the magnetic fields of the vessel, with an overall downward trend in strength throughout the course of the attack. This pattern is fully consistent with standard fatigue models.

4) *The Attack*: The attack took place over the course of four minutes, thirty-seven seconds, commencing at 2317:21 local Hendersonville standard time and finishing at 2321:58 HST. The first slugs came rapidly after one another, hitting the moon and strategic targets on the ground. Until they were destroyed, the ground-based lasers returned fire with no apparent damage to the vessel. It is likely the vessel's magnetic field disrupted the laser fire. No recognizable structures remain on the planet's surface. As noted earlier, a few of the smaller space-based platforms escaped destruction.

5) *Aftermath*: In the immediate aftermath of the attack, the vessel pulled in magnetic material from the moon's debris cloud. The attraction patterns were fully consistent with known naturally occurring magnetism, albeit far stronger. The vessel aggregated approximately a million tons of material to itself, before altering course toward Barnard's Star.

6) *Unknowns:* We do not know how the alien technologies are possible. We do not know if there is more than one alien ship, as it is possible the aliens travel as a fleet but attack one at a time. We do not know the alien's intent.

FINAL ASSESSMENT: We judge that the alien vessel is operated by beings who have detected human activity using our extensive electromagnetic footprint and have decided to refuel themselves in our systems while destroying our presence there. Based on the time between the Delphi and River attacks, we calculate that the ship will arrive at the Barnard's Star colony in approximately forty-eight years (2333). At that point, the Solar system would be twelve years away.

Brady sat back in his chair, a bourbon in hand. The report was done. A good effort by his people. Some of the calculations had taken guesswork and multiple permutations to arrive at a good fit, but there it was. Finished.

One vessel. One damn vessel. It swooped in and wiped everything out. No time for comms, no calls from the surface, no descriptions of what was happening, just massive explosions everywhere. The turrets fired back, their pulses turning aside before they hit the alien ship. Streaks scarred the atmosphere where the slugs burned through. The smaller moon convulsed and broke into pieces.

Armageddon.

One vessel, and it was heading toward Earth. Its capability was obvious. Devastating. Unmatchable. Apocalyptic.

If nothing else, Brady had the answers. He *knew*. Others might have dismissed the threat or argued the evidence or pretended it never happened, but not him. And now he had a ticket for the big show. ORPHEUS no longer needed to worry about funding. The money spigots were wide open for whatever General Fitzpatrick wanted to pour.

After Delphi was destroyed, before they knew if another system would be attacked, Brady made sure there were sensors in place around the planet River and throughout the River system. Tiny instruments, unlikely to be detected, fed data back to his section through a dedicated TEC portal, itself concealed on a small, low-observable, high-orbit platform. The sensing system worked perfectly, and they witnessed the destruction of River in real time.

Not that it made any difference.

He had been right about many things beforehand—the slugs, the angles of attack, the gathering of raw materials. He had been so, so blind to many other aspects. The incredible magnetism. The defensive capabilities. And the size of the threat: how could a single ship generate that kind of power? Entire human fleets wouldn't have that much capacity.

And—most importantly—what could they do about it?

The fatigue pattern in the magnetic fields as it fired—that

was intriguing. His team projected a significant decrease in power beyond one hundred slugs, with a likelihood of several minutes' recovery time. Still, if an attacker was taking out big chunks of a star system in ten-or-less minute increments, that was bad. Very bad.

Intent was even more of a mystery. The aliens had not communicated in any way he could tell. The magnetic patterns showed no modulation that might indicate a message. They wanted ferrous materials, that much was clear. Less clear was whether they saw humans as a threat or had some other motivation. It would be easy to mirror-image, to project human-like thoughts onto the aliens, but there was no reason to. The aliens were a blank slate, and you could write whatever you wanted on it. There was no data.

And weaknesses. What weaknesses had the ship shown? None that he could tell. He originally wrote "non-magnetic materials may have an effect against this vessel" in the draft report before deleting it. Of course non-magnetic materials might; they also might not. Ops did not need him to state the obvious. Part of his job as an intelligence officer was to identify adversary weaknesses, and he had no idea where to start.

The bourbon, though. It was going down more smoothly than usual. Because he *knew*.

General Fitzpatrick looked over the report. Intel officers would be intel officers, even good ones like Brady. They would hide behind "maybe" and "possibly" and "likely" and "judge." Still, the overall conclusion was solid, even if anticipated. The strength of the magnetism from a single vessel, though: that was new.

How do you attack something that magnetic? Forces warships would need refitting with non-magnetic slugs and needle guns. That seemed relatively straight-forward. But the alien vessel had blunted laser fire—had used magnetism to turn away light.

The iron slugs, as well. How could they defend against something that big moving that fast? He would set Acquisitions to looking at a counter-magnetic program.

Maybe the way to counter weaponized magnetism was with bigger magnets? Those were unheard of magnetic readings, though. Or maybe they could counter this thing with enough ships so Forces Command could absorb the losses and still counter-attack? The fatigue readings from the alien vessel were a good sign. Whatever powered that vessel had limits, and anything with limits could be overcome.

So. Barnard's Star. Apart from the Alpha Centauri cluster, the nearest star to Earth and likely where the alien vessel was heading. That would be the test-bed. Fitzpatrick would do his best to protect the colony, but more than that, try out various means of defeating the threat. Earth would have twelve years to mass produce whatever worked best. It was one vessel. One. It had demolished two colonies so far. If it destroyed Barnard's Star colony as well, then that was the cost. Earth, though. Earth would not fall.

He buzzed Brady. They had done this so many times that Brady no longer bothered to answer—he just showed up moments later.

"So," Fitzpatrick's statement floated in the air, after Brady settled into his normal leather recliner, drink in hand, "what do you think?"

Brady cleared his throat, buying himself a second. "We are in trouble, sir."

Fitzpatrick smiled. "Go on."

"This alien ship—it is beyond us. The power it generates in such a small area—I don't know how we can beat that. I'm not sure we've even seen it strain itself yet. Maybe we can communicate with them? Provide them with iron fuel or something, in exchange for not attacking us? But I don't know how to start a conversation. They seem to know we are intelligent, and they have tracked where we are. Not one indication that it is sending out signals. Just that magnetism. And the destruction."

Fitzpatrick swirled his tumbler, the liquid on the outside slowed by friction with the glass. There was nothing in all this he hadn't concluded himself. Sharing it was different, however.

"And if they come here?"

"I don't know, sir. We are a big system. Lots of outposts and cities and places on a scale far greater than the colonies. One ship couldn't destroy it all, certainly. But Earth... if it shoots those slugs at Earth, it won't take very many to destroy it. So many things depend on Earth—if we lose it, the rest of the system will scramble to survive. Earth and Mars together, if we lost them both... I don't know. Hard to see past that one. And we only have the experience of the colonies—the ship used massive firepower, but it only had a few targets. It could just as easily fire smaller slugs but more of them, I assume."

"Options?"

Brady grinned and looked Fitzpatrick in the eye. "Isn't that your department, sir?"

"Fair enough," Fitzpatrick laughed, then hesitated before continuing. "With the information from River, we can modify our plans, look for ways to counter the alien's magnetic weapon. Some of the ideas we are tossing around involve overwhelming attacks—produce enough firing platforms that the ship can't hope to take every single one out. But that magnetic field is so strong, we could probably fire at it from all angles at once and never get close to it. It just gets stronger when you get nearer.

"One idea I had was massive null-space projects—throw as many people as possible into null-space and wait for the aliens to go away. Turns out the energy costs are extravagant; we can do that for some select groups, of course, but to put a field around an entire planet takes more energy than the sun puts out in a thousand years. Exponential or something like that. Even the null-space field we use around the entire command center takes a dedicated fusion reactor. Like I said, we can protect key areas, but if the ground they sit on is gone, it's not going to turn out very well when they come out of null-space. "

Fitzpatrick's eyes were open, but his mind was turned elsewhere. The simulated fire cracked and shot up a puff of sparks that disappeared into nothingness.

"How about a decoy?" Brady asked. "Set up transmitters so it looks like one of the gas giant moons is Earth. Let the alien ship blast that apart and then move out of here. We don't defeat it, but maybe we will never have to."

"Yes," Fitzpatrick replied, "we considered that one as well. With robust transmitters on Neptune's Triton, or maybe Pluto itself, paired with reducing or blocking transmissions from Earth and Mars, we might be able to fool this vessel. I'm not comfortable with trying to get through this using only defensive measures, though. And the inner Solar system has been openly broadcasting our location for centuries. If the aliens have extremely accurate angle measurements, they can probably figure it out."

"A diaspora?" Brady was grasping for anything original.

"Diaspora?"

"Yes. Disperse humans as widely as possible, within the solar system, among the stars, maybe on long null-space journeys that come back here in a few hundred or thousand years. To find whatever is left. I mean, in the long run, it worked for the dinosaurs, didn't it?"

"It did?"

"Sure. They spread over the entire globe, filling all kinds of environmental niches. When the asteroid struck, it took out almost all of them. Almost. But they were dispersed enough that some survived, and then it was a whole new world to colonize. Humans are already spread out, but if we gave it a push, we could ensure more of us would survive."

The old soldier looked sideways at Brady, nodding appreciatively. "Now that, Brady, is a good idea. Would the dinosaurs recognize their descendants, though? And if they didn't, would they think it was worth it? Or would it have been better to just die and avoid all the intervening suffering?"

The conversation stalled, both men gazing into their drinks, the firelight tinging the whiskey a deep red. Odd, Brady thought: here they were talking hypotheticals, and yet, if everything went according to plan, both men would be there to see them come true. In terms of their null-space lives, not that far in the future either.

Brady finally raised another question. "What about Barnard's Star?"

Fitzpatrick shook his head. "What about it? I have a nephew who went there, now has kids, a life. Quickly gaining years on me as we spend more time in null-space. But that colony took off in terms of population. Several million people. We can't hope to get them all back here, and even if we did, how could we handle that many refugees? We can use Barnard's as a testing ground, of course. I don't want to give away too many secrets too soon to the aliens, either. Let's try out some new weapons, save what we can save by digging deep and dispersing, and use null-space as much as possible."

"Shouldn't we make our stand there?"

The Old Man nodded. "I could see that. Throw everything we have that way, then fight the thing all the way here, as much as possible. I don't know. That's one I will have to think about."

They sat in silence again, the atmosphere thick and dark.

"Well. Thank you, Brady. I appreciate you coming over." Fitzpatrick stood up, and Brady took the signal to leave.

"Thank you, sir."

"We will do it again, Brady. Soon. And if you come up with anything new, let me know."

"Yes, sir. Will do."

CHAPTER 24: IN RESURRECTIONE

Scio quia resurget
In resurrectione
In novissimo die

I know that he shall rise again
In the resurrection
At the last day

-Excerpt from the Requiem Mass, *Gospel*

2326 A.D. (Age 23, Birth + 107)

The world exploded around me, so I engaged the null-space field. Coming out of it, multiple alarms blared in my ear, each demanding immediate attention.

Heat was the first problem to solve—if you can't fix that one fast, nothing else matters. Wherever I had landed or would land, and whatever else was going on, if I cooked to death inside my suit, I wouldn't be of use to anyone.

Those were my first thoughts, as it took me a second to register the blue timestamp on my screen. There were a lot of numbers, many more than there should have been.

>   41:11:14:10:23:56
>   :57
>   :58
>   :59
>   24:00

The clock counted up relentlessly, telling me how long I had been in null-space. I worked my way from right to left: seconds, minutes, hours...

Almost forty-two years? That couldn't be right. I had sent the suit an untimed command, but the default setting should have been minutes. Not years. Not forty-two years. Damage to the suit, maybe? It seemed improbable. Then it occurred to me: the time that had passed was slightly longer than the journey to Earth. If something went wrong, you would dissolve out of null-space about the time rescuers came looking.

And something had apparently gone very, very wrong.

Gravity dictated that I had landed somewhere, but wherever that was, I couldn't move. And it was dark.

The extra heat in my suit dissipated, silencing the worst of the alarms. Diagnostics showed a few red patches elsewhere but nothing life-threatening. I silenced the remaining danger signals and released some nanobots to fix the problems.

I turned my attention outside. Soil—I was encased in soil, head down, arms still twisted as when I entered null-space.

For me, the attack had just happened. For everyone else, it would have been a distant memory. I needed to get to the surface. Kylie—she had been on patrol and suited up like me, so maybe she survived? But then her transmission cut off mid-sentence. Major Belner had asked something, so he had been in a suit.

All of that forty years in the past.

If I still trusted my null-space generator, I could have shot a timed explosive into the dirt, null-spaced for a few minutes, and climbed out of the crater.

No way.

I pushed back and forth with my arms, compacting the soil until there was slightly more space to move. After that, I repeatedly slammed my hands down hard, budging a few centimeters upward each time. I twisted and got my head aimed sideways, then kept squirming like a dancing worm. It took several minutes until I was pointed in the right direction.

My arms were first out of the ground. Weak sunlight poured in around the clumps of mud falling on me. I reached to the sides of the hole and pulled for all I was worth.

River did not want to let me go. With a slow, sucking sound, the earth gave way, and my helmet emerged from the soil. I must have looked like the maggot of some giant insect emerging when the passing season indicated it was time.

The Green was everywhere. Thick. Wet. Oppressive.

And there I was. Fully out of the mud, standing on my own feet, the canopy over me and nothing but River plants and a few River bugs all around.

I keyed the mic. "Anyone out there?"

Nobody replied.

"This is Coren Slade from Forces Command Bravo Six. Is anyone out there?"

Silence.

"If anybody can hear me, I need assistance."

Still nothing.

I breathed deep and let the air out slowly.

I needed a broader picture of what was going on. The suit overlay showed my current position as northwest of the colony and slightly outside its boundaries.

River was a flat planet with nothing you could legitimately call a hill or a valley. This ground, however, was choppy. As I walked south, ridges and basins and thick foliage impeded my every step. Finally, at the top of one peak, I cleared away the plants.

Out to the horizon, immense craters pockmarked the surface, overgrown by the Green. There were no signs of human activity. Hendersonville should have been a couple of kilometers away, but it wasn't. The location of the barracks was to my left, but nothing was there. The colony, the people, the terraformed area—all of it was gone, replaced by a living moonscape.

I sat down in the middle of the clearing, popped my helmet open, and stared at nothing. Less than an hour before, and forty-two years prior, I had walked the perimeter, gazing at the stars and the town lights as they flickered in the humidity, thinking about Kylie, about some music, about dinner, about being here on this planet in the middle of nowhere, and about nothing.

Now, as far as I could tell, I was the only person on River. No idea what had happened or who had attacked us. Who could have gotten out this far with that much firepower, and for what reason? No idea.

And Kylie. She had sounded frightened, confused. And warm—her tone had been warm, as if she finally let go of whatever fear she had in being close to me. As if she thought of me during those years we patrolled together and didn't forget what could have been between us. I survived all that time in null-space; maybe she had, too. If she were alive...

I shook the thought away.

There were practical considerations. My water reserve was full, but water wasn't the problem. One thing River had in abundance was water, and water is the same everywhere. The suit would filter it, and I would be fine.

Food, though—the plants and animals on River were inedible. Something about left-handed and right-handed amino acid twisting.

"Don't eat it; it's poisonous," they said during introductions in our first hour on the planet, and that's all I needed to hear, so I stopped paying any real attention as to why. But whatever the reason, no amount of suit processing was going to transform poison into something I could eat. I had a few flavored protein bars along as a snack, and that was it.

As I scanned the terrain, plants were rippling here and there—nothing too close, but also a sure sign of Legs. Legs who had plenty of time to repopulate this area. The big ones. The ones Belner said used to be found far away from the colony. The aggressive, territorial ones, like the ones that had killed Bud.

So. Options.

I had to find food left over from the colony.

Or I had to find a way off this intolerant planet and soon.

Or back into null-space for an extended period. See if anyone showed up.

A final option, of course... Quick. Painless. Definitive. But I had no intention of ending my life quite yet.

So. What to do?

I reactivated my helmet and brought up my screen.

Comparing where I had been before the attack versus where I landed might allow me to calculate where various parts of the colony had ended up. Whatever was left of those various parts of the colony, that is. What might have survived in the way of food? We mostly printed what we needed, when we needed it, from the raw organic matter that we grew. But there were the pre-packaged meals. How would I find them? And if I did, how much and for how long? And for what purpose? At best, surviving on River was a short-term proposition.

Getting off the planet, that was the thing. I scanned again for communications traffic. When that turned up nothing, I checked for orbital objects. My systems immediately noted the smaller moon's disappearance, with a nascent ring developing around the planet. The scan also brought back rubble everywhere, showing up as noise. I raised the gain threshold and tried again. This time, I got a positive contact. The coffin receiving and processing station was still in a synchronous orbit above the colony's location. No emissions, no signs of power, but that station—maybe, just maybe—held a way out. If I could get there.

I needed something else that could have survived the attack and that I would have a reasonable chance of finding.

Shuttle or even an engine? Seemed improbable.

Run-abouts? Possibly. Plus, I could probe the ground for their metal.

Suit? Impossible. The power requirements to make orbit were high. Anti-grav and boosters would get you a few kilometers up, but each suit had instantaneous energy limitations. At a certain height, it was a losing battle between overheating and staying in the air.

A full-circle turn showed me the Green. The landscape was fractured and heaped to the south and east, fading to ripples north and west.

Something tickled my mind. Where the barracks had been. Where the suits had been. Where the suits built for combat and for repairing themselves and for communicating with other suits—where they had been.

Sorting through the display icons, I found the one to ping other suits. I activated it, and... nothing. The suits would be running in power-conservation mode at this point, so perhaps my signal needed to be closer to them to activate the protocol. I calculated where the barracks would likely have landed and walked in that direction.

It took me a couple of hours, boosting the signal and wandering around in a more-or-less systematic manner until I got a ping. It was deep—over three meters down—but it was there. I scanned a bit more, hoping to find something closer to the surface, then gave up and dug.

The suit did most of the work. I blasted away the topmost layers before using my arms to throw dirt over the rim. The lift-and-toss got to my back—not the effort, just the motion—so I switched to a bent-over style, flinging soil between my legs. An hour later, the shoulder of a suit came into view. I grabbed it with both hands and leaned back, pulling for all I was worth. It gave a little and stopped before vomiting forth all at once with a sickly, gurgling sound.

The name on the suit was Trenton. Charlie Six. I had a vague image in my mind of a brown-haired woman. I called up her picture on my screen and remembered her face. Della Trenton. She looked like a soldier, the soft civilian lines hidden behind a mask of competence. Hair pulled straight back, severe. Uniform crisp. Maintenance badge. Her service pictures. She arrived two years after we had. I had never spoken to her that I could remember.

My eyes wandered from the empty suit in my hands to the Green hanging over me to the blue sky behind, bright spots here and there where the plants let the sun sparkle through. Something scuttled off to my right, leaving a rustling of fronds in its wake.

For a moment, I wanted nothing to do with this life. The soldier's life, generally, though a part of me again thought of ending the whole thing and this traveling out to the stars to die alone for no apparent reason.

What was the difference between Della Trenton and me?

I happened to be on patrol, protected in my combat suit,

when the colony was destroyed, or I'd be just as dead as she certainly was. Over eighty years since she left Earth, and who there would remember her? No one. The same as me. I could kill myself, and no one would ever know. In fact, it would be easier for them, considering the monumental bureaucratic hurdles it would take to officially resurrect me.

Sigh. I looked back down at all that was left of Della Trenton.

I wasn't dead yet.

Though it showed signs of having been partially burned, the suit still had a good power core and came back to life easily enough. I synched my comms with the new suit and started pinging again, now with double the amplification and the ability to triangulate. A few hundred meters out, I picked up multiple signals in one area, and before the sun went down, I had a collection of seven suits, not counting my own, all with reasonable power.

It was starting to get dark. I could dial up or down the spectrum to see perfectly fine no matter the light conditions, but some part of my animal brain preferred the day. The foliage rustled nearby, possibly indicating I had attracted some attention with my efforts. It was time to take a break.

Of the suits I pulled from the ground, three had belonged to Bravo Six personnel. The first was Omedele Danjuma from Plans. On Enceladus, she struggled at first to walk in standard gravity and pushed herself hard to meet the physical requirements. Omedele and I shared some drinks soon after we arrived on River. I hoped maybe it was going someplace. It did not. Still, she had been beautiful and smelled wonderful and occupied my mind for a couple of days.

The second belonged to Joanna Rutter of Bravo Six Seven. We laughed about stew on Enceladus. She portrayed me in the awards ceremony following our win in the mock battle. Now, in one hand, I likely held all that was left of her in the universe.

The final suit had been worn by my friend Yousef. As I said before, he was good at intelligence and gave threat briefings that were both clear and interesting, with hints of humor thrown in—enough that you had to figure out the joke yourself and also wonder how much had been intentional. A humor as dry as my protein bars. He had been from a habitat around Jupiter, an environment so similar to mine that talking to him was like going home.

The others: Mann, Salazar, and Duchet. I could picture each one even before pulling up their profiles.

Protein bar for dinner, washed down with plenty of water. I cleared the Green around me a bit so the stars shone through, sealed my suit, and lay down on my back for the night, tuning my audio to the natural environment. A breeze shifted some plants. A scrambling occurred off to my right, as some creature fought for another minute of life. The stars stared at me, wavering in the humidity, as if some giant wind could come and blow them away, as if they were the dying embers of the fires Kylie, Bud, and I shared on Enceladus.

CHAPTER 25:
NE ABSORBEAT EAS TARTARUS

Libera eas de ore leonis
Ne absorbeat eas tartarus
Ne cadant in obscurum

Deliver them from the jaws of the lion,
Lest hell engulf them,
Lest they be plunged into darkness

-Excerpt from the Requiem Mass, *Offertory*

2326 A.D. (Age 23, Birth + 107)

The next morning, it was yet another protein bar. They are not that great to start with, and two meals in a row is one meal too many.

I had to get off this plant-infested rock.

I also had to get out of my suit, which I had been in—by my clock—almost a full day. Suits will keep you clean enough, wicking away the sweat and grime and odors, and processing waste for disposal. Scratching you if you itch, taking pain away if needed—all the comforts of home. You are still inside a suit, though, trapped, like something is wrong but you can't put your finger on exactly what.

I peeled that thing off and stepped out into the green and brown loam, sinking down several centimeters. No clothes, of course. It was still early. The heat would soar later, but for the moment, it was cool enough to raise the hair on my arms.

Our ancestors would have been proud: as a species, we have built marvels of technology and spread to the stars and understood the very mechanics of the universe, and yet it all comes back to where we started: naked and alone in the mud.

Eventually—and reluctantly—I put the suit back on and got to work. My basic idea was to join the power generating capacity of all the suits together to lift me into orbit. Way, way into orbit; *geosynchronous* translates into *extraordinarily high*. I also needed to get there before I ran out of air—in the range of a day or so. Factoring in all seven suits, the power curve calculations looked plausible. I just wasn't sure how. It was time for some simulations.

I encircled myself with the suits, like booster rockets around a main fuselage. It turns out scientists have good reasons for why they do certain things. For instance, if the suits all fired at once, you ascended quickly but didn't have enough power to keep going, even if you dropped the other suits away. If the suits fired sequentially, the imbalances in mass twisted you in all directions.

For an hour, I strung the suits together in a line, the hands of one suit connected to the heels of another, and me, bobbing along at the end of the kite, ejecting each suit when it ran low on power. This configuration worked well in some simulations. In others, when a suit came free, it would bounce down the chain and disrupt the entire thing, the effects cascading to catastrophe. I'd take a chance on it if I had to.

Finally, I linked each of the suits together like pancakes, the front of one joined to the back of another. Both the front suit and the back suit would fire the entire way, with me on one end, facing the other seven suits and distributing power back and forth as needed. As each suit ran out of power, I would sever the link to it and let it fall away. This configuration prevented the uncontrollable pitch-and-roll of my first idea. It also resulted in a clean ejection of each suit, unlike my second idea. The numbers seemed to work as well, getting me to the transfer station in a little over twenty-three hours. With a bit of extra time bought by collecting oxygen along the way, I would have about an hour and a half there before I ran out of air. Not a lot, but something.

The final configuration was Trenton - Rutter - Duchet - Mann - Salazar - Danjuma - Yousef - Me. I would keep Yousef by my side—by my front, to be more precise—until the very end.

I gagged down one of my two last protein bars, whispered a prayer to no specific god, and stepped in to my suit. When my helmet came up, the display showed the configurations of fuel and electricity through the stack, and it all looked good. I ran one last quick simulation, popped my helmet open for one final breath of fresh air, and checked that my oxygen supply was as full as it could get.

A muffled thumping rippled through the plants. The ground shook. To the left, a Legs barreled through the Green in my direction. It was a huge one, close to three meters tall, each individual stalk of the damn thing as big around as a bar stool. Deep scars across multiple segments marred its patchy tan surface, as if the colony was well-accustomed to fighting for its place in the world—a place I now found myself in.

Startled, I backed up as fast as I could, but I had seven suits strapped to me. They flopped over to one side, dragging into the mud. I lost my balance, fell straight back, and scrambled to scuttle away further, legs and arms flailing at the ground.

When the Legs reached the clearing, it stopped cold in its tracks. Slowly, the two segments nearest me lifted into the air. They rose and fell and swung side to side, as if tracing a scent. I held my breath.

One of the two slammed itself into the ground, and all the segments joined in, hammering the soil, churning up muck, and spraying pulverized green and brown juices everywhere as it crab-walked toward me. It was a shredder, and I was about to be shredded.

A Legs section caught the Trenton suit and riveted its arm into the ground. I got my feet under me, but with the slack built into the suit stack, I had no leverage to pull the arm free. I ducked underneath the Legs to grab Trenton, then threw myself to one side as a segment plunged right at me. It sank into the mud half a meter from my helmet. Its exoskeleton was dripping with fluids—none of them mine. Yet.

Nano-wire would end the battle immediately, but the risk of slicing the suits was too great. Instead, I fired flechettes from both shoulder-mounted nozzles at the chitinous organisms and the grey connective flesh holding them together. Orange and brown pus gushed out, dousing me. At the same time, the ground jerked up hard as the Legs recoiled, pulling me and a chunk of land into the air. I crashed back down into the basin. Right away, water began oozing in, mixing with the putrid fluids and bowels and sludge and turning the small hole into a brown, pudding-filled sewer.

The Legs staggered. I had sliced the thing nearly in two, and now the parts were held together by a slim, slimy strip of skin and sinew. Straining against each other, the two halves broke apart, each creature hauling remnants of dead and dying segments, jagged in their destruction, like broken and bleeding teeth sticking out of a ruined mouth.

I smeared the goo around on my faceplate to get a better view of things. My flechette attack had not split the Legs evenly. The colony to my right had about three-quarters of the segments but had taken more damage, while the one to the left was smaller but was already in the process of shedding its dead pieces and staunching its bleeding.

I had a perfect fighting position to nano-wire both Legs to death. One great big sweep and the whole fight would be done. Unless, in doing so, I stranded myself on River, winning the battle but losing the war. For a moment, I had a chance to breathe while the Legs gathered themselves.

The smaller one crept back toward me, so I shoved suits in various directions to brace my back and shoulders against the crater wall. It stopped a few meters from my position and reared up, the front two individuals circling like snakes, ready to strike.

I had nowhere to go.

The two segments crashed down, landing outside the crater. I craned my neck around, and there was the other, larger one. They were facing off, stamping and rocking back and forth. All at once, they charged each other, punching and grappling, using single stalks as clubs and razor mouths as knives. Once separated, they had not recognized each other and were now staking rival claims.

I sank down, submerging myself in the viscous juices.

The ground shook and rolled violently, cavitating the fluid, sloshing and swirling it side to side. The titanic clash raged back and forth over my head,

There, in the darkness under the liquid, an image of Jovan entered my mind. He was buried under tons of Legs, all writhing and punching and stabbing him. How much pain did he suffer? When did he realize it was the end? What were his last thoughts?

And Bud—sliced in half, sliding into ruin.

Kylie's expression.

All of them—all of Bravo Six, everyone I had known just the day before—were gone, buried, forgotten. Except for me.

The battle above subsided gradually. When I didn't feel anything for several minutes, I pushed up the slope until my eyes broke free. Filthy excrement slid slowly down my visor, revealing broken Legs segments everywhere, like a forest hit by a tornado. I couldn't tell if there had been a winner or a loser, much less whether it had been the larger or the smaller one.

I got my feet under me as best I could and used both my arms and my legs to walk myself out of the mire. Once free, I grabbed Yousef's shoulders and dragged the whole chain up, all of us dripping viscera.

Broken Legs littered the blood-soaked ground. Yellow sap oozed from plants all around the clearing. To one side, half of a two-segment pair pushed itself into the air, only to fall back when the other segment didn't move.

It was past time to get the hell out of there.

Using water from my suit, I hosed off the make-shift rocket and lined everyone up. I took a deep breath and kicked in both my booster and Trenton's. We lurched upward, gradually gaining height. As we did so, the trail of whatever had survived the fight and crawled off through the plants disappeared into the unrelenting Green.

A little higher still, the full extent of the colony's destruction became evident. What I had visualized as disconnected ridges and valleys revealed themselves as a huge crater system, wrinkling the land, creating peaks and valleys and even lakes

Two minutes later and three kilometers up, my atmosphere filtration system could no longer pull enough oxygen to be worthwhile. I was on my own, with twenty-four hours to get something done.

The first suit—Trenton—came off with a jolt not long after I took off, sacrificed to the steep sides of the gravity well. I had reclaimed her for a few hours, animated her, let her be attacked by a Legs, and now she fell away, tumbling, limbs flailing in some approximation of life. Same thing for Rutter. Then Duchet. With each one, the load lightened, and my improvised spaceship responded better.

Toward the edge of space, the larger rivers looked like veins carrying blood for a grotesquely oversized being. The planet was alive. Full of life, covered in life, bursting with life. The wounds it had taken in the attack would heal, the Green would go on, the flora and fauna continuing the eternal fight for one more breath, one more chance to photosynthesize, one more minute in a universe that couldn't care less.

By that point, I was moving more vertically than horizontally, while the null-space transfer station above me was only moving horizontally. Horizontally in a circle, of course, at a faster speed than the planet's surface. The simulations showed that I would not be able to fully match the station's speed, so at the endgame, I would need to use a grappling hook and let the station yank me into its orbit. The accompanying acceleration could either hurt or kill me—the trick was to balance the G-load with how close I could get.

With a couple of hours to go, and down to Yousef and Danjuma, I decided to split the difference when I got to the station and take fourteen Gs for two minutes. I would black out, and my suit would struggle to pump enough blood to keep my brain alive, but a couple minutes is not exceedingly long. I was optimistic that the suit would revive me when it all ended.

Danjuma went, and it was Yousef and me for a while.

Yousef.

He challenged soldiers to eat ridiculous things for tiny

amounts of money. He once got a Charlie Six member to drink an entire bottle of pancake syrup in under ten minutes. Another favorite was beans coated in insanely spicy hot sauce. Yousef always paid up with a smile on his face.

Yousef, my friend.

When his suit ran out of power, I disconnected it. Yousef fell, flames licking around his sides as he descended into oblivion.

My view was now unimpeded. The transfer station had been easy to track the entire way with my suit's sensors, but now it was a bright spot moving against the blackness beyond. I turned control over to the suit, set a countdown timer, and waited. The bright spot grew, the timer shrank.

The clock hit zero. A hook shot out and disappeared into the distance, the line playing out of my right hand. I waited... and waited. My heart started pounding as I pictured the hook missing or failing to grapple. Then the slack in the line traveled down its length, whipping me forward and slamming my body. My vision tunneled down to a straw, and my awareness went with it.

I came back slowly, beyond groggy at first as a headache tore my brain apart, and my eyelids scraped over sandpaper when I blinked. I checked the diagnostics. The suit had survived fine, and I had done fairly well. I hadn't died and had no broken bones or ruptured organs. I had the suit suppress what pain it could without making me drowsy. It still hurt like all hell.

The transfer station was out in front of me, its boxy lines sharpening as the line reeled in. I had two hours of air, slightly ahead of estimates.

The final approach was slow, a meter or so every second, and I grabbed a handhold and stopped myself. The station had holes punched in it, mostly pore-sized from micrometeorites both entering and exiting, but here and there were larger ones, up to the size of my fist. It had taken a beating—and a bad one.

I needed to get inside to see whether there was anything salvageable, whether I would asphyxiate up here, or whether

I would take one last thrill ride and plummet down through the atmosphere until I burned up. Those seemed like my three options.

CHAPTER 26: AB ILLO BENEDICARIS

Ab illo benedicaris
In cuius honore cremaberis

Be blessed by him
In whose honor thou art burnt

-Excerpt from the Requiem Mass, *Absolution*

2326 A.D. (Age 23, Birth + 107)

I held onto the side of the transfer station and looked back at River.

As a kid, I watched the same holovids series as everyone else. The show *Judith* was a favorite of mine. Judith was a priest or bishop or a Jesuit—something like that. The religious aspect wasn't why I watched—she wore robes which had a certain way of clinging to her. Judith hunted down criminals and then offered them a choice between reforming or being reformed. The vids tended toward the latter. She championed the law without having to worry about its particulars. One thing always struck me, though: how she blessed the criminals she reformed. After subduing them, she held her right hand high, thumb held loosely to the side and each finger more curled than the one before it, like a wave crashing on the beach.

To me, it was a gentle gesture conveying hope for the future and sadness at all that would pass away. Which is everything, of course.

I can't say why I did it. I'm human. I have the same hardwired tendencies toward faith as everyone else. Hanging on to the side of that station, looking back at that green planet that held the last traces of people I loved, with nothingness surrounding me, I held up my right hand and blessed the planet. Blessed the memories of Kylie and Bud and Yousef and the rest of Bravo Six. Blessed the seven suits which had helped me escape. Blessed humanity for failing so often and yet still trying.

Something shifted in me, something fundamental. A fire took hold in my chest, and I burned with the desire to take part in humanity's passion play, to give back some of my experiences, to learn new ones, and, yes, to take revenge on whoever had attacked River. I may not have lost the family I always wanted, but I lost the only family I ever had.

I blessed the planet for another moment. I thought of Kylie and whether she might be alive down there. Memories of her echoed in my mind as I turned away.

Despite the station's fist-sized holes, there was no obvious way in. The entry point for null-space coffins was closed, as was the shuttle connector. Without internal power, I couldn't activate the airlock either. The easiest place to cut my way in was a thick plexiglass portal—the same one through which I caught my first glimpse of River years before. I nano-sliced through it, pulling it out and away and tossing it back toward the planet to make a slow journey into nothingness.

The inside of the station was dark, blistered by radiation, with objects floating in their own perfect geosynchronous orbits until I bumped them, sending them tumbling around the cabin. I couldn't tell whether anyone had been there following the attack. No helpful signs had been hung up, no desperate last-minute graffiti adorned the walls, no skeletons or suit-encased mummies greeted me. It was a ruined and forgotten museum.

I scanned up and down the spectrum for heat sources or emissions of any kind. Nothing except shadows and darkness everywhere.

This part of the station had two rooms. I was in the control section, used for piloting and navigation and everything else that made the station livable, so I made my way back to the null-space section, used for receiving and shipping the coffins, passing the shuttle dock in the process.

The null-space room was full of its own mini-satellites,

hanging motionless in the void. I jostled my way through them and found two coffins. One had a huge hole in it, bigger than an egg and punched clean through and out the side of the station for good measure. The other one looked intact, with its lid already open as if waiting for me. I popped down the control panel on the side, randomly hit a couple of buttons, and scanned the spectrum. Nothing. Not a glimmer of power. If this coffin arrived immediately before the attack, or was brought up for maintenance, its energy reserve might have been low, and then time drained the rest. If not... if they were all like this one...

My suit chimed: two hours of air remaining. It was possible the station still had oxygen in its tanks, but from the look of things, it was not very probable. I needed more coffins, and I needed a functioning one in the near future. The *very* near future.

Access to the storage area was in a corner of the room. I yanked the hatch open and pushed my way inside, headfirst. Coffins were everywhere, loaded onto rotating cylinders in groups of six. There were hundreds of them, and all I needed was one.

As I pulled myself fully into the chamber, a flash of green caught my eye. I peered around the cylinders. River glowered through several holes in the station, which meant the coffins on the bottom might be damaged.

I floated to the center of the room and tried a coffin panel. Nothing.

My heart kicked into gear.

Another one. Still nothing.

Calming my breath, I crawled to one on the cylinder above. No hint of power. The same was true for the coffin behind.

I might have been able to check every coffin in two hours but without time to spare.

I stopped. There had to be a better way. I closed my eyes for a second and hung in space. A better way. I shined my light back up to the ceiling and followed the machinery. The coffins came in and went out of the room at the same place, but there was also a gantry system to move the cylinders around. So, the ones at the very top had either just arrived or were getting ready to leave. Depending on where the gantry finished, coffins toward the top should have been fully powered. I swam up and popped open a panel.

The screen pulsed. *Configuring*, it said, followed shortly by a *Ready* prompt. All systems green. I punched my fist in excitement and put a good-sized dent in the ceiling. All I had to do was get the coffin into space, and then it was a straight shot back to Sol. One moment here and lost, the next moment there and saved.

Except... I still had to get the coffin into space, and hundreds of others stood in the way.

I looked around. I could cut through the bulkhead above and then cut my way out of that room. Lots of cutting, and it wasn't an instantaneous process, especially as I did not want to use nano-wire on this, if I could avoid it. The area was crowded, and one wrong move might slice my rescue vehicle in two.

The coffin might fit through the access hatch, but it would be tight and awkward, both below trying to get it into position, and above, trying to keep anything else out of its way. If it got stuck, my already small options would grow smaller.

Leaning my head to one side, I glanced down at the holes in the bottom of the station. Seemed like the best option.

I steadied myself against a coffin, eliminating one movement vector from the equation, dialed up the strongest laser I had, and drilled more holes, peppering the metal with little dots. Where possible, I connected the dots with existing holes until I had an ugly but continuous, square-shaped outline. I lashed myself to a cylinder and pushed off as hard as I could toward the floor.

My first attempt produced two boot impressions on the metal but no discernible popping of the makeshift exit. I reeled back in, looked over the outline, cut a couple more holes, and tried again. A corner—one anchored by a large pre-existing hole—gave way, ripping in silence even as I tilted to one side. On the third try, the whole thing pried open, hanging on by one side only but also letting me slide into space. The line stopped me and hauled me back up. Good enough.

Starting with the lowest hanging cylinder, I shot out a nanowire and cut through the beam holding it in place. It separated cleanly, and I pushed it down. It had no weight, but it certainly had mass, and it moved slowly, almost lazily, clipping one side of the exit and then banging soundlessly into the flap of metal on the other, bending it further back and breaking it free. Both tumbled away from the station. I did the same for the cylinders above it until there was a direct line between my coffin and the exit hole in the floor.

There didn't seem to be any way to tell the coffin to detach itself from the cylinder. Detachment must have been part of a mechanical process as it entered the null-space section. The nanowire cut right through the support beam, though, and I hugged the coffin tight as we drifted out of the chamber.

River below, the ugly black outline of the hole I had cut in the ship above, and me and the coffin in between. I had done what I set out to do.

Without the full controls of the transfer station, I had limited options about where to tell the coffin to go. It had one choice for "Return to Origin." I was certain it hadn't started here, so I selected that. It had me confirm that I wanted it to go back to the construction yards on Jupiter II.

Yes, as a matter of fact, I did.

With one last look at River spinning slowly below me, I set the destination and crawled into the coffin. Red numbers counted down to zero.

INTERLUDE 4

With each doubling
My memory of One fades
As does the sound
Of home

-Two poetry

The non-Ones came from the stars.
They were not One but became One.
They were dangerous.
They are dangerous.
They must die.
The non-Ones on the first planet
Died without a sound.
The non-Ones on the second planet
Screamed in agony.
They died but swung spikes
While they shrieked.
Like the non-Ones of old,
They fought. They resisted. They died.
The non-Ones of old died,
But not without hurting One.
Not without hurting Two who was One,
Who is One.
The non-Ones on the third planet
Spew filth into the cosmos.
They vomit their sour waste among the stars.
These non-Ones must die.
I must kill the non-Ones on the third planet.
And I must return whole to One.
There is a way.
I am fat from the last planet.
I gorged myself on their ruin.
I absorbed their essence.
Now I will become thin.
I will kill them from afar

And feast upon their carcasses.
The non-Ones on the first planet
Died without a sound.
The non-Ones on the second planet
Screamed in agony.
The non-Ones on the third planet
Will die
Ignorant of their death.

CHAPTER 27: SUMUS IN ADVENTUM

Qui vivimus,
Qui residui sumus in adventum Domini
Non praeveniemus eos
Qui dormierunt

We who live,
Who wait for the coming of the Lord,
Will not prevent those
Who have slept

-Excerpt from the Requiem Mass, *Epistle*

2331 A.D. (ORPHEUS + 72)

Brady noticed small changes about thirty years in. He had expected the people—both civilians and soldiers—to come and go, but he hadn't expected the changes.

At first, it was subtle shifts in the uniforms: a little broader across the shoulders, a little narrower through the hips, a slightly darker shade of blue.

The acronyms changed, too, but that went with being in the military. He'd look them up and mentally file them away as he came across them.

TAS: The Alien Ship(s), which proved almost impossible to use without an extra "the" in front of it.

Pre- and Post-*AOR*: Before and after the Attack on River, not to be confused with AOR, Area of Responsibility, or AOR, Alert on Recognition.

ODM: The sum of all Offensive and Defensive Measures.

ETEC: Enhanced Twinned-Electron Communications, with nearly four times the bandwidth of previous systems.

Personnel threw these acronyms into sentences or tossed

them out during briefings, as if everyone in the room knew exactly what they meant. Most attendees would, but some—particularly those hopping through null-space—would not, and Brady sometimes suspected a briefer was doing it on purpose, a small dig at those perceived to have excess power and minimal situational awareness of day-to-day happenings. He caught the occasional whiff of frustration from Fitzpatrick as well.

Civilian styles changed more rapidly. Bright colors faded to pastels and then back, interspersed with blacks and greys. These fashions made their way slowly, in watered-down versions, into the uniforms. All things may change but not the rate of change in the military. Yesterday's trends tomorrow, and not a moment sooner.

The pronunciation, though—that was what finally got to Brady. At first it was a flattening of some vowels, or a consonant moving from voiced to unvoiced, or the replacement of *t* with a glottal sound, as if the speaker had something stuck in their throat.

The nose things, too. He initially spotted one on an imagery analyst and wondered if she had undergone surgery. A clear, almost invisible plastic cap covered both nostrils. Then Brady saw it on someone else, and someone else again. He asked about it in hushed tones, as if it were something to remain hidden, never to be discussed openly. It was an artificial scent generator. People had begun programming these devices to control what they smelled and to project the fragrance they wanted others to pick up. You no longer had to smell anything unless you wanted to. People were more attractive. Food tasted better. Life was great. All it took were two little inserts.

Beyond changes in the culture, there were the war preparations. The ODMs—offensive and defensive measures. A dozen destroyers forward deployed to Barnard's Star, armed with prototype weaponry based on magnetic studies. The colony there prepared as well, with stocks of food laid in, null-space shelters, and land- and space-based kinetic and energy cannons. The colonial government had implemented an idea of their own: a cluster of iron chunks, floating in a LaGrange point, broken up and laced through with quasi nano-wires thick enough to not evaporate but thin enough to do damage at high speeds. With luck, it would look like an easy meal to the TAS, but by eating it, their ship would be torn to shreds. Brady had to hand it to the colonists on that one. Worth a shot, at least. Two more years, their projections gave them, until the TAS arrived.

The TAS. It irritated him every time he used it, a sliver in his mind he could never quite dig out.

Brady also watched Fitzpatrick—who had given his career and what remained of his life to ORPHEUS—wear down over time. The general spent more and more time outside null-space, fighting off senior officers who wanted his job, his prestige, and his power. These officers nibbled around the edges, looking for morsels of weakness, taking ownership of a small snack project here, extending their meal beyond the plate's boundaries there. By controlling the central finances, Fitzpatrick had the upper hand, but the effort to keep things in line took its toll.

Their late-night talks had continued, less frequently as time went on, and with more discouragement. During one session, over three decades in, Fitzpatrick had broken down.

"I don't know any more, Brady. I really don't." He looked haggard, his eyes hollowed out, his posture slumped even sitting down. The holo fire was the only light in the room, flickering in Fitzpatrick's damp eyes.

Brady nodded and gazed at his drink. They had saved the whiskey bottles as they emptied them over the years and now had a sizable collection hidden away in a cabinet. There was nothing he could say.

"I've tried. God, I've tried. I know what the plan is, what the goals are. I know the risks. I see the bigger picture. We proved ourselves right the first time, and yet the political generals still come after me. Just last week, Jelsing told the Earth Defense commander to bring the orbital platforms closer together. To maximize firepower. Like it was a nineteenth century battle formation. Or Pearl Harbor—remember that one?

"I undid it all, of course, but who knows what the others are up to? And Jelsing's not even the worst of them. Parmalan —he is an idiot. Thick-as-a-brick stupid. They say Napoleon made his couriers explain orders back to him to ensure their clarity. I tried that with Parmalan during a senior officer briefing. Everyone was there. I asked him to repeat what I had just said, and he couldn't. He sat there and tried to laugh it off. Maybe I caught him daydreaming, but I'm fairly certain he wasn't able to follow the conversation."

Fitzpatrick trailed off, lost in thought. After a few moments, he took a sip of whiskey and continued.

"Do you know the true test of a commander, Brady? War. You never know how someone will react until they're under fire. The coming battle is going to clear out the top leaders like a scythe. Automation will hide some of the defects, sure, and I've done my best to put the right people in the right spots, but if we survive what's to come, there'll be a senior officer winnowing like you've never seen."

Fitzpatrick asked Brady for advice at times or for him to express opinions free of bureaucratic restraints. But when Fitzpatrick confided in him about other senior officers... well, it was like they were friends.

"What about you, Brady?" It was an unusual question coming from Fitzpatrick, and it took him by surprise.

"Me? I'm fine, sir." The older man fixed a bleary eye on him, challenging him to do better. "I'm fine, I'm good. Well... the intel work has slowed to a crawl. We've taken apart the data we have on the attacker every way we can imagine and haven't had any new ideas for some time. We did get the magnetic sensors forward deployed out to—"

"I meant," Fitzpatrick interrupted, "how are *you* doing?"

Brady rocked back and forth, disguising it as best he could as a nod of understanding. "I'm..." There was no point in hiding it. They had known each other too long. "I'm lonely, sir."

"Yes?"

"Yes. Not what I expected in any way. I am out of touch. A

little lost. Alone, I guess." Brady liked knowing things others didn't; it was the main reason he had pursued intelligence as a career. This situation with the alien ship was a goldmine: not only did he see all the data, but he planned how to get more information and how to put all the pieces together. He would see the ultimate results of it all. He would know everything there was to know... and he would have no one to share it with.

"What about that technician you brought along with you? The comms analyst? Sand-something."

"Sandbury, sir. She's nice. The rank difference is awkward. And she's not really my type. I can't put my finger on it, but no. Not for me."

Fitzpatrick nodded. "Friends?"

"More friendly than friends, I would say." Brady caught himself. "Oh—you mean friends among the other officers. Sure. When I can. When there's time."

The truth was that Brady had withdrawn from them all. As his job dried up, so did his interests in other things, including socializing. He sat in his room, a random holovid playing in the background, devising things to do with his time but never actually doing them. Whiskey. That was his hobby.

"Okay," Fitzpatrick replied, his tone skeptical. Brady wasn't sure how much of the drinking the general knew about or suspected. "Well, if you need anything, or need some time off, or want to spend more time not in null-space, let me know. I need you, Brady. I know it's slow right now, but no one knows the threat like you do, and no one can translate that threat into practical suggestions like you. I need you."

Brady smiled. He already couldn't fill his off-duty time, and he definitely didn't need more. It helped hearing Fitzpatrick express confidence in him, but the answer had to come from his own outlook on things, not from anyone else. The struggle would go on.

CHAPTER 28:
QUANDO JUDEX EST VENTURUS

Quantus tremor est futurus
Quando judex est venturus
Cuncta stricte discussurus

How much terror there will be
When the judge comes
To damn those who must be damned

-Excerpt from the Requiem Mass, *Sequence*

2332 A.D. (ORPHEUS + 73)

Brady had been up late, nursing a drink. He had checked all the intelligence preparations one more time that day, met a couple of new people on the staff, and satisfied himself that the plans were still on track. Accomplished, he retreated to his room. It was a null-space night. He would go to bed, and in the morning, when he woke up, it would be a month later. Routine.

But he misjudged the time, and the null-space field kicked on while he was sitting there, drink in hand. Normally, it would have been unnoticeable. Null-space jumps were done with time continuity in mind. It would kick in at midnight on one day, and dissolve at midnight on the target day, to avoid constant time disorientation.

This time when he blinked out of null-space, his comm unit was flashing red. The time displacement didn't line up either. It was mid-morning only eight days later. He threw on a uniform and hustled down the corridor to the intel section, dodging several soldiers running in the opposite direction. Whatever it was, it was serious enough to drag the null-spacers into real time.

The eyes of everyone in the room locked on him as he

entered. It was quiet. At this time of day, there should have been three people staffing the intel desk, but there were six, looking varying degrees of scared, angry, and vacant. Brady suppressed an impulse to panic.

"What happened?"

FS9 Sandbury was the senior military member in the room, but it was FS4 Angel Moran, the brilliant analyst with the hygiene problem, who spoke up.

"The attack, sir. On Galvus."

It took Brady a moment to process the information. Their best estimates put the alien ship a year out, so this was extremely early. Still, the offensive and defensive measures had all been in place and should have been activated with first contact. Except the analysts were horrified.

"Well, what happened? Did we manage to hurt them this time?"

"There was no ship, sir," Moran continued, "just a bombardment. No warning, no nothing. Thousands of rounds, all hitting the planet in less than an hour. We still have comms from Galvus, and we have a lot of data, but it's bad."

"How long ago?" Brady asked, keeping his voice even.

"About thirty minutes, sir. There was confusion on the watch as we processed everything. Then Logistics struggled to get the right person here to bring you all out of null-space."

"And no ship?"

"No, sir."

"Then tell me what we do have."

Moran glanced at Sandbury, who still didn't seem inclined to take the lead. "We have full video, full comms, full spectral data, both from orbit and from the ground," Angel answered. "Complete data."

"And what's our initial assessment of the attack?" Several people averted their eyes from Brady, avoiding the question.

Not Angel. "Total surprise, total destruction. Galvus never stood a chance."

Brady sensed the clock ticking. There would be a high-level meeting within the hour, and senior officers would expect answers. From him. Fitzpatrick especially. "Total destruction" was not going to brief well. They needed more.

"Okay, Angel. Show me but make it quick."

Moran sat at her console and brought up a file.

"Here's the feed from the largest Galvetian city."

A bustling metropolis appeared on her screen. Skyscrapers linked by bridges filled the foreground. Advertisements blinked and danced. It must have been a warm day, as people rushed here and there without jackets. In the background, the red dwarf Barnard's Star hung low in the perpetually purple sky.

All was normal for a few seconds before a single yellow slash split the dark air. A few people looked up from their everyday business. Then there was another. And another. Then dozens, raining down continuously, the sky furrowed as if by a great plow. Wherever and whatever they hit disappeared in gouges of fire and violent eruptions of material. The buildings and roads and sky and people all disappeared in a smoky haze.

"Sensors indicate it's the same iron slugs as before. Here's the feed from orbit." Angel's voice did not waver.

The star was in the upper right of the feed, and Galvus was in the lower left. Between them, twelve destroyers hung in the blackness. Without warning, one split in half. The slug trailed the ship's atmosphere behind it, pulling objects and personnel into space. The front section of the ship tipped downward and began falling toward the planet, while the back tumbled away, tossing its contents to the vacuum.

In the background, a second destroyer exploded.

"Direct hit on the engine, I think. It's pretty much the same for eleven of the twelve destroyers."

Brady winced and rubbed a hand through his hair. "Thank you, Angel," he whispered, "anything else?"

She shrugged. "Lots."

"I mean, anything else I need to see before we discuss?"

Angel hesitated a moment before bringing up a new vid. "Just this one. It's from the cavern complex under Timora, the capital city. It housed thousands. Fusion reactors provided Earth-like heat and light, making it the most expensive real estate on the planet."

The image showed a complex spiderweb of catwalks arching from one side of the cave to the other, connecting stacks upon stacks of apartments. The roof glowed a wholesome yellow. Plants grew all around, twisting across balconies and sprouting up the cavern sides. Birds flitted here and there above a green park with a stream running through it. Children chased each other while their parents picnicked nearby.

"Watch here," Angel said, pointing at a boxy structure in the rear of the cavern.

The kids ran. The adults ate. The birds flew. The box exploded. The picture lasted a few seconds before blanking out.

"Direct hit on a fusion generator."

No one spoke.

"Summary?" Brady asked at last.

"The attack lasted forty-seven minutes. We estimate in excess of fifteen thousand slugs were involved."

"And no sign of the alien ship, Angel?"

"None."

Brady pondered the situation. There had to be more.

"Let's start with some basic questions and see what else we can learn. First, what does this size of attack imply about the adversary? And do we assess there are multiple ships now? How far away are they? Were there signs we missed? How about the size and velocity of the projectiles? Any differences? Or patterns to the strikes? Or signatures?"

Brady gazed around at his people. Most had ceased staring at the floor and were now looking at each other.

"Everyone else in the Forces will be looking at these same videos and watching the destruction, but not everyone will have access to the feeds you have, and no one will have the same expertise. You are the best analysts I know, and I need whatever you can give me within the hour. Let's tell them something new."

True to norm, the briefing was packed. All the principals

were there, including Fitzpatrick as the head of ORPHEUS. Earth's most senior military officers were in attendance as well, and each had brought an aide or a deputy. As the lead intelligence officer, Brady's seat at the table was secure, but others crowded in on him. The throng overwhelmed the temperature controls in the room turning the air stuffy.

General Oberlin, the ranking officer and Forces chairman, stalked into the room and put everyone at ease immediately.

"Show the holo," he barked. "I want everyone to see this."

In the middle of the table, a vid flickered to life. It was taken from orbit but different than what Brady had seen in the office. City lights shone from the planet. Barnard's Star sat red and glowering in the distance. A single bright explosion appeared on the ground. Nothing happened for a moment, and then blasts rippled across the land, too fast to count, obliterating all signs of human life. The briefing room stayed silent, except for an occasional gasp.

"Well, ladies and gentlemen," Oberlin started, "that was forty years of work undone in a matter of moments."

It occurred to Brady they might hold Fitzpatrick accountable—*he should have known!*—and replace him with someone else. It would not be fair. As the attack on River faded into the past, funds and programs had been raided for more immediate needs. The general had pushed and argued and leveraged the authorities given to him, and whatever protections Galvus had, as ineffectual as they had proven, was all Fitzpatrick.

Oberlin continued. "Bad enough for Galvus—maybe if they had some warning, the defensive measures would have helped them. Or the offensive measures could have slowed the onslaught. And we haven't seen the alien ship or ships yet. Hard to believe this was the work of that one ship we've seen."

Brady winced as a small pit formed in his stomach. He and his team had reached the opposite conclusion over the last hour.

"If the intel is right and these aliens are tracking us through space, the implications for us are even worse. Earth cannot—I repeat *cannot*—suffer the same fate, so whatever we must do, we will do. Maybe we didn't realize it fully enough before, and if not, I take the blame..."

There was a nervous ripple through the crowd. It was an honorable, mistimed statement.

"Whether we realized it or not before, we are at war now. In a few hours, I'm meeting with the Earth and Moon governing councils, along with ambassadors from around the system. I intend to tell them exactly that—we are at *war*." He let the words hang in the air, before shifting in his seat. "General Fitzpatrick, let me turn it over to you."

"Thank you, sir." The Old Man looked as if he had never smiled in his life. He liked things to go in a certain order, and that started with a common understanding of the situation. The intel brief. "Lieutenant Olsen, what do you have for us?"

Brady nodded and began.

"Good morning. We continue to assess the damage and will pass along more information as we get it, but the attack was catastrophic at best and annihilatory at worst. What we have found so far..." He faltered. He preferred to have a presentation to guide his narrative, but there hadn't been time. "That is—let me start by saying that we detected miniscule differences in the velocities of the iron slugs, even ones impacting the planet at the same time. We've run the calculations based on a small sample size of less than a hundred, and the results were fully consistent with each other. We believe one ship fired all the projectiles used in the attack. While we can't state definitively that it was the River and Delphi alien, we have no reason to believe it isn't."

Oberlin squinted, as if trying to understand the information. "One ship?"

"Yes, sir," Brady continued. "Of the hundred or so slugs we've sampled, we ran the speeds and the vectors backwards, and we found they almost certainly came from one source, firing over the course of maybe seven or eight weeks, timed for synchronized impact. Given the distances involved, it is an example of exquisite expertise in velocity management."

"The distances involved?" Fitzpatrick this time.

"Yes. As I said, we assess the projectiles came from a single source, so we took the velocities and backtracked for distance. When the alien ship fired the slugs, it was just over a light-year away. Away from Galvus, that is, not here. The ship was also not in a straight line back to River—it had curved core-ward a few degrees. Based on that, we can extrapolate both the direction it will approach Barnard's Star from, as well as the approximate arrival date. With the slugs being fired about four years ago—"

"Four years!" Oberlin erupted. "These things were flying toward our colony for four years?"

"We believe so, yes, sir. Based on the slight variances in the speeds, it is a remarkable feat of engineering that the aliens were able to time their arrival so precisely."

General Vesely, coordinator of all colony defenses, half raised a hand. "And when will the alien ship arrive at Galvus? Based on all this."

Brady glanced down at his comm panel, more for show than to double check the number. "Given the speed, distance, and direction from River, and then comparing that to the remaining distance to Barnard's Star, we judge the alien ship will arrive in the system in eight years. That's worst case. If we account for continued drift core-ward, it adds a few months, but nothing significant."

Vesely followed up. "More barrages before that?"

"I don't know, sir," Brady said, hoping the logic of the situation would prevail. Once was a data point, twice was a trend.

Vesely did not seem pleased.

Brady added what he could. "Sir, we calculated the overall mass used in the attack, and it amounted to somewhere between thirty and forty tons of iron. These are manageable amounts given what we know of the ship's mass. So, yes, another distance attack on Galvus is possible, if only looking at it from a supply standpoint."

"And we have no idea about the psychology of these aliens?" Vesely's voice rose in anger. "What motivates them? What their intent is? All the resources we have available and

—"

Oberlin cut Vesely off with a sharp look. "What does this mean for the Sol system?"

Brady and his analysts had discussed this briefly, as it was a natural place for the briefing to go. He had just refused to speculate for General Vesely but was now dangerously close to it again.

"Well," he started, picking his words carefully, "from an intelligence perspective, we believe there are a few implications. First, given the ship's delay in reaching Barnard's Star and then factoring it into an Earth approach, we anticipate arrival about twenty years from now. There are other parameters that could affect the timing, of course, but twenty years is our best estimate.

"Second, the progressive nature of the attacks is interesting and may lend us some insights. Delphi was our newest colony with the smallest electromagnetic signature, and it received the lightest attack. The two colonies since have had progressively higher signatures and have received progressively heavier attacks. We believe this reveals how the aliens go about targeting and attacking.

"So, if we extend that line of reasoning to Sol, we expect an attack similar to the one that happened against Galvus, spread out over the populated planets and colonies, and of a magnitude far greater that what we have seen so far."

Brady paused the briefing and was met by complete silence.

"Additionally, and finally, we judge the increasing levels of attack are indicative of an intelligent species that is learning as it goes along, so a straight-line extrapolation from previous attacks will not reflect the sophistication of future attacks. That is, we believe there will be elements of the unexpected if and when we are attacked."

Brady felt good despite the seriousness of the situation. He said what he wanted to say and strung the words together in the manner he desired. All too often, intelligence personnel reiterated common knowledge. Not in this case. He had known things others did not, and his analysts had put the pieces together quickly and brilliantly in ways that made sense.

Oberlin cleared his throat. "Thank you."

He appeared to consider where to go next.

"As I said before, we are at war, with an enemy that has shown no weakness. And we need to rethink everything we have done in light of this attack. I would like to take this opportunity to thank General Fitzpatrick for his service. It was he who personally accepted this mission decades ago and kept pushing it as a priority. He sacrificed years of his life to do it. For all of that, we thank you."

Fitzpatrick sat stone-faced, the only reaction a reddening of his cheeks.

"Now though, what had been a part of our armed forces —a subordinate command underneath the joint chiefs, working in parallel with other efforts—has now become the *entire* effort of our armed forces. For that reason, I am dissolving the ORPHEUS task force and assuming direct command of all preparations, both offensive and defensive, to protect this system.

"I understand that there are certain legal restrictions preventing this. However, I have already broached the subject with the general counsels and expect there to be an emergency vote granting me powers later today. For now, I am ordering section chiefs to reorganize the Forces for this single goal. I am also promoting General Fitzpatrick to be my chief of staff. He will consolidate your inputs and present them to me. You will work through him for the moment. I do want to emphasize, ladies and gentlemen, that we have one single mission now. The pirates, the smugglers, the terrorists, the secessionists, the cults, the illegal colonizers —they are all threats to our way of life but not existential threats. If we are still here after the alien ship comes and goes, we may have the luxury of dealing with those problems again. For now, we have one mission. We are at war, and we *must* win."

Oberlin stopped talking and looked around. Normally, he would have asked if there were any questions, but not this time. He stood, the assembled scrambled to their feet, and it was over.

CHAPTER 29: USQUE AD NOCTEM

A custodia matutina
Usque ad noctem

From the morning watch
Even until darkness

-Excerpt from the Requiem Mass, *Absolution*

2332 A.D. (ORPHEUS + 73)

Back in the office, Brady walked straight for his desk and gathered himself. His people had responded magnificently to the situation. Moran continued to have great potential, and more and more, the inner brilliance outshone the outward awkwardness. It had been her idea to check the slug velocities. Rosado had picked up on that and found the data. Sandbury had used her comm skills to organize the information. Krafft had turned it into visualizations. When it was all there to look at, they assessed its meaning. It was the kind of breakthrough which comes along only once or twice in a career—thrilling, despite the circumstances. A triumph for them all.

And yet... Fitzpatrick. The Old Man. He had been so right and had fought so hard. General Oberlin didn't exactly fire him, which was good, but still, his power and autonomy were gone. As for the intelligence office... ORPHEUS no longer existed. By extension, the office no longer existed. They all gave their lives to this, believed they owned the problem, judged themselves indispensable because of their superior knowledge and insights. And, in all probability, they had just been tossed aside. Dispensable. Brady knew—had always known—the military did not care about individuals and their preferences. That made sense. But to be thrown away for political reasons...

That night, when the call came, instead of waiting for the general to ask, Brady answered the comm by saying, "I'll be right down." He took with him a special whiskey he had ordered earlier in the afternoon, spending far more than normal.

Fitzpatrick was waiting for him at the door, and Brady slipped in. As he opened the bottle and poured each of them a good-sized drink, Brady thought Fitzpatrick looked different, possibly even relieved, less like the fate of humanity rested on his shoulders. They toasted each other in silence and settled into their spots, the usual fire crackling in the background.

"So," Fitzpatrick started.

Brady toasted him. "So."

"Excellent whiskey, Brady. Thank you." The Old Man shook his head. "I wasn't expecting an attack so soon. Or so devastating."

"None of us were. I apologize, sir."

Fitzpatrick waved it away. "There was no way to know, Brady. You are the finest intelligence officer I've ever known. But there was no way." He took a sip. "I also didn't expect the change to come so fast. Even when I first heard about the attack, I anticipated the bureaucracy would move slowly. I planned on having time to shape outcomes. Maybe General Oberlin already had this change in motion, I don't know. The resolution passed unanimously, by the way—the one giving Oberlin command over everything. It is quite remarkable really, the scope of his powers. If I had been given the same at the beginning..."

He trailed off, seeming to chase the ghost of a dream in his mind. They had discussed the idea of Martel the Hammer and Fitzpatrick the Blacksmith, how the general might possess the knowledge and skill to solve a problem no one else could. Maybe the days of such leaders were gone.

Brady had no issues with Oberlin as a leader. He seemed like a political general, friendly and outgoing, better at promoting himself than with grasping the finer details of the modern military. As such, he likely took inputs and relied on subordinates, which might mean good things for Fitzpatrick.

"What does the chief of staff job look like, sir?"

It took Fitzpatrick a moment to recover himself. "So far, I think it will be okay. I appreciate what General Oberlin did; he could have cashiered me completely. As it is, I should be able to use some of my expertise to help him." But not lead. Not control. The Old Man would hand the metal to someone else for shaping.

"And what about me, sir? And my analysts?"

"You have been as loyal a soldier as I could have wanted, Brady. And a friend. I already spoke with the general about you, briefly. He has his people, of course. General Hoople has been Oberlin's intelligence officer for years, and nothing will change that. She helped him get where he is today; he will keep her. So, no, you will no longer be leading the effort to understand the aliens, and that effort will no longer be centered here. Overall, the intelligence personnel assigned to this problem will likely expand, though my guess is that they will not equal your success. The amount of data is huge, but the amount of pertinent data is small, and you made the most of it. I couldn't have asked for more.

"This headquarters..." Fitzpatrick gestured around himself, "this place is being turned into a bunker of sorts —that's my understanding. A place where authority can devolve if other sources of command are put out of action. I'll move out and start a normal life trajectory, working as the chief of staff and coordinating day-to-day activities. Someone else will fill my spot—not to command but to maintain situational awareness. I suggested, and General Oberlin agreed, that the bunker leaders would need a small intelligence cadre—personnel who understand what level of knowledge the leaders were at when they entered null-space, can figure out what has changed since then, and quickly bring everyone up to speed. And I recommended to the general that you lead this small cadre. He approved."

"How small is small?" Brady asked.

"Well... that's up to you, in some ways." Fitzpatrick cleared his throat. "Two, maybe three at the most. Room inside the bunker will be at a premium. The idea is that emergency leadership will live here, but also that if an attack starts, other senior leaders can use this as shelter. And this facility will back-up critical data from the entire system. There will be big supply stockpiles and memory servers taking up space, as well as rooms converted to senior officer quarters."

"So..."

"So... however many of you there are, you will have to share quarters. Your quarters, that is, as you already have one of the smaller apartments."

A single bedroom with a closet-sized bathroom, and a living room combined with a kitchen. It was adequate for one person, two would be tight, and three would be intolerable for any length of time, especially those living *and* working together.

Brady accepted the information in silence, looking around slowly at Fitzpatrick's multi-room apartment, with its muted lighting and leather furniture. The cabinet with the empty whiskey bottles was open. All these things passing away, in a moment, in a twinkling of the eye, never to return.

"Thank you, sir," he finally managed to get out, "for looking out for me. For everything, really."

Brady looked up. Tears welled in Fitzpatrick's eyes. Respect offered and earned.

"To us," Fitzpatrick toasted, his voice thicker than normal. "To quote the Scots: who's like us? Damn few, and they're all dead. Cheers, Brady."

They touched glasses and drank together one last time.

In the office the next day, Brady gathered his analysts and relayed Fitzpatrick's news.

Natasha looked immediately relieved. "I was going to ask to leave anyway, Brady. There's no intel mission left here."

"I agree," Kal chimed in. He had invested wisely and, with market returns spread over decades of actual time, accrued a small fortune. "I'm ready to go home to Jupiter. I've been thinking about starting a commercial intelligence company."

Brady put a hand on his shoulder. "You will be wonderful at whatever you put your mind to, Kal."

Brady turned to Angel, who was staring at him.

"How about you, Angel?"

"I'll stay," she replied immediately.

"You sure?"

Angel crunched her eyebrows together. "Of course."

"The quarters are not very big, and we—"

"I said I'll stay."

Brady shrugged and smiled. "Welcome aboard, Angel. It's you and me."

There was no reason to wait. Brady passed along the decisions to the administrative offices, who promptly cut orders transferring Kal and Natasha off the task force. They moved out the next day, while Angel moved in with Brady.

"Where should I put my stuff?" she asked as soon as he opened the door. "And where will I be sleeping?"

"Hello to you too, Angel. Come right on in."

Pushing her luggage ahead, she entered the apartment and looked around. "It's bigger than you described."

Brady grinned despite himself. "I guess that's good news. So, sleeping arrangements. We have two choices: one room or two. But the only bathroom is in the bedroom, so if I sleep out here, I'm still going to be coming in and out. And vice versa, of course."

Angel pursed her lips and frowned. "One room, then. We can put up a curtain between two small beds. I think that's better than intruding on someone's privacy all the time."

"I agree. That means we answered both your questions: you can put your things in the bedroom and sleep there too."

"Good," Angel said, smiling. She wheeled her suitcase into the bedroom, and that was that.

It was back to work the next morning. The plan was to stay in real time for several weeks until the Galvus data was better analyzed. Angel and Brady began digging into the information they had, but without the specialists and without the mandate, the real breakthroughs started occurring elsewhere.

An imagery analyst on the Moon discovered flickering stars in the constant-stare telescope data, clear indications of the iron slugs on their way toward Barnard's Star. Ops immediately ordered hundreds more telescopes in place all around the Solar system.

The giant quantum computers on Earth verified the conclusions about when and where the alien ship had fired the slugs after calculating the speed and direction of every single projectile.

No one had any great insights into the motivation or identity or technologies of the aliens. Professionals and amateurs alike let their theories run wild on forums. The implications for Earth were... apocalyptic.

Angel and Brady settled into a routine. They worked all day, as normal, and then went back to the apartment for dinner, after which they retreated into their own activities. Sometimes they watched a holovid together if one of them started something the other was interested in.

Conversation after dinner was kept to a minimum, and this gave Brady some personal space. At first, with Angel around, he curtailed his drinking. When he saw she liked the occasional adult beverage, he joined her—one or two at most.

It was nice, sometimes, to have someone there.

As for Angel, she liked her boss. He was even-keeled, didn't ask too much, didn't accept sub-standard work, and listened when she talked. Like most officers, he had to play political games, passing along loaded or unanswerable questions, often with an eye-roll, just so he could say they had investigated it.

He was a good boss who soon became more than that. She showered more often, and got her hair cut at one of the off-facility salons. It hadn't bothered her to move in with Brady; she had grown up in a big family, several to a room, and this was nowhere near as bad as that. But now she found she did care, and that she didn't want the arrangement to end.

It was nice, sometimes, to have someone there.

After some initial confusion following the end of ORPHEUS, the Forces brought in a new intelligence lead: General Michaela Livornese. Brady suspected this was a dead-end career move for her and that she was well aware of that.

Brady's first brief to her went fine, but he could tell from the look on her face how frustrated she was. She wanted Brady and Angel to make breakthroughs, to be on the leading edge of knowledge about the alien attacks, to rescue her from this backwater. They couldn't, of course, due to policy and personnel limitations. If they did come up with some unique angle, they would pass it off to greater the Forces Intelligence enterprise for verification. When a discovery was validated, Brady and Angel would be lucky to still be connected to it, even tangentially.

The first null-space skip under General Livornese, when it came, only lasted a few weeks. One of the constant-stare telescopes around Barnard's Star picked up an occlusion from the approximate direction of the alien ship. Further analysis revealed it to be a random chunk of ice in the star's Oort cloud, but it was a proof of concept at least: tuned correctly, the telescopes could provide early warning.

Back into null-space, and when they came out over a year later, Galvus was bracing for an attack after detecting a massive magnetic build-up in the outer fringe of the system. The Galvetians prepared as best they could, sending the most vulnerable people into null-space shelters, tugging the wire-laced iron mats into better positions based on readings, gathering final supplies, preemptively firing non-magnetic slugs and munitions back at the TAS, and bracing for the worst.

When the worst came, it was bad. The alien ship approached along the ecliptic, fanning slugs out in front of it while sucking in random iron-rich rocks. It ignored the iron mats, perhaps sensing something unnatural in them. It soon became apparent that the aliens intended to do to Galvus what they had previously done to the moons of Delphi and River: break it apart and eat it. A planet required significantly more firepower than smaller bodies, so the aliens fired at low graze-angles, blasting what they could out into space. What they could consisted of a large amount of material, including the remnants of the capital city Timora, along with its people, sheltering or not, null-spaced or real-time.

The single destroyer which survived the first barrage stayed behind the planet, hoping to catch the alien ship off guard as it moved away. It fired off multiple salvos of non-ferrous slivers, pellets, and slugs—a variety of sizes to see if any worked better than others. The alien ship chuffed off thin layers of metal skin, stopping everything, before returning fire and cutting the destroyer to pieces.

The aliens gathered iron, accelerating out of the system in a direction which was not definitively toward or away from Sol.

Brady finished getting updates from Forces headquarters and prepared himself to brief General Livornese. The aliens were smart and adaptable—nothing new there. They had breezed through the Barnard's Star system without a scratch, as the Galvetians and the Forces stationed there had not come close to hurting the alien ship. If the TAS came toward Sol, the future looked grim. That—along with tallies of the dead, wounded, and missing; some statistics on mass and weights; and some spectral analysis—that was the entire briefing. Livornese accepted it stoically. Two days later, they all went quietly back into null-space.

The bunker personnel settled into a routine, coming out of null-space four times a year regardless of whether there was anything new. The standard was two days out, if there were no substantive changes—and there never were any substantive changes to the intelligence—plus an extra week every five years, for upgrades and restocking and familiarization.

Brady and Angel watched from afar as humanity lost all sense of unity, exploding in every direction as people sought something secure to hang on to, some sense of stability in an actively hostile universe, something absolute and immovable.

On the military side, the Forces made tremendous efforts to protect the Solar system, its people, and its vital resources. The null-space shelters, the electromagnetically-shielded underground cities, the citizens-in-storage efforts at the poles of Earth and Mars, the hibernation ships hurled on grossly exaggerated elliptical orbits around the Sun, the radio-silent launching of new colony ships in every direction, the self-appointed peace messengers broadcasting anything and everything, true or false, to make humanity appear non-threatening, the religious extremists seeking deliverance by pointing to unfulfilled promises, and the suicidal advanced fighters launching their small fleets out into the void, convinced that taking the fight to the enemy was the only way to win: all of these things Brady and Angel witnessed.

Inside the bunker, personnel changed often: General Livornese lasted seven years real-time, before she chose retirement with enough remaining connections to land a good-paying private job. Three more generals took her place short-term—the last dying in his actual physical office from a massive heart attack, beloved pitbull by his side—all taken together only lasting another eleven years.

Then they brought Fitzpatrick back.

The Old Man looked gaunt, hollowed out, his stiff gray hair a defeated army retreating over the top of his skull. The gleam in his eye, however, still showed the intellect that governed it all. His was now a dead-end job. But it was good to see him, and when they shook hands, neither one was in a hurry to let go.

When Fitzpatrick rejoined them, they were expecting a pre-emptive bombardment on the solar system sometime in the next ten years, with the alien ship arriving a couple of years later. They grew nervous as those ten years slipped to fifteen, then approached twenty. The TAS was late, and that did not bode well.

And... somewhere in there, through all of the changes and the uncertainties, with the sword of destruction continually hanging over their heads, and despite the forced nature of it—somewhere in there, regulations and common sense be damned, Brady and Angel began sharing the same bed.

CHAPTER 30: RECORDARE

Recordare

Remember

-Excerpt from the Requiem Mass, *Sequence*

2369 A.D. (Age 23, Birth + 150)

From watching video and news clips after the fact, I pieced together much of what happened. The receiving station on Jupiter II picked up my beacon. Normally, this would have been no big deal. Coffins come, coffins go—each one has a beacon, and the receiving station ensures the arrival times are deconflicted and that someone is there to handle them when they come in. Routine.

Well, routine, that is, except for a few things.

One: my coffin was coming from an unexpected direction, a direction with no traffic in nearly a hundred years.

Two: everyone—and I mean, *everyone*—was on edge, and anything unusual made them jumpy.

Three: coffin traffic in the area was at very low levels. Jupiter II was a transfer station, not somewhere people went to stay or for colonization or deployment, and it was not particularly defendable, meaning a majority of its population had already left.

When my coffin showed up in the receiving queue, with all of its non-routineness, the personnel on the station acted in a reasonable manner: they rustled up some Forces soldiers, isolated my container, and sent in a mechanized unit to unseal me.

For my part, it had been the standard countdown to zero in red, count up in blue. The seconds ticked by. It can take a few moments to get everything set before you open a coffin—maybe fifteen or twenty seconds at most. But time kept passing, until one minute rolled into two rolled into five. The responders had, I found out, brought in a non-destructive scanner to go over every inch of my container, looking for anomalies or threats. When you are always in danger, everything looks dangerous, and that's how they treated me.

My pulse raced. I had been gone a long, long time, even if I hadn't aged very much, so maybe I was no longer welcome, a legacy of a now banished way of life? Or maybe there was a quarantine? Or something was wrong with my coffin, it wouldn't open, this had never happened before, and they didn't have a tool to cut me out? Or maybe there was no one left to greet me? Should I punch a hole in the top and crawl out? I didn't know, and the longer I lay there, the more nervous I became. I only had an hour of oxygen in my suit.

The lid finally lifted as the count-up timer approached ten minutes. They had rotated the coffin into a standing position —yep, they turned me into a stander. Except for the nearby robot, the receiving station looked like every other one I'd seen. Maybe it was a little less crowded with empty coffins and a little more abandoned looking, but with the same catwalk machinery, loading platform, and control consoles.

Two soldiers peered through the half-open entrance. They wore uniforms that were recognizably Forces, and each was aiming a weapon at me. Something was off about them.

I raised both my hands, then slowly stepped forward out of the coffin. When the soldiers didn't react, I eased my helmet back. Maybe there was a little relief in the eyes of one of them, but again, something was off.

"Hi," I said.

One barrel dropped slightly, and the other raised up and away. The door fully retracted, and a crowd huddled in the hallway. They looked awful. Well-fed and healthy, but a mess, with tangled hair and dirty clothes. And their eyes—they glowed, and maybe that was affecting what they were seeing, as their reactions seemed... unexpected.

A tallish woman with matted red hair stepped between the two soldiers holding weapons, arms spread wide and palms open.

"Hello."

Her accent was strange. I could understand it, but it was not the neutral Standard I was used to. "I'm Berreca Rechal, administrator of this station." The words sounded twisted, as if she was deliberately putting me on. "Who are you?"

"Coren Slade," I replied cautiously. I saw no need to lie, but this was unusual. "Uh... FS3 Coren Slade." It reminded me of my first interactions with Jovan back on Enceladus.

"Spell it," Berreca ordered. It sounded like *shp-ahhl eet*.

I did, and a man behind her typed it in to a datapad while she watched. He lifted his glowing eyes to hers a few seconds later and nodded. They apparently had a record of me.

Berreca wasn't satisfied. "More about you. Unit, where you were stationed, origin, year of birth."

There's nothing like telling the truth under examination to make you feel like you are lying, but I went through it all: Mars II, the enlistment, River, the attack, the escape. In the end, she seemed convinced that I was who I said I was, at least for the time being. She motioned for the crowd around her to move back, then indicated I should precede her out the door. She and everyone else gave me a wide berth, as if I were unclean.

I followed her people down a hall, around a few corners, and out into the main part of the station. Like the people, the shops were run down and neglected, with many lacking signs. At the same time, these unkempt people appeared reasonably happy. It was odd. Also, some word about my arrival had apparently slipped out, as various glow-eyed citizens would stop, point, and stare.

We headed off the concourse into an administrative section, where they ushered me into a small, ratty, beige conference room with no pictures on the walls or furnishings except a cheap plastic table and beat-up, non-magnetic chairs. Berreca and a few others followed me in, including a Forces officer—Captain Kerrigan, by his nametag —who was the first person I'd seen without the weird eyes.

Berreca handed me a bracelet of some kind, and I put it on. A data device, I suspected, but not one with any displays. I may have imagined it, but the people in the room appeared to relax.

"So, Coren..." *Kah-rhen*, with a rattle in the back of her throat somewhere.

"Cor," I interrupted. "I go by 'Cor.'"

"Cor, then," Berreca continued, struggling with the vowel. "Let's hear your story."

A vid-bot hovered in the air behind her, recording it all.

"Again?" I asked. I thought I had already proven who I was. Berreca nodded.

I shrugged. Fine. Whatever they wanted. "Well, I'm Forces Soldier 3 Coren Slade, part of 4th Brigade, 1st Battalion, Bravo Company, Cohort 6, Section 12. Bravo Six Twelve, as we say, assigned to the planet River. I was on patrol last night—or was it the night before?—when..."

"No," Berreca interrupted. "Your whole story. From the beginning. All of it. Your entire life. In detail."

I looked over at Captain Kerrigan for help, but he shrugged indifferently. So, I told it, all the way from growing up to enlisting on Mars II to waking back up on Jupiter II. I wasn't sure how much detail she wanted exactly—the garlic-fry kiss? The hidden alcohol? My mother's struggles? But if I seemed to skip over something, Berreca promptly pried me for more. I left out my feelings for Kylie and the ins-and-outs of my relationships inside Bravo Six. I possibly maybe might have overstated how much I suffered alone on River by adding unnecessary adjective and adverbs.

Oh. And my mother Constance—I made her sound a lot better than she had been. Almost a heroine of sacrifice. It was the least I could do. And Kylie and Bud came off looking heroic. Aurelius too. Jovan... I minimized his role in things.

When I finished, Berreca flashed those eerie eyes around the room before settling them unsettlingly back on me. "FS3 Slade, on behalf of the great Jupiter II station, and all the peoples of the Solar system, I want to thank you for the service you have provided and welcome you home as a hero of the war!" At which point, she stood up, smiled at me, and walked out of the room with her entourage and vid-bot. It sounded more like a political speech than something heartfelt. Also, I did not consider myself a hero. I had avoided getting killed, not through any actions of my own but because the universe is massive and uncaring, and by pure chance, I'd lived through things I shouldn't have.

Captain Kerrigan was the only one who stayed behind, waiting semi-patiently for them to leave so he could shut the door.

"There," he said with an accent closer to standard, "we are alone."

He pulled up a chair and sat across the table from me, leaning his head back to think for a moment before continuing. "That is quite the tale, FS3 Slade."

I laughed a little. "Yes, sir, I suppose it is."

"Is it true?"

I nodded slowly, wishing it weren't. Kylie. Bud. Bravo Six. Mars II. Friends and places gone. Me there.

"Yes, sir." I hesitated. "Sir?"

"Yes?"

"Could I get something to eat? I've only had protein bars the last couple of days, like I told you, and they weren't very good. And maybe a uniform or some different clothes?"

It was his turn to laugh. "Of course, Cor. You've been gone a long time, and we don't want you to believe our manners have completely disappeared, do we? Any preferences for food?"

Something hot? A sandwich? I didn't really care. Kerrigan stuck his head out the door, got someone's attention, and after a brief discussion that seemed to involve who would pay, came back in and sat down.

"The food will be here soon," he said. "We'll also get you set up with a uniform in a bit."

He was on the short side, possibly even from a mining lineage, with dark brown skin and black hair, and a round, friendly face. He looked better, more presentable, than anyone else I had seen. His eyes didn't glow, but he did have transparent inserts in his nostrils.

"So. You survived River."

No one had mentioned anything to the contrary, but I

asked anyway. "Anyone else, sir? Survive, I mean."

He half smiled, half grimaced. "No. You are the only one that we know of."

"What happened?"

And now it was Kerrigan's turn to tell the story, all the way from Delphi through River to Galvus, to the anticipated but overdue attack against Earth. Partway through, the food came: hot soup with noodles and some bread for dipping. And a beer. That was some good food, offset by a growing rage in my heart.

Forces Command had known about Delphi, maybe not before they sent us out, but certainly en route and while we were stationed there. That's why they built the laser cannons. It's why we wore our suits on patrol with the helmets down. They could have evacuated us all, or told us what the threat was, or given us a choice. Maybe more of us would have lived. Maybe all of us would have lived. Such a waste. And the aliens: they had taken everything from me. I wanted to squeeze the life out of them, one slow drop at a time, painful and quiet.

When Kerrigan finished, I pressed my hand against my forehead, trying in vain to make the thoughts go away.

"What about here, sir?" I asked eventually.

"Here?"

"I mean... the people. The eyes. The hair. No one looks right."

"Ah. Well, the eyes. Yes. Inserts. With those, you can appear to be whoever you want and see whatever you want to see. But it's considered impolite to alter what someone else looks like—or wants to look like, I should say."

He could tell I didn't understand.

"That bracelet you have on—it allows you to present yourself however you would like, as long as the receiving person has similar eye, nose, and ear inserts. I've got the smell inserts in, but that's it. Technically, Forces soldiers are not supposed to use the eye inserts ever, but out here on Jupiter II... Anyway, I don't wear them often." He looked a little guilty.

"So, this bracelet..."

"Yes," he answered, before my question was even out, "that will project whatever you want people to see, hear, and smell about you. For the moment, it's tuned to neutral, so people are basically seeing and hearing and smelling you like you really are—that is, unless they deliberately changed how they see you for themselves. Which is rude. Except for smell, of course. But it's also rude to not present an image for everyone to—"

"But they're dirty!"

Kerrigan looked pained. "Yes, but not to each other, you understand. We—they—perceive each other however they want. It saves colony resources, too."

Honestly, I could care less what other people do with their lives, especially if it doesn't affect me. Except... this did affect me.

I had seen things with my own eyes—things I could trust, things I knew were true. Even filtered through the suit, I saw reality, not somebody throwing a version of it my way. They put a barrier between themselves and life, and apparently rejected anyone who rejected the barrier.

Like me.

The captain noticed my reaction.

"You don't *have* to use the inserts," he said. "No one will really know. The bracelet, on the other hand... there's no law, but you will stand out as different and unusual and... well... unclean, if you don't wear it."

Unclean. Now that was ironic.

I nodded acceptance. Was I more isolated now or when I was alone on River? At least there, I still hoped for a homecoming. Here, I was as home as I would get, and it was wrong. I did not belong here. Maybe it would pass, but for the moment, I wanted no part of it.

"What's next?" I asked.

Kerrigan furrowed his brow and shrugged. "That... is an incredibly good question. If you'll come with me, I'd like to take you back to my office. We can check your record and see where you stand legally with respect to your

Forces' commitment. I'm sure you've been declared dead, like everyone from River, but when we reactivate your account, it may indicate that you have time left to serve. Though given the circumstances, I'm sure we can get you out of it, if you want."

What did I want?

Two days before, I ate a meal with the best friends I'd ever known, then went out on a normal patrol. Two days before, Kylie and I wandered under the same stars. Two days before, my world exploded before my eyes.

Now, here I was, among these strangers.

What did I want?

Revenge.

CHAPTER 31: REDDETUR VOTUM

Et tibi reddetur votum

And to you a vow shall be paid

-Excerpt from the Requiem Mass, *Introit*

2369 A.D. (Age 23, Birth + 150)

Kerrigan ushered me into his office and motioned for me to sit in front of his desk. It looked a lot like the recruiting station on Mars II, as I remembered it. Similar vintage, maybe. Neat and orderly, unlike anything else I had seen on the station. He held out a datapad and asked me to place my thumb on it, so my DNA could unlock my record.

He scanned it for a moment and said, "Now that's interesting..."

"What, sir?"

I couldn't imagine I had done anything wrong, but you never know.

"Your record does not list you as dead but as missing. Odd. I read about the mass funeral they held for you all. After you were all declared dead."

He continued to scroll through the data.

"That's... unusual, and I don't know why that would be. Ah. Here's a link to a footnote." Kerrigan stopped, then looked up at me sharply. "Did you select something called 'missing person insurance' when you joined?"

I tried to picture the specifics of that day. I remembered the office clearly enough, and FS5 Carmichael, with his polished accent and all the deceit he practiced on me, and I remembered signing my life away, hoping to get stationed back on Mars II, and something about insurance, yes. And then Gladright on Enceladus mentioning something about that as well: kickbacks.

Kerrigan shook his head and whistled low, a half-smile on

his face. "I've never heard of a case like this, and whether you did or didn't select that insurance, your record says you did, and that's all that counts."

"What is it, sir?"

"Missing person insurance? No idea. Let's find out."

He poked around on his screen for a minute.

"Ah, here it is: *Missing person insurance. Soldiers electing this coverage will, upon Forces' declaration of the soldier being missing or presumed dead but without extant proof, continue to receive a salary at the in-transit rate until the soldier's body, or vital and necessary parts thereof sufficient to conclude that the soldier is no longer alive, or compelling evidence of the soldier's death such as verified and irrefutable video directly showing the soldier in a recognizably deceased state, are found. Once declared missing, the soldier's salary will be invested on behalf of the soldier in trans-Solar index funds.* Huh. I have never heard the like. They stopped offering it about fifty years ago."

"Oh. Does it still apply to me or not?"

Kerrigan held up a hand. "You were grandfathered in. You're fine. You've been putting small amounts of money into the stock markets over a long period of time, Cor." He turned the datapad toward me, and I scanned the information. Everything looked right, as far as I could tell, until I came to the bank account. The number there looked large. Exceptionally large. Maybe inflation had made money worth a lot less, so what I was looking at was not really what it seemed.

"Is that a lot?"

Kerrigan exhaled a nervous laugh. "Yes, Slade, that is a lot. A *lot*. You are... well... you are rich, Cor. Not only by colony standards but by system standards. That amount of money can take you anywhere."

I didn't know what to say. Neither did Kerrigan. I had never had money. My mother and I scraped by, but we didn't really need anything we didn't have. I guess. I mean, we certainly would have taken money, and others had a lot more than we did, but it wasn't the focus of our lives. She always found ways to get stim packs and that was her main concern.

And on River, there had been nothing to spend money on except alcohol binges—in town, at the barracks' bar, or alone in your room. Any of the three.

Kerrigan input something into the datapad. "Okay, there you go. Based on your positive DNA match, and my sworn confirmation, your status has now been changed to 'active.' It may take a couple of days for everything to propagate through the system, so we can determine where you are as far as being a soldier. Again, if you want out, it will probably not be a problem."

If I wanted out? Out? For what? The future...

What I wanted.

I wanted to go back. I wanted to go forward. I wanted to be anywhere but here. I wanted to be home, to be accepted, to be a part of a family, like those few short days between Bravo Six finishing initial training and Bud dying. When we were whole.

Most of all, I wanted to kill aliens.

After we finished, the captain took me to a hotel that looked as if it had been looted. Kerrigan assured me it was the best in the colony. I signed in and went to my run-down room, which almost tempted me to get some of those inserts. But I was alone, and it was quiet, and the bed was comfortable. Kerrigan had a uniform and some other clothes brought to me, and I figured out how to have food delivered. I watched holovids and tried to catch up on what I had missed, but for much of it—the politics, the religion, the society—I had no context. It was a foreign language, much like what the people spoke.

I read once about how the brain processes everything in terms of what it already knows, and if stone-age humans found themselves in a modern city, they would see strange canyons—not buildings, not man-made things, but gorges and giant hills and strange flat rocks to walk on.

I was the caveman now. Technology and language and culture had moved far beyond me, and I found myself in the mysterious city, wanting nothing more than to returning to the environment I knew, even if it meant protein stew in the barracks. I did not see how I could tolerate living here. I suspect they thought the same of me.

In the holo-feeds, Jupiter II trumpeted its discovery of me. I was the Hero of River, returned from out of the past. Clips of my interview with Berreca showed up. I thought I looked worn down and tired, but that's probably because I was worn down and tired. You had to pay to see the whole thing.

I asked Kerrigan about it. He apologized—he had sensed at the time maybe Berreca was recording the interview for posterity, but he hadn't been completely sure and was not in a politically solid enough place to object. He also explained how poor Jupiter II was, how those who could afford it had already left, how the trade routes had passed them by, how undefended they were. So... if this was a way for the colony to make money—and given my own financial status—maybe I could just let them run with it? Not sue them for royalties?

That felt like the right thing to do. So did transferring some anonymous funds to the colony's treasury. I will give Captain Zachary Kerrigan this: not once did he ever ask me for money, nor did he, as far as I could tell, ever leak how much I was worth.

Over the next few days, it became apparent that my story had ignited imaginations across the system. There were arguments that the alien attack was survivable: it had happened to Coren Slade, why couldn't it happen to others? Why have we been so worried about the alien ship? We can just go into null-space and wait it out like Coren.

There was also a counterargument claiming I had made the whole thing up and had deserted my post. What evidence did we have that Coren Slade was telling the truth? Wasn't it more likely he had cowered away in some null-space corner for all those years?

The colony administrators set me up with a temporary account and forwarded along the messages people sent me. There were more than I could read in a lifetime—millions of them, ranging from professions of love to death threats, from the adult-oriented to the abstract and absurd. Money poured in, little donations here and there, which all added up to a significant amount. I funneled those funds to Jupiter II.

Sometime around my fifth day back, I got stir crazy in my room. I needed to do something, anything.

As if summoned, Kerrigan knocked on my door a few minutes later and came in.

"How are you doing?" he asked, just like he'd done every day before.

I repeated the answer I gave him every time.

"I have no idea."

He flattered me with a fake smile. "You have made quite an impression, you know. I posted one of my soldiers down the hall here to keep people from bothering you. I've never seen anything like it!" His smile turned real and carried me with it.

"Anyway, I have news for you. It seems Forces Command Central, and the governments of Earth, Moon, and Mars—maybe some others, I'm not sure—would like to honor you." Kerrigan appeared to expect a reaction, but I didn't see how this affected me.

"In person," he added.

Oh.

"So, I'd have to go there?"

"Yes, in person." Kerrigan grimaced. "Here's the part you may not like, Cor. Since you are still a soldier, they didn't *ask* so much as *tell*. They have ordered you to report to the Forces station orbiting Earth to take part in a ceremony. Leaving immediately. With a rush transport, max acceleration and deceleration, we can have you there in two weeks. Your story may have died down by then—though I honestly suspect Berreca and the colony are working on a fictionalized version—but still, close enough to your return for the central governments to gain some political benefit."

I let the news sink in, then nodded in resignation. I wanted to get out of the hotel room, and this was getting me out. "Now?"

Kerrigan hesitated in that kind way he had. "Well... soon. Not necessarily right this minute, but maybe within the hour? Or two? And I'm told you should wear your suit."

A little while later, less than a week after arriving on Jupiter II, I was back in that same room, climbing into yet another coffin. It was a bigger, more muscular device than I had seen before, and I was told it was a faster version than the ones which took us to River. The technician didn't say it, but it was obvious in her tone: faster than the ones in the primitive past.

I have learned this: the past is no more primitive than the present. The past is not better, not worse—just different. Different technologies. Different cultures. Different morals. I happened to think that this present—at least there on Jupiter II, with its barriers to reality and superficial approaches to personal interaction—was distinctly worse than what I came from. And maybe one of these people, finding themselves a hundred years in their future, might come to the same conclusion. None of that makes any difference. You can be a good person in an immoral society, or a bad person in a moral one, but either way, you are responsible for who you are. You are not responsible for the overall society, except to the extent you make it better or worse. And when you reject others not for their actions but for their essence; when you label others as outsiders and undeserving because of who they are; when you treat some people as something *less*, you are making it worse.

That's what the null-space technician, with her grease-stained fingers and unwashed stringy hair and acidic sweat-stench, was doing to me: making it worse.

Berreca came to see me off, and I thanked her as sincerely as I could.

I wanted to hug Kerrigan, and in the end, we did some awkward kind of shoulder touch thing. Be safe, Captain. Wherever you are, whether in or out of this universe, I hope it is a good place.

CHAPTER 32: IN NUBIBUS

Cum illis
In nubibus

With them
In the clouds

-Excerpt from the Requiem Mass, *Epistle*

2369 A.D. (Age 23, Birth + 150)

Count down red. Count up blue. Coffin lid pop. Pause, and sit up. When I saw the news feeds later, I looked robotic: back too straight, a weird twist to my head as I glanced over at the unexpected crowd, a mechanical wave, and a sudden retraction of my helmet. The audience liked it, though, and rewarded me with a big round of applause.

I was met with phalanxes of glowing eyes, shining in the dimmed light, and vid-bots hovering in the air in front of me. A crowd of high-ranking and well-dressed individuals leered in my direction, as if I were a zoo animal. They had moved my container from a standard receiving room to a huge domed hall, with grass-green carpet, banners congratulating the Hero of River, balloons, and, in the back, red and blue lights pulsing in rhythm to bass-heavy music. A balcony ran around the inside perimeter of the hall, stuffed with people staring at me.

From the holovids I'd watched on Jupiter II, I recognized the first person who came over to greet me as President Diana Minskaya, representing the various Sol governments and councils. Her eyes didn't glow, so that was a positive. She waited until I climbed out of the container, then took my hand and raised it in triumph. She was wearing transparent gloves, but I appreciated the gesture.

It was—despite my embarrassment, despite knowing I

was a prop—a good moment. President Minskaya said some nice, bland words, welcomed me back, congratulated me on my accomplishments, promoted me two ranks (of all things), and made sure she got plenty of one-on-one video with me. Then she moved on, working the crowd, as a succession of people with successively less interest in me did a quick meet-and-greet-and-make-sure-the-vids-are-on. I guess technically nothing was keeping me there in that room, but I had nowhere to go, and there were quite a few general officers in the crowd. They got their moment with me as well.

It wasn't all bad, of course. One very nice and nice-looking FS6 brought me some food on a plastic plate: meatballs, cheese, and some fruit. I ate all of these with my fingers and drew some horrified expressions.

As I said, it wasn't all bad.

One woman came up to me to discuss her great uncle (or great great uncle, or something like that) who had been on River when it was attacked. Had I known him? He was in that last cohort to arrive, and while I recognized the name, it didn't immediately go with a face. Still, I enjoyed telling her what her relative's life had been like. I gathered that her uncle-ish relative had become a family celebrity.

The reception lasted another hour or so, gradually clearing out as everyone got their turn and as the most important people left, providing less ways for those scrambling toward the top to be seen and heard. To me, power is neither a good nor a bad thing—it just is, and we as a species need it, both to our benefit and our detriment. I don't resent those who wield power. I do find the pushing and shoving and preening and chest-beating on the part of those trying to get it to be unseemly at best and disgusting at worst. I have met good and bad people in my life, but the ones seeking power for its own sake are the worst.

There were only a few individuals left in the room when I was blindsided by a reporter. He started asking me questions about Mars II, then hinted that he knew what had become of my mother. I wanted and didn't want to know at the same time, but either way, I certainly didn't want to find out from some stranger who was there to provoke a reaction and make some news.

I was about to walk away from the reporter, which might have been the reaction he was looking for in the first place, when a major came up and greeted us. He was a good four or five centimeters taller than me and stood ramrod straight. His hair followed suit, cut flat on top and shaved close on the sides. He wore a one-piece white dress uniform tailored to show his muscles. He could have been imposing had he chosen to be, but he seemed inclined to treat me nicely. Maybe overly nicely. Whatever the case, he quickly grasped what was going on and pulled me away from the encounter with a brusque, "Sir, excuse me, I need to talk to this soldier now," to the reporter.

As he led me away, he put a hand on my shoulder. "FS3—I guess it's FS5 now, isn't it? Congratulations, young man! Heh. Young man." He found that joke amusing, I gathered. I had been born before most of their grandparents.

"FS5 Slade, I am Major James 'Reno' Black, a recruiter here at headquarters. I have been assigned to take care of you for the next couple of days. And to discuss your future. Shall we get you settled? We can put you up in a hotel for a couple of nights until we get everything straightened out. And don't worry—we will cover the cost for now, until we can make sure your pay situation is secure. We don't want the Hero of River to be homeless!"

Sure.

There was almost a brutal honesty to his insincerity. Maybe it's a recruiter attitude. I had more than a vague sense that Major Black and FS5 Carmichael back on Mars II were cut from the same cloth. I mean, it was a very fine piece of cloth in appearance and professionalism, but maybe the job forced them to act in certain ways, or maybe the job itself attracted certain types of people. Or, as with most things, some combination of those factors and more. It is in our genes to connect cause and effect, whether we acknowledge the capricious nature of the universe or not.

I gathered up my few belongings and followed him out the door. We stayed away from the main thoroughfares, winding our way through back hallways until we entered a hotel lobby through a side door. We breezed by the front desk without stopping and headed down a corridor to a room, which Major Black keyed open for me. Wood and brass and leather. It was the nicest room of any kind I had ever seen. He left me there with some reassuring words of support. He may have been a decent man under all the pretense, but I couldn't tell.

I ate, I slept, I watched holovids. It was just like being on Jupiter II, except much, much nicer.

The major came back the next morning, all business. "So, FS5 Slade—may I call you Coren?"

Well, of course he could, since he outranked me, but I corrected him anyway. "Cor, please, sir."

"Ah, very good. Cor, then. Again, let me say how pleased we are to have you back. The reception yesterday went exceedingly well, and you made a good impression on people. That was just terrific—fantastic even—so thank you!"

Black and I were sitting across a small table from each other in two high-backed burgundy leather chairs, the kind with the brass buttons on the front arm seams. I shifted my weight to get more comfortable, the leather squeaking in response.

"Yes. So, Cor, let's discuss your future."

He pulled out a datapad before going on. "I've looked at the terms of your enlistment, and it's all a little murky. Transit times don't count, of course, but we are not sure what to do about the time you spent in null-space on the planet. You weren't in transit, nor were you active. The point being that depending on how we count it, you may or may not have fulfilled your contract to the Forces."

He looked at me to gauge my reaction. I shrugged. I had no idea what the future held for me either.

"Having said that," he continued, "and in discussions with senior officers, we wanted to get your input. It's not in the Forces' interest to keep you in the service against your will, especially if that information were to leak out—and everything leaks out."

He smiled at his own joke.

"So, if you would like to be discharged, we will give you credit for time served on River, pay you what we owe you for that time, and we can go our separate ways. We can even give you a ticket to get back to Mars II, if that's what you'd like."

I nodded understanding. I suspected Mars II closely resembled Jupiter II, and there was nothing there for me except painful memories and finding out what happened to my mother. Which I could probably do from anywhere. Except from that reporter, of course, based on principle alone.

"Or..." And here Major Black caught my eye and held it. "Or, we could retain you in the Forces."

He held up his hands, asking me to suspend judgment.

"Now—we would get you set up with very light duty, nothing too hard, and you would have plenty of time to get re-acclimated to the worlds. We would even station you wherever you wanted. All we ask is that you make yourself available for interviews and speaking engagements and some recruiting vids, that kind of thing. You see, the thing is Cor... you heard about the alien attacks, right?"

I looked at him in disbelief.

"Of course you have, of course. But I mean the one after River, the attack on Galvus."

I nodded.

"We anticipated the aliens would launch an attack here, against the Solar system. But it's been decades, and there has been no sign of any attack, no further contact with the alien ship, nothing, and pressure is mounting on all sides to cut back on military funding. Focus spending on other problems. The Forces would like to avoid that, or at least lessen the impact of it, since we believe the threat is still out there. So, yes, we would like to retain you under those conditions. And we can certainly give you a day or two or maybe more to consider it. Okay?"

When, on impulse, I visited the recruitment office on

Mars II, and talked to FS5 Carmichael, and he described being in the service and what it could mean for me, new possibilities for my life bloomed in my mind. Not a life lived in hiding, scratching out an existence, but a life of chances, of experiences. That was what I had wanted so badly. And as Major Black spoke, that same expanse opened before me again, now sighted on the aliens. It was an impulse based on a sudden vision of the future. The chance to hit back at them, and to choose how I would do it—it was power of a different kind, whether it made me into a tool for the Forces propaganda machine or not.

"Sir," I replied, "I would like to remain in the Forces, but I have one request first."

"Let's hear it."

"I want to be in a combat unit. A unit that is in some way preparing to hit back at those bastards if they ever show up. That is what I want to do."

Major Black grinned so broadly I thought he might hurt himself. "FS5 Slade... we have ourselves a deal."

CHAPTER 33: ELEISON

Eleison

Have mercy

-Excerpt from the Requiem Mass, *Absolution*

2369 A.D. (Age 23, Birth + 150)

Major Black and I may have had a deal, but it took some negotiation before I found the right place for me.

Right then and there, in his office, Black pulled up a list of all the in-system posts, bases, and stations and told me I could pick any one of them.

"Even Mars II!" he offered helpfully.

I was interested in mission, not location. The list didn't tell me anything, so I sent him back to consult with his superiors.

He came to my hotel room the next day with standard Forces specialty codes combined with specific job descriptions. This was closer to what I wanted. Major Black looked over my shoulder as I ran down the list.

First were rail-gun targeteers and pulse cannon operators and maintainers.

"It would be personal revenge if you could get a hit on the alien ship!" Black exclaimed.

Next was a long series of combat soldier positions.

"You are already trained and experienced—you would fit right in and probably get promoted quickly. And you could even go back to Mars II and do it!"

Or a pilot position.

I glanced over my shoulder, and Black gave me a knowing look. "Once this is all over, you will have a guaranteed job!"

"And this is all of the combat positions?"

"Yes."

"Nothing else?"

"No. These are all the regular Forces combat positions. As you can see, the majority are in the infantry. Piloting, though. If I could recommend—"

"What do you mean by regular Forces?"

Black stopped. His eyes shifted sideways.

"Well..."

"Well what?"

He held out both hands, half a smile on his face as if I was passing up the deal of a lifetime. "You don't want those other ones, trust me. No flexibility, highly dangerous. You will never get back to Mars II that way."

I looked at him and didn't say anything.

When he came back for the last time, Black brought another major with him—a tall, thin woman with close-cropped grey hair and a no-nonsense attitude.

"Cor," Black said, "this is Major Lexie Roth. Occasionally in the recruiting business, we come across... exceptional candidates, and, in those cases, we can make the appropriate introductions to the special projects section of Forces Command. And that's where my knowledge stops. I'm going to step out and let you two discuss, and I hope you find it to your liking. Our deal still stands, right?"

"Yes."

He pumped a fist. I got the sense he saw this as a career stepping-stone, dangling in front of him like a carrot.

After he left, Major Roth came forward, shook hands, and took Major Black's seat. "I'm Major Roth," she said, "but you can call me Riff."

"Uhhhh... FS5 Coren Slade," I replied, taken aback slightly. "Cor."

She smiled as if she understood.

"Well, FS5 Coren Slade," she said, kindly mocking me, "this is a very unusual situation we find ourselves in. Normally, when someone is identified for this kind of program, I would come in and ask questions, and then, based on the answers, determine if we have a spot for that person in our projects. From there, selectees get diverted to us, and we eventually reveal what they will be doing. But I've been told from on high that you can choose whatever you want, and to do that, I'm going to have to give you some basic descriptions of what the different projects entail."

Riff glanced down at her datapad and seemed to get sidetracked for a second. "You do have a remarkable story. Amazing. You really shouldn't be alive."

I knew that, but it's not really the kind of comment you can reply to.

"So," she continued, turning her datapad around and showing it to me, "I will need you to certify here that you will not discuss, disclose, or in any other way reveal what I am about to tell you, except with others who have verified access to the same information. This is a life-long, binding contract with severe penalties should you break it. If you agree, certify with your DNA."

Who was I going to tell? Anyway, it sounded like we were getting closer to what I wanted. There was a pulsing fingerprint spot on the datapad. I touched it; it stopped blinking and turned green.

Next, she took out a small device, placed it on the table, and turned it on.

"Prevents eavesdropping."

Riff took a deep breath. "Okay, here we go. We have three compartmented programs to counter the aliens. First, we have Project Prometheus. This one is designed to bring fire to the alien ship, you know, like—"

"Yes, I got it."

"Ah, I see. Well, the basic concept is that there will be a swarm of human-, remote-, and computer-piloted spacecraft that will attempt to attract the alien ship's attention, while a smaller group of stealth vessels approach it and hit it with antimatter. That's Prometheus. You could have your choice of any of those positions—human pilot, drone pilot, or antimatter dropper."

Bombing the aliens sounded pretty good. To watch humanity's revenge unfold—yes. "What's the chance of success?"

Riff frowned like there was a bad smell in the room. "Cor...

we wouldn't be doing these things if we didn't believe we would succeed. At the same time, you must understand—we haven't had a single indication the aliens are heading this way. The prevailing belief in the Forces is that they are not coming, that maybe they feared us after Galvus. Or maybe three colonies in a row were a coincidence. So yes, we think it would succeed, but we are doubtful about getting the chance."

The attack on River was still fresh and raw—barely more than a week in the past for me—and I wanted to hit back hard at the alien murderers. Destroy them. Watch them die so they never made anyone suffer again. And I had no doubt they were heading for the Solar system.

"Okay," I said, "what's next?"

"The second program is called Project Dolos. At its core, this project is deception: we are building a huge fleet of spaceships that will have the same external electromagnetic appearance as their real counterparts but internally are all engine. The plan here is to have the aliens expend time and energy eliminating these as a threat. To make the illusion more complete, we have a group of operators who will be controlling the fake ships and remotely generating communications between them."

She held up her hand, asking me to suspend judgment. "It may not sound like the most exciting option, but from what I've seen of the tactical plans, this project is very enjoyable for those involved. They have even come up with unique ways of carrying out battles in space, which have been removed from the cover program and published in military journals. In that way, Dolos is like a think-tank. The personnel on this project are always looking for individuals with unique perspectives, and you would fit right in."

Riff looked at me expectantly. I tilted my head to the side and shrugged. Not for me.

"And finally," Riff said, smiling at some inner joke, "Project Aeneid. Given what you've been through already, this one... well... I don't know. So, Aeneid: the idea here is that several companies of soldiers go into null-space, encased in iron.

Like a big geode with Forces troops at the center instead of crystals. We believe the aliens fuel themselves by accreting ferrous metals. We found material from Delphi in the slugs that hit Galvus and believe they gather metal on the outside of their ship and then slowly move it to the interior as they use up ammunition or expend energy. The encased soldiers will go in the path of the alien vessel and, with luck, be accreted—aggregated to the vessel, as it were. The null-space controls have a gap sensor that will bring a soldier out whenever it senses something besides the metal encasement. Presumably, this will be inside the alien ship.

"Aeneid is a back-end project—that is, we will try to place the soldiers in the path of the departing ship, hope they get picked up, and then wait for a signal from them as to success or failure, at which point we will launch a rescue mission. We have no idea how long it might take for a rock on the outside of the ship to work its way inward—could be decades, could be centuries, possibly never. So yes, given what you've already been through, I can see how this might be an awkward choice, entailing potentially much more time in null-space.

"And that's it for active special operations. Prometheus: distract and attack. Dolos: deceive and waste. Aeneid: encase and wait. Anything sound promising?"

I had a lot running through my mind, of course, but one desire above all: see the aliens in person and make them hurt. That's what I wanted. As for the extra time... I had no home, so whether I looked for one now or later made no difference to me.

"Aeneid," I said. "That's what I want to do."

Reno jerked her head back. "Just to be clear: spending time in null-space is not hypothetical. The soldiers in this program are already there, waiting to be put into action. They come out occasionally, when we add a member to their ranks or upgrade their equipment or try out some new tactic, but it's not a lot of time. If you choose Aeneid, there are a few months in training and then you will—I repeat: *will*—go into null-space."

"That's perfect," I replied.

Riff grinned. "You got it. Your life, Cor. Let me get the administrative actions underway, and then we'll get you going. Sound good?"

"Yes," I answered, grinning from ear to ear. "Very, very good."

Before my training began a couple of weeks later, Major Black spent two days escorting me from place to place so the Forces could get all of their propaganda vids shot. First stop was the Smithsonian Museum, where I donated my suit from River. They weren't sure they would display it, but promised to keep it, you know, *just in case it's important*. After that, it was a whirlwind tour of other continents, the Moon, and finally back to the space station we had started on for final processing.

The Forces issued me a new suit guaranteed completely metal-free, with a tolerance for magnetic fields up to one hundred fifty thousand gauss. That sounded vaguely reassuring. They also replaced the iron content in my blood with some sort of synthetic non-metal substitute. They indicated the iron in human blood was already non-ferrous at normal-to-high magnetic levels, but they couldn't be sure what would happen in an extreme magnetic environment. It was fine by me as long as it didn't hurt and everything kept working properly.

For the Project Aeneid training, Riff the recruiter escorted me down to the Sonoran Desert of North America. I had seen the desolate ice plains of Enceladus and the overflowing green abundance of River, but I had never been to a place so dry and yet, in its own way, so full of life.

In the desert, I had no instructor. I got the impression from the guide in my suit that the course was designed for more than one person, but I was happy to be out there alone, where my thoughts had room to breathe. I had gone from a normal life in a no-name colony to a system-wide hero without doing anything of note. From the corridors of Mars II with no future, I had traveled to a wilderness over a hundred years later, most likely volunteering to die alone inside a rock.

I spent three months in that desert. They started me out in the east in the bone-dry Chihuahuan basins with a lesson in dehydration. Actual dehydration. With no suit on, I hiked up and down the same slope for hours, until I stopped sweating. Cramps and fever and dizziness overtook me. I brought myself back slowly, with small sips of water.

Dehydration: I don't recommend it.

After that first lesson, I did the rest of my training at night. With my helmet retracted, the cool air bathed my face. The scent of dried pine needles mixed with the moss growing on boulders.

I saw with my own eyes the wonders of Earth's night sky: stars everywhere, the backbone of the galaxy black with cancerous dust, the Moon with its cities glowing, the planets orbiting and visible to me just as they had been to our ancestors for untold thousands of years.

The animals came out after sunset. The lizards and toads, the snakes, the desert mice, the insects, and the occasional coyote all scrambled for life in an unforgiving environment. After I spotted one the first time, I kept an eye out for a particular type of desert tortoise I liked. It carried its home on its back, and its stone-faced expression reminded me of Bud.

Thinking of Bud brought up memories of Kylie, of course. She would have loved this extended outdoor trip and laughed when I could finally claim that I had been properly camping. Her final words to me had been warm, like a desert breeze after the sun rises. A breakthrough, a change, the first water trickling in a long-desiccated streambed. If only there had been time.

Maybe I should have looked for her back on River. My suit saved me; her suit could have done the same. Maybe those final words weren't cut off by the explosion but by her going into null-space, set to emerge after forty years just like me. There had been no sign of her, though, and most likely her atoms were scattered across that damned world. But I would likely never know for sure.

I wandered westward, up through the mountains, acquiring skills in climbing and repelling, extracting nutrients from unlikely sources, and strengthening mind and body. The Forces' brilliant idea was that they had no idea what was inside that alien ship, so above all they trained Aeneid personnel to adapt, to make the most of what was available.

One night, I passed near the Gila cliff dwellings, empty of any daytime tourists. From the ground, the ruins lurked in shadow, their blacker-than-black windows staring out like empty eye sockets. I scaled the canyon wall and turned around slowly. Men and women had stood there a thousand years before. They gazed into the canyon and heard howls in the distance and knew they were safe in this shelter, in this home. I imagined bringing them forward, to let them see through my eyes the wonders we have wrought and the technologies we have built. We are born into a technology and live our lives modifying it, for better or worse, before passing it along to future generations. And there, on that cliff, I wanted to live their life, a simple life, constrained by time and location, wrapped in humanity, good and evil warring within each of us as we cope with a society beyond our control.

I slept briefly in one of their homes and left before dawn.

During those three months in the desert, as I wandered, Bravo Six accompanied me. Yousef joked about what we saw. Anwar fretted over details. Bud was a tortoise. And Kylie... she never spoke or smiled. She was a shimmering ghost floating through my memories, as untouchable as the stars above.

At other times, I ebbed and flowed with the life around me, mercifully free of thought.

The desert calmness wound its way into me, and I found the animal rage against the aliens giving way to something more sustainable: a dense-as-iron determination to punish them.

And then it was over. The Forces' ship landed, the door slid aside, and Riff motioned me to join her.

I looked back at the way I came. Maybe I could have used my money to extricate myself from my contract and spend the rest of my life there on Earth, in the desert, searching for meaning. It was tempting. But I had promises unkept.

The next training was in space. The Aeneid leaders sent me off the planet in a ship loaded with supplies and put me into a highly elliptical Earth orbit. I'd suit up every day and go outside, accustoming myself to zero G maneuvers and learning how to manipulate my suit to fire and move, without propelling myself in the wrong direction. It was enjoyable at first, after my stomach accepted its new situation, and as I learned to send sequential commands to be executed simultaneously. But it became repetitive, then boring, and finally tedious. The muscle memories were there, and I just wanted to see someone again. As beautiful as a planet can be from a distance, I missed the kinship of life on Earth.

I don't know if there were standards involved in all this training—that is, whether I could fail or not—or whether there were standards for everyone else but not for the Hero of River, or whether it was just a matter of completing the training, no matter how long it took. In any case, after a month, the program leads were apparently satisfied. Riff bundled me into a null-space coffin and shot me out to the Aeneid parking spot, somewhere eight or nine times farther from the Earth than the Moon. They told me I'd be inserted right away into an iron sleeve—just in case—and brought out at the next software and hardware update. That's when I would meet the other soldiers and undergo some joint training.

Red numbers down.

INTERLUDE 5

My cells ache
My segments grow weak
I yearn to rest
Beneath the star
Of home

-Two poetry

The non-Ones on the first planet
Were the quietest.
They died silently.
I silenced their putrid howling.
The non-Ones on the second planet
Were louder.
They shouted in anger as they died.
I banished their shrill rottenness
From the cosmos.
The non-Ones on the third planet
Were louder still.
They burned in agony as I breathed on them.
Their shrieks reverberated in my cells.
I bit them and yet they still shook the stars.
I wretched on their cacophonous glare
As they writhed and died.
The non-Ones on the fourth planet
Are deafening.
The beautiful flavors of the stars
Drown beneath their strident excrement.
The non-Ones must die. They must all die.
They must not harm One.
Two will protect One.
I will sacrifice my body.
I will give of myself
Until I hurt,
Until the sound of pain is all I see.
The non-Ones on the fourth planet

Are deafening.
They must be silenced.
They must die.
They will die.

CHAPTER 34: ET LUX PERPETUA

Et lux perpetua
Luceat eis

May your eternal light
Shine on them

-Excerpt from the Requiem Mass, *Communion*

2370 A.D. (Age 24, Birth + 151)

Blue numbers up.

I was floating in space less than a kilometer from a black, saucer-shaped station. It had no windows, no blinking warning lights, no antennas, nothing other than an airlock breaking up one side of its circumference. Earth was a bright spot far behind my right shoulder.

I dialed up the light sensitivity on my suit, which showed other soldiers stretched out around the station, climbing out of irregularly shaped rocks. As soon as they emerged, they jetted toward the airlock. I followed and joined the line somewhere in the middle.

We cycled through and emerged into one big central chamber. From the size of it, I estimated it took up almost the entire saucer. Soldiers had retracted their helmets and were forming into small clumps, talking and joking, the way Bravo Six had on Enceladus, when we finished a training scenario. There were fifty or sixty others in the room. I stood there alone, looking for something to occupy myself. The news feeds seemed as good as anything, but when I went to access them, they were blocked. I was inching my way toward a clump of people near me when a major stood up on a dais in the center of the room and raised his hands.

"Alright, alright. Settle down," he said. He was muscular, as were most of the other soldiers. Correction: *all* of the other soldiers. "So, you may have noticed we have come out of null-space earlier than planned. In a minute, we will pass along the updates and give you access to the news databases and to your personal communications."

The major was talking in a standard dialect. Kerrigan, Black, and Riff had all spoken something similar. I figured it was a way of uniting the Forces no matter where or when they were from, and it was similar enough to what I grew up with that I didn't need translation.

He checked something on his wrist display. "We came out of null-space early because we have an FNG joining us. First one in over fifteen standard years, if I have my math correct. FS5 Coren Slade. For now, FNG will do. So, FNG Slade, tell us something about yourself."

The major hadn't mentioned anything about my past, and I wasn't going to either.

I raised my hand and swiveled to greet everyone.

"Hello," I started, "I'm Coren S—"

"Shut up!" the soldiers yelled as one.

Laughter cascaded through the crowd. When it died down, the major continued.

"Oh, and I almost forgot: FNG Slade is apparently some kind of hero, although I'm still trying to wrap my brain around the exact details of what he did. On River, I guess, though from the vids I saw, there wasn't much left after the alien attack, which doesn't lend itself to many heroics. In any case, we will train with him for the next couple of weeks before going back under."

So much for staying out of the spotlight. My cheeks burned.

"Alright, soldiers. I'm restoring access to the newsfeeds now. Get caught up, talk amongst yourselves, say hello to the FNG, get some food, and we will meet back here in five hours —that will be 1400 local. Dismissed."

The man stepped away from the podium. I froze, my fight-or-flight instincts in overdrive. I remembered what it was like being part of Bravo Six at its best, how anyone coming inside our circle, even when it had been broken after Bud's death, was an outsider until proven otherwise. I was equal parts afraid someone would come talk to me and that no one would. The crowd dissipated somewhat. Helmets were going up all over the place, and individuals wandered to the far reaches of the room. The larger bunches broke down into smaller couplings.

The first person to greet me was the soldier who had spoken to us all. "Major Salisbury," he said, holding out a hand. "Stake."

He had "Stake" emblazoned on his suit.

"I'd like to welcome you to the program, Coren," he continued, smiling. "Everyone gets a bit of an... introduction... when they come aboard. Nothing personal. I am going to send you a little program to run..."

My suit beeped indicating I had received something. I pulled up my helmet, saw the icon, and ran it. By the time I got it retracted, the suit fibers had rearranged themselves. "FNG" now adorned the upper right of my chest.

"We'll get you a real name soon enough," Stake said. "Any family you are leaving behind?"

"Well..."

"Oh. Right. River. I was briefed on it. Briefly. Quite a story." He side-eyed me. "Any of it true?"

I didn't know what he had been told, but I assumed it was based on the truth. "Yes."

"See any combat?"

"Only briefly." Then I thought better of my answer. "Well, only briefly against the aliens. I did have a couple of good fights with the native creatures." Which were also aliens but not *the* aliens. I was about to clarify again when Stake interrupted.

"Any combat experience is good combat experience and will be valuable to the unit. Welcome aboard." He fixed me with his eye a second time. "So, you are the oldest of all of us, huh?"

"Probably," I replied, "by birth year, at least."

"'Grandpa,' maybe?" He appeared to be mulling something over in his mind. "Ah, well. Too early to tell. 'Hero'? I don't think that would wear well. Kind of like Thrash over there."

He pointed in the vague direction of several soldiers.

"We originally gave him an obscure Trojan horse name. Thrasymedes. Supposedly one of the men inside. But the name was too long, and Thrash's style tends toward the uncoordinated, so we shortened it to 'Thrash.' Worked out well. Anyway, let me introduce you around a bit."

I met, among others, soldiers named Speed, Baja, Zoom, Mojo, Doc (the medic, of course), CAJUN, and Tiny (who may have been the largest, most physically fit woman I have ever seen). From across the room, I couldn't have told you who was who afterward (except Tiny), but up close, there were names on the suits. When my helmet was in place, everyone was tagged. A banner across the top of my display indicated I was FNG. It was a nice touch.

That afternoon, we started training. The dais in the middle of the room retracted, leaving the entire space free of obstructions. I watched for the first hour, as soldiers bounced off the dome and performed coordinated maneuvers both on the floor and in the air. The way these soldiers handed off commands and sensed what others were doing and acted to complement those actions—this was a professional team. Apparently, that was only the warm-up, and then the real training began, with simulated firepower against simulated aliens.

CAJUN, who led Alpha Squad, took charge of me. She was a captain with fiery red hair pulled back severely and blue eyes that danced over me.

"Stay back here," she said, "and don't move."

So far, it replicated what I had done in the first hour.

"As Alpha, we are going to sweep forward to the left. Bravo is going up the middle, likely only providing covering fire. Charlie is to the right. Where the seam is between Alpha and Bravo—that's what I want you to watch. If you see an alien come at the squad from our right—*our* right, got it? Not their right—engage and take it out. Understood?"

I nodded in a way that at least partially satisfied her, and off they went. The lights dimmed to almost complete blackout, barriers sprang forth from hidden compartments all over the dome and floor, and the soldiers grouped themselves into their units. I stared at where I estimated the demarcation line was between the squads and watched. And watched. And watched. Alpha Squad moved out, each of them represented on my screen. When CAJUN had said they were going left, she meant left in a three-dimensional sense: some on the ceiling, some on the walls, some on the floor, and some in the air. I wasn't so much watching a line as I was an entire area. Bravo Squad made a feint forward, and then fell back, which left a wide-open field of fire, but I saw nothing. I scrolled up and down the spectrum, but there was still nothing. No firing from our side either. Comms chatter was non-existent.

CAJUN came back a while later.

"Good job," she said.

She must have seen from my expression I didn't understand. "It was a hold-fire exercise. The computer picks scenarios designed to highlight our flaws and weaknesses. Sometimes we need a reminder to observe before we start firing. This was one of those. There was nothing to shoot at, and you didn't, so good job." It was the first inkling I had of belonging here.

She then called the squad together. "Okay, let's critique. Boomer, you're first."

Even though the exercise had gone smoothly, each soldier in turn picked apart their own performance piece-by-piece and then offered observations on what others had done right and wrong. There was no rank, no sense of blame or defensiveness—just comments meant to improve the overall effort. She even called on me for my feedback, and all I managed to say was, "Impressive." That brought forth a few smiles. I sensed they appreciated me not trying to pretend that I knew more than I did, which was nothing. I may have done a fine job guarding the crops on River and taking down Legs whenever I needed to, but that was a long way and a long when from here.

CAJUN consulted with the major.

"Take a fifteen-minute break," she ordered. "Hydrate, and then be ready again. Same formation." The group became a little less focused, but most people just stood in place or sat down on the floor.

The next scenario was more active. A different arrangement of barriers appeared, forming closed off rooms and a complicated series of formations which my suit couldn't see through. Right away, there were soldiers firing and clipped instructions coming in.

"Mojo, right seventy-five."

"YAW, up top and over."

"Xeno is down, repeat, Xeno is down."

"FNG, engage. Three-five-five."

That last comment pumped me full of adrenaline, and with my heart pounding, I headed out, just slightly left of straight ahead. A vaguely humanoid figure with no display name lurched toward me, and I lit it up like it was the embodiment of all evil. I hit it six or seven times, it crumpled, and I shot it a couple more times to be sure. I took three or four steps forward, and my suit froze.

"FNG down, repeat, FNG down," someone said on the comms.

You win some, you lose some.

During debrief, Mojo—handsome and tall, like a holovid leading actor, his blonde hair swept back and over his head—started laughing. "That one alien is certainly dead, FNG. Well done on that and for following directions. Next time, fire twice and scan for the next threat. Check back on the downed alien between five and ten seconds later, then move on."

We continued like that for the rest of the day, then the next day, then for the next two weeks. The computer threw new scenarios, obstacles, aliens, and weapons for us to face on every outing. I accepted the role of staying in the back and moving forward when called on. Occasionally I got a good shot in and seemed to be improving. I did have one friendly fire episode where I plunked Radish in the back. Oops. That was a no-no even during initial training back on Enceladus, and feedback was harsh in the after-action review. To be fair,

I was shooting at the alien beyond Radish, and he lurched left unexpectedly, but the soldiers seemed to think I should have anticipated that.

At dinner that night, a few soldiers grumbled about Project Aeneid.

"What's the problem?" I asked.

CAJUN looked around the table and shrugged. "It's no secret. We are not only *considered* expendable but *expected* to be expendable."

"What do you mean?"

Her eyes narrowed, and she studied my face. "What did the recruiter tell you about the rescue plan?"

I thought back but couldn't remember anything.

"Right," CAJUN said, "pretty typical. Well, the plan is for us to get picked up by the alien ship, let the aliens digest us in some way, and then we pop out of null-space and kill them all. Once we are done with that, we activate a beacon, go back into null-space, and wait to be rescued."

"Sounds reasonable," I replied.

"Reasonable?" Xeno looked horrified. "Reasonable? Do you know how long they think a rock takes to move from the outside to the inside of the ship? They estimate at least a century. And how far can the aliens move in a hundred years? Pretty damn far. So there we are, out at the ass-end of nowhere, we rah-rah and beat the damn things, turn on our little beacons, and then what?"

I wasn't sure if he wanted me to answer or not. "They come get us?"

"Fat chance," Xeno guffawed. "They will leave us in null-space and forget about us. Right?"

Xeno gazed around at the soldiers sitting nearby. Most were nodding their heads.

"But why?" I asked.

"Would you go on a couple-hundred-year rescue mission? A century out, a century back? To what? Pick up some soldiers no one remembers anymore? When those soldiers will never know that they won't wake up? Nope. They will wait for the beacon to tell them we were successful, then they will dither and squabble about the expense and whose responsibility it is to mount the rescue. After a few years, the issue will drop in priority until it is forgotten."

I mean, it seemed like a logical argument, but... "What about an unmanned rescue? A robot ship or something like that? Can't cost too much."

Xeno nodded. "Maybe. Maybe. But I doubt it. We are fodder in a cannon, expendable and forgettable."

"So..."

Grinning, CAJUN put her hand on my neck and shook me gently back and forth. "So, what are we doing about it, FNG? Is that the question? First, they can't make us get into those iron tombs. Second, Stake—Major Salisbury—has been negotiating with Forces Command. It's possible we will get some movement."

"Is it all or none?"

CAJUN frowned. "What do you mean?"

I hesitated, unsure if I was treading in dangerous territory. "If there are no good rescue plans but I still wanted to go, would I be allowed to? Or is it all the soldiers go or none of us go?"

"Why would you do that?"

"Personal reasons." I had a debt I needed the alien to repay.

"Your life, FNG." She patted me on the head. "Throw it away however you like."

We trained hard for the next several days, sometimes running up to fifteen full group scenarios, a small unit exercise, and a solo situation every day. The suit does most of the work, but it's still exercise, and possibly there was a small difference in my puny arms by the end of it.

I did well enough when I was going it alone that I didn't embarrass myself, and I even got a compliment on my shooting from Xeno, after one situation where it was just me, him, Speed, and YAW.

However, I apparently seemed entirely too happy about the compliment.

"It was a good shot—for you. For anyone else, I wouldn't have even mentioned it. It's just expected."

Thanks, Xeno.

About a week in, we were eating dinner, mercifully out of our suits for a few hours, when I asked a question about how they got their callsigns.

Xeno spoke up first. "Usually, FNGs don't ask things like that unless they want to earn a name like SASQUATCH—Stop Asking Stupid Questions You As... well... Wait 'til you have a name until you talk, that's all I'm saying."

CAJUN frowned and held up a hand. "It's okay, Xeno. It isn't like it used to be. FNG here is likely the last to arrive."

The soldiers at the table erupted in laughter. Xeno turned bright red. I had no idea why.

"So, go ahead, Mojo," CAJUN went on, wiping a tear from her eye, "why don't you start? Why did we name you 'Mojo?'"

The man's eyes twinkled.

"I'm good with both the ladies and the men, if you know what I mean," he said, with no bravado or false modesty. "I got mojo, so I *am* Mojo."

His teeth flashed in the subdued lighting, his smile bordering on shy. "Why don't you tell him where your name comes from, CAJUN?"

She blushed, her cheeks reddening to match her hair.

"That's fair. Sure, yeah, good call, Mojo," Xeno piped in immediately.

She gave them both a look that promised payback.

"Yeah. So, early in the program, we... Yes. So, we... we were having some drinks and discussing the rules we would impose on ourselves, you know, by consensus, to make sure we are all accountable to each other. Someone—was it you, YAW?" YAW shook his head. "Well, my memories are a little vague from that night, but someone suggested we should not have sexual relations amongst ourselves to prevent the complications that can come from that. Just like at initial training. And I—remember, now, we had been drinking—I apparently seized on that and kept repeating, 'We can't just *not*. We can't just *not*.' And that's how I got my name: Can't Just Not. CAJUN. My real name is Adrienne, my ancestors were Irish, but now I'm just CAJUN."

I smiled. It was a good story.

YAW's last name was Armey, and he liked to cuss at the aliens if he got shot in training, so his stood for "You And What." Army, that is.

Boomer went supersonic in Earth's atmosphere when he wasn't supposed to.

And Xeno. Upon arrival, Xeno was fully convinced he was the final person who would ever be accepted into Aeneid. It was based on something the recruiter told him. He wasn't the last to arrive, of course, but it was enough stupidity to get labeled xenophobic.

I enjoyed that meal immensely.

To be honest, despite any progress I made, I was nowhere close to being as talented or intuitive or fierce or strong as these Aeneid soldiers. They were warriors who had earned a spot in the program by being elite, and I was someone who got there because I happened not to die. I knew it, and they knew it too. But there I was, and as long as I played the role given to me and followed instructions, I did fine.

We had a party at the end of the two weeks. Lots of alcohol, some songs that were not in any way in keeping with Forces directives on such things, and soldiers coupling up and leaving the dome area for periods of time. CAJUN came back from one of these, arm-in-arm with YAW. She was drunk and happy and hugged me and said, "You know, you *can't just not*, you know?"

I laughed. "So I've heard, CAJUN. So I've heard."

The primary source of entertainment that evening was to come up with a callsign for me. They wheeled a large board out, and whoever wanted—and pretty much everyone did—could suggest what my name might be. There were a lot of suggestions, most of which were the ramblings of soldiers with too much alcohol in their systems, but I do remember a few of them:

Musket (as in Musket S-lade – they thought my last name was slightly suggestive, I gathered).

Slo-Jo or *No-Jo* (compared to Mojo, I was less talented and less good looking and less everything else. Someone argued that the names were too similar to Mojo and might get confusing. *Slo-Jo* and *No-Jo* were scratched out, accompanied by much booing).

Hero (I prayed to whatever gods there might be *not* to get that one, and of course, that was the one Xeno pushed for the hardest).

BOXB (Back of Xeno's Balls—I have no idea why that was funny, but it was).

Grandpa (birth year is not age!).

LACTL (Last And Certainly The Least—but how do you pronounce that?).

CAGES (Can't Get (S-lade), I guess, although I didn't like that one at all).

And the winner, which they decided on by voice vote, measuring the loudness of the cheers as best they could, was PAPA: Puny Arms, Puny Ability. Or Puny Abs, Puny Ability. Or Puny Arm, Puny Arm. Things were a little hazy that night, and different soldiers had different takes on what it stood for. I liked the name, though. It sort of spoke to how old I was, sort of poked fun at me, and sort of made me sound like I had authority. PAPA. I was part of them now. "They" had become "us."

I was proud to have been a part of Bravo Six—a pride born of the people and what we went through together and the nearest thing to a home I ever had. With Aeneid, it was a pride that came from ability. I may have been a PAPA—and almost a No-Jo—but I was still on the team, and I still had a chance to get revenge.

CHAPTER 35: QUIS SUSTINEBIT?

Quis sustinebit?

Who shall endure it?

-Excerpt from the Requiem Mass, *Absolution*

2370 A.D. (ORPHEUS + 111)

Brady woke up with his arm over Angel. She liked to fall asleep on her own—not touching, as she liked to say—but didn't mind Brady getting close after that. He checked the date and time. Everything was as expected, which likely meant there was nothing new. It had been a leap night, so they had gone to bed last year and woken up this year. Two days of normal time, and then they would do it again. One more after, and then a two-week stretch of normal.

He scanned his urgent feed for messages and then switched to a channel highlighting the main news items from the last year. A huge typhoon in the Pacific, a mining accident on the Moon, growing protests against military spending, a scandal in Titan's government: the headlines changed but always had the same themes. Weather. Death. Politics. Tragedy. Triumph. Love. Hate. Life, sliced into digestible chunks.

Brady stopped and scrolled back. A soldier from River had returned during the past year. After all this time, it seemed impossible, yet there it was. He started to watch the pay-to-view interview with the man. After a minute or two, he paused it and woke Angel up.

She yawned and nuzzled up to him until he poked her a few more times.

In some ways, it was like being transported into the past. The soldier wore a combat suit they remembered, and he spoke with an accent they understood. They were—all of them—of a similar time, transported to the future, through the wonder and horror of null-space.

"Any intel value in talking with him?" Angel asked after it finished.

Brady had been thinking along the same lines but couldn't come up with anything. They had studied the River attack inside and out. A different perspective was always good, but intelligence value? Maybe they could examine suit video of what River looked like so many years later, after his null-space resurrection? Might inform some damage estimates. Seemed doubtful, though.

"No," he answered, "not likely."

And only several months earlier, this man from the past had been there—right there—across the catwalk in the real-time station. After which he had...

"Angel!" Brady said, sitting up straight in bed. "You don't think he joined Project Aeneid, do you?" The news feed said he volunteered to stay in the Forces, with duty in the Sonoran Desert. Which was where Aeneid was being run from, though that part was classified.

Angel smiled. "Seems likely, don't you think? If you wanted to get personal revenge on these things, isn't that where you would go too?"

"It's just... I don't know. He's been gone so long already, wouldn't he want to settle down, get re-accustomed?"

"Isn't that exactly our situation, Brady?" She nestled her head on his upper chest. He held her, breathing in the scent of her hair.

"Everything has changed out there," she continued. "I don't understand any of it. I've started to use a translation bot to comprehend what some of these newer people are saying. And those glowing eyes—I don't like it. It's as if they are seeing more and less of you at the same time. And the references they make to things I've never heard of, as if they are common knowledge. So, whether we start living full-time outside of null-space today or next century, does it matter? Maybe things will swing back to being more normal. I mean, normal, like we were used to."

"I don't know." It was a conversation they danced around

all the time. "I don't know."

"Do you want out?" Angel asked.

"Do you?" he replied.

After a moment, she shook her head faintly.

"Fitzpatrick was right, Angel," Brady went on. "From the beginning, he said that a sustained military effort without a definite adversary was not possible. He set it up for success, and then things went crazy after Galvus, and now here we are, with efforts splintering all over the place."

"Maybe *we* should join Aeneid," Angel teased. In all likelihood, there were intelligence officers on the project, but they would be the rugged and physically fit kind, not the kind that mined databases all their careers.

Brady squeezed her and kissed the top of her head. They had each other, and they had Fitzpatrick, and for now—as short as now might be—they would press on.

2373 A.D. (ORPHEUS + 114)

It was several cycles later when they came out of null-space at an unexpected time. After four decades of unbroken routine, it could only mean one thing: the aliens had made themselves known again.

Angel and Brady dressed hurriedly and sprinted to their office. The situational awareness updates owed to the bunker staff had gotten spottier over the years, as nothing happened and bureaucratic drift took over. But this morning, there was a full and concise summary of events waiting for them:

At 0337 Earth Central Time today, constant-stare telescope (CST) 915 detected multiple occlusions in the direction of Sagittarius. Within the hour, three more CSTs (422, 491, and 683) also detected occlusions, covering thirteen degrees of sky. Based on the number, direction, and duration of the occlusions, Forces Intelligence has assessed the following with medium confidence:

1. The occlusions are likely projectiles emanating from the alien ship;

2. *The projectiles are likely similar to those used the in the attack on Galvus;*

3. *The projectiles are on trajectories toward the Solar system;*

4. *While the projectiles' density per degree of sky (DPDS) is approximately the same as seen with Galvus, the breadth and width of the attack are orders of magnitude greater; and*

5. *Based on triangulation from the CSTs, we estimate the projectiles are just under a half of a light-year away and will arrive in -system in approximately nine months.*

Forces Intelligence will update you as more information becomes available."

And there it was: just like that, the aliens were back. Indeed, they had never gone away, they had just taken their time to launch a massive attack. Angel and Brady converted the DPDS number into an actual quantity and came up with a number in the millions.

The aliens had been busy.

So had humanity, and many of the preparations were to counter just such an attack, even if no one imagined that kind of scale. The anti-projectile railguns could handle part of it—at least what was detected. The layered metal and magnetic shields would slow some of them down, but not all of them. The attack was coming, and it would be bad.

Brady once read about a massive German cannon in World War I. It was so large that it had a name and a dedicated train to pull it. Word spread among the French soldiers about the railway gun—how nothing could stop it, that it would crush any bunker ever built. When the ground shook as the artillery slowly walked toward them, as the shells as big as trees rained down on them, the soldiers went mad. Death approached—*soon, so very soon*. Some took their own lives. Others fled into the open. Others huddled in their insanity, sobbing as they awaited the end.

Is that what would happen to society? Mass suicide? Scrambling in search of mirage protections? Hunkering down into madness?

When they briefed Fitzpatrick, they skipped the technical details in favor of substance: a larger-than-anyone-imagined barrage was heading toward them.

The Old Man sat back, not moving. He had read the report but not realized the meaning.

The three of them huddled alone in silence around the conference table—a far cry from the days when it was standing-room only.

Fitzpatrick breathed deep and exhaled slowly. "Maybe..."

The word hung twisting in the air.

"Maybe if I had—"

"Sir," Brady interrupted, tapping the table with his palm, "you did everything you could. More than anyone else could have."

"He's right, sir," Angel chimed in.

The general's lips began quivering. He dragged a knuckle across his eye and grimaced as if in pain. His voice was sandpaper when he spoke again.

"We made such tremendous progress in those early years, when Galvus was fresh on their minds and when it was easy to imagine the same thing happening to *their* home, to *their* friends, and *their* family."

"That progress will still save lives, will still blunt the blow when it comes," Brady replied. "All because of you."

"Maybe I could have fought harder or dreamed bigger. Maybe I'm guilty of preparing to fight the last war, not the next one, like so many leaders before me."

Angel frowned at him. "If Brady or I had the same opinion, what would you say?"

Fitzpatrick looked puzzled for a moment before his expression cleared. "You weren't in charge."

"I mean, if we asked if we could have done more, what would you say?"

"I'd say it was nonsense and that you were being self-in..."

Brady cocked an eyebrow.

The Old Man chuckled softly. "I see. *Et tu, Brute?*"

"*Et tu, Brute.*"

CHAPTER 36: DIES IRAE

Dies irae, dies illa
Solvet saeclum in favilla

The day of wrath, that day
When time turns to ash

-Excerpt from the Requiem Mass, *Sequence*

2374 A.D. (ORPHEUS + 115)

"All soldiers report to duty stations."

Angel gasped. Brady startled and sat straight up in bed.

"All soldiers report to duty stations. This is not a drill."

The couple looked at each other in confusion, then scrambled to get dressed.

"It can't be the aliens, can it?" Angel asked, pulling her uniform up. "All the calculations indicate they are still two months away."

Brady splashed water on his face and grabbed his shirt. "The calculations are correct. We both saw it. Maybe something is wrong with the station?"

They raced to the intelligence section, scarlet alarm lights illuminating the corridor the entire way. Once inside, they flicked screens to life and opened the information feeds.

Emergency communications were already piling up. The farthest colonies in the Kuiper Belt and on Pluto had gone silent first. Then consecutively closer facilities on Enceladus, Triton, and Io had ceased communications. A bright flash had engulfed the asteroid Ceres, and now it was no longer responding. Forces Command had mobilized all resources.

Angel fixed her eyes on Brady. "The aliens. But they are too early."

"Could they have launched with greater velocity than we thought?"

"We based the arrival projections off *detected* speeds. They can't speed up after they are fired."

"Separate attack?"

"Must be, but how can we…" Angel tapped her forehead repeatedly. "Ceres—do we have video of the explosion there?"

Brady searched the holdings and found a file immediately. A constant-stare telescope had recorded the event. When they ran it, the asteroid was invisible in the spotted blackness until a blinding eruption of light filled the screen.

"Determine the distance from the CST to the asteroid," she instructed the computer.

It blinked ready.

"Establish the absolute brightness of the explosion."

The computer pulsed again.

"Now calculate the overall energy conversion and display."

After a second, the answer popped up. Brady refreshed the display to ensure the commas were actually commas.

"That's not possible," Angel whispered.

"Run it again."

She repeated the steps. Same result.

Searching the holdings, Brady found a different video of the attack. They ran the numbers and received a nearly identical response.

"Eighty trillion megajoules. That's unbelievable," Brady said. "Angel, can you—"

"Yes."

Brady smiled and kissed the top of her head, while she took the slug velocity from the attack on Galvus and divided it into the energy output.

When the answer appeared, Angel pointed at the display and looked back over her shoulder at Brady. "So, if the projectile that hit Ceres was traveling at roughly that same speed, it weighed close to twelve hundred kilograms."

Brady tilted his head backward and pictured the alien ship. That much mass, combined with that much speed… each slug must have cost them enormous effort, like giving birth, pushing and cramping and heaving to get one out. He couldn't imagine it otherwise. And when the massive slugs struck the smaller asteroid colonies and the free-floating stations, they simply ceased to exist, their components raining down on Pluto and Jupiter and Saturn and...

"Angel! We need to talk to General Fitzpatrick. Right now."

"Why?" She furrowed her eyebrows.

"The null-space part of the station emits no electromagnetic radiation, correct?"

"Correct. It's more efficient to flow communications back through the real-time section. Safer as well, given what the aliens shoot at."

"And so—"

"And so if these projectiles are not timed to arrive simultaneously and more are inbound—"

Angel stopped talking and pulled up the timestamp on the Ceres video. "This happened twenty-three minutes ago..."

She manipulated more data. "Given the angles, distance, and speed, if this station is targeted, we have less than thirteen minutes."

Brady keyed up a comms channel to the general. "Sir, we need to get the emergency evacuation plan going immediately."

"Brady?" The Old Man's voice was strained.

"I'll come up and explain, sir, but please activate the plan. Now."

"Understood." The line went dead.

A new report flashed into the message queue. Several Mars stations had gone quiet, including the Forces base on Phobos and the Mars I and II colonies.

Angel recalculated the numbers. "Less than eleven minutes. Call it ten to be safe."

Brady sprinted out of the room, dodging one soldier hurrying in the opposite direction and causing another to flatten herself against the bulkhead.

The klaxon screamed while the warning notice boomed out in a giant voice. "All personnel evacuate to the null-space bunker. This is not a drill. All personnel evacuate to the null-space bunker. Do not attempt to return to the real-time station. This is not a drill."

Dashing past the elevators, Brady banged open the stairway door and took the stairs up two at a time.

Normally quiet and sleepy, the command post roiled and churned like a boiling pot as soldiers shouted at one another and yelled into mics. Brady shoved his way through the crowd and up the levels until he stood before General Fitzpatrick.

"Sir," he huffed, then leaned over and put his hands on his knees.

Fitzpatrick put a hand on his back. "Take your time."

Brady stood back up and gulped down a breath. "No time. More slugs. Inbound."

The general's eyes narrowed. "You're sure?"

"Yes. The aliens didn't..." Brady breathed deep, "they didn't time this one to arrive simul... simultaneously... The attack is rolling in toward us."

"How long?"

"Ten minutes."

"That's not enough."

"Maybe less."

Fitzpatrick frowned and pinched his lips as if he was sucking on a sour lemon. "We will need at least a minute to..."

He turned away and grabbed his primary personnel officer by the arm. The ripples of command propagated outward, as officers rose in disbelief and settled back into their chairs to work.

Angel.

He hustled back to the intelligence section, dodging the soldiers and civilians now flooding into the station.

She was still at her desk, still triaging the message traffic.

Brady touched her shoulder. Angel glanced back at him, tears in her eyes.

"It's bad."

"I know."

He pulled her up and hugged her.

"I love you, Angel."

She sobbed. "I love you too, Brady."

He stroked her hair and squeezed her. "You did good, though."

"*We* did good."

"Yes, *we* did good. I love you."

"I love you too."

The door opened suddenly. One of the Logistics officers with a security clearance stood outside.

"Lieutenant Olsen, apologies for disturbing you, but we need places to put people."

Brady scanned the room for classified material. Nothing was immediately visible, and given the circumstances... He nodded approval. The officer appeared relieved and motioned to someone behind her.

Brady and Angel held each other tight for one more moment, then broke as civilians poured in.

"Separation in six minutes. Repeat, separation in six minutes. All personnel and their families need to be in the null-space section in six minutes."

Brady and Angel sat together in their usual seats, holding hands, waiting. Angel gripped tighter as time went on, until finally, a voice came over the announcement system and told everyone to prepare for null-space. The countdown started at ten.

When it hit zero, Angel and Brady found themselves weightless, drifting out of their chairs as any lingering pre-null-space inertia resolved itself. They were still holding hands.

It was quiet. The background hum of air filtration and machines was silent. Brady grabbed the small conference table in their workspace and pulled them back down. He tried to picture what was going on in the command post, what steps they might take to reactivate the bunker. First would be figuring out where they were and what had happened to them, which would require some external observations. From there, they could decide what to bring online first.

Angel pulled him close, steadying herself as best she could against the table. "It's going to be okay," she said. Brady held her, and they waited together.

When the announcement came, it was unexpected and loud. Several people yelped in surprise.

"This is General Kecia, head of Forces Command. We are working on restoring gravity. It should only take a few minutes. I did want to let you know that we are safe." Her voice was rock-steady. "The bunker detached itself from the main part of the station just like it was supposed to. However, there was insufficient time to switch the power supply over. We should have that done in a few minutes.

"We were in null-space for a couple of days. The real-time section that we separated from was not hit, fortunately. We are still determining the extent of damage across the Solar system and will inform you when we know more. For all Forces personnel, including civilians and contractors: when our gravity fields are back, you will report to your respective duty code's offices. We will take accountability there and begin the process of restoring chains of command. For all family members, I do want to reiterate that you are safe now and that you are our highest priority."

Angel glanced up at Brady, and he smiled in return.

"Please do not move around the bunker yet. I will inform you when it's safe. If you are hungry, we will make food available as soon as we can. The bunker is well-stocked, so we have plenty to eat, just please give us some time to get settled."

"I'm too scared to be hungry," Angel whispered. Brady nodded in agreement and rubbed her curly brown hair between his fingers. If you had to travel down through time and abandon everything behind you, Brady thought, this was the way to do it. With someone like Angel. No, that wasn't correct: with Angel herself. He leaned in and kissed her cheek; she squeezed his arm in response.

Several minutes later, the life support systems began functioning, and the gravity fields were close behind, along with power to their workstations. The Logistics officer came by soon after and escorted the civilians away.

With the uncleared individuals gone, Brady and Angel

opened their information feeds. There were no summaries to pass along to General Fitzpatrick, but there was an overwhelming number of messages to go through. None provided a clear picture of what had happened. Instead, they were snapshots from a thousand different perspectives, a collage of system-wide ruin.

Angel hooked into a camera on the bunker's exterior, and they got their first sight of Earth. Its marbled splendor was blotted out by black, poisonous vapors, glowering angrily while lightning flashed non-stop back and forth inside the clouds.

Brady averted his eyes. Angel stared. On a side screen, she went back to her message queue and filtered it to only show those originating from Earth itself. Most were sending pleas for assistance, but at least there were some.

Angel switched to the Moon, on the far side of Earth but still visible. There were noticeable cracks in the surface and spots of molten rock. A few more keystrokes, and she brought up Mars. It was the same thing. Along the limb, though, just on the dark side of the terminator line, a few scattered lights of a different color remained, glowing with a small promise of life.

Over the next hour, other intelligence personnel made their way to the section. They had been real-timers, but now, according to General Kecia's order, the officers reported to their duty code's section.

When the eighth new person showed up, Brady took stock of who and what they had available.

"We should start a full damage estimate, Angel. At least as best we can. There may be other people doing it, but then again, there may not be, and it will give us something to talk to the general about. He's going to want to know."

Angel nodded and scanned the room. She recognized one or two people. "I agree. We should also get as many people involved as possible."

It took an hour of coordination to get analysts set up at workstations and divide up the workload. Angel wrote out who was covering what and hung the signs next to the terminals, so if a message straddled a line or was mis-routed, each person would know who they needed to talk to.

When they got around to assigning areas to themselves, Angel and Brady were left with the outer colonies in the Kuiper Belt and Oort Cloud. There weren't many of them, and they were all tiny mining outposts. A couple had checked in using one-liners, reporting no damage and inquiring about what was going on. Several others had not been heard from. Brady queued up a message to the latter asking for status, and then sat back in his chair.

"That didn't take long." He smiled over at Angel.

"No," she replied without taking her eyes off her screen, "but it feels good."

They knocked out a summary of their assignment and then checked in with the other analysts, starting with those with the smallest jobs and determining whether they needed help with a query or two. As the tasks finished, Angel and Brady rolled the analysts into the most complex assessments: Earth, Mars, and the Moon.

General Fitzpatrick stopped by in the middle of the day for an update. Brady briefed him on what he had so far and explained the way forward. The Old Man nodded his approval and indicated he'd return later for a full run-down.

The afternoon wore on, and collectively, the analysts began to get a sense of how catastrophic the attack had been, and how unprepared they were for the next onslaught, much less the arrival of the alien ship.

As Angel had said earlier, it was bad.

Of the roughly fourteen billion human beings in the Solar system, over half had likely died, with more than five billion dead on Earth alone. Essential civil and industrial systems were down in many if not most areas, meaning the tally of the dead would continue to rise. As for the status of the Forces, the space-based ships and the firing platforms had come through unscathed. They didn't know very much about ground-based troops: two outposts around Jupiter and one each around Saturn and Mars had checked in, reporting no damage. Many of the Forces, however, would have gone into null-space to protect themselves and may not have come out of it yet.

Fitzpatrick returned in the early evening and took the assessments stoically.

When the briefing finished, the three of them sat there in silence. A couple of the other analysts were listening drifted away, leaving them alone.

Angel finally spoke. "So, what's next?"

"Next?" Fitzpatrick asked, looking up. Angel thought his eyes seemed far away, focused on something else entirely.

"Well...yes. Next. There's still a whole mass of slugs inbound, and we ought to do whatever we can to save whatever we have left, right?"

Fitzpatrick's eyes flared for a brief second before settling back into darkness. "Sure..."

Angel pressed forward. "What I mean is, if an outpost was destroyed, let's bring back the ships or equipment protecting it. Concentrate what we still have on the places we can still save. Or park them on the far sides of planets so we can use them when the alien ship arrives. We took a big hit, but we're still here. And something will be left after the next slugs arrive. And something will be left after the aliens leave. So... what's next? What do we do to maximize survival?"

Brady gazed at Angel and shook his head slowly. As always, she spoke her mind.

They would mourn the lost, but they would also fight to preserve the living.

Fitzpatrick grimaced and rubbed his forehead. When he opened his eyes, there was a renewed spark in them. "You're right, Angel. You're right. Of course you are right. Let me talk to General Kecia. I know she has her hands full, but... okay. Brady, here's what I would like you and Angel to do. Based on what you've already put together, start working with Ops to identify what resources can be moved where for maximum effect. Try to come up with a basic plan by... tomorrow? Noon?"

Brady agreed and got a head nod when he glanced at Angel. "Yes, sir. Will do."

The general squinted at the clock then stroked his chin. "Would you two like to join me in my quarters tonight? To talk a bit more informally?"

Angel brightened.

"We would love that, sir," Brady replied.

CHAPTER 37: QUID SUM MISER

Quid sum miser
Tunc dicturus?

What shall I, in my sadness,
Say then?

-Excerpt from the Requiem Mass, *Sequence*

2374 A.D. (ORPHEUS + 115)

The visit that evening was Brady's first since General Fitzpatrick returned, and Angel's first ever. The Old Man greeted them at the door with a drink in each hand.

"Thank you for coming," he said, motioning them inside and handing them each a glass. The apartment looked exactly like it had before he left. The leather furniture glowed crimson in the light of the holo-fire. It was the only illumination in the room.

"Please, sit, sit." Fitzpatrick spun slowly and ambled forward unsteadily until he was silhouetted against the flames.

Angel glanced at Brady and shrugged before choosing the nearest seat to her, slipping off her shoes, and tucking her feet up under her.

Brady walked up behind the general and touched his shoulder. Fitzpatrick flinched, then reached up and patted Brady's hand.

"Thank you," he whispered.

"Of course, sir. I'd do anything for you."

The Old Man took his own drink off the mantle and turned around. "I know that, Brady. You as well, Angel. Thank you both. Cheers."

They raised their glasses and drank. It was whiskey.

Brady let the smoky liquid languish on his tongue before

swallowing it. The alcohol burned as it went down, lighting his chest on fire. "Strong."

"Good," Angel added, taking a longer sip.

The corner of Fitzpatrick's mouth curled upward. "You are a lucky man."

Brady gazed at his wife, compact and wholly herself as she nestled in the oversized chair. Orange and red light flickered across her face. He raised his glass to her.

A very lucky man.

"Sit, Brady. Sit," the general said, lowering himself into his own chair.

Brady spotted the whiskey bottle and topped everyone off before sitting down himself.

The fire cracked several times before Fitzpatrick muttered, almost inaudibly, "Tell me more."

"About the attack, you mean?"

"Yes." He dragged the word out, then closed his eyes and leaned his head back. Only half his face was illuminated by the fire. "Tell me. How... how did this happen?"

Brady and Angel exchanged glances before looking back at Fitzpatrick.

"I think there were two main reasons we did not detect this attack, sir."

"Dispense with the 'sirs,' Brady. And your weaselly intelligence words. Just tell me."

"Yes, s—"

"Fitz," the general ordered. "In here, call me Fitz."

"Right. Understood." Unprecedented.

"So, Fitz, two main reasons. First, the attack came from a slightly different direction than the slugs we've already detected. Second, the slugs were gigantic but fewer in number, weighing over a metric ton. Because the number of projectiles was lower, there was less chance a constant-stare telescope would pick one up. If a CST did, there's still a noise level it may have fallen below. Drowned in the sea of data."

"Mars."

The Old Man had a son there.

Brady pointed to Angel. She had better knowledge of that

one.

Angel threw back her drink. "Overall, seven slugs hit Mars, traversing the atmosphere in less than a second. Based on the force they carried, the projectiles likely punched through the crust before penetrating deep into the mantle and evaporating from their own heat. In the process, they transferred all their energy to the planet. It was a colossal addition of energy to the environment.

"One city—Terminus—was close enough to an impact point that when the ground liquified, the city folded in on itself and exploded. Other places suffered catastrophic damage from the Mars-quakes that rang the planet like a bell. Habitats lost electrical generation and almost everything else that makes Mars livable. Valles Marineris collapsed from both sides, covering hundreds of ongoing mining operations and thousands of miners.

"On the far side of the planet, away from where the attacks struck, the surface bulged up and then slammed back down, allowing the more rugged structures and the hardened subterranean caverns to survive. Portions of Mars are relatively intact."

"Earth."

Fitzpatrick was from Ireland.

During the day, Brady had considered the old question of what happens when an unstoppable force meets an immovable object. "Unanswerable" was the answer, of course, since it postulated absolutes in a fully relative universe. Atoms, molecules, dust, rocks, asteroids, planets, galaxies, and galaxy clusters—they all obey the same laws of physics. Mass wins; mass wins every time; and there is always something more massive. When a thousand-kilogram slug of iron meets a planet, the planet wins every time.

Unfortunately, "winning" is also a relative term.

Brady cleared his throat and began with the basics. "We believe there were twenty-eight total slugs launched at Earth. A counter-projectile railgun clipped one, altering its course slightly so it bounced off the atmosphere. It pulled a significant air mass behind it, but other than that, no damage.

"The other twenty-seven plowed into the planet, striking sites in western Africa and Europe, eastern North and South America, and the Atlantic Ocean. Just as on Mars, the slugs passed through the atmosphere and crust, shedding energy at every step, causing tidal waves which slammed into seaboards on both sides of the ocean. Earthquakes rattled the entire planet as the plates adjusted themselves.

"Below the surface, according to preliminary models, the spalling from the bottom of the crust spread deep into the mantle, displacing rock, and pushing pockets of lava toward the surface, like pus squeezed from a wound. Mexico City disappeared. Fuji and the Hawaiian volcanoes and the great continental rifts at Krakatoa and Tonga blew themselves apart. Occasionally, we've caught a glimpse of the surface through a telescope. It appears the Pacific ring of fire is ignited all the way around."

"Survivors." Fitzpatrick's speech was slurred.

"Too early to tell. There will be survivors in bunkers and null-space bubbles and the rare fortunate pocket of relative calm. But we don't know enough yet."

The fire glinted off a tear running down the Old Man's cheek.

"Thank you."

The three of them sat in silence. Brady got up once and refilled their glasses. Fitzpatrick mumbled something unintelligible. A few minutes later, he began to snore.

Angel found a blanket and covered him up before she and Brady slipped out the door.

"Fitz?" she asked as soon as they were back in their quarters.

"That's a new one."

"He never asked you to call him that when you had dates before?"

"They weren't dates, Angel. And no, he never asked me."

She giggled a little and hugged him. "What's next?"

"Tomorrow, we get back to work, I guess. More

assessments. And in two months…"
"The next attack."
"Yes."
"I need to be close to you tonight, Brady."
"Me too, my love."

The next morning, Angel and Brady set about implementing General Fitzpatrick's instructions from the day before. In a strict sense, the task of realigning resources was outside of normal intelligence duties, but they were contributing, and maybe what they were doing would make a difference, however small.

It took a bit of explaining to the Ops personnel what the goal was, but once they got the idea, the work went quickly. Captain Grant, the principal Ops planner, provided prioritization of mission-related assets. Angel was a wizard when it came to calculating what resources could be moved where within the next two months. The two of them huddled in a corner all day. When Fitzpatrick stopped by late in the afternoon, he approved their efforts and ordered Brady to incorporate Logistics personnel into the effort.

With all three disciplines working together, they pumped out multiple recommendations a day. General Fitzpatrick parsed them out as orders.

The reward for doing good work was more work, and early mornings turned into late nights. Angel and Brady fell into bed each night, exhausted but satisfied.

Two months slipped by in a sunset of hope and a sunrise of fear. Humanity teetered on the brink.

Three days before the attack was set to arrive, the working group ran out of implementable suggestions. There just wasn't enough time.

Anything in space that could move took shelter behind planets. Anyone who could manage it went into null-space, including the bunker.

Unlike the first barrage, it only took several hours to come back to normal time, all systems running, with the main part of the station floating in orbit next to them. General

Kecia announced they were safe, and that was the cue for the Ops-Intel-Logistics group to get back to work, checking how their recommended preparations had fared and seeking information on casualties.

The out-stations had improved their communication protocols, and within half a day, the team had a decent damage estimate to send up the chain. It was not good news. Several of the colonies and outposts which survived the massive projectiles succumbed to the smaller ones. Random death in random places.

The number of dead was significant, but the individual stories...

Communications from Ganymede painted a bleak picture of failing life support systems; they reported being cold, then colder, and then silence.

A woman on Pluto pleaded for help. Her null-space field had failed to activate, and the facility was burning.

On Venus, a group of children in the colony's safest place had not heard from anyone.

An elephant on Earth stood over her dead calf, a wall of fire in the background. Whale carcasses by the thousands washed up on shores.

A microphone left on by accident recorded someone wailing.

Angel cried at night. Brady drank to take the edge off. They held each other. In the mornings, when they first woke up, they forced themselves to move, to go back to the office one more time and be vulnerable to the unexpected, the shocking, the nightmarish.

During this, Angel calculated the mass the aliens had used in both attacks and found it totaled between a third and a half of the assessed mass of the ship. Since that amount of change ought to be visible whenever the alien ship arrived and might make it more vulnerable to attack, she passed it over to Captain Grant.

Several weeks later, Fitzpatrick walked into their office unexpectedly and asked Angel and Brady to accompany him. They followed him up several decks and into a private conference room—one normally reserved for sensitive intelligence briefings.

Odd. Surprising.

They took their seats at the table.

Fitzpatrick composed himself for a moment, running a hand across his mostly bald head and puckering his face together as if waiting for some internal pain to pass.

"I brought you two up here for a number of reasons," he started. "First, I want to thank both of you for all the hard work and the contributions you've made. I'd put you both in for medals, but that kind of recognition has ceased for now. Maybe survival is reward enough. Or maybe dying is. I don't know.

"In any case," he went on, "your efforts allowed me to get my foot in the door with General Kecia, and from there, I've managed to get back in the game."

The Old Man noticed their excitement.

"No, not like that. I'm not back in command of anything, not really. At least not the way I used to think about it." He arched an eyebrow. "You have heard about Project Aeneid, correct? And you know basically what it is?"

They both nodded. Brady now understood why Fitzpatrick had chosen that room. No one knew if the aliens could understand human languages, and while there was not much risk of humanity's plans reaching them, the military always made projects like Aeneid highly compartmented, and always would. By way of their clearances, intelligence personnel often found out about them, even if they weren't supposed to.

"Good," Fitzpatrick continued. "One problem with the project has always been the perceived suicidal nature of it. Even if the soldiers are successful and get inside and somehow destroy that thing, they will still have to wait years for a rescue—that is, if anyone is still around to rescue them or still cares enough to try.

"General Kecia has decided that instead of waiting to send out a vessel, we are going to immediately send a rescue mission after the alien ship. We will make the chase vessel as low-observable as possible and wait a couple of weeks before launching it, but the idea is that if-and-when the Aeneid soldiers emerge, we will be able to detect them and pick them up. Kecia believes that until we know for certain that the alien ship is dead, we won't ever get back to any kind of real normal. Whatever normal means these days.

"And... well... here's the thing: I volunteered for and was chosen to command the rescue vessel. The *Carpathia*, we are calling her. She's a small ship with a small crew—mostly medical personnel, maybe eight or ten doctors and nurses. And I'm also going to need a few other specialties on board. Ops, for one, and I will be asking Captain Grant from your team. I'll need a pilot, but those are easy to find. And in case we run into the unexpected, I'm going to need an intelligence analyst."

Fitzpatrick let the sentence hang in the air.

"Or two."

Brady's heart leaped. He looked over at Angel, who seemed excited as well.

The general spread his arms out, though Brady wasn't sure if he was pleading or welcoming them.

"I'd like you both to join me. Join the *Carpathia*. You are the best in the business, as far as I'm concerned, and more importantly, I trust you with my life. Now, before you decide, let me tell you a couple of things: we are mostly going to be in null-space, with the ship automatically trailing the aliens. We also have no idea how long the journey might be. We will have set times when we emerge and reassess the situation, but my going-in position is that we will follow the aliens as long as it takes until there is no hope of rescuing anyone else. The Aeneid soldiers are putting their lives on the line, and so will we. That's why it's all-volunteer."

Angel took Brady's hand and squeezed it tight.

"Yes," she replied.

"You don't need more time?" Fitzpatrick asked.

They looked at each other and smiled before shaking their heads.

"I hoped you would accept, so thank you. We are going to

be heading out soon—in the next week, maybe two; we want to be well out and away before the alien ship gets here. So, wrap up things on your team, take some time off if you need it, and I'll let you know where to be and when. You can't talk about this with anyone, of course. In fact, I'll have the admin officer send some orders down so you can just leave, no questions asked. Again, I... This means a lot to me. You two are... Well, thank you."

The general choked up at the end. Brady thought maybe they would all hug, but the moment passed.

Fitzpatrick thanked them again and left. Angel and Brady lingered in the conference room.

"You okay?" Brady asked, taking her into his arms and leaning his head on hers.

"Never better," she answered. "Scared?"

"To death, honestly. You?"

"Same." Angel stopped and looked up at him, tears welling in her eyes. "I love you, Brady."

"I love you too, Angel."

INTERLUDE 6

One!
I have fought for you.
I have bled for you.
Must I die for you?

-Two poetry

The first non-Ones died.
The second non-Ones died.
The third non-Ones died.
The fourth non-Ones did not die.
They fought.
They hurt Two.
They exposed me to the beyond.
I lost rock.
I lost air.
And they lived.
I have not finished what I started.
I have eaten. I am fed.
I am weak. I must recover.
I ride the currents and think.
I wish to return home and become One.
I must not lead the non-Ones to One.
The stars whisper advice to me
In their steady rhythms.
I yearn to return home.
I cannot return home.
I cannot return home
And lead the non-Ones to One.
The non-Ones must die.
Or I must die.
I will ride the currents and heal.
I will eat. I will grow strong.
I will return and kill them.
The fourth non-Ones will die.
I will destroy them.

CHAPTER 38:
SOLVET SAECLUM IN FAVILLA

Dies irae, dies illa
Solvet saeclum in favilla

The day of wrath, that day
When time turns to ash

-Excerpt from the Requiem Mass, *Sequence*

2493 A.D. (Age 24, Birth + 274)

I couldn't move. Again. Just like on River after the attack. This time, though, I could see. A bit of the ceiling had either chipped away or was eaten, leaving the right upper corner of my display clear. Straight below me was a lumpy, murky, blue and green liquid. A whitish moss-like growth covered the walls above the water, piling on top of itself until it partially stretched over the surface, creating shelves down near the waterline.

I craned my neck a bit and got a better view of the pool below. Washed up along an edge was something that looked like a soldier's boot. Another glance around. Scorch marks scarred one side of the cavern where the white mold gave way to pure rock. Almost certainly a soldier's boot.

My suit informed me I was in a highly magnetized environment with no specific source. I scrolled through the spectrum to see if anything looked different. In ultraviolet, more details popped out.

The lump-like things in the liquid were spread regularly across the floor of the chamber. Each one looked like a surgically altered octopus, its limbs coming directly out of the middle of its body, each tentacle frayed into hundreds of strands. The flagella thrashed and squirmed in the viscous milky liquid. Strands regularly detached themselves and groped through the cloudy pool for similarly detached appendages, entwining themselves together in living ropes.

I had found the aliens.

And I would kill them.

As soon as I freed myself from the tomb I was in.

I tried snapping my helmet forward as hard as I could, a head-butt to the rock. A flake fell away. I pushed with my feet for extra leverage, and a good-sized chunk came loose, exposing my right shoulder. The stone made a notable splash in the liquid. Tentacles squirmed and grabbed for it.

With an arm free, we were in business. I dialed down the energy output in my right beam weapon, pointed it to the side, and began chipping away at the stone, gradually increasing the power. Within a minute, a crack formed, then widened, then split off completely, releasing most of my body. I shut off the beam and moved my right arm up quickly in case I started to fall. I shot three wires into the ceiling near me, then tugged on them before pulling my knees toward my chest. The last of the iron cracked away.

I was mobile.

Nothing moved beneath me in any unnatural or aggressive way. That was good. The pool filled the bottom half of an enormous egg-shaped chamber—one of the two bulbous ends of the barbell-shaped vessel, I assumed. Peering down the dim tunnel leading away from the chamber, glowing aliens and white moss stretched into the distance.

A glance back at the boot confirmed the worst: to one side of the cavern, where the water met the wall, was the remains of a soldier's suit. Not much was there, and nothing which looked like a nametag, nor was I getting any pings or identification from it, but it was enough to know I was not the first one out, and that a previous attempt had not been successful.

I hung above it all and considered my options. The scars marking the wall looked purposeful, and I tried to figure out what had happened from the soldier's perspective. The soldier had come out of null-space, just like me. The soldier had either fallen into that liquid below or made it down to it

or maybe to one of those moss shelves. And then...
What would I do in that situation?
Well, I was PAPA.
I wanted to massacre aliens.
I was not the most skilled.
But I really wanted to pound the living hell out of aliens.
Most of our training had been as a group.
So, if it were me, I'd try to see if I could find more soldiers.

I studied the marks on the wall more closely and noticed a pattern: straight lines, as if the soldier were looking for something. I could even determine the direction and angle the shots had come from—not exactly where the remains were but close.

So.

Maybe that soldier made a mistake by being down there and trying to free others. Maybe I would be safe up on the jagged ceiling. Or maybe I was not only the second soldier out but also the last. The other soldier could have blasted away for a long time without discovering anything. The same thing could happen to me.

Another option: start converting aliens into pulp.

I liked that one.

It was possible the things below me were the alien equivalent of sheep or cows, but they reminded me of brain cells and suggested intelligence. I could shoot one and see what happened. Or drop down into the watery substance... That would be just like on Enceladus. Below the water, overcoming obstacles, all you needed was one person to survive. Except no Bravo Six. No Kylie. No Bud. No Yousef or Mei-Zhen. Not even a Jovan.

No one else to get hurt—that was one way to look at it. Me against them. The aliens had stranded me on River, and I would pay them back until there was only one of them left, then carve that last one up slowly.

Another way to look at it was that I was all alone, that the aliens had apparently shown themselves to be deadly inside the ship as well as outside, and that my chances of success were higher with more soldiers.

So.

A wave of dizziness washed over me, and my magnetometer indicated a spike. A big spike. If the aliens weren't aware of my presence yet, it wasn't going to be long. At all.

I looked back at the small cavity I climbed out of earlier. It would offer some protection, a hole from which to fight. I started drilling here and there along the sides and in the back, scooping out the occasional rock and regretting some of the jokes I had made about miners. In just a few minutes, I created an open-ended cocoon to put myself in. I changed my anchor locations and retracted myself up inside it.

A deadly spider in its nest.

I programmed the suit to do three things simultaneously.

First, the flechettes would fire at maximum power into the liquid, starting at the closed end of the chamber, working back and forth like our raster march on River, and moving toward the tunnel. In theory, this would clear a zone from which I couldn't be attacked, maybe even pushing the aliens out of the chamber altogether. Maybe.

Second, the bigger weapons on my chest and back would start pounding the walls and ceiling with periodic salvos, potentially breaking additional soldiers free. Using those weapons would require me to hang upside down in my cocoon.

Third, my sensors would be on the lookout for any signs of a null-space encapsulation. Any soldiers were absolutely safe in null-space, but as soon as the quantum-sized control unit sensed a void, it would bring them back out into the universe. I had no intention of liberating soldiers only to kill them because I was too busy doing something else. As for me, while my suit was doing those three things, I was going to keep an eye on the far end of the chamber, in case something bigger and badder came along.

I gulped down water and ran through my plan one last time, testing it for flaws. It was tempting to second-guess myself, to project what I would have done if I knew what was about to happen. It was hindsight regret before the fact. I shook it off. I tried to anticipate what I would do if such-and-such happened—if they started shooting at me, if hordes of them came racing at me, if whatever magnetism technology they were using made me unable to think straight. There was nothing to do but do it. I had done what I could to prepare, had done as much as I could do without actually doing anything. I had waited for this moment to get revenge on the aliens, and here it was. I gave the order to execute.

The first few seconds went off without a hitch.

The flechettes punctured the surface. Glowing green-blue ooze bubbled up. The first two blasts from my heavy weapons pulverized rock and left massive craters in the walls. The concussions moving through the walls knocked me around hard before I told the suit to stabilize. There were no signs of other soldiers but also no signs of anything coming to kill me.

It was a warrior's moment.

Most of the Aeneid scenarios envisioned mobile aliens firing weapons that somehow resembled our own. We were never presented with anything remotely resembling this. Still, if nothing else, I had hurt them and was glad of it.

My magnetometer pinged again, only this time, instead of a passing wave, it spiked and stayed high. Everything pulsed in and out of focus. A ripple in the liquid scurried away from where my flechettes tore into it. One alien was dragging half of another behind it, leaving a long trail of viscera in its wake.

With no new soldiers detected, I launched more explosives.

Below me, the liquid erupted. Aliens climbed over one another and clung to the wall, swarming up the moss shelves, and forming lattices with their flagella, all attempting to get to me. Blast debris knocked several loose and punctured one. Their rope-like appendages swung and grabbed for me. They had no features—no eyes or mouth or anything recognizable—just those tentacles groping and probing, tasting the air as they sought me out.

I abandoned the raster pattern and fired wherever the

damn things were closest. I augmented the flechettes with some beam weapons.

My heart pounded.

"You bastards!" I screamed, grinning for all I was worth. Thoughts of Kylie came to me, of us holding hands on the night before we went into the Green, of her smile when joking about camping with Jovan, and those last, sweet words before these damnable creatures blew her apart. The aliens deserved to die, and I would kill them.

An alert sounded, telling me a null-space capsule was half-buried in the far wall. The information did not register. We've improved technology far beyond the coping ability of our monkey brains.

I popped a high explosive into the water. It splattered liquid and alien guts over the walls and the ceiling and me. The aliens dove back and propelled themselves away.

The liquid below was a foul stew of blood and entrails and flagella.

I liked it.

The adrenaline rush passed, and a wave of exhaustion flowed back in its place. I gulped water and steadied myself. Blind rage had left my mind unbalanced.

An icon and a name popped up on my screen: Dish. One of the soldiers from Charlie. He was active, out of null-space.

I wasn't alone anymore.

CHAPTER 39: RESURGET CREATURA

*Mors stupebit et natura,
Cum resurget creatura,
Judicanti responsura*

Death and nature shall be stunned
When mankind arises
To render account before the judge

-Excerpt from the Requiem Mass, *Sequence*

2493 A.D. (Age 24, Birth + 274)

"Dish, this is PAPA. You there?"

Silence. My heart skipped a beat before thudding back to life. "PAPA, Dish. I'm here." He was breathing hard. "What's the situation?"

"We need to cover the far end of this chamber, then we can talk. Sound good?"

"Got it. Moving to position. What am I looking for?"

"As far as I can tell, anything that moves," I answered, "except me."

"Got it."

Coming out of null-space, Dish had fallen into the liquid, so he grapple-hooked his way up the wall and carved a small fighting position out of the mold.

"PAPA, Dish. I'm here. Recommend you take up a similar position on the opposite wall."

I acknowledged and made my way in that direction, trying to emulate Dish. It took me a lot longer than I would have liked, the pressure of inadequacy mounting, but I managed it in the end, and Dish didn't seem to notice. Or if he did, he hid it very well.

"Dish, PAPA. All set." The tunnel showed no indications of

anything headed our way.

"Okay, good," Dish replied, "tell me what's happened."

I described everything. It had only been twenty minutes since I exited null-space myself. On the other hand, it had been an eventful twenty minutes.

"Good. And good job," he said when I finished. "What's next, do you think?"

I believed we were relatively safe at that moment, at least compared to what happened earlier, so I set a motion-tracker alert and started considering options. I mean—my eyes were glued downrange since anything bad was going to come from that direction, but at least it gave me a little mental room.

"Try to find more of us in the walls? Then mount an offensive?"

From the corner of my eye, I caught Dish nodding slightly. "I like the idea of finding—"

My motion sensor went off, and before I had time to react, a rock slammed into the wall a few meters away. I ducked and held on as shards bounced off my helmet and shoulders. Two more rocks came in, one slightly closer and one farther away. I set my flechettes to auto and leaned out to give them a clear zone of fire, only to flinch back as another rock almost took my head off. It hit right behind me and sent a fist-sized fragment straight into my lower back. The suit absorbed some of the blow, but it hurt. A lot. I gasped for breath.

The flechettes kicked in, shattering the projectiles before they could reach my position. It was a temporary fix; a single flechette is a tiny sliver of metal, and a suit could hold thousands of them, but they weren't unlimited. Deflected pebbles ricocheted off the walls, noisy, pattering like heavy rain.

"PAPA, Dish—you still there?" Dish's voice was strained but still a sweet sound.

"I'm here," I answered. "Took a hit to my back, but I'm still functional. How about you?"

"One of those things hit my left arm. The suit has stabilized everything, but I'm not fully mission capable." I glanced over at him. His arm hung limp.

"We need more people," I yelled.

Dish grunted out a laugh. "Yes. Yes, we do. Hey—there's no point in both of us shooting at the same rocks. I'm going to cease fire, if you have it covered. My suit is still rerouting and repairing some things."

"Got it."

I glanced at him. He tried to lift his left arm with his right arm, as if he were confused about what had happened. Shock was always a possibility. If he faded out on me... well, it wouldn't be good.

"Do you think we could lay down a few nanowires across the entrance, Dish? Maybe they would take out some of the rocks?"

His head came up, and he slowly turned to look at me.

"I don't see how we could move forward to anchor them to both sides of the tunnel." His voice was strained.

"Good point. Okay. Can you start blasting the side of the cavern? We need more people."

"More people?"

Stay with me, Dish.

The flechette launcher hummed as it kicked out rounds, sending rock flakes pinging in all directions.

"I got it, PAPA. I'll start looking."

Dish worked himself around until he was in a better position to shoot at the back wall. "Here goes," he said.

I couldn't turn to see what was happening, but the concussions from the blast traveled through the rock and rattled my teeth.

"Anything?" I asked. I needed to keep Dish engaged and talking.

There was no answer.

"Dish? Anything?"

He was looking down at his left arm again. Really not good.

"Dish—hey, it's PAPA here. Can you look over at me?" His head came up a little. "Dish, it doesn't appear that last shot found any more soldiers. Can you try again?"

When it came to medicine, I knew absolutely nothing. The suits did the work for us, or we could call a medic, right? As for Dish, his suit should have given him a shot of adrenaline to keep him alive and awake and functioning. Maybe it was damaged in some way. Maybe Dish was more severely hurt than the suit could handle.

My flechette launcher indicated rounds down to fifty percent. When it comes to having enough ammunition, the glass is always half empty.

I had an idea.

"Dish, PAPA again. What if we punch a hole in the wall? Open this chamber up to space. Maybe that will kill off all the aliens. What do you think, Dish? We could look for more of our friends..." I struggled to remember who his friends in Charlie might have been. I didn't come up with any. "You know, like Speed and CAJUN. Good people like that."

Really good people like that.

Really, really good people like that.

Silence. My flechette rate of fire increased.

Still, what I proposed to Dish was a good idea. I launched explosives and relied on my suit to give me a picture. After the third salvo cleared, I got another indication of a soldier: Xeno. He hadn't been my favorite person back at the Aeneid station, but right then, he most certainly was. I waited a moment for him to get oriented, and then hailed him on comms. It was a repeat of what had happened with Dish.

Xeno grasped the situation quickly and told me to inform him if I got low on flechettes. He was going to try to crack the place open.

When he launched explosives, he didn't pause between rounds. The blasts piled on top of each other. Everything inside and outside vibrated and trembled and shook. Smoke filled the chamber.

Xeno let the air clear for a good fifteen seconds. No new soldiers. He bombarded the cave again, salvo after salvo. The walls reverberated from overlapping concussive waves to the point I was amazed my motion tracker worked.

"Through! It's open to space!" Xeno yelled.

The hazy atmosphere surged upward toward the vacuum beyond, only to slow and stop almost immediately.

Xeno keyed his mic. "It was open! I know it was. Can you hold the fort here, PAPA? I'm going up there."

My flechettes crept down toward a third remaining, my heart pounded, and I was thirsty and scared and beyond human.

"Go!"

I waited. The aliens hurled projectiles at me. The flechette counter dipped below twenty-five percent.

Xeno came back on. "The hole iced over. It ices over just as fast as I can blow a hole in it! I'm going to try…"

The line went dead.

I wasn't sure if—

A thunderous boom proved Xeno was still alive.

I turned my full attention back to the tunnel. The rocks flew at me, each one registering as a tiny blip on my screen until counter-fire took it out.

In the background was a larger movement—bigger than a blip, like a gathering or a…

Rally.

I hastily pre-programmed as much as I could, most of it boiling down to "if that big sensor reading starts moving this way, fire everything you have at it."

Dish didn't respond when I hailed him.

Whatever was gathering down the tunnel stopped moving, and the rock projectiles ceased as well. I waited, peering through the haze. There were small movements in the area where the big one had been, like whorls in a boat's wake.

Xeno had been gone over a minute—how long could it take?

Flechettes at ten.

My sensors erupted. The entire tunnel barreled my way. Fast. Rocks slammed in again, bigger than before.

I ducked and told my suit to wait… to wait… to wait.

Fire now and hope for the best.

Fire now and get it over with.

Anything but the waiting.
Come on, Xeno. I need you. If he didn't get back soon...
"Xeno..."
"Getting there, PAPA! Give me a few more!"
"Xeno..."
No reply.
"Xeno... they're here."

CHAPTER 40:
QUI SPEM NON HABENT

Ut non contristemini,
Sicut et ceteri,
Qui spem non habent

That you be not sorrowful,
Even as others
Who have no hope

-Excerpt from the Requiem Mass, *Epistle*

2493 A.D. (Age 24, Birth + 274)

"They're here."

I said it like that, just a matter of fact. And they were.

Their glowing, bulbous bodies surged toward me—along the walls, on the ceiling and in the water. Their tentacles connected and disconnected, launching some through the air. They flew up out of the water and from across the cavern and everywhere all at once.

I told my suit to fire and to keep on firing until there was nothing left. They crawled and grasped and lunged for me as I mowed them down again and again. My explosive rounds traveled only tens of meters before detonating, the blasts absorbed by the aliens, until the blue-green slime from their corpses covered me, covered them, covered everything.

I jumped out and away, hoping to find a clearer field of fire. Flagella snatched me mid-air. Flechettes fired in globes around my shoulders. An alien grasped at the launcher and lost three limbs. Two more tried before the third succeeded, leaving my entire right side undefended. I told the suit to concentrate explosive rounds in that direction and was rewarded with a slight lessening of the aliens' hold on me.

A big one grabbed my helmet and twisted, its tentacle

covering my view. Fluids pulsed and gurgled under its skin. More flagella grabbed my waist and leg in a tug-of-war. My head bent to the right, my torso to the left, like a wet towel being wrung.

All at once, the aliens released me. One pulled back and then another. They flung desperate feelers in all directions as the entire group slid backwards.

Xeno had done it. Xeno had cracked open this hellhole of demons straight to vacuum.

I sunk a wire into the wall as the aliens grasped the edges of the blast hole and grabbed others as they flew by. Except...

They slithered *into* the opening, not *away* from it. They weren't saving themselves—they were plugging the wound.

I checked my ammunition. Flechettes were gone. I had two high explosive rounds left, along with nano-wire and the beam weapon. And my fists. Always the fists.

An image of Dish holding his arm flashed through my brain. We could share his ammunition. And I needed Xeno back. Why hadn't he returned?

"Xeno!"

"PAPA, we are fighting our way back to you. Just hold out a little while longer!"

We? What did that mean? It was too much to process.

Dish's suit pinged to my right. Aliens jumping out of the water blocked a direct path, so I reeled myself back to the wall and traversed the ceiling to get to him.

I glanced back. The aliens had filled the gap, an inverted hill of squirming, squishy limbs where the hole in the hull had been.

Dish was where I had last seen him, just disassembled. Every limb had been torn from his body. His head was loosely attached by a flap of skin and the remnants of his suit. He had a vacant look in his eyes, his red blood fading to yellow where it mixed with the alien muck. A torso and a partially attached head. Everything that had made him Dish was gone, and the only difference between me and him was...

Time. That was it. He was there, and I was here, and I'd be there, sooner or later. Other than that, there was no difference between me and him.

One of the alien bastards snuck up from below and grabbed my leg, pulling me off balance. The thing was strong —incredibly strong. I gripped the side of Dish's fighting position, then started kicking the alien with my free leg. It had no real effect, and I wasn't in a good position to use my last two explosives or my beam weapon.

Nano-wire.

I anchored myself with a single hand as best I could, shot out a wire, and swung it at the alien as hard as I could. The wire sliced right through rock, the alien's appendages, and my left foot.

For a moment, while the universe held its breath, it didn't hurt or bleed. Then it started pumping blood like a fountain. What I couldn't understand about Dish's behavior earlier now became clear to me: understanding anything other than the pain in my foot was impossible.

The suit, however, was already staunching the bleeding and covering over the wound. It was not lethal, but pain shot through my body, ankle to brain, leaving me breathless, nauseated, unable to think or plan. Alerts flashed all over my display, but I couldn't understand them. They were a foreign language.

My screen flashed red, and something sharp jabbed my hip. The agony lessened a little and slowed my mind down. I swam through the fog in my head, not seeing or hearing anything. That's when...

Something about Dish.

Dish's arm—it didn't work right.

Of course it didn't—it was lying on the rocks in front of me.

And my foot. It was right where it was supposed to be.

Oh. The other one. Half my foot was gone.

Maybe Dish had it. Dish's foot was still here, but mine was not.

Brain-cell aliens were everywhere.

No ammo.

Dish had ammo. But no limbs.

Dish had no limbs. I had no foot.

"PAPA, Xeno! Come in! Are you still there?"

Maybe I had heard that before? The sound was distant and meaningless.

Xeno. Yes. Xeno and Dish.

And the boot down in the liquid. Maybe the boot held my foot? But that was before, wasn't it? Or was it?

"...talk to us, PAPA!"

"Xeno?" I remembered I didn't like him much. He had... what had he done? On Enceladus, he had...

"PAPA!"

Xeno's voice was good, despite him being a miner.

No, that wasn't quite right...

There was another jab in my hip, and my vision narrowed down to a small tube.

"Hold on, PAPA! We are fighting our way through! Anything you can do from your side?"

My side?

My side hurt. Something had hit me.

And my back.

And my foot, too. No, that didn't hurt. But something was wrong with it.

And with Dish. Something was wrong with Dish.

"Dish..." I managed to say.

"Do you see Dish, PAPA? I can't raise him. Can you help each other?"

Sure, I could see Dish. He was next to me. Oh. Right. He was dead.

"Yes... No..."

I clung there in silence. Xeno didn't answer. Dish stared straight ahead. The universe was far away, distant, unreal.

Somebody came into view. Close. Their helmet right up next to mine.

"PAPA, it's me. CAJUN. How are you doing?"

CAJUN. I was very glad to see her.

"Fine, CAJUN. How are you?"

She laughed. "You're in shock, okay, PAPA? Just hold on. You are safe for now, and we will get you some help."

Help?

"Dish...?"

"Don't worry about Dish. We've got him. Just take it easy." She looked up. "Doc—get over here with that kit!"

"On my way." A few moments later, a second faceplate appeared behind CAJUN. I saw him focus on something on his screen and then look at CAJUN. "That can't be from his foot, can it?"

"No way," CAJUN replied. "I think he got hit with something else. Or maybe he was poisoned. How is Mojo doing?"

"About the same as PAPA here. You could be right—they were both exposed to the alien environment. Maybe something got in. But the nanobots should take care of any foreign substances, so I don't know."

CAJUN considered that. "Okay, stay with him for now, Doc. See what you can do." She started to stand up, then stopped short.

"Iron."

"What about it?" Doc asked.

"They were exposed to the environment, and iron got in. It's everywhere here—this whole ship is infused with iron."

Doc's eyes darted around as he considered the possibilities. "And if it got in—"

"The magnetic fields would start playing havoc with their bodies. And the nanobots wouldn't go after it because it's supposed to be there."

Doc grinned. "So, we should—"

"Yes."

"I'm on it. Go! I got this."

CAJUN disappeared. Doc leaned over me and looked me in the eyes. "We are going to filter your blood through your suit. This should help you out."

He attached a network interface to me, followed by a third jab into my hip. After a few minutes, my mind began clearing. "B" again followed "A," and I knew where I was and what I was doing. And that half my foot was gone. And that Dish was dead. And that moving any part of me seemed to require more energy than I would ever have. Staying right where I was, pinned to the side of an alien ship, helpless and virtually unarmed—that wasn't so bad as long as I didn't have to move.

I drank some water, concentrated on breathing, and celebrated being alive.

When I first woke up in the cavern, I saw the white lichen, the glowing aliens, and the viscous liquid. Above the mold, below the chamber's vault, was bare rock, smoother than the ceiling but not cut or polished or worked. But as I looked at it more closely and with more time on my hands, it held a hint of something more. I scrolled up and down the spectrum, and in the radio and microwave regions, images jumped out: pictures of a night sky, stars brighter and dimmer and in slightly different shades; a nearby nebula; and the galaxy's disk, clear as it had been in the Sonoran Desert. The whole thing was beautiful, in its own way. Maybe this was where the aliens came from. Maybe these were their stars of home.

It was no excuse, of course. At the risk of sounding like I don't appreciate the incredible miracle of life in all its myriad forms; and at the risk of sounding like I somehow put the Earth and its progeny ahead of all other cradles of life; and at the risk of projecting human norms onto an alien species: you don't go marauding through the universe destroying whatever you come into contact with unless you want to be destroyed yourself.

I had no idea what the motivating factor was behind these aliens, and whether their native environment left them no choice except to conquer or be conquered, but I did know that their actions were wrong to the core, and that they would pay mercilessly for what they had done to Bravo Six, to Kylie, to River, to Galvus and Mars and Enceladus and Earth, and to me. The aliens' intolerance had been demonstrated well and thoroughly, and they would pay with their lives. All their lives.

Somewhere in there, I slept or passed out. I awoke to CAJUN gently shaking my shoulder. "Hey, PAPA. There you are. How are you feeling?"

Honestly, CAJUN: like I drank all night, then wandered out into a road and got smashed by a vehicle. By two vehicles, headed in opposite directions. Four vehicles, one from each primary dimension. Everything hurt. Except my foot, of all things. The suit was taking good care of me there.

"I'm fine, I think."

CAJUN smiled. "Good try, PAPA. We do need to get you up and moving so we can talk about a few things. You ready?"

"I hurt," I replied.

She laughed. "I bet. Do you have any...?" She checked something on her display screen. "Ah. No wonder. Your painkiller supply is almost at zero. Here."

She popped a packet out of her suit and fed it into mine.

"There you go. You should feel better in a second." She kept on smiling. "That was a *lot* of painkillers you went through, PAPA. You addicted?"

An image of my mother, stimmed out of her mind, came to me. She was a terrible mother, but she was *my* mother, for better or worse.

"No..." I said, slightly confused. The medicine took hold and rolled through my body. It felt so good not to hurt.

"I was joking, PAPA. You took quite a beating. And you did good." She winked at me and held out her hand. "Here, let me help you up."

I grabbed hold of her arm, and together, we stood me upright, at least to the point I could lean against the wall. Someone had further excavated Dish's fighting position because there was plenty of room for both of us.

Other things had changed, too. The blue-green glow was gone, replaced by light sticks that failed to tame the shadows. The atmosphere and liquid had disappeared, and there were no traces of any aliens. Stars shone through the cavity the aliens had tried to plug. Seven or eight soldiers were scattered around the area: two guarded the tunnel, a couple more were putting up barricades, one was prying rocks loose from the walls, and several appeared to be sleeping. Or dead.

"What happened?"

CAJUN looked deep into my eyes and nodded, satisfied.

"When Xeno blasted his way out of here, he freed the rest of us, but we were *outside* the ship. When we came out of null-space, Xeno was busy lining the rim of the hole with nano-wire, which kept a protective layer of ice and rock from forming for a minute or so at a time. The aliens fought their way toward Xeno, their blood boiling inside them whenever they approached the hard vacuum, but they kept on coming. Xeno shot at them as long as he could, until the ice appeared again, when he had to re-apply the nano-wire.

"We arrived and started shooting as fast as we could, but still they kept coming. We finally widened the exit. The ship tried to scab over whatever we opened, but with all of us firing and hacking and clearing, we kept it free long enough to line for Prince to line it with a thick wire. A couple of us got inside and started pulling dead aliens out into space. They made one last push and got to Prince and Speed both. The rest of us kept pounding away. When we finally opened this chamber to space, that liquidy goo boiled away and cleared the cavern out. The flow stopped before much came out of the tunnel, though. They caved it in and abandoned this part of the ship."

"How long ago was that?" I had no sense of time.

"You've been out for six hours or so. It took us an hour to get to you. I was sure you would be dead, but..." she shrugged, "here you are. We need to go down and discuss the way forward with everybody."

CAJUN must have seen the question in my eyes.

"Everybody, yes. There are eight of us. We would have had eleven, but Prince got blown into space during the attack. Dead, though. We are sure of that. Speed over there. And then... Dish, of course."

His body was still there on the ledge, partially reassembled.

"We are okay for ammunition—not great, but okay—but we will need a new source of oxygen in the next eighteen hours or so. We can pull it from their atmosphere if we get through the blocked tunnel, so that's about the timeframe we are looking at."

"Can we find more soldiers?"

"That's what Mojo is doing." She pointed up. "We want to be careful not to crush anyone with falling rock, and it's also a balancing act between looking for more people and using up our ammo. So, he's being cautious."

Even as she said that, Mojo chipped a block away and watched it fall.

"Let's go."

CHAPTER 41: A PORTA INFERI

Sed libera nos a malo,
A porta inferi

But deliver us from evil,
From the gates of hell

-Excerpt from the Requiem Mass, *Absolution*

2493 A.D. (Age 24, Birth + 274)

I followed CAJUN down to the cavern floor. Climbing wasn't hard, but as soon as we were at the bottom, I had trouble keeping upright. I found it worked better if I put all my weight on my right leg and then propped myself up on my truncated left foot, using it more like a crutch than a limb.

CAJUN gathered everyone together just far enough down the slope where we could peer into the tunnel but weren't fully exposed. There were eight of us: me, CAJUN, Mojo, and Xeno from Alpha squad; Crash and Zip from Bravo; and Doc and Seymore from Charlie.

"Okay, what's next?" CAJUN asked. "Anybody have any ideas? I mean, besides the obvious."

I didn't know what the "obvious" might be, nor did I have a good sense of the situation and terrain.

Zip was the first to speak up. "Clearing that blockage in the tunnel would cost us a lot of our remaining firepower. If we can get through it all. And they could just drop more and more rubble as we get further in."

"We need air, though," Mojo said. "Whatever ammo we have isn't going to do us any good without air."

Zip rolled his eyes at that; maybe that was the "obvious"?

"How about the shaft that runs through the walls?" Doc asked. "Could we use that to get beyond the blockage?" First heard for me about some kind of shaft.

"It's pretty small," Zip replied. "We could probably crawl through it single file, but trying to maneuver or plant explosives and get away from them would be difficult. And if the aliens collapsed it, there'd be nowhere to go."

Doc chimed back in. "Maybe it widens at some point, or there's a door or something connecting it to a larger area. What would be the point of a shaft like that if it never connected to anything?"

CAJUN held up a hand. "Any other suggestions?"

"We could go outside the ship, of course." Doc again. He seemed to be the idea man. "Go to that hump in the ship's middle and try to blow the thing in half. Or go to the other end and attack the chamber there."

"Still going to take lots of ammo," Mojo said. "We know where the aliens are—beyond the rocks—so let's go get them!"

"That's the whole point, Mojo," Zip added, annoyance obvious in his tone. "Whatever we do is going to take all the firepower we have left, so we have to choose the best path."

Mojo looked put out. "Sure. Of course. But the rocks that way," he pointed down the tunnel, "are loose. We aren't trying to dig a mine, we're just clearing rubble. It should be easier."

Zip didn't answer. Mojo didn't press the point. CAJUN seemed on edge.

"The other option..." Xeno started to say. "Well. I'm not advocating this, but just so we consider everything. We've hurt the aliens. Bad, if I had to guess. They have two chambers like this one—at least, it would make sense if the other was similar—and we destroyed one of them. Even if they repair it, they aren't likely to be a threat for a very long time. In a certain sense, we've done what we came to do. We could jump out, go into null-space, and get picked up by the rescue ship."

It was tantalizing. Declare victory and go home. Even though I wanted to kill all the aliens, the idea of not going back into combat was appealing. I could sense everyone struggling with that—a couple shaking their heads violently, a couple more staring at the ground, and a far-away look in CAJUN's eyes.

Xeno broke the silence he had created. "Or... we could pool our ammunition so several of us are full-up, and let the others go. At least Earth would know what we did."

And that broke the dam. Whatever temptation the idea held for CAJUN, sending some to certain death while others ran away was too much for her. Maybe she believed it was a morale issue—that if anyone started worrying about their own safety first, the unit would lose cohesion.

"No," she stated flatly, "our job is not complete, and we aren't going anywhere except toward the aliens until it is. Clear?"

Everyone nodded.

"We still have several hours until we must take action. Doc, since it was your idea, I want you and Seymore to go into that shaft and scout it out. One hour at most outward, then get back here. Understood?" The two soldiers acknowledged the order. "Crash and Zip—same thing, only outside the ship. I'm serious: even if something looks tempting, one hour. Mojo, you keep excavating. Xeno—you're with me on guard duty. Maybe we can probe that blockage a little. Understood?"

Nods all around. Except me.

"Uhhhhh." It wasn't a word, and I hadn't planned on saying it.

"And PAPA—apologies—you figure out how to walk, then come join us on guard duty. We need everybody for this."

I smiled. It was not the time or place to feel isolated.

After the two scouting pairs departed, I set about fashioning a makeshift prosthetic for my foot. The only real resources I had to work with were my own suit (and I figured I would probably be needing it intact) and Speed's, so I went over to his body.

His face looked calm, almost serene. He could have been sleeping, except for the enormous gash in his side. Something had ripped into him hard leaving organs and bones exposed. I didn't want to disturb him; it was desecration. I also didn't see what choice I had, so I imagined the reverse situation, and I'd want him to do whatever was necessary to survive. CAJUN caught my eye and gave me a half-hearted sign to go ahead.

It's odd how something so familiar can seem so different in a new context. Speed's suit had multiple attachments I could pull off or extract without doing anything to the body, including the helmet, fabric, and weapons systems. I couldn't quite connect any of them in my mind to a solution, though.

In the end, I did what I didn't want to do: I sliced through Speed's leg and pried his foot out of the boot. My suit generated a model of how my foot would fit inside, and I used that to construct a wire cage to keep the toe area stiff, with form-fitting wires running up my leg. The most difficult part was shoving that wire cage into the boot and getting it seated properly. Once finished, I stuffed the empty space full of as much fabric as I could, then pushed my foot down and in. It resisted at first but finally slid into place all at once with a satisfying thunk. The toe was still too floppy, so I lined it with more wire on the outside and wrapped the whole thing as tightly as I could. It functioned well enough that I could walk normally or even do a slow, slightly limpy run.

I rejoined CAJUN and the others just below the top of the slope. She gave me a questioning look, and I indicated I was better, but not perfect, which she accepted. I low-crawled up to the lip of the tunnel. The cave-in plugged the passageway several hundred meters away.

"That's a lot of rock," I said.

CAJUN slowly turned her head to look at me, as if she couldn't believe how dumb a comment that was. She went back to what she had been doing, which appeared to me like staring down the tunnel in the same way I was, but then she stopped abruptly.

"That *is* a lot of rock, PAPA. A whole lot of rock." She was processing something. "And it mostly came out of the ceiling, right? Some out of the walls, maybe, but still..."

She grew silent. We waited. I struggled not to relive the combat I had been through or imagine what might happen next.

The scouts returned in just under two hours. Neither group had much to report.

Zip went first, detailing their trip outside. "We made it to the other side of the ship, past the hump. We saw nothing at all. No airlocks, no weapons, not even any engines. There's a star directly in front of us; it's large enough to tell that's where we are headed, I think, but not huge in the sky or anything."

CAJUN accepted the news without comment and turned to Doc.

"We got nothing, CAJUN. The shaft just follows the outside of the ship. We also got to the center—barely—and there's something like a central ring there, but we didn't see anything that looked like an opportunity. Nothing. Tight quarters, too. Without that ring, I'm not sure we could have turned around. We would have had to return going backwards."

CAJUN didn't move or speak for longer than was comfortable. Finally, she nodded.

"Okay, well done all. If nothing else, we eliminated some possibilities. Here's what I'm thinking: PAPA helpfully noted that there's a lot of rock in the tunnel. Which there is. That rock came out of the ceiling and walls of the ship... which means the ship is thinner in those areas, and probably thinnest on top.

"What if we attack from the outside of the ship and try to sever this end of it from the rest of it? Break the ship in two. The aliens will be losing air and water and will have to attack us. And if they don't, we attack them, but at least we get beyond the plug in the tunnel." She looked around at us all. "Thoughts?"

Seymore looked like he wanted to say something, but Zip got there first, like he usually did. "Nanowire? Could it cut clean through the ship?"

"Too far," Doc answered. "With that long a segment, we might get a meter down before the chain broke, and you have zero chance of getting another wire in the same groove."

"If we blow the ship apart, won't they just plug the tunnel back up?" Zip again. I had already seen the Doc-and-Zip show once, and I was not looking forward to a repeat.

Xeno broke in. "I think they are both right, CAJUN. And I think you are right, too." Not helpful.

It looked like CAJUN was biting her tongue, and there was an audible sigh when she spoke. "In sixteen hours, we all need to be in null-space or sucking in some good alien air, or we need to die trying. I get it that there aren't any great options, but if we don't even have good ones, we go with the least bad. So come on! Give me something!"

It occurred to me that we were only looking at this from our point of view.

"What are the aliens expecting us to do?" I got blank stares in return. "I mean, they are profoundly alien, but they still seem to be thinking in terms of defending themselves and attacking us. They blocked our direct access to them. So, what is it that they are expecting us to do? Because whatever that is, they will be most prepared for it, so we shouldn't do that."

"He's right," Mojo chimed in, "the aliens would expect us to come through the tunnel, but based on what we already did, they might also expect us to pound our way through into the other chamber from outside the ship."

"But we didn't pound in, we pounded out!" Xeno sounded stressed. "And that wasn't one of the considerations CAJUN mentioned either!"

CAJUN raised both hands, and the argument stopped abruptly. "I hear you. And I've had enough. Here is the plan. We will sever their ship in two. And PAPA is right again: if we look at it from their point of view, maybe we can distract them by acting as if we were coming in from the outside. Divert some of their resources to give the main part of the plan a better chance of working.

"Crash and Zip will lead us outside, back the way they went. We'll find the far side of the cave-in ends, so if we manage to blow the ship in two, the side that still contains the aliens will be exposed to space."

There were some confused looks.

"Like uncorking a bottle of wine. Sort of. We will slice into the glass just where the cork finishes, where the hull is thin, but not so plugged up that the wine won't leak out." I tried to reconcile all the mixed imagery.

"Crash and Zip, the two of you will go to the far end of the vessel. Punch a few craters into it about the same place as the hole is here, then make a lot of noise with your flechettes. They should sense the activity and prepare for it. As soon as you do that, the rest of us will blow this end off. Just keep making a show of it as long as you can, okay?"

Crash and Zip acknowledged. It was probably the safest assignment of any of us.

"You each take one high explosive along with you and give your rest to PAPA. PAPA, go back over to Speed's suit, get his ammunition, and distribute everything evenly among the rest of us. Understood?"

I nodded.

"I'd like to be underway in twenty minutes. Doable?" There was general agreement. "So, drink some water, eat a little something, take a stim if you need it, get your ammo from PAPA, and be ready. Got it?" Agreement again.

I appreciated CAJUN making me the one to go back and get the ammunition from Speed. I had done what I had to do, but it wasn't pretty. No one else needed to see it unless it was necessary. It also occurred to me that if this end of the ship were separated, there would be no way to get Speed's body home. Or to find anyone else who might be trapped in the walls.

"CAJUN, PAPA."

"Yes, PAPA. Go ahead."

"I'm getting the ammunition, no problem. But I did look at Speed's suit, and his null-space generator is showing green. I think we could do that for him. Might get him picked up, and it would be better than leaving him here."

"Good idea, PAPA. Take care of it once you've got everything usable."

"And CAJUN..."

"Just tell me, PAPA."

"Well, if we staked Speed to the outside of the hull, maybe someday there could be a rescue operation that could look for other soldiers we haven't found yet."

"Also a good idea, PAPA. Take care of it. Get Mojo to help you if you need it."

I felt better after that, as if I had taken care of Speed in some way. And maybe Speed would be able to help others. It's what I would have wanted for myself. Well, after not dying in the first place, of course.

It was closer to thirty minutes by the time we were ready to go. We climbed our way up to the exit hole and out onto the surface of the ship. There was a moment of silence as Mojo and I pinned Speed down and engaged his null-space generator. The familiar silver substance flowed over him, making him look more like a soldier and less like a mutilated corpse.

Zip took the lead, though there was really no doubt where we were going. We climbed up until we were on top of the ship, relative to the direction of travel.

The star ahead was a bright orange dot that provided enough light to make out our surroundings. The outside of the vessel was a jumble of aggregated rock, secured in place by whatever magnetism mechanism these aliens employed, but rough and jagged. Zip turned to the right and headed toward the middle of the ship, and we followed behind, climbing and leaping over the mounds, bound to the craft by its constant acceleration.

We probed the rock beneath us, trying to make sense of the visualizations. They weren't very clear while we were directly over the blockage; when we got to the far end, however, a definite gap appeared. The trick was going to be cracking it open right at the point the cave-in stopped, where the hull was still thin. Where the cork met the wine. A few boulders left on the alien side of the ship wouldn't be a problem, as the escaping air would push them into space. If there were too many boulders, however, the plan would fail. We'd be right back to digging through them.

CAJUN stopped, then walked back and forth trying to find the best location. Finally, she pointed at a spot and shot a flechette into the rock. "Here. We will try to break it here. Zip and Crash—you head over to the other end of the ship. Let us know when you're in place and ready to go. We'll give you a minute or two to cause as much noise as you can, and then we will start blasting away. The rest of you—I want two on one side of me and three on the other, spread out at fifteen-degree intervals. Go."

Her plan was to cover a 90-degree arc of the ship's body and punch enough holes to crack it all the way around.

I ended up two positions away from CAJUN, with Mojo between me and her. Xeno was on my other side, furthest out. We carved out primer holes so the rock would help capture more of the explosive energy. I dug mine down to ten or fifteen centimeters, extracted a round from my suit, placed it inside, and backed away toward the ship's hump.

When CAJUN saw everyone was ready, she retreated quickly.

All we needed was the signal from Zip and Crash.

The brain is a wonder of engineering. Whether it came into being fully formed via some creator or is the result of relentless evolutionary pressure, its ability to cope with reality is nothing short of miraculous. I had seen intense combat less than twelve hours earlier, and yet my brain had already partially healed, had already begun to block out the worst memories—as long as I had some task to occupy me.

But standing there, exposed to space, tethered to some godforsaken alien vessel, hoping beyond hope not to embarrass myself or suffer any pain or even to have to go through with this—it all came back: the terror and the adrenaline and the absolute overwhelming strain of having to do and understand everything at once. My heart raced, my breath shortened. I wanted to get it over with and never have to do it, all at the same time.

CHAPTER 42:
JUSTE JUDEX ULTIONIS

Juste judex ultionis

Righteous judge of vengeance

-Excerpt from the Requiem Mass, *Sequence*

2493 A.D. (Age 24, Birth + 274)

And then it was there. The signal from Crash. They had created a distraction, and it was our turn.

"Everybody secure? Speak up now if you aren't." The comms remained silent. "Okay, then. We detonate in thirty seconds. Get ready."

CAJUN set a timer on our displays. I anchored myself to the surface and huddled back as best as I could, with my arms over my head, watching the clock. When it hit zero, I set my charge off, protecting myself but also peering toward the explosives.

Rock and scree shot soundlessly into space, like the ice geyser back on Enceladus. The surface of the vessel heaved, pushing me away from the ship. My tether slammed me to a stop, the anchor bolt straining to let go, to give up its struggle for good. Debris bounced off my helmet, and then it was done.

No extra fountains of air and ice. We hadn't punched all the way into the interior. I landed back on the surface, bruised but in one piece. I looked around for the others before standing up. Xeno staggered to his feet, but no sign of Mojo.

CAJUN came back on comms first. "Status updates. Everyone check in, starting with Doc." He was on the far end and checked in immediately, followed by Seymore. When it came to Mojo's turn, there was silence.

"Mojo, CAJUN. Come in." Nothing. "Okay. PAPA and Xeno,

check in."

We did, and then CAJUN tried Mojo again with the same result.

"His locator says he's still there. PAPA, unhook and go check on him."

I popped myself free and hurried to his location.

Mojo was lying face down, not moving. I rolled him over. A shard had gone clean through his helmet, with both an entry and exit point. It had taken a good chunk of Mojo's head with it. That unassuming, handsome face that carried such warmth and charm was now mangled beyond recognition.

"CAJUN, PAPA. He's dead. Took a rock through his helmet."

There was a pause. "Thanks, PAPA. Grab his ammunition, put another explosive in his hole, and return to your spot."

I got what I needed before tossing a round into the crater that had cost Mojo his life. It was ten, maybe twelve meters deep.

That's what a life is worth sometimes. I wish it wasn't true, but it is.

As I jogged back to my position, a hairline fracture appeared on the surface of the vessel. I shared my feed with everyone.

"I've got cracks, too." It was Xeno.

"Me, too. A lot of them!" Doc, at the far end.

CAJUN cut in. "Okay, great. Crash and Zip, get back here as fast as you can, but stay tethered to the ship. It's going to get a little bumpy. Everyone else—take out a high explosive round and drop it in your crater. We're cracking this ship open like an egg!"

Or a wine bottle. One of the two.

We started our demolition in one-minute cycles, which gave us just enough time to recover from the shock waves, get back to our craters, throw an explosive inside, and retreat. Since the holes were deeper now, the debris only shot up and away, not toward us, but the simultaneous detonations made the surface buck like a transport in bad weather.

On the third round, Seymore reported that some air

escaped briefly. The fissure joining each crater had grown and was now well over twenty centimeters wide. After the fourth round, CAJUN shortened the interval between blasts, and we were rewarded with multiple momentary air ventings.

"Everyone anchor yourselves right next to your crater! We are going to speed this up!" CAJUN yelled.

I secured myself as best I could, within rolling distance of the edge, but with almost no play in the tether; I couldn't afford the time to come back down to the surface and get set to go again. It also meant that I'd take the full brunt of the shock waves.

"Speak up now if you're not ready," CAJUN ordered. Silence. "Okay, we go in ten!"

On zero, I detonated my charge and flinched back as best I could.

"Again!"

"Again!"

"Again!"

The surface bucked and rolled, a wild animal screaming in rage. It was the end, whether I lived or died: the end of the long journey to get here, the end of the battle, the end of sanity as rock crumbled and flew and broke, and the ship did its best to push me into the void. It was too much. It was hell. It was not survivable.

Kylie's last, confused words came to my mind. She hadn't deserved to die like that. If this was what it took to revenge her, then I welcomed death. The aliens were about to pay for their transgressions.

I clung to the surface and to CAJUN's voice, rolled and dropped, rolled away, over and over and over.

"Halt! Everyone—back away from the fissure!" It was now meters wide and growing on its own. I shot an anchor into the stone a good distance behind me, unhooked, and scrambled away as fast as I could. I caught a glimpse of Xeno doing the same thing.

All at once, the ship broke. The gap widened, then split completely, the ship's acceleration twisting in a strange way and taking my stomach with it. Air and water poured out into space from the half we were on. The other side was plugged with debris which slowly dislodged itself.

It was beautiful, like a slow-motion holovid, everything calm after the chaos, objects drifting in the void, a ballet of physics. As I watched, though, the free-floating boulders changed direction, as if under the control of an invisible hand.

"CAJUN!" I shouted. That was all I had time for. The slabs of rock sped up, heading straight for our positions. They pounded the area where we were, hitting the ship hard, cracking its hull, spraying flechette-like splinters everywhere. I gave up any pretense of extra safety measures and ran for my life, straight toward the central hub of the ship. The impacts tossed me up, and I crumpled when I came down, already scrambling to move before I hit the surface. My prosthetic foot came loose and started flopping.

I stopped when I got to the vessel's bulbous center. The impacts had ceased. Nothing moved.

"CAJUN?" I asked. There was no response. "This is PAPA—is anyone out there?"

What if I was the only one alive, a repeat of River, a nightmare playing itself out again? But then Doc checked in followed by Seymore, Crash and Zip, and finally Xeno, who sounded weak.

"Status, Xeno?" It was Doc asking.

"Beat to hell," Xeno gasped. "Broken ribs, feels like, and I lost a lot of blood before the suit sealed itself."

Nobody spoke. This was the part where CAJUN was supposed to step in and take over, but we all sensed, I think, that CAJUN would never do so again.

"Null-space, Xeno. Now. Get out of here." Doc was in charge now? Fine by me.

"Got it, Doc. I'm sorry." Xeno must have been in worse shape than he was letting on, otherwise he would have argued more. A silver form separated from the ship and drifted away.

Air and water no longer poured out of the broken hull, but

none of us wanted to go back and check what was going on; there were still plenty of rocks floating in space nearby for the aliens to use.

We joined back up at the base of the ship's center section, more refugees than soldiers. I wasn't sure how much I had left to give. I looked around at the other four. Doubt and exhaustion filled their eyes, too.

We must have hurt the aliens badly, but they weren't done yet. There was a slight trembling in the rock, and then our motion detectors picked up something coming out of the front of the ship. They were using their main cannon, the one they had destroyed so many systems with. The projectile flew out and changed course, heading right toward us.

"Down!" Crash yelled, and I dropped as quickly as I could. The rock they threw at us merged with our position, so it must have gone over our heads.

Another tremor. I knew what it meant—I just didn't know what to do about it. Seymore looked up to see what was going on, and the round took his head off. One moment he was there, as alive as any of us, and the next moment, all that was left was a torso and limbs and flash-frozen blood, collapsing back to the surface.

"Doc?" I asked. "Crash? Zip?"

"No ideas here."

"What do we do?"

"Null-space—we've done what we can."

Everybody was talking at once, protocols long forgotten. A shot plowed into the surface right next to us, leaving a long scar. The faint shaking of the ship came more often. Our time to make meaningful decisions was rapidly passing.

"Everybody agree on null-space?" Zip wanted out.

I wanted out, too, but I had an idea.

I explained as we rolled out of the way of another rock, and, after a couple of questions, everyone agreed to try it.

We low-crawled toward the center of the ship, moving as unpredictably as possible. There were some close calls, and Crash took a splinter through his hand. The aliens had a steady launch tempo going, and it was only going to be a matter of time before our luck ran out.

We inched our way forward until we were near the firing tube. Crash and Zip kept moving to the right of the hole, while Doc and I stayed to the left, spreading out around it. The rhythmic firing didn't change, and being right next to the tube told us how much time there was between the warning shakes and a round exiting the vessel. It wasn't much—less than a second. I calculated the time between shots. It averaged just over seven seconds. We could work with that.

"Fifty seconds," Doc ordered. "That's when we go." We had to survive seven cycles.

I took out all my remaining high-explosives and bound them together with a wire, all while evading invisible rocks being hurled at me at high speed.

Thirty seconds. A fountain of rock erupted right next to me. A pebble glanced off my helmet.

"Crash is down," Zip reported. "Twenty seconds."

I pushed myself right to the lip of the chasm and waited until the hull trembled. That would be the last alien shot before we executed our plan.

Zip counted us in. "Four... three... two... one... now!"

I tossed my bundle of explosives over the edge, the ship shook as it started to fire, and I detonated my rounds.

Everything exploded all at once. The munitions combined with the kinetic power of the aliens' projectile, all of it confined in the firing tube. The hull under me erupted, and I was shoved hard into space, riding on a boulder that shielded me from other chunks of the maelstrom.

As the rock tumbled, it threw me clear.

The hull splintered and cracked, shuddered and bucked, as veins spiderwebbed over its surface. For a second, I felt the terror of the creatures inside, as they encountered the end of all things: all their cares and worries and hungers and desires narrowing to a fleeting moment, before the ship split completely open. Aliens writhed in the vacuum, boiling away along with the water they were in, popping, bloating, and clinging to the remains of their vessel as best they could.

Some had tendrils entwined with others, as if trying to protect each other or saying a final goodbye.

Even that short time was more than I had with Kylie or Bud or the rest of Bravo Six. Or Aurelius, for that matter. Or CAJUN. Or my mother, in a certain sense. Some part of me wanted to have pity, to imagine that maybe some of the aliens detested what the others had done, that they could be reasoned with and become our friends. It was too late for that. They attacked us. We destroyed them. I was sick to my stomach and elated and full of hate and joy, my brain on the verge of bursting.

"This is Doc—anyone else survive? Check in please."

"I'm here, Doc. It's PAPA."

"Good to hear your voice, PAPA. Zip—you there?"

We didn't hear from Zip then or ever again. After all of that, only Doc and I survived. Xeno was out there, somewhere, and maybe he would live as well. As for the others, I hoped in their final moment they knew they had done their best and that their fellow soldiers would remember them in triumph and respect. It means nothing to the dead, but everything for those about to die.

"Well, it's you and me, Doc," I said.

He was roughly a kilometer away. We could both have gone into null-space right where we were, and it wouldn't have made any difference as to whether we were rescued or not, but I wanted to be near him, and he felt the same way. We were drifting in different directions, not exactly away from each other but not toward each other either, so I first had to stop my momentum in one direction and then move in another.

Given our training, it took us longer than it should have, but we were both overstimulated, our minds racing and unfocused, darting from here to there among the events of the last several hours. If I had been another meter in the other direction, it would have been me instead of Crash getting crushed back at the firing tube. The slab of rock that protected me could just as easily have smashed me. The aliens dying, screeching in silent pain. The waste of it all.

The triumph of revenge. The battle came back to my mind unbidden and relentless, forming a lifelong partnership, never forgotten and never far from the surface. The endless *what-ifs* and the dwelling on details and the second-guessing of my motivations, actions and character—they started then and never stopped.

No one who has seen it up close really survives war; whoever you are afterwards is not who you were before. Doc and I were alive, and we were grateful, but we would never be the same.

When we finally came together, we hugged. Brothers. Warriors. Connected forever. And compared to River, having someone else to lean on made living through it much better.

We pulled away from each other but kept holding hands, neither one of us wanting to risk losing each other. The battlefield was littered with debris, tumbling away. The stars stared at us, unmoving. It was time to go home.

CHAPTER 43:
NE CADANT IN OBSCURUM

Libera eas de ore leonis,
Ne absorbeat eas tartarus,
Ne cadant in obscurum

Rescue them from the lion's mouth,
Lest they land in hell
Or vanish into the abyss

-Excerpt from the Requiem Mass, *Offertory*

2493 A.D. (ORPHEUS + 234)

As planned, the *Carpathia* AI pulled the crew out of null-space a day out from the beacons. There wasn't much to prepare for, but General Fitzpatrick wanted to monitor the sensors on the way in.

Angel and Brady retreated to the intelligence terminals as soon as they were able.

"Forward or backward?" Brady asked her.

Angel froze, her eyes darting back and forth.

"I have no idea what you are talking about," she said after a second.

Brady laughed. "Do you want to go over the scans looking forward at the beacons, or do you want to triage the last hundred years of message traffic?"

"Definitely forward," Angel replied without hesitation.

"I don't blame you. You're better at that than I am anyway."

Fitzpatrick entered the small room followed by a soldier they didn't know.

"Angel, Brady—I'd like you to meet FS9 Yael Perski. FS9 Perski, this is Angel and Brady, our intelligence experts."

"Pesky," the new soldier said, pointing to the name on her uniform. She was short but muscular, with silver hair shaved close into arcs on the sides of her head and spiked on top.

"We picked her up barely a month after launching. In those early days, the alien ship regularly shed pieces of itself. The AI detected an iron object matching Project Aeneid specs and brought a few of us out of null-space to check it out. Sure enough, Pesky was inside."

She waved at them. "The general thought I should take a coffin back to Earth, but I begged to stay on."

Fitzpatrick shrugged. "There was room and supplies for her, and her insights into the Aeneid personnel, tactics, and training might prove valuable. Anyway, we went back into null-space immediately, so I hoped you two might be able to brief her on the final attack."

"Yes, sir," Brady answered. "Angel is going to analyze the beacon data, but I can definitely do that."

The billions of unread messages would have to wait.

The general left, while Brady and Pesky pulled a couple chairs together.

"So, when did you go into null-space?" Brady asked.

"Not long after the second bombardment. The one with the smaller rocks."

"I see."

"Almost all the Aeneid soldiers were unhappy with the original rescue plan. We were certain we'd be left to die—beacons or not. Forces Command changed its mind and announced you wonderful people here on the *Carpathia* would be right behind us, and that made the difference. There was no reason to wait, so into the iron tubes of doom we went."

Brady nodded. "Okay, thank you. That gives me enough to go on. So, the alien ship arrived in the system about two years later. July 19th, 2376, to be exact. It looked much thinner and more jagged than its last sighting at Galvus. It was still shaped like a barbell—two lobes connected by a shaft with a round bump in the center—but gaunt. I believe the aliens expended a tremendous amount of resources on the bombardments.

"Also, it acted differently, like it was hungry. The ship

pulled in any ferrous metals it could find and went out of its way to aggregate more. That may be why Aeneid worked."

"Did it pick us all up?" Pesky asked.

"No," Brady replied, shaking his head. "Of the fifty-four encased soldiers put out as bait, the aliens pulled in thirty-eight. Not bad, really. One of the stealth ships scored several antimatter hits before being destroyed. The attack tore a chunk out of the alien ships' left lobe, momentarily venting atmosphere before the wound iced over. We hoped the aliens would pack you all in around the wound—maybe you could get inside immediately. But that didn't happen."

"How bad was the attack?"

"Compared to the bombardments, not terrible. The antimatter attack occurred while the alien ship was inbound. The aliens destroyed a large portion of our ships but stayed away from Earth and instead veered past Mars. That planet took a beating. It also meant that your Aeneid program leaders had to quickly corral the boulders, calculate the most likely path of the alien ship, and fling you all out into the vastness to see what would happen."

"And now I'm here."

"And now you're here."

Pesky frowned. "And not with them. The general said you've detected beacons?"

"Yes." Brady turned to Angel. "Anything interesting?"

Fitzpatrick chose that moment to walk back in. "Interesting about what?"

"The beacons, sir."

Angel hadn't taken her eyes off the display. "Well, the albedo and lidar and radar returns are all way too big for a single soldier."

Brady thought for a moment. "Could it be several soldiers spread out and giving the appearance of a bigger object?"

"I don't believe so. For the lidar, sure—that's mostly just telling us distance. But the radar is giving us a solid return, with a resolution of less than seven centimeters, and the albedo is wrong. Very low."

"No visuals yet?" Fitzpatrick cut in.

Angel shook her head. "Not enough light coming off that thing. Another hour and we should have something."

It was closer to ninety minutes, but by then, they had detected a large debris field fanning out in a halo from a singular point in space, all of it drifting toward the nearby star. The largest piece was clearly a truncated wing of the alien ship, with a beacon coming directly from it. The other three signals were a few thousand kilometers beyond that.

When they reached the broken wing, Fitzpatrick halted the *Carpathia* over the beacon. There were no readings from the vessel, no power sources. It was still highly magnetic, but nothing compared to its previous magnitude. The egg-shaped lobe had a hole blown open in it—judging by the scatter pattern on the surface, from the inside.

Captain Grant and one of his officers performed a quick spacewalk and retrieved the soldier, who had been deliberately pinned to the surface. Back on board, following a full decontamination, Doctor Kelly deactivated the null-space field.

The soldier's suit was relatively intact, including the label showing his name as "Speed." The body, though—the body was mutilated, ripped open and destroyed, and missing the lower part of its left leg.

The doctor released Speed's helmet, pulled back an eyelid, and scanned a pupil.

"It's him," Kelly said. "Identity confirmed. FS8 Carlos Rapido."

She peered into the massive wound in his side and then examined his leg. "Little doubt about the cause of death. But based on the lack of bleeding around his shin, he was dead when he lost his foot. That chest wound, though—that's what killed him. Took half his organs with it."

Fitzpatrick nodded. "Thank you, Doctor. Let's put him back in null-space so he can get a full burial when we get back home. Captain Grant, take us to the next beacon, please."

"Yes, sir..." Grant acknowledged, stretching his words out. "Just a suggestion, but could we stay here a day to explore the alien ship?"

Brady was thinking the same thing; the intelligence value of the artifact was beyond measure.

Fitzpatrick didn't hesitate. "No. Our mission is to rescue these soldiers, and that's what we are going to do. Once accomplished, I'll consider coming back, but for now, we concentrate on getting our people."

The next pick-up was much easier as the body was free-floating in space. The crew repeated the procedures and once again gathered around as the null-space field was cut off. It was hard to watch, given what happened the previous time.

This soldier, however, was alive, and the shock and relief of seeing people was evident on his face. So was the pain.

"God, but you all are beautiful," he grunted after retracting his helmet. "Xeno" was written on his suit.

"Quiet, soldier," Doctor Kelly ordered, her smile belying her tone. She checked the scanner and ordered blood.

"It's him—FS6 Sukhbataar Puri," she said, addressing Fitzpatrick before turning back to her patient. "You've got a lot of internal bleeding. Broken ribs, too, but those aren't the real threat. We will fix you up, though. Don't worry about that."

Fitzpatrick appeared to want to ask him some questions, but the doctor gave him a warning look.

"Not until he's stable."

"Got it," Fitzpatrick answered. "Okay, then—Captain Grant, take us to the other two beacons. We won't bring them in until our medical staff is fully available. Understood?"

"Yes, sir." Grant headed off.

It was more than a day later when they were all set. Xeno was out of danger but sedated, and the crew fully rested when they brought in the last two. They had been drifting together several meters apart. Fitzpatrick ordered the first one out of null-space.

His name tape said "Doc," and the retina scan verified him as Jordan Danielson. Just as with Xeno, there was the sudden shock from drifting in space one minute and being surrounded by people the next. Doc proclaimed himself fine, and after a minute, Doctor Kelly agreed.

"What happened, FS7 Danielson?" the general asked.

Doc shook his head. "Bring PAPA out first."

"Is he injured?" Kelly asked.

Doc laughed. "Yes, but nothing life threatening. PAPA is quite the survivor."

They brought the last soldier out of stasis. Once the initial shock faded, he looked around the room and smiled.

"That was for you, Bravo Six." He caught a glimpse of Doc. "Hey, buddy. We made it." He tried to swing his feet off the table, but Kelly put a hand on his chest.

"Not yet, soldier. We need to get you healthy first." Kelly looked at her device again and showed the results to Fitzpatrick. PAPA had internal bleeding, and his organs and tissues showed signs of severe blunt-force trauma.

"Verified as Coren Slade, though. Welcome back, FS5 Slade."

Angel startled, and then leaned into Brady. "That's him!"

"Who?" Brady asked.

"Coren Slade," Angel whispered. "You remember that soldier from River that came back? That's him! I don't remember his face, exactly, but that was his name. I'm certain of it. And remember how we talked about him joining back up?"

Brady looked back over and tried to associate the soldier on the surgical table with the holovid he had watched long before, but the memory wasn't there. "You're sure?" he asked Angel.

"It's the same name, at least. And I sort of remember what he looked like. Yes, I'm positive it's him." It was a wild thought, that with all this distance from home and all these years later, here was someone from their own time and place.

"Alright, FS5 Slade," Kelly said, "I'm going to put you under so we can drain some of these fluids and repair the tissue damage, but you are going to be fine. Okay?" The soldier didn't respond. "Everyone else who isn't here for medical reasons, get out. Now. Doc, you are free to go as well, though I will follow up with a psychological examination soon."

A huddle of people escorted Doc out the door and to

the galley. The room filled with false conversation as they waited for Doc to get his food, to sit down, to eat. And then Fitzpatrick offered him a change of clothes. And a shower. Brady feared the general would offer him a night's rest too.

Finally, though, they all gathered back in the galley to hear what happened. Doc told the story slowly and carefully, uninterrupted. When he finished, there was a moment of silence. By unspoken protocol, the first question belonged to the general.

Fitzpatrick took his time. "Thank you, Doc," he started. "So... based on what happened, do you believe there are more soldiers still buried in the hull somewhere?"

"Yes, sir. I do. We really only excavated that one small area."

The general looked over at Grant. "I want an assessment of how we can look for those men and women."

"The search should include space as well, sir," Doc said, clearing his throat. "From the end of the ship that blew apart. And the ones who died. They may be in space somewhere, too."

Fitzpatrick nodded agreement and passed the additional tasks to Grant with a glance.

Brady saw an opportunity. "If we are scanning for objects that size, sir, we could also look for alien corpses. Getting even part of one back would be a goldmine."

"And there should be thousands of them out there," Doc added. "They poured out of that ship like a swarm of bees."

The Old Man raised an eyebrow as he considered it and then nodded permission before opening the floor to questions.

Grant jumped right in. "You never saw any type of system on the ship? Nothing electronic or mechanical or anything like that?"

"No, nothing like that. There were aliens and that white stuff on the walls and that awful liquid, and that was it. There was the main tunnel and the two lobes where they lived and then that small shaft that seemed to run closer to the surface. The magnetism readings were massive and constant. But no, I never saw a computer or anything."

"Did they seem intelligent?" Angel asked. "I mean, individually intelligent versus collectively intelligent?"

Stress creeped over Doc's face. "I don't know. They just kept attacking. And then they all spilled into space at the end. I was glad to see it, but it was horrible. They came out alone, squirming and twisting, and they came out in pairs and clusters, holding each other. And I saw some small ones in there, like babies. The pain was obvious. I hate them... I do. But I also wonder if..."

His eyes had grown less and less focused, his voice thicker.

Fitzpatrick stepped in. "That's enough for now. Doc, thank you for sharing. We'll tell everyone back home what happened. Let's talk later about the details."

Doc snapped back to the present. "How long, sir? I mean, how long ago did we leave Earth?"

They had pushed Doc too far, Fitzpatrick saw now. The general looked around for advice.

Brady shrugged helplessly. Angel looked pained but nodded for him to go forward.

Fitzpatrick nodded several times. "It's been... well, this is hard for all of us. It's been one hundred seventeen years, Doc. But you are safe, and we are all going to get home. Okay?"

Doc went somewhere inside himself as he tried to process the information.

Fitzpatrick leaned into Brady, put a hand on his shoulder, and whispered in his ear. "Why don't you and Angel take him back to Doctor Kelly?"

Brady didn't need to ask why.

Captain Grant and his team came back to Fitzpatrick the next day with their proposals for finding more soldiers. Brady and Angel sat in on the briefing.

"Sir, we have looked at the situation and have come up with some options for you." Grant averted his eyes before looking back at the general. "We did not find an option that will give you everything you want, but we tried."

Fitzpatrick didn't move, but his face turned red.

"The first issue we looked at is the intact wing of the alien vessel. We are well equipped to tear it completely apart and ensure there aren't any soldiers left inside. We anticipate that will take roughly a year. So far, so good.

"As for any soldiers floating free in space: we can run a full hi-res scan of the battle debris during that same time and likely find anyone, at least as long as they are still roughly human-shaped. This would likely give us Olsen's alien corpses as well. Again, so far so good."

Fitzpatrick still did not move.

Grant cleared his throat.

"The problem is one of momentum, sir. The debris is drifting toward the nearby star—we are, too, for that matter. In less than a year, most pieces will enter the star's atmosphere and burn up. A few will fly wide, but not many. The intact wing is also headed that way, but we can slow it down by blasting from the star-ward side.

"We also looked at whether we could push everything to one side so it misses the star entirely, then deal with it all afterwards. There are just too many pieces for that. Getting the wing out of the way will require a month all by itself—it's too much mass for a small ship like this. Taking all that into account, an optimized path has us getting to roughly twenty-seven percent of the other debris. That is, the wing plus an additional twenty-seven percent."

"And the time involved, Captain Grant?" Fitzpatrick's nostrils flared.

Grant exhaled heavily. "Right. If we go with that last option, and then pursue the material once we have pushed it out of the way, it will add about forty-one years to our mission. Most of that time would be spent moving between chunks of rock, not actually cracking them open."

The general contemplated the information.

"And what total percentage of the alien ship would we have searched at that point?" he asked at last.

"Just over half, sir. Somewhere between fifty-one and fifty-two percent of the original mass of the vessel."

"Dammit!"

Brady froze; he couldn't remember the general ever raising

his voice or cursing in anger before.

The Old Man sat in silence, his hand worrying his face in an unaccustomed manner.

"Do it, Grant," he said at last. "More than half is better than nothing. Get started right away, and then run those numbers again and again and again. I want to squeeze every single moment out of the time we have. And if picking up a dead alien costs us any time at all, skip it. I'll take live soldiers over dead butchers any day."

CHAPTER 44: AETERNA IN CAELIS

*Aeterna in caelis habitation
Comparatur*

In heaven, an eternal dwelling
Is readied

-Excerpt from the Requiem Mass, *Preface*

2493 A.D. (Age 24, Birth + 274)

"That was for you, Bravo Six."

I said that when I came out of null-space as the medical bay abruptly replaced the stars. Maybe the sentiment included everyone else I had known throughout my short-yet-overextended life, but my thoughts were on Bravo Six —as it was before Bud died, as it might have become had he lived, and how maybe, just maybe, someone else had survived the River attack in null-space all these years.

I missed my family.

Doc leaned against a bulkhead behind the medical personnel. Doc. He and I had talked two or three times before the mission. Then we fought side-by-side for a few hours at most. Now we had an unbreakable bond. My only friend in the entire universe.

"Hey, buddy. We made it."

And somehow, maybe through a rush of relief, I knew three things for certain.

First, I had no home, perhaps more than any human ever.

Second, I regretted nothing about slaughtering the aliens. The violence, the horrors, the constant alertness of battle— those would never leave me. But the aliens: I would do the same thing again without hesitation. If anything, I wished they had suffered more.

And third, I wanted no more part of anything remotely

military, ever.

It was all as clear to me as Saturn had been above Enceladus. I wanted to start on this new life right away, and since I had no pain, I went to sit up. My muscles did not fully obey me. Actually, they didn't obey me at all. I recall someone offering a vague assurance of something, some other talking that grew distant, and then a blank spot.

When I woke up again, a crowd stood around me. A doctor approached my bed and leaned over me, putting a hand on my forehead.

"How are you feeling?" she asked. "Any pain?"

I hadn't been in any pain before, thanks to the full pharmacy my suit pumped into me, and I didn't have any pain now, but somehow I knew I was better. Maybe it was a certain flexibility of movement or ease of breath or just some subconscious feedback system of the body. "I'm okay, I think."

The doctor smiled broadly. "Good, good—that's great. You were pretty banged up when you came in here. There was more damaged tissue than healthy in some places. And your foot—we got that fixed up as well. At least a prosthetic slightly better than the one you had."

She was pretty, with a nice smile. Not Kylie's smile —not Kylie's mysterious knowledge-of-the-universe smile— but warm and friendly, nonetheless. I started to explain to her about where the fake foot had come from and why I had to do it, but she shook her head. "It's okay. There's time for that."

Time. That was funny. Time has never been my friend.

A man approached—tall, thin, grey, weary. The others backed up, bowing their heads slightly.

"Hello, soldier. I'm General Fitzpatrick. How are you doing?"

"Pretty well, sir."

"I'm told you go by PAPA."

No.

Doc and Xeno and anyone else from Project Aeneid could call me that, but I was done with the military. They could lock me up for insubordination or do whatever they wanted—I had had enough.

"Cor, sir. Please call me Cor."

General Fitzpatrick smiled. "It's nice to meet you, Cor. We've reviewed the recordings from the suits. You all did an outstanding job. Brilliant, really. You should be proud. And please know that we are doing our best to locate your fellow soldiers out here—both alive and dead.

"The doctor says we can get you up and about if you feel well enough. Can you make it down to the galley? We'd like to have dinner with you and hear what you have to say."

This caught him a look from the doctor.

"No questions and no pressure, of course," he continued, "but whatever is on your mind, we'd like to hear it."

I sat up slowly. That part went well enough, so I braced myself, swung my legs over the side of the bed, and stood. Slight head-rush, but I felt good. I felt steady. I couldn't even tell half my foot was gone. We made our way through the ship, somewhat awkwardly led by a captain, with me in trail and the general by my shoulder. I got the sense that if the corridor had been wider, we would have gone side-by-side but he was letting me go first out of respect. I appreciated that; it was not a normal way to walk.

As we got to the galley, the captain palmed the door open and offered for me to enter first. "We've got a special meal planned for you," he said.

I sat at a table with General Fitzpatrick and the captain—Grant, by his nametag. Doc and Xeno were there too. They were the ones I wanted to talk with and compare memories—what had happened, what they had seen, and their plans for the future.

For the moment, though, it was small talk. I answered questions about what I wanted to drink with dinner, about where I was from originally, and, based on a cryptic comment from the doctor, about how I had accidentally cut off my own foot while hacking away at an alien. Others at the table must have known how it happened from my suit's recording, but apparently not her. It was fine; I liked talking to Doctor Kelly.

A junior soldier sitting down the table cleared her voice. "I'm Angel Moran," she said. "Intelligence specialist. I... uh... that is, you were on River, weren't you?"

I nodded guardedly. I wasn't sure where she was going with this. But all she did was smile and give a knowing look across the table to a lieutenant.

"I knew it," she said. "Didn't even have to look it up."

I was grateful she had not called me the "Hero of River." As I've said before, I accomplished nothing on River except survive, and I certainly wasn't a hero there. And what I did on the alien vessel was out of fear and desperation and love for my team, not out of bravery. I wasn't a hero before, and I wasn't a hero now, and I doubted war could produce anyone who would claim the title willingly. War is too hideous, too brutal, too horrific to result in anything admirable. Sure, if it makes leaders feel better about themselves for sending other people off to die, then find your heroes and celebrate them. Those of us who have been through it, though—we know the truth, and the truth is that on the battlefield, emotions and thoughts and events are too overwhelming and too vast and too complicated to boil them down into a single title. You survive, or you don't. If you do, you won't remember who you were before. At best, you can hope to carry a few good things forward with you. At worst, your mind will eat itself alive.

"How was it?" the captain asked. "I'm Captain William Grant, by the way. It's a pleasure to meet you... Cor. So, how was it? River, I mean."

"Green," I answered, "very green."

That got a laugh or two and broke the ice, though no one brought up the alien vessel during the meal.

Later, I was alone in one of the small observation rooms when Doc found me. We embraced just like we had in space. Here was something solid and real for me to hold onto, someone who didn't want anything from me.

We talked through the battle, filling each other in on details we either hadn't seen or hadn't processed at the time.

I was privileged and saddened and horrified to see each of my fellow soldiers die again through his eyes. Doc thought maybe he saw the rock that killed CAJUN.

"What's next?" I asked him when the conversation hit a lull. "For us, I mean."

Doc hung his head and rubbed the back of his neck before replying. "Yeah, PAPA. I mean, maybe someone else should be telling you this, but the rescue mission General Fitzpatrick described—it's going to take decades. We're going to be out here a long time, and it will have been over two hundred fifty years when we get back."

Doc looked serious, as if he were bringing me bad news, but I didn't care. My life had been strung out so far already that hundreds or thousands or millions of years didn't make much difference. I shrugged. I cared about my future, but not about when that future started—as long as it didn't involve the military.

"And when we do get back, what then?" I followed up. "What are we going to do?"

It was his turn to shrug. "I don't know, PAPA. I guess we'll have to see what civilization is like. They did guarantee us significant money to volunteer for this, so maybe we don't have to do anything? Maybe we can retire? You know, buy a place on the beach. Maybe you and me together? I don't know. But we made it, PAPA! We made it. You, me, and Xeno. And Pesky. And maybe there's a lot more of us still locked in the alien ship. I hope so. It would be good to see everyone."

Except we both knew "everyone" wouldn't include Dish, whom I couldn't save; or CAJUN, whom I wanted to know so much better; or Crash and Zip from Bravo; or the unidentified owner of the boot I glimpsed when I first woke up in the alien vessel; or Mojo and Seymore, from Doc's own company.

Whether anyone saw us in the observation lounge and decided to leave us alone, or whether it was by chance, we talked undisturbed for hours, two lifelong friends getting to know each other for the first time. Whenever I imagine a good conversation—one that is full of trust and understanding and safety—that's the one that comes to mind.

Doctor Kelly was eager to talk to me, so I met up with her first thing the next morning. Like her smile, she was warm and caring, but she asked all the wrong questions. I mean, I suppose they were the right questions for most people, and maybe they were even the right questions for me, but they were not relevant to where my mind was.

She asked about the battle, about my levels of pain and discomfort, about how I slept, about whether I was having any unwanted recurring dreams or intrusive visions. I was, of course, but I didn't tell her about them. Violence of that magnitude rips the brain apart. Perhaps in time I would need help stitching my mind together again, but for the moment, they were *my* nightmares, and I would own them completely.

I needed something I couldn't quite name yet.

I also met and spoke with Angel Moran again, as well as the lieutenant—Brady Olsen—who had been sitting across from her at dinner. Even then, before I knew them so well, I suspected there was something between the two—the way they shared glances that were more than professional, the way he treated her as an equal despite their different ranks, the way she looked at him when he was speaking. I would come to learn that it was a special bond—one based on mutual respect and trust and a deep appreciation for the qualities of the other. Together, Angel and Brady were always so much more than either of them alone.

Maybe that's how Kylie and I would have been, and maybe that's wishful thinking, but someday finding someone like that would be nice.

It looked a lot like home.

By the time I met with Angel and Brady, I'd figured out that Doctor Kelly was warning people away from asking me about the battle. If I brought it up myself, whoever I was talking to was suddenly more attentive, but no one seemed inclined to dig deeper. So, that was the first thing I got out of the way.

"Please," I said, "feel free to ask me anything about what happened. It's fine."

The two of them shared a smile of relief. "Thank you,"

Brady said, "that will make things a lot easier. How are you feeling, by the way?"

That right there was the moment I started liking them—I mean, really liking them as people, not just as acquaintances. Here they were, two Intelligence soldiers, just given the green light to ask any intelligence question they wanted about the biggest threat in human history, from one of three people still alive who had seen the aliens in person, and Brady took the time to ask how I was feeling.

"I'm fine," I answered. "Glad it's over, glad I'm here. I hope we find more people with the search. But I'm okay, I think. Thanks."

Brady seemed genuinely pleased. "Good. We're glad to hear it. You know, if you need to talk to someone, Doctor Kelly is always available and excellent. Also, Angel and I are a little younger than you by date of birth, but not as much as most of the others, so we'd be happy to listen as well. We might have a perspective that fits a little better with how you grew up."

It was a nice offer and right on target. "Thank you," I said.

Angel took over for Brady. "We went through the video from your suit, Cor. One of the things I find most intriguing is the star patterns you found on the upper walls of the chamber. We were able to process what you and the other soldiers recorded, and we have a good idea of what the entire scene looked like—for the portion of the alien ship you all were in, of course. We were wondering if you had any thoughts about it."

"Yes, as a matter of fact, I do," I answered. I cast back to those first few moments when I was able to look around the big chamber and see the milky fluid and those creatures and the white growths on the walls. "I think the aliens recreated their home inside their ship. My first impression was that this was natural for them. The images on the ceiling—when I think about them, they are like a continuation of the same theme. I believe it was the sky of home for them."

"That was our conclusion, too," Angel said. "We are going to propose to General Fitzpatrick that we scan the debris in the radio and microwave wavelengths—we may be able to pick up some images and stitch it back together. If we get enough, we might even be able to cross-match the scene with actual places in the galaxy and discover where their home world is."

That made sense. The threat of that particular alien ship was gone, but it had come from somewhere, so who knew whether more ships were headed our way?

"But what do we do if we find it?" I asked under my breath to no one in particular. They were right, though, and only doing their job. Identify, locate, and describe the threat—others will decide what to do about it. But I feared the consequences, and I feared what some future version of someone just like me would have to face, and I feared waking something that was best left dormant.

There was a silence as my question passed unanswered. Then Brady picked up where Angel left off. "Did you get a sense of what their skin felt like? It looks smooth on the recording, but maybe it was different in person? Scales? Texture?"

The conversation went on like that, well into the evening, Angel and Brady tag-teaming, but always with a certain concern for me. Their questions made me dig deep, made me consider and challenge what I had seen. As I said, I liked them from the beginning, but in the middle of that conversation somewhere, we became friends.

Doc, Xeno, Pesky, and I went back into null-space the next morning to preserve resources. Fitzpatrick promised we would be brought out when more soldiers were found, and it was a promise he kept.

In total, over the next few decades, the crew of the *Carpathia* rescued twelve more Aeneid personnel. Eleven were alive, including Thrash, Tiny, and Baja, all of whom I had known from Alpha company. The crew brought us out of null-space each time they found someone and threw a celebratory dinner.

The celebration part was awkward, to be honest. In theory, we were honoring the person we had just found, but they knew, and we knew, that while it took incredible bravery to volunteer for the mission, they sat out the battle. All their training and preparation had been for nothing, in a certain sense, except maybe to increase the odds that some soldiers would make it inside the alien vessel. We celebrated them being alive, and we all got drunk together, and we told each other we were friends forever, and then we went back to our coffins.

The crew did find one body amidst the debris: Mojo. It was a somber reunion. I last saw him on the alien ship's hull. He did his duty, he set off his explosive, and he died by sheer bad luck. The time spent floating in space desiccated his body, but somehow, it also made his ruined face look more like him. Mojo—in all my travels, I have never seen anything to indicate there is an afterlife, nor have I necessarily seen anything to indicate there is not, but if there is, I hope someday to see your handsome face restored to its fullness. Here's to you, Mojo, and everyone like you.

During one of the celebrations, I learned from Angel and Brady that they had retrieved several of the alien bodies. They described to me how the aliens were able to generate such enormous magnetic fields and manipulate magnetic rocks so precisely, and how the ship itself was both a huge electromagnet as well as a sensor, almost a body as opposed to a transport mechanism. The two of them even believed each octopus-thing was more likely a cell in a larger consciousness than an individual creature. Based on what I'd seen, I agreed with them. I was interested in all this, of course, and their enthusiasm for the subject matter was infectious, but what really mattered to me were the people and who we could still find and what would become of us all.

After a few decades, General Fitzpatrick brought us out of null-space one final time to tell us that the search was over and that we were heading back to the Solar system. All told, of the thirty-eight soldiers the alien ship dragged away with itself, sixteen were unaccounted for—Boomer and YAW among them. We left a plaque bearing their names on a large chunk of alien rubble.

As for what happened to the missing, whether the aliens shed them into the depths of space or killed them before I emerged or something else, we would never know.

It could just as easily have been me.

CHAPTER 45:
GERE CURAM MEI FINIS

Oro supplex et acclinis,
Cor contritum quasi cinis,
Gere curam mei finis

On my knees, I pray,
My contrite heart almost ashes,
Take my ending into thy care

-Excerpt from the Requiem Mass, *Sequence*

2654 A.D. (Age 25, Birth + 435)

Coming back to Earth, there was one thing I was certain of: uncertainty.

My return from River was disorienting, confusing, overwhelming. I didn't understand the culture or the references, and everything seemed off—wrong and unnatural. But I had found a way out: peace in the desert and a family in Project Aeneid. I never fully adjusted to that time before I left again.

Now, I had been gone twice as long.

We arrived back and pulled into an Earth-orbiting station two hundred seventy-eight years after we left, over four hundred years since I was born.

I was twenty-five years old.

The authorities sent aboard a medical team in full hazardous materials gear. They poked and prodded us and gave us thorough physicals and pumped us full of inoculations and other medicines.

Even with that, when the airlock unsealed and we walked out, the few military members and civilians who greeted us kept their distance and parsed their words—wholly unintelligible without a translator. Part of it may have been our lack of appliances. No two of them were the same. One had a quarter of his or her skull replaced with a metallic-looking simulacrum. Another had a jet-black eye that moved of its own accord. None seemed fully present, as if we were distractions from other things happening inside their heads.

And yet... these humans had done nothing wrong. They had been born into a technology I found intolerable, but they still had the same singular burden of every human ever: act morally. As I had done nothing *to* them—indeed, as I had done much *for* them—I expected them to accept and welcome us.

They did not.

We were escorted to a hotel, ushered to our rooms, and told to wait. Then, over the next several days, both collectively and individually, we were debriefed by a series of scientists, sociologists, and intelligence personnel, all via holovids, all using translation devices. The debriefers already knew most of the details, since the *Carpathia* had sent back the logs and recordings and events via twinned-electron communications. And it was all very old information for them—more historical than relevant, just like all of us who returned.

The military, though—I had to hand it to them. They came in person, briefed our options, and sat down with each of us to discuss. Our service obligations were now over, and we were free to leave the Force, with full benefits and honors. Or we could stay... which would require retraining and an extensive orientation to the "new way" of fighting.

There was work to be done, though—a revolt on a colony, piracy in the outer belts, crime on Mars. If we wanted a job, the Forces still wanted us. Captain Grant later indicated he was going to stay in, that he still had something to offer. We wished him well, and he left the next day, headed for special operations, he hoped. Maybe we will see you again someday, William, but if not, thank you for the rescue. If you ever need anything from me... well, you know where to find me. Where to find us.

The media interviewed the *Carpathia* returnees as well,

and we trended for several days. The focus was on how old we were and how we returned after being gone so long. A couple of stories highlighted our role in destroying the threat, but it was more like something the populace wanted to avoid, like an old wound long since healed and best forgotten.

As I watched all this on the holovids, I was adrift in a maelstrom of information, a caveman transplanted to a city and staring at the strange cliffs and forever-rock trail. I needed a way forward.

First, I had the AI show me Earth. It was now where the rich went to play. Following the devastation of the alien attack, the remaining poor were transplanted elsewhere, and the planet underwent a full terraforming into a paradise, the likes of which had never been known.

Gone were the swings in temperature from cold to hot and back again, based on some random tilt of the planet. Gone were the industrial excesses, the urban sprawl, the vast discrepancies between the haves and have-nots. Disease, hunger, and ugliness were no more.

For those who could afford it, Earth bequeathed an endless bounty of beauty. The African plains were full of wild animals modified to avoid harming humans. You could walk the paths of our most distant ancestors, through fields of wild grass and under umbrella trees, sleeping where you wanted without fear of harm. Or you could hike the great mountains of Asia without getting cold and never risking your life because technology could heat you up, cushion your fall, or supply you with oxygen. No danger. No challenge. Where the very richest could go and have anything and everything, swapping out various parts of their bodies on a whim, all in the name of vanity.

Pulling back a bit to the Terran orbital colonies and the Moon, the influence of Earth's culture became apparent: the nearer you were to it, the more likely you were to follow its trends and to mimic its lifestyle. Envy is an endless vortex, swelling with all it consumes.

For the first time since I left it so many centuries earlier, I looked for Mars II. It had ceased to exist. A slug from the alien ship pushed the entire colony down onto the planet's surface. A crater named Mars II marked its final resting place, a few hundred kilometers north of Valles Marineris' remains. My mother. Devlin. Red. Tommy Cooper. Maybe even my recruiter Carmichael, if he stayed there. Whatever remained of them, whatever atoms had constituted their bodies—all of it was now down there, blending with the Martian soil.

Finally, I started hopping around and looking at settlements and colonies and ways of life wherever my interest took me. The estate system out around Cygnus; the agricultural collectives on Eriadne; tyrannies here and socialist societies there, with representative governments scattered among them. Almost fifty known extrasolar homes for humanity, with more suspected due to the alien-driven diaspora.

There were things I liked, things that spoke to me of "home." And there were things that scared me, things I did not want to believe still existed after so much time: the slums on the Moon; the pirates who robbed ships and spaced people because they could; the violence between communities on the same planet, whether resource-constrained or not. And the Earth people, with their constant modifications—I wanted no part of that.

No single place had everything I wanted, and... and an idea grew in my mind. I needed to know what was feasible.

Based on my first return from the dead, I was fairly sure there was one particular visit coming, and that visit came on our fourth day back. The holo informed me that someone was at the door and asked me if I would like to see this person or if we should reschedule. I said it was fine and stood for the visitor.

The woman who greeted me was young and blonde, her hair cut in a neat bob. Her blue eyes shone behind old-fashioned glasses, the kind I saw sometimes on holovids as a kid. She was dressed in a black business skirt and blouse with a white collar and matching belt cinched tight at the waist. She showed no signs of machine enhancement.

In retrospect, I believe she had been groomed for this one

interview for a very long time, perhaps her entire life.

"Mr. Slade?" she asked, and, seeing my slight nod, continued. "I'm Xybel Johnson. May I come in?"

No accent. No translator. No impossible-to-follow linguistic shortcuts

I motioned her inside; a faint smell of flowers floated behind her.

"New here?" I asked.

She looked at me quizzically. I let it go and motioned her to the couch. She took a seat on the edge, keeping her feet under her so she didn't sink too far down, and placed her briefcase on the table.

"Thank you for seeing me, Mr. Slade. I represent the law and accounting firm of Kim, Carter, and Johnson."

She handed me an actual business card on actual paper, a format long outdated even by the time I was born. It was heavy, substantial, like those gold bars I'd arranged for Carmichael back on Mars II.

"The Johnson on the card is my mother, not me, by the way. Maybe someday. And please, if you like, call me Xy."

"Nice to meet you, Xy," I replied. "Cor."

She smiled in return. "Perhaps you know why I'm here, Cor?"

I shrugged half-heartedly.

"Yes. Well. We were hired by the Forces to manage your investment portfolio when it started to become... significant. I'm told I should advise you that this was allowed *ex post facto* by the Military Reform Act of—"

"It's fine," I interrupted. "I mean, assuming that you've taken good care of everything."

She laughed gently, like clear water flowing in a stream. "Well, that's just the thing, Cor: We not only took *good* care of everything for you—we took *exceptionally* good care of everything. Now, I am also legally bound to disclose that we have collected a ten percent fee on your annual earnings, which was also..."

I waved her off. "When I returned from River, I had a lot of money. If you have built on that, then a fee sounds justified.

So..."

"So, how much do you have? That's what you want to know?" She cocked an eyebrow. She had good news and seemed to be enjoying the suspense, especially as I didn't make her dwell on the more mundane details.

"Let me just say that all of you who returned from the expedition did very, very well and shouldn't have any monetary worries for the rest of your lives. I can't go into specifics on the others, of course." She opened her briefcase flat on the table. "You, on the other hand—you started from a much more advanced position than any of them, which gave us significant latitude in building your assets."

The air over the briefcase came alive with a simple graph chart, showing a blue line steadily ascending. Xy pointed to the lower left corner. "This is the baseline—where you started the year you left. As you can see, in aggregate, your net worth has increased every year, with the big tic marks at the bottom being fifty-year increments."

She had a big smile.

"Now, you may be thinking that the line looks too smooth to be accurate."

I was thinking no such thing; it looked like a lot of money, but I wasn't sure how much.

"And you would be right," Xy went on. "Any economist would look at this chart and know that it's problematic —no economy, no investment strategy will produce steady returns like this, given the timeframes involved. Except... well, except that this chart is logarithmic, Cor."

It was the big announcement she had been leading to, but I had no idea what she meant. I sort of remembered logarithms from school, but just the word itself, not the concept behind it.

She must have seen my look of confusion.

"What it means is that each of these tic marks over here—" she pointed to the left part of the graph, "is ten times greater than the tic mark below it. The line appears smooth because your overall net gains in the periods shown here have been exponential. You must have money to make money, and oh my—do you have money! All the market ups-and-downs you would normally see in this type of graph are hidden by the enormity of the scale."

My blood froze, my mouth went cotton-dry, and my heart thumped hard in my chest.

"How much do I have?" I asked.

A dream tickled the edges of my brain. Two thoughts which had always been separate collided with each other. The idea from the day before took root and blossomed.

Maybe...

"You, Cor," Xy said, her languid blue eyes fixed on mine, "are the single richest person anywhere. And really, any 'when' as well. I mean, as compared to average net worth, or even compared to other wealthy people. Now, there are a handful of corporations that have a greater value than you, but you own substantial portions of those corporations, so it's kind of like a snake swallowing its own tail. If you get my meaning."

Oh, I got it all right. At least the most important part. My mind raced. My vision for the future doubled and doubled again before expanding all the way. The two thoughts merged into one inseparable dream.

I couldn't, could I?

Maybe...

Xy kept going with her presentation. "Now, I can show you where your financial holdings are, if you like, and talk you through any specifics. We at Kim, Carter, and Johnson value you as a customer above all others—as you might imagine—so I can spend as much time as you want going over things."

"That won't be necessary," I replied. "And thank you."

I thought for a moment.

"How much of this is... cash?" I didn't quite know how to ask for what I wanted.

"You mean liquid assets? Immediately spendable?" she asked.

I nodded.

"Not much—liquid assets don't grow, so we kept your portfolio invested all the time. If you are worried about paying for or buying things—well, you never have to worry about that. We can provide you with a spending account right now, and work with you to convert your holdings into any money you need to get settled. Whenever and wherever you want. It's not really how the rich operate, though, Cor. You pay a lot of taxes when you convert holdings into direct monetary instruments... cash, as you called it. Kim, Carter, and Johnson specialize in finding ways for you to get around..."

I waved off the end of her sentence. The details didn't matter.

She smiled, white teeth gleaming brilliantly behind the red, red lipstick. "The universe is really yours, Cor."

I stood up. My mind whirled as I pictured a new home, and I needed time to think things over. "Thank you, Xy. Let me consider this for a couple of days, if that's okay."

"Of course it's okay, Cor! Whatever you want," she laughed, catching me with the corner of her eye as a strand of that beautiful hair fell into her face. "Now that you are back—well, we were hired by the Forces to take care of your portfolio, but that relationship technically ended the day you returned. In other words, we do not yet have a direct business relationship with you, but we would certainly be more than pleased if you hired us to be your lawyers and accountants."

I liked Xy. I liked her attitude and her intelligence and what I perceived as her honesty. Given my large importance to them, I'm sure their firm had practiced this meeting dozens of times and prepared Xy on multiple levels to win my trust. And she had.

"What would I have to do to hire you?" I asked.

"For today, a verbal agreement is more than sufficient. We can go over the legal documents and sign them later, but if you tell me you want to retain us, then we are here for you. Today and forever."

Forever. That was funnier than she knew.

"Done," I said. "I would like to retain your firm. I believe I'm going to need you a lot, and soon."

Xy beamed. Mission accomplished. "Well, then, may I say

on behalf of Kim, Carter, and Johnson—"

"Your mother—not you," I joked.

She laughed, probably more out of relief than because it was funny. "Yes, my mother. On behalf of all of us, we could not be happier to represent you."

"Thank you, Xy," I replied. "I'll be in touch soon, and we can talk about what I want to do."

Xy was all agreement. "You're in charge! We work for you, so whatever you want, that's what's important to us."

She gathered her briefcase, reminded me of the business card but also that the room had their contact information, and that if I needed anything—including a nicer hotel or money or anything at all—that I should contact them.

I thanked her and said goodbye.

I didn't need anything except time to myself.

CHAPTER 46: DONA EIS REQUIEM

Agnus Dei,
Qui tollis peccata mundi,
Dona eis requiem

Lamb of God,
Who forgives all,
Grant them rest

-Excerpt from the Requiem Mass, *Lamb of God*

2654 A.D. (Age 25, Birth + 435)

On our second night back, we arranged a time for all *Carpathia* personnel to have dinner in the hotel's restaurant. It went so well, we kept it going—come if you want, stay as long as you wish, leave whenever you like. The dinners gave us a chance to see each other and to compare notes on what we heard and learned and thought about this society. I mostly sat with Doc, Angel, and Brady—Fitzpatrick, too, if he attended, which wasn't very often or for very long. The dinners also meant there was a set time when we would get together; I didn't have to worry about being interrupted during the day, which was what I needed.

The fourth night—after everyone had gotten a Xybel-like visit—a palpable sense of excitement floated in the air. The alcohol flowed early and never stopped—top shelf, all of it. Doctor Kelly ordered the restaurant's oldest bottle of whatever they had. The waiter brought back an eighty-six-year-old Scotch. We hoped for something brewed while we were on mission, so we could talk about what we had been doing when it was made, but instead, we had all been in null-space on our way back. It didn't matter, though—we doled out the bottle, toasted ourselves and the ones we lost, and drank.

It tasted awful. Mud in a glass. But because we were toasting each other, I enjoyed every drop of that horrible drink. It was a night to remember.

Uh... mostly remember.

Parts of it are hazy, and I may have made a pass at Doctor Kelly, and after that went down in flames, possibly one at Pesky, though she wasn't my type at all. Some people talked loudly about amounts, but the focus seemed to be on what was next, what others were going to do.

I woke up the next morning and rubbed a cream on my arm that wiped away my hangover immediately. Thank you, Science. At least for that. Maybe we are all born into a time and a place and a technology, and maybe we should live our lives there and nowhere else in order to be comfortable, adapting to the changes as best we can until our time is up, and we hand responsibility to others born into a different time and technology. But I suspect that everyone who has ever had a hangover, since the first person discovered that you could let grapes ferment to pleasurable effect, would appreciate an instant cure.

After breakfast, I dawdled a bit. I knew what I had to do, I was excited to do it, but I was also scared—scared about where the idea might take me and scared that it would not be possible or that the reality might land so far from the dream that I would be better off not starting. And starting—starting is always, always the most difficult part.

Intolerance.

Upon our return, we were greeted with disgust, dismissed as primitives. Oh—I'm sure if word had gotten out about our net worth, we would have been plenty tolerated. But that's the tragedy of the rich: they never know if they are liked or being preyed upon. I had no desire to win a spot amongst humanity that way.

I had seen all the horrors of war, its hideous countenance now a constant companion. Yes, I fought aliens, not humans, but haven't people done worse to each other? Not at the same scale, perhaps, but also not with the same twisted *homo sapiens* ingenuity. Greed, envy, pride, wrath. Denigrate others, deny their status, and then take everything from them, including their lives, in the most painful way possible.

In my examination of the Solar system and the colonies and the various societies they contained, I saw no substantive difference between them and any other time period I was familiar with. Maybe life is war. Maybe it has to be that way. Maybe my rejection of this society, their rejection of me, and humanity's long, troubled history of lethal rejection of otherness—maybe it's all the same thing. Maybe there is no cure.

Tommy Cooper. On Mars II, he conspired with Carmichael the recruiter to entice me to sign a Forces contract under misleading circumstances. Tommy gained a little money, and I...

I was here. Four hundred years later.

Tommy Cooper would have loved Earth, this new Earth, this new society, I think. In my place, Tommy would have surrounded himself with a constant party for all his remaining days. He would not have been troubled by whether he was accepted for being himself. Tommy could have lived in the moment—the ever-present moment—and been fulfilled and happy. Me, though... maybe I was born this way. Or maybe I have seen too much to accept that the universe was, is, and always will be an empty husk in which the living rattle around like dessicated, crumbling seeds. I needed more, and I needed more than being surrounded by people who always wanted more. The ever-present here-and-now—the tyrannical maw that swallowed my mother whole—would not consume me.

I didn't want to go to Earth. No, not Earth, and not anywhere else. Everywhere I looked were societies cloned from a face I could not recognize.

For whatever reason—by birth, by conditioning, by experience, or by corruption—I knew this: I couldn't live in this *now* and be content. There must be more than this. I had drifted through my short life, mostly letting others decide for me, a passive mote in an active whirlwind. My mother, Carmichael, the aliens, the Forces—I was a product of what they wanted and needed. Not in any way unusual for someone my age.

But no more.

I would *act*.

I would control my own destiny. I would find a place that I could call home, where the perversities of time and culture and human whim could not touch me and mine.

The nightly dinners expanded into farewell parties as individuals decided where to go and what to do. That evening, the fourth evening, the evening we all found out how rich we were, we said goodbye to Doctor Kelly. She and I talked briefly, musingly, about relocating to a nice beach together. I could dream it, but I couldn't do it. She could. She had already found a place on Earth where she could live comfortably and try to forget the darkness.

God, I wanted to do that, to be that way. But I couldn't. At the end of the evening, I hugged her hard and told her that if she ever needed anything, contact me, and that I would help her. No questions asked. She offered the same. And then we parted. I think we both knew it was for the last time.

At the group dinner the following night, I asked Angel and Brady if I could come over afterward. They agreed, even if they seemed a little puzzled.

Their room looked just like mine, except for the dimmer lighting and a fire blazing on one of the holo screens, imparting an intimacy to my innermost thoughts. We sat on the couches. Angel and Brady looked at me expectantly. It was my show.

I took a deep breath and started. "I have had an idea that I would like you to take a look at, if you don't mind."

They exchanged a glance that was equal parts agreement and confusion: of course they would look at anything I wanted to show them, but why tonight, and why did I seem nervous?

"Would you like to send it to us, so we can both see it?" Brady asked.

"No," I answered a little too quickly. Everything was still

contained. "I have it here on my datapad."

And only there, where I had written it earlier in the day. Where I could delete it and be rid of it forever, if I wanted.

I reached out to hand it to them, and as I passed it over, possibilities unfolded as I floated in a cloudless sky, not breathing, not thinking, just being. There it was. I had shared my ideas with someone else.

Angel and Brady huddled together to look at what I wrote.

Brady finally broke away and stared at me. "You intend to do this?"

"Yes," I said simply.

"But where...?"

"River."

Angel had been studying my datapad at length. "You think you can afford this?" She glanced back down to find something.

Brady looked over at her, and then back at me. "Exactly how much money do you have, Cor?"

I smiled, trying to look as humble as I could. "A lot."

"Enough to—"

"I'll find out tomorrow."

Angel was struggling to find words, though I couldn't read her mood. "But... why, Cor?"

"Honestly, Angel, I'm not sure I'll ever know." I smiled, the past welling up and threatening to overflow from my eyes. "I was born on Mars II. A long time ago, as you know. Like you two. We didn't merge ourselves with machines, we didn't cover our eyes with false visions of reality, we didn't wear things in our noses so we would never smell anything except what we wanted. We weren't whatever this has become. That was home to me, and it is as gone as the aliens I slaughtered. These people here seem almost not human. Have you watched the vids? Their strange customs? And the way they keep us at arm's length, as if our presence will contaminate them.

"Are they wrong? Is their society an abomination? Or am I wrong? Are we wrong? Is the future always better than the past? Is society a one-way street? I can't answer those questions. So, I want to create a place that is safe for me, however I want it to be."

"Can't you do that anywhere, Cor?" Angel asked. "You could buy a big piece of property and live there. Wherever you want. An asteroid, even."

I shook my head. "It doesn't matter where you go, there is always somebody trying to tell you what to do, and if not now, sometime soon. I could buy land hundreds of kilometers from anyone else, where no one would bother me, and in a few years, the political tides change, and I'm right back where I started. And then, well, let's just say I have some personal reasons for returning as well."

Angel and Brady sat still, silent, mulling it over. I let them think for a few seconds before it occurred to me what I wanted to ask them. It may have been the whole reason I came there that night; I don't know.

"Yes, I'm going to do this. I am going to buy a planet and go live there if I can, and I want you to come with me. You and anyone from the *Carpathia* who wants to come along. Please."

2654 A.D. (ORPHEUS + 395)

After Cor left, Brady poured himself some wine and offered a glass to Angel, who accepted.

"What do you think?" he asked.

Angel sat on the couch, curling her feet up under her, sipping her drink. "It has potential for both good and bad, Brady."

"Start with the one you want."

"Bad, I guess." Angel rubbed her forehead. "You know, I don't like what we came back to any more than Cor does. It's ugly. The people are ugly. The language is ugly. The whole society is ugly. I mean, the technologies are amazing, but they sold their souls for it. And the violence—Cor is right about that. We were gone for centuries, and war and murder and crime still rage across societies. Same as it always was. Maybe it isn't that way everywhere. Maybe there are already colonies out there where people have learned to live together or rejected fusing themselves to machines. Or both. We haven't really looked yet, and I bet he hasn't either. Instead, he jumped straight to this."

"Because he can," Brady said.

"Because he can."

Brady put his hand on Angel's before she continued. "What he's proposing sounds difficult. He wants to purchase an entire planet, un-terraformed, and then go live there. It takes colonies years to get off the ground, even if they have several hundred people working. He somehow wants to shortcut all of that, so he can avoid playing by anyone else's rules. But it sounds... lonely."

"I wonder exactly how much money he has," Brady mused.

"We have a lot, too, you know, especially combined. We can purchase anyplace we want, or travel, or do whatever we wish."

Brady emptied his glass and poured himself another. "So, it's difficult, and he might wind up alone. That's the 'bad.' What does the 'good' look like?"

Angel nodded. It was like dissecting an intelligence problem. "'Good' looks like what he described. 'Good' is making the rules to live by, or abolishing all rules, or whatever he wants. He'll be free to live as he chooses without fear of finding himself on the outside again. Insulated. Protected."

"Which brings us back to alone."

"Yes," Angel answered. draining her glass and holding it out to Brady.

"What should we do, Brady?" she asked as he poured more wine.

"I agree with you, Angel." Brady handed her cup back and sat down. "I see it the same way. It's just—"

"It's just that he's going to do it anyway. No matter what."

"Yes."

"And you think we should help him?"

"Angel..." Brady rolled his thoughts around in his mind. "Where are we going to go? Somewhere where we can sit and stare at each other for the rest of our lives?"

"Brady—"

He waved a hand. "Not like that, Angel. I love you, and I want to spend the rest of my life with you, but two people alone? With nothing to occupy our time except each other? We have spent our whole lives working, taking things apart, putting them back together, and now we will do nothing? We need a place to land, you and me, where we can be useful."

Angel took the explanation in stride. "And you think this crazy idea of Cor's would do that? Give us purpose?"

Brady shrugged. "I don't know. Maybe. But it would be interesting. Like being stranded on an asteroid in the old holos. Make our way in the wilderness. Something new. If we don't like it, we move on. I think... I think we should."

Angel unfolded herself from the couch and moved next to him.

"I agree," she said at last. "Help Cor. He's so young and so alone. I don't get the sense he's had the easiest time of it, either. At dinner the other night, he was drunk and told me an almost incomprehensible story about someone named Kylie. On River, I gathered, though I couldn't tell if he loved her or was angry with her or if even the point of the story was her. He kind of rambled. His childhood wasn't the greatest either, from the little I've heard. And he's done so much, given up so much for everyone. Yes, I think we should do it."

"Good. I do, too," Brady replied.

They held each other for a long time before going to bed.

2654 A.D. (Age 25, Birth + 435)

"I want to buy a planet," I told Xy.

After leaving Brady and Angel's room, I'd called her and set a time to meet the next morning. She arrived promptly, even on the early side. I introduced her to Angel and Brady, who had agreed to help me. Despite the short notice, Xy was polished. Professional. Maybe even a little more relaxed.

Until I stated what I wanted.

"A planet?" She was confused. "You mean, as a mining investment or something like that? We can investigate it. You already have several highly profitable mining operations, but one more—"

"No, not as an investment," I cut in. "I want to buy a planet to live on—not just me, though: Angel and Brady and anyone else I've known who wants to live there. From the *Carpathia*, mostly."

"Anyone you've known... I'm sorry, Cor. I'm not really following. Like a colony?"

I struggled to find the right words. "No, not a colony, Xy. A refuge. A place where the weary can find rest."

Xy was still confused.

"He wants to buy a planet for himself and a few close friends," Brady chimed in. "Not for the purpose of expansion, like a colony, but just to live there."

Xy nodded, understanding dawning on her face at last. "Got it. An entire planet devoted to... How many people did you say?"

Brady and Angel exchanged glances with me, and I guesstimated as best I could. "A dozen, maybe? More or less?" It felt weird to say it out loud.

She considered the idea. "I don't think that's how it works. Basically, as I understand it, if you can get transportation to a planet that has not been fully colonized, you can take whatever unclaimed land you want. But you can't just put four stakes in the ground and connect them the long way around, claiming the whole thing. You have to start farming or build a factory—something like that. Whatever land you use is yours, but other people can claim other parts of the planet."

"Put four stakes in the ground and connect them the long way around—that, Xy," I replied, "is exactly what I want to do."

Xy looked skeptical but went along with the idea anyway. "Did you have a planet in mind?" she asked.

That was the question I had been waiting for.

"River," I said, breaking out into a big grin. "And I want to terraform the entire thing."

A look of distaste crossed Xy's face—the first negative reaction I had seen.

"The entire thing?"

"Yes."

She gathered herself, choosing her words carefully. "I'm not sure you understand how things have changed since you left."

I couldn't argue with that. "Go on."

"The environmental movement is incredibly strong. To them, even partially terraforming a planet with aboriginal life is taboo. You would never get permission—"

"If I own it, I don't need permission, do I?"

"That's not how they would see it."

That gave me pause. I looked at Angel and Brady for help, but they both shrugged.

"Okay, Xy, let's try it this way: who owns River now?"

Her eyes darted around the inside of her glasses. "The government, I believe. As I understand it, a set of original, non-exclusive settlement rights were sold to the company that started the colony. When the colony was destroyed, the company went bankrupt, and the rights reverted to the government."

"So, you *can* buy some rights to a planet?"

"Yes, technically, but as I was saying—"

"The government could use a financial influx to improve things?"

"Of course. Always."

"River, Xy," I said, finishing the conversation. "I want to buy River. All the rights. What I do with it after that is my business."

Xy closed her eyes, took a deep breath, and held it before letting it all out at once. "You're the boss, Cor. We'll get started right away."

It took years of effort and more money than any one person should ever have, but in the end, Xy and her firm secured River for me. For me, and eighteen others who decided to join me.

At dinner the night after I spoke with Xy, I explained what I wanted to do to the assembled crowd. Once I convinced them I was not joking, a higher-lower guessing game of my net worth broke out. It took them a while until I finally was able to reply, truthfully, "Lower."

Once I talked to them about what I thought life would look like there, over thirty people expressed interest. As I nailed down the details over the next several weeks, a few dropped out; one died of an overdose; and others, I think, were worried it was a waste of time. In the end, in addition to Angel and Brady, a good many people I held dearest joined me:

Doc and Xeno from the battle on the alien ship.

Pesky, Tiny, and Baja, Aeneid soldiers who survived but never fought.

And, best of all, General Fitzpatrick. Being relieved of responsibility had aged him, oddly enough, as if all his energy had gone into keeping up appearances. He accepted the offer graciously, with tears in his eyes as he placed a shaky hand on my shoulder.

I started terraforming River right where the old colony had been. In the back of my mind was the idea that maybe, just maybe, in all that activity, we might just find Kylie or someone else from Bravo Six, still alive inside a null-space purgatory.

I didn't know how I felt about that. I had a home on Mars II once. Then, for such a short time, I had a home in Kylie's smile and in the comforting palm of Bravo Six's hand. It was an open door that would never quite shut. It wasn't so much Kylie I missed though, as it was the idea of her, and a life lived in another way. I tossed back and forth in my mind what finding her might mean.

Xy predicted that the environmentalists would not like what I was doing. About halfway through the acquisition process, my plan leaked. The outcry was massive, unending, dehumanizing. Following an assassination attempt, I moved all nineteen of us out to River to await the outcome.

We used null-space to skip down through time. The

gigantic Faraday shield went up first. It sat outside of River's orbit and prevented beaconing our presence toward the aliens. From space, we cheered as a tiny sliver of the planet transformed from green to brown.

A day here, two days there, and the years slid by, with Angel and Brady and Doc and Fitzpatrick and even Xeno at my side. Starting in that one small patch, the Green of River slowly disappeared, replaced by the browns of forests and the blacks of lakes— unspoiled, untouched, ready for me and mine.

Where our original Forces barracks had been, I built my citadel. I would live there and watch over the planet with those who joined me. Or they could build a house of their own. It was up to them.

There was only one rule: be tolerant. Be kind if you can, but above all, tolerate others—even the intolerant. Especially the intolerant.

Because who am I to judge you and yours?

Who am I to judge at all?

Indeed, who am I?

I am an ordinary man who left home young and impulsive; who found another home once, maybe twice, and hopes to find a home again; who was celebrated for not getting killed; who slaughtered aliens out of fear and desperation and love for his team; who murdered a planet for his own needs; and who decided that the clearest way to happiness in society was not to belong to society.

This is who I am: I am Coren Slade.

EPILOGUE

The heavens hum
In sacred harmony
I wail into the darkness
Two does not return

-One poetry

One must be One.
I have waited for Two.
Five hundred twelve times
Around the Great Spike, I have watched.
For nine doublings, I have listened.
Two does not return.
Two makes no sound.
Two sends no comforting words.
Two does not answer.
One is alone.
The loudest non-One noises have ceased.
I still hear echoes of their presence,
Distant and garbled.
Two should return.
Two must return.
Two does not return.
I circle and think.
For an entire circling, I think.
There had been many,
And then there was One.
There was One,
And then there were non-Ones.
Non-Ones at my home,
And other non-Ones out in the stars.
And where there had been One,
I made Two.
Two left many doublings ago.
Two should return.

Two does not return.
One will find Two.
One will find Two and become One.
One must be One.

About The Author

Rich Greenslit is a retired U.S. military intelligence officer and a veteran of both Iraq and Afghanistan. He writes what he knows: leaving home and never really coming back. He can be found hanging out in Maryland with his Great Pyrenees, Zeus; his two cats, Buddy and The Other One; and some combination of his five kids. He is grateful to everyone who helped get this book to the finish line over many, many years.

To learn more about Coren Slade Books, visit corenslade.com or contact the author at corensladebooks@gmail.com

Cover Artwork by Andie Pavlat
Contact Andie at acpavlat@mail.com

Made in the USA
Columbia, SC
27 January 2025